EDGE

PLAY

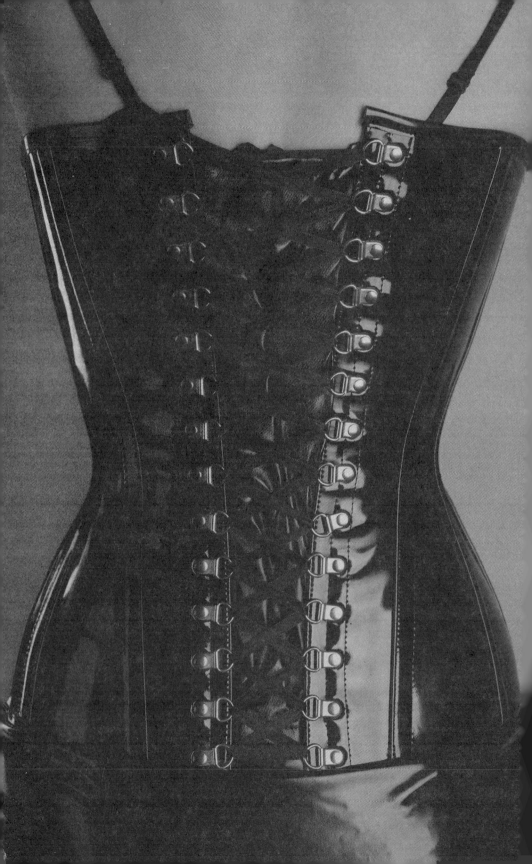

EDGE

A NOVEL   JANE BOON

PLAY

Regan Arts.

Regan Arts.

First Regan Arts paperback edition, July 2020.

Library of Congress Control Number: 2020933765

Paperback ISBN 978-1-68245-132-8
eBook ISBN 978-1-68245-134-2

Cover design and overall art direction by Richard Ljoenes
Interior design by Daniel Lagin and Richard Ljoenes
Cover photograph by Elisanth/Shutterstock
Author photograph by Bradford Rogne
Printed in the United States of America

For Norm

CORRECTION

Correction [k*uh*-rek-sh*uh* n]

1. A sharp decline in market price following a rise, a reversal

2. Punishment intended to rehabilitate, chastisement

Roubini saw the correction coming, so did Schiff. Burry made bets that earned a billion. I wish I'd possessed their foresight. I spoke in hushed tones about my concerns to my boss, I nudged the analysts to dig a little deeper, but I was no Cassandra with the gift of prophecy. I heeded the Big Swinging Dicks who said everything was normal. So when the markets crashed, I was stunned and then I was crushed. The beating was devastating. My group was at the epicenter of the financial crisis and the massive correction that followed. If only Xanax had been enough, but something stronger was required.

In the dungeon, there was a different kind of correction. Between the whips and the paddles, the ropes and the chains, I was meting out punishment instead of taking it. The very men who had caused the crisis, those same Big Swinging Dicks, the bankers and their lawyers, were suddenly naked in my presence and paying dearly for the privilege. They begged me for mercy, their cocks hard and their faces filled with need. I warmed to their howls and thrilled to their grunts. Male privilege came disguised as sexual submission, and I wanted to hurt them all, selling misery along with orgasms.

CHAPTER 1

A WOMAN OF QUALITY

By late 2006, I really began to worry. I'd been fretting for a year, but that was when the nightmares started. The housing market was struggling, with prices falling and foreclosures mounting. All the forecasts had assumed the housing market would chug along as it had since the '30s. Up. Up. Up. Only now, it was faltering.

We had every reason to believe housing prices would continue to climb. My parents had made that bet thirty-five years ago, when they bought their arts and crafts style bungalow on a small lot in Burlington, Vermont. Dad worked as an operator at Burlington Electric. It was a union job that paid by the hour, so his financial future was predictable and solid. Given the minimal risk of default, the bank loaned my parents the sixty thousand they needed, at a reasonable interest rate, to complete the deal. Back then, a local bank kept the mortgages in the community, taking the interest paid and reinvesting it locally. Neighbors helped neighbors.

As expected, my parents paid down their mortgage monthly and their home appreciated steadily. Burlington was no different than most cities in the U.S., where housing prices increased year over year. The mortgage that my parents had taken out had given them shelter and an expanded financial cushion. And the bank that had loaned them the money had made a modest profit on the deal.

What was once simple, however, had become complicated. Instead of local mortgages remaining local, mortgages went national where they were bundled into broad securities partitioned by risk. In turn, these securities were sliced and diced, sold and resold.

In the industry, they sneeringly called my corner of the world "shadow banking." Our products were complicated, synthetic, and often required a Ph.D. in mathematics to understand. The business was hidden, mysterious, and all but unregulated. I thought I knew what we were doing. We all did. Only we were mistaken.

Jon Brenner, my boss, had anticipated the market and our firm, *Banque Fédérale de Belgique* (nicknamed BFB for short, or "Big Fucking Bank") was among the first large investment banks to structure and underwrite the deals.

Jon and I had worked closely since he hired me as a summer analyst when I was still an economics undergrad at Harvard. At the time, he still had all his hair, and I had no idea what an investment bank did. I'd grown up in Vermont, and Wall Street might as well have been on the moon. The prospect of spending a few months in New York City, pretending to be an adult, had been enticing.

That first BFB internship included the obligatory scut tasks, like picking up dry cleaning and fetching coffee, but my boss also invited me to think. There were endless pitch books to consume and charts to digest. And instead of schmoozing with my peers and checking out restaurants in Soho, my nights and weekends were spent doing a deep dive into the sexy world of debt.

Jon valued my willingness to do his bidding, so he invited me to return to the bank after graduation. Having that offer was a huge relief. I loathed interviews. Wearing my faux-Armani suit by Ann Taylor and trying to sound like the person I aspired to be always made me feel like an impostor or a fraud. And besides, I really liked Jon.

Except for a brief interlude back at Harvard for my MBA, my career closely followed Jon's. We had clicked during that first summer. It wasn't sexual, we never fucked, but I understood him, and he appreciated me. That analyst position turned into an associate position. And as he ascended, earning fresh responsibilities and big bonuses, I was always part of his team, getting promoted in turn. His strength and vision made him a Big Swinging Dick, but to me, he was Lance Armstrong. Jon was the lead cyclist, where I was a key member of his personal peloton, pushing and sacrificing myself and enabling his performance. But as he moved forward, and I gained strength and confidence, I was searching for opportunities to sprint. I wasn't going to be his *domestique* forever, but fate always seemed to thwart my breakaway.

For years, we were in and out of each other's offices constantly. "Jon, what are those San Francisco guys doing?"

"The hedge fund guys? They're sponsoring deals. They're making us a ton of money."

There was this peculiar hedge fund based in San Francisco named Pulsar that had come to us, pushing hard for riskier deals to invest in. They were like nymphomaniacs, always needing another fuck, and it baffled me. Only, they were nymphomaniacs seeking the dirtiest, most outrageous opportunities. They weren't looking for nice, clean investments. Their tastes were edgy. They were the market equivalent of guys looking for rough trade.

"Jon, are they crazy? Is there some angle to this?"

"Amy, they're crazy. Fuckin' crazy. And we're gonna make tons of money off 'em. The twenty-eighth floor says to hunt elephants, so get out your bazooka." He leaned over his desk and patted my hand. "Don't worry. You've got buyers for the balance, right?"

"Of course, Jon." My database was filled with eager buyers. Pulsar could gag down the nasty bits, while pension funds, other banks, and insurance companies would consume the boring, low-risk remainders.

Our deals were sold in slices rated by risk. The more risk, the more the expected income. If someone wanted a piece of the U.S. mortgage market, I had something to serve them, from "utterly safe," to "proceed with caution." Pulsar swallowed the most dangerous slices whole.

"Just remember, there's only one Johnnie Kahn." Kahn was a mythic figure in the hedge fund world. He'd transformed a small fund of only $25 million by accruing returns of 25% per year. There were rumors half his gains were illegal, and the other half were voodoo. "Half these hedgies are below average. These Pulsar guys are strictly bottom of the barrel."

"I know. Somebody's gotta buy this stuff."

"Exactly. Trying to get into the head of a hedgie is pointless. Focus on the fact they're doing us a favor."

"Thanks, Jon. I just don't get what they're doing."

"Life is full of mysteries. Relax."

"I'm trying, Jon. I'm trying." And I was trying desperately to relax. It was disorienting feeling so much anxiety. In the past, I'd had no qualms about our deals. I rushed at opportunities full tilt. I wasn't just a "yes" woman, I was a "Hell, yes!" woman. But the times and the deals felt different. "It's just been nagging at me for months. Who's the manager on this?"

"Birch Advisors. They're pickin' all the bonds."

"Birch—so if they pick the bonds, that means they're the ones responsible to the investors. . . ."

"Exactly. They're on the hook. If these suckers bomb, the investors blame them, not us. We're good."

"Right. I get it. But Birch also gives Pulsar cover, and Pulsar has an appetite for some pretty gnarly shit. They're gobbling back risk the way your kids scarf peanut M&Ms."

"Amy, I realize civilians may have trouble accepting all this complexity, but this is just how Wall Street works. There's nothing out of the ordinary here, so we're not going to get any calls. Birch is doing the picking, so *they* are responsible."

"And that's how it works in theory. But you and I both know who'll be answering the phone if these suckers blow up. It won't be Birch, and it won't be Pulsar. It'll be us."

"They won't blow up. We won't get any calls." Jon's voice exuded cool. I wanted to believe him.

"Who's Birch anyway? Never heard of 'em. Are they decent?"

"Firms like Birch are a dime a dozen. Birch is fine."

"It's just that these deals are weird, Jon. We have so much Pulsar exposure. Isn't this a good time to reduce our risk?"

"Amy, every deal is weird, and we can't just leave money on the table. The twenty-eighth floor would fuck me up the ass if they knew we'd held back, and our bonuses would feel the reaming."

"I know. I know. But these deals are keeping me awake at night. We are swimming in Pulsar."

"They're morons dining on gristle. Just cut back on the espresso, take an Ambien, and forget about it."

"Ambien's not working anymore. Maybe I should try Lunesta."

"Maybe you need a fella who'll leave you exhausted. Prolactin, baby, works every time."

"That only gets released when you *men* have orgasms. We women don't get sleepy."

"Hey, whatever it takes. When I'm not gettin' laid, Johnnie Walker works for me."

"I'll keep that in mind. Now about these Pulsar deals."

"Don't worry about 'em. Just sell the good stuff to our best clients."

"Right, boss." In the past year, Jon had taken to teasing me, saying that I worried enough for the entire team, that I'd become another mother.

"By the way, Amy, Susan wants you to come to dinner on Saturday. There's a fella." I made an exasperated noise and raised my hands. "I heard what you said about prolactin, but he still might help you sleep."

"If he's putting me to sleep, there's something wrong with him."

"Oh, come on. They're not that bad. Susan says this one's special."

"Please, Jon. Not again? They're always 'special.'" Jon's wife was always trying to introduce me to someone—a lawyer from the tennis club, some random executive. The overtures pained me. The prospect of sitting in the Brenner dining room, making small talk with some well-intentioned guy, filled me with dread.

"If you don't wanna come, you gotta tell her yourself; otherwise she'll have my nuts." Jon picked up his cell phone. "Hey, Susan, Amy's here. Tell her about Mitch." He handed me the phone.

"Hi, Amy!" Susan always sounded happy to hear my voice. Then again, she'd studied drama at Yale. I once tracked down her guest-starring episodes in *ER*, and she'd been superb, portraying a visiting surgeon with a drug habit. She could convey seriousness, compassion, and fragility with just a flutter of her eyes, but she'd told me she hated the perpetual hustle. After a few years of eking out a living, she'd left performing in favor of fundraising. Susan was no slouch—she'd led a successful capital campaign for Yale, but Jon has a way of bending people to his will. When he proposed, Susan opted to perform the complicated and nuanced role of Jon's wife. She'd gone from being the lead actress in her own drama to being a supporting actress in Jon's. Susan and I were each tasked with different aspects of his care and upkeep, so we weren't rivals in competition, but Jon enacted barriers to how close we could become.

I made a face at Jon. "Hi, Susan. Jon says there's a someone?"

"Yeah. Mitch is fantastic. A cardiologist. I know you're sick of lawyers."

"Busted! The last three guys were all JDs."

"Hey, we live in Greenwich, what do you expect? And I know better than to introduce you to bankers."

"Is this one a divorced dad, too?" At first, the men were never-marrieds, but once I hit my thirties there weren't any left.

"Yes. But only one kid. Shares custody with the mother who lives nearby. Sweet guy. Went to Columbia. Did his residency at Mass General. Excellent reputation." Susan ticked off his accomplishments efficiently.

"So, he's impressive."

"Very impressive."

"But is he cute?" Jon should suffer through some girl talk if he was insistent about me joining them for dinner.

"Very cute! He's about six foot, no paunch, all his own hair. You'll like him. If I weren't married, I'd want to date him."

"Understood. I'm sold. I'll get a car to bring me out. What time?"

"Drinks at 6:30, dinner at 7:30. You'll be back home by 11."

"Okay, I'm in. You drive a hard bargain, Susan. Can't wait to see you and the kids."

"They miss you, Amy. And we should have lunch again in the city, soon. No boys allowed."

"That'd be great, Susan. It's been way too long."

"See you Saturday."

I handed the phone back to Jon. "Don't find me a husband, find me a Susan. Someone who'll keep me fed and watered . . . Someone who'll be nice to everyone so I don't have to be. Can you and Susan track down one of those?"

"Sorry, Amy. Susan's taken. You'll have to find one yourself."

I always played my part, bringing flowers or a bottle of Pinot Grigio, but the bland, vanilla guys in their khaki pants and checked shirts left me unimpressed. It was easier to be a solo operator than to make nice with some guy whose idea of a great life was quiet weekends on the beach in Montauk.

Jon knew I despised these rituals, but he invited me anyway. It was his way of reassuring Susan that we weren't doing anything naughty during our late nights together, or during all those sales trips to London or Dubai. And her concerns were legit, because Jon did have girlfriends, it's just that I wasn't one of them. This was one of the reasons I loathed the setups they engineered. I liked her, and having to pretend that Jon was a good husband rankled me. I was the woman on Jon's day shift while Susan worked nights and weekends, and though we both dedicated ourselves to serving Jon's needs, only one of us had to be dishonest while doing so.

Often, I was Jon's alibi; he'd say he was out with me when he was actually spending time with some chick. I cringed whenever he asked, even as lying to Susan became a routine part of my job. Playing along made me squirm, but it was far easier than finding a new boss. At least Jon treated one woman at work reasonably well: me. Which was one more woman than most of the men in the bank.

We had lunch in Jon's office two or three times a week, eating sandwiches from Au Bon Pain as we sat opposite one another at his desk. We spent much of our time strategizing about the deals, but we also spent long stretches figuring out how to keep Jon's mistresses away from his wife. Both puzzles required considerable time and effort, but the girlfriends began to gnaw at me. I resented their intrusion into our lengthy workdays, and the ethical compromises these affairs required of me.

"Fuck, Amy, what should I do? Mirasol's threatening to call Susan."

"Jon, steer clear of models, they're children."

"Oh, come on. I avoid the teenagers. They're all in their twenties."

"That still makes them kids. Fuck the lovely thirty-somethings who're trying to sell you stuff. Those women will respect your private life."

"I know, Amy . . . I know. I'm working on it, but it's hard to find the complete package. You got any leads for me?"

"No! You're on your own with this hunt, buddy. Find your own bimbos."

"Bimbos are too easy. I want a woman of quality!"

"You're *married* to a woman of quality. You sure you're not looking for a slut?"

"Well, I have that taken care of. This one's crazy hot and hungry. She just told me she wanted a new pair of tits, and I closed the deal as fast as I could." Jon had a voracious appetite for models. There was always a 22-year-old appreciating his company and the way he threw around toys and gifts. There was the Ford model who got a Cartier necklace, the Elite model who got dresses at Saks, and the Wilhelmina model who got a week at Cal-a-Vie.

He may have been a cad, but he was generous with his women. Susan had a brand-new, lipstick-red Mercedes 550 convertible. She ignored what a cliché the car was as she drove it back and forth to the Greenwich tennis club. He was generous with me, too. One year, for Christmas, he got me a top-of-the-line set of clubs, a platinum membership at the Golf Club at Chelsea Piers, and weekly lessons with his favorite pro. "I want you in my foursome, Amy. Deals happen on the greens, you know. But your swing's for shit."

For years, Jon was like the big brother I never had, and I became his work wife. There was never much distance between us, physically or intellectually. He had the market instinct, and I helped him refine and implement it. Risk was my second language, and between us, we made sure the analysts and traders stayed focused and ravenous. As the only woman in a group filled with testosterone and "bros," Jon took care of me.

"We're lucky we found each other," he'd sigh. "Most women can't handle this stuff. And most men don't want a woman like you around. You're an 'E' with me, baby. You exceed my expectations every fucking day."

The bank rated us on a scale. The top 20% were rated "E" for exceeds expectations. The middle sixty were rated "M" for meets expectations. The bottom twenty, however, were rated "N" for needs improvement. Or, as we called it in the trenches, "needs a new job."

Jon had always rated me highly, but he was the exception. BFB was notorious as a toxic workplace for women. There were scores of misogynistic assholes up and down the food chain, and if some unlucky woman got one of those guys for a boss, she'd be lucky if she lasted a year.

BFB gave lip service to improving the number of women in their investment banking teams, but the results were pathetic. Every year, there'd be a fresh batch of MBAs that always included a few eager women. The senior executives patted themselves on the back, and yet there was no program for transitioning these exotic creatures into the hyper-masculine environment those same executives cultivated.

At first, I mentored a few, trying to coach them on how to deal with the idiots and the assholes. What do you do when somebody leaves a dildo in your desk? It's helpful to prepare for that. What's the best answer when you're invited to a meeting in a strip club? It depends on who issued the invitation, and how you feel about weak cocktails and bare breasts. And once a month, whether there was someone on the line or not, use your most threatening voice and yell expletives into the phone with your office door open. Thankfully, the jerks were predictable, so it was possible to anticipate, sometimes even to preempt, the hazing and the harassment.

I chaired meetings on how to draw more women into the bank, and I actively recruited women at the best B-schools, but it was agonizing work. To be a forceful advocate for women put me at risk of being labeled a ball-busting feminist, which was career suicide. Part of my success was due to my ability to fit in. Jon had little interest in closing the gender gap. He just wanted to close deals.

I served two purposes. I could close. Asking for the sale was something that was comfortable for me, and I did it well. But I also gave him cover. He was one of the good guys so long as he had me around. I was a human shield, deflecting charges of sexism over the eight years we'd worked together.

Most of the women lasted only a year or two. No managing director ever wanted more than one "skirt" on his team, making the promotion of other women a zero-sum game. Especially for me. If I groomed the wrong woman, I might have taught my replacement. It was almost tempting to stop trying. After all, if I could figure it out, so could they, but that would be admitting defeat to the bros. The patriarchy may have bought my silence, but they hadn't purchased my acquiescence. There were discreet ways to tilt outcomes. "I know, Jon. You're the best!"

Most of the traders, and Jon was no exception, had been towel-snapping jocks. Jon had played squash at Princeton, where he was known as the guy whose shots only narrowly missed his opponents when he took them off the back wall, and the guy whose elbows almost always made contact when someone was in his way. He'd been a notorious member of Tiger Inn. One "Viking Night," he'd led a midnight raid of the Colonial Club and stolen all their liquor. He was the King of the Bros, but I learned to play along and laugh at the fart jokes. "If it weren't for me, you'd probably be reading balance sheets. You'd still be paying off your school loans."

"I *am* still paying off my loans, Jon." Jon came from money, he didn't have a clue what it was like to receive financial aid. Despite my salary, I lived on a budget. My salary was more than just a way of keeping score. "It'll be years before Harvard's done with me."

"The bonus pool should be bigger this year. You'll get a chunk, I promise."

"Thanks, Jon." And I knew there'd be a piece, but the allocation of bonuses is a bit like the famous pirate game. If the head pirate is given a hundred pieces of gold, he doesn't share evenly with the lesser pirates. He only gives them the minimum he can get away with, while keeping potential mutineers in line. Jon approached bonuses like Long John Silver. His share was always ten times greater than mine, while mine was greater than the analysts. I didn't like it, but until I was at his level, I couldn't carve up the pool to my advantage, and he was always one rank ahead.

I pushed for more responsibility and authority. Jon said as soon as he got his next promotion, I'd slide into his spot and run the group. There were forty of us, and I wanted to be the person making the choices and implementing the strategies, not merely the person offering advice. I wanted to divvy up the spoils. I wanted to attend the meetings on the twenty-eighth floor. I wanted more—especially since I was doing most of Jon's work already, even if I had to pretend otherwise.

CHAPTER 2

DOUBLED DOWN

In order to exceed expectations and remain a BFB "E," my life was monastic. Our hours were crazy. Twelve hours a day, six days a week, was routine, and it was far worse when we were closing a deal. Every few years, someone would self-destruct and have a heart attack at thirty-two or wind up in rehab with a nasty coke habit. The addicts were easy to spot. They'd disappear for long stretches during the day, and come back glassy-eyed as they screamed into their phones. I'm a grinder, so I'd always led that life, which inoculated me from its rigors.

It could be lonely. Dating was too distracting, and I didn't make friends easily. In my freshman year, the residence hall gods had been kind. I connected with one of my three suitemates, Erika Grieg. They called us "the twins."

Erika and I didn't look identical, but we were both tall, slim, and we both had long, dark hair. If you caught us from behind, you'd struggle to figure out which one was which. From the front, however, it was easy.

Erika always had an edge to her appearance. She was from LA, but she was no sunny surfer. She kept her skin a pale white, and with artful eyeliner and deep red lips, she looked like a gothic bombshell. I grew up in Vermont, where my hair was in a perpetual ponytail and my skin was left bare. Though I lacked her polish and glamor, she didn't mind. She tolerated me, letting me tag along to nightclubs or gallery openings. Even then, I had a fuzzy notion she was giving me experiences that would help me navigate through a more rarefied social milieu.

It was an education, to go out together. She always held herself with an unnatural maturity, and as a consequence, she could get us in pretty much anywhere. When you're eighteen and you've led a cloistered life, this was huge.

I still remember the time junior year when we went to the Capital Grille. We had dressed up for the day because Erika was very specific about what to wear to visit the art galleries on Newbury Street. My hair was wavy and polished, my makeup was subtle but present. I wore a tight cream turtleneck dress, accessorized with one of Erika's belts, and my only pair of black Nine West pumps. Erika was her usual, witchy, self. She wore a black shirt, black skirt, black stockings, and pointy black high-heeled booties. After we had explored the various galleries, admiring the works and being treated with respect by the *galleristas*, Erika announced she was hungry.

I followed her over to Boylston Street, thinking we were going to the food court at the Copley Place Mall. Instead, she led me into the steakhouse where we took seats at the bar. I followed, warily.

A quick glance at the menu told me that I had no business being there. Ramen noodles and Diet Cokes were my typical snacks, not fancy cocktails and raw oysters. My budget had no place for extravagance. And neither did Erika's.

I leaned over and whispered to her, "Erika, even the sodas here are expensive. Let's go someplace else?"

"Don't worry. I got this."

"You got this? How?"

"Watch." Erika then discreetly unbuttoned the third button on her blouse, and she reapplied some of her trademark blood-red lipstick. "Put some on yourself, too. Your coloring is perfect for this shade."

I was skeptical, but curious, so I complied and smeared some of the vampy red across my lips. The bartender came over to take our order. Erika went first, and she spoke loudly. "I'll have a martini. Make it dirty and really, really cold."

"Very nice. What would you like, miss?"

I looked at Erika. "I'll have the same."

The bartender never asked to see our IDs, to verify that we were twenty-one. He just accepted that we belonged on those barstools. Erika knew how to convey that kind of confidence.

Erika leaned in and whispered in my ear, "So, we're going to laugh a little too hard at each other's jokes. Okay?"

I got the drift and giggled noisily. "Oh yes, I understand. Shame on you." We just blathered and giggled, giggled and blathered. It only took a few minutes before a pair of men who'd been sitting together at the other side of the bar wandered over to say hello.

"Hi, ladies. Beautiful day," said the tall one with the brown curly hair.

Erika spoke up. "Gorgeous. We were just shopping on Newbury Street. What brings you gentlemen out today?"

"This is my 'hood. I live in Beacon Hill." The tall one stuck out his hand to Erika. "I'm Alan, by the way. And this handsome man is my brother, Brad." We all shook hands.

Erika took charge of the conversation, learning that Alan was a doctor and Brad was an accountant visiting from St. Louis. Having decided they were suitable, she then invited the men to sit down beside us.

"You need to buy us a round, Alan. We're poor students. We shouldn't be here." Erika grinned as she ran her fingers down his lapels and floated them across the crotch of his khakis.

Alan understood what was required. He leaned over to the bartender, and had everything put on his tab. Immediately, I permitted myself to feel thirsty, while also recognizing that Brad was my job.

"So, Brad, do you like accounting?"

"Yeah, it's okay. Finance offers lots of intellectual challenges. It's not the dull work that a lot of people think."

"Really. I've been thinking about trying finance. Maybe investment banking. Good idea?"

"You're still in school?"

"Yeah. But it's time to pick a career. I'm studying Econ."

"You could do worse."

"That's no ringing endorsement. Maybe we should talk about something more exciting."

"More exciting? I like excitement. What did you have in mind?"

He threw me with his question. Someone with more panache would have a good answer. Instead, I asked, "Like, what keeps you amused back home in St. Louis?"

"Hockey."

My clunky repartee was mortifying, but I tried to make the best of things. "Hockey? I don't believe you. Open your mouth." Brad opened his jaw and I reached over and ran my fingers across his teeth. "See, you can't play hockey, everything is still in place." Brad grabbed my hand and pulled me into him for a kiss. His soft lips touched mine tentatively, but then I opened my mouth and let my tongue give him a tiny lick of encouragement. He put his hand to the back of my head, deepening and intensifying the kiss. Then he released me, and we sat back on our stools.

"Oh. That was nice." I purred, encouragingly.

"Yeah, and I'd like to do it again."

"Again?"

"Yeah. You're cute." My face grew warm while I delighted in the attention of a non-student male.

"Let me think about it, okay?"

"I'll let you think about it through dinner. Why don't you and your friend join us. The steaks here are great."

"Are you sure? I have to check with Erika. We may need to be back on campus."

"No problem. Do that girl thing and run off to the bathroom together. Discuss my invitation."

I stood up, gathered my clutter, and nodded to Erika, who was nuzzling at Alan. She righted herself and we scurried to the bathroom. "Well, they want us to join them for dinner."

"That's what I was hoping you'd say. What do you think?"

"I dunno. Brad's cute. Can you stand Alan?"

"Sure. He seems very nice. And I'm hungry. The steaks here are great."

"We might as well. Uh, dumb question. Do we have to fuck them?"

"No, silly. We'll take their business cards and promise to be in touch."

"Is that it?"

"I mean, you can, if you want. But you really don't have to."

"Okay. But what's in it for them?"

"Dinner with two pretty girls . . . the possibility of more . . . If we really want to make them crazy, we can paw at each other."

"You're awful, Erika!"

"The worst. Now, put on some more lipstick. Yours got smeared." She handed me her Chanel lipstick, and in the bright white light of the Capital Grille ladies' room, I readied myself for dinner and dessert.

It went exactly as planned. Erika and I were flirtatious, but we didn't over-promise. I followed her lead, teasing Brad a bit between courses, but otherwise, retaining some mystery. Erika and I snuggled together on the banquette, her arm draped around my shoulder suggestively as I leaned into the side of her body. We hinted at lesbianism, without actually having to perform it.

The men were enticed and aroused, and they picked up the tab for her porterhouse and my filet. They even wanted cheesecake, so I let Brad feed me a spoonful of his, and I licked the cherry topping off his fork with a suggestive slurp of my tongue. Erika looked longingly at Alan. I gazed admiringly at Brad.

Afterward, the four of us stood on the street, the crisp fall air making sure we didn't linger. Brad and I kissed, as I pushed my body into his, enjoying the feeling of his hands massaging my ass and breasts beneath my leather jacket. Before things could progress, Erika pulled me away and we crossed the Charles into Cambridge. We giggled all the way back on the T. Mission accomplished.

"Oh my god. That was so fun."

"I know. I do it all the time."

"You do what all the time?"

"Find a restaurant I want to go to, and then pick up some guy at the bar who'll pay."

"And that's it? Just a meal? You don't do *more*?"

"Well, I might choose to do more. After all, anything could happen. But I never have. I like the hunt and the tease more than the sex."

"Okay . . ."

"But my openness to the possibility of more is something the guys can taste. They know, if they play their cards right, *more* is possible."

"You're insane."

"I may be insane, but I'm very well fed."

While I didn't go out on many improvised dinner dates after that, it was always an education to hang with her. Erika had a knack for getting what she wanted, and I admired the way she approached a problem, like wanting to try the roast chicken at Hamersley's Bistro.

Erika and I remained close. She wound up staying at Harvard and doing a Ph.D. in art history. When I was first working in NYC, she'd come to the city and crash in my microscopic Chelsea studio. We'd go visit galleries and museums together, and then get trashed at some dive bar in the Meatpacking District where Erika would find some guy to buy us round after round of tequila.

We stayed connected during my MBA. I liked my Harvard cohort. My classmates were bright and focused, but the prospect of spending evenings with them at Jillian's playing pool, or at Pho Pasteur eating summer rolls, held little appeal. It was bad enough I had to compete with them daily, trying to squeeze in some clever answer for the professor on whatever case we were studying in Strategy class. Thankfully, Erika was around. We didn't hit guys up for meals any longer. She had funding, and I had savings, so we could afford a cheap Indian dinner in Central Square without much difficulty. While we smeared our samosas with mango chutney, we each feigned interest in the other's classmates and professors.

When she finished up at Harvard, Erika got a job with Larry Gagosian, selling Basquiats to billionaires. It was a relief to me that we wound up in the same city again. I had visions of double-dating, or just going out prowling with her, but the reality of my job was that most evenings were consumed with work. If I was in Manhattan, I was at my desk until eight or nine. If I was on the road, I was crashing in my hotel room. BFB was relentless, and the pace taxed most casual relationships.

I often joked that the reason I was still single was because I wanted a wife like Jon's. Someone who'd play the role of dutiful spouse, while simultaneously pretending not to notice if I failed to come home. Jon actually had a small couch put into his office so that he could tell Susan he'd crashed there, even though he was usually at the Four Seasons with some hot young Brazilian he'd picked up at Bungalow 8.

As one of the only women who'd had the stomach to ascend to my level at the bank, I didn't have that luxury. I'd always made a point of being one of the first to arrive in the morning, which meant getting up at 5 a.m. so that I could be in the office by 6:30. Jon's pace was more leisurely. He didn't roll in until 7, which gave me time to read any emails that came in overnight from Europe, and to make a call or two to Shanghai. We'd get up to speed on any deal news, check our Bloomberg terminals for any flashes that might cause indigestion, and then we'd get on with the day.

With my first real promotion, I moved from my crappy, cabbage-scented studio in Murray Hill, to a small one bedroom in Soho. I should have bought, but even with my bonuses it was a battle to save for a down payment.

The paradox of the six-digit salary is that it's never enough. It was always a stretch. With every bump in income, there was a corresponding increase in expenses. Better apartment. Better clothes. Better vacations. Even my sheets were better. But I also needed to pay someone to clean my place and change those Egyptian cotton, high thread-count sheets, and to pay someone else to pick up my dry cleaning and replenish my fridge, because I simply didn't have the time. Without even realizing it, the cost of my comfort increased.

As for a social life, forget about it. I might as well have been married to my job. It's not that there wasn't the odd offer. Susan tried to fix me up a few times a year, and there were clients or colleagues who'd make a run at me, but I spent so many hours toiling for Jon that I never met anyone who wasn't somehow linked to my occupation.

The first couple of years at BFB, I struggled with the solitude. My friends had all paired off, emitting contentment, instead of pheromones, and it pained me. Every time an expensive, gilt-edged wedding invitation arrived in my mailbox, it left me feeling left behind. All the same, I accepted and went with a thoughtful gift and an open heart. My mother had always said weddings were a great place to meet someone special. And given the cost of attending these events—my B-school classmates only seemed to marry in exotic places like Mumbai or Lake Como—I was fully invested. There were designer dresses and rhinestone-decorated Jimmy Choos. I flirted with whoever was at my table of singles. I got down to everything from hip hop to Bollywood show tunes. And despite my best efforts, it was hard not to conclude that the window for pairing off had already slammed shut.

For all the talk of having it all, I couldn't find a single role model. There were women at work with kids, but the single mothers looked depleted as they warriored forward on behalf of themselves and their brood. The married women seemed similarly joyless on the job, despite the best efforts of their baby nurses and nannies. I'd heard rumors of stay-at-home dads, but these exotic creatures eluded my notice. There seemed to be an impossible tension between a meaningful family life and a career on the ascendancy. And having failed to meet Mr. Right in grad school, I consoled myself by doubling down on work.

CHAPTER 3

TAKING ON
THE CLIFFS

For years, I tried doing the things my mother had always coached me to do with the opposite sex—to be friendly and available, flattering and nice, and to downplay my intellect. While this had worked for her, my parents had been high school sweethearts and forty years later, they still adored each other, this approach had no more success for me at BFB than it did back in Burlington, where I was chronically uncool.

I'd known most of my classmates since we were in kindergarten, and by the time we all hit our teens there was no mystery, let alone, desire. At least none directed at me. Some of the girls in my class got their first kisses as early as sixth grade. I had to wait until tenth. Ken O'Doherty had just moved to the area when his dad accepted a faculty position at UVM, so he hadn't spent a decade observing that I was an unpopular dork and fearing I'd destroy the curve in math class. Instead, he thought I was smart and pretty.

Ken was a little smaller than most boys, with sandy brown hair and glasses. He excelled at physics, where math was my natural habitat, so we had plenty to discuss. He passed me notes written in Elvish, a trick he'd picked up reading Tolkien, and I answered in a simple cipher code. We were two nerds in a pod. It took weeks, however, of sitting adjacent in the lunchroom, before one of us had the nerve to make a move.

One chilly Saturday in mid-October, I suggested we go to Red Rocks

Park. There were trails leading along the shore of Lake Champlain. The leaves were just changing color, and the golds and reds of the maples were spectacular. Ken had grown up in Tampa, so it was his first time experiencing fall in the Northeast.

Ken met me at the park wearing a heavy black leather jacket and a green striped toque. It didn't feel particularly cold to me, so I wore a burgundy Harvard sweatshirt. Even then, I knew where I wanted to go.

We gave each other awkward hugs, and I grabbed his hand. We raced around the paths together, kicking at the leaves that had already fallen and playing hide-and-seek around the massive, gnarled Wolf Pine whose branches jutted and menaced.

I knew the park intimately. My mom would take me to its beach in the summer. To outsiders, the Red Rocks beach was nothing special, but my mother adored its surrounding pines and wildflowers. There were large clumps of yarrow, with its elegant white blossoms, and lots of goldenrod exploding from the ground. After our cold water swims, Mom always snuck a few stems for a vase on our kitchen table.

My father, however, preferred the cliffs. He loved describing the geology of the area and how, five hundred million years earlier, a violent act had pushed tons of rock upward along the local fault. It delighted him that one long, hard thrust had exposed the rock of the cliffs, the shore of the lake, and all the rugged, ragged, beautiful things in our environment.

Ken and I wound through the park, and I led him along the narrow paths closest to the edge. In the summer, a few of us would sneak down from the trails, over to the high cliffs, and then hurl ourselves into the lake. It was terrifying and thrilling. Every other year, there was an accident, and even the odd fatality, because you had to fly past roots, stumps, and stones that jutted into your path on the way down. Then you had to land where the water was deep enough to be safe.

When you peered down, you could see rocks submerged in only a few feet of water, until the bottom of the lake dropped down as suddenly as the cliffs above. It required guts and aim, but my dad had grown up doing it himself, so he taught me to ignore the warning signs. Then, when I was ten, he showed me where to run and how to hit the water. There's a technique to landing safely in the lake after you've dropped seventy-six feet through the air.

When my mom learned what he'd done, she was hysterical. I was their only child and he couldn't put my life at risk like that. She made Dad promise never to do it again. My father was apologetic, but I was undeterred. After that, at least once a summer, I'd sneak off to the highest cliff. It took only a moment to work up my nerve and my speed, but never longer.

Risk is something I can analyze and internalize. It doesn't trouble me the same way it does others. I've always been able to size up situations readily, and then act. When a challenge is in front of me, my instinct is to throw myself at it. And what I learned on the cliffs is that challenges may be dangerous and fraught, but taking on something big and terrifying is actually exciting. The best moment was the run—the instant between the commitment to act and the cold, wet plunge. I adored that rush into emptiness, just as the void was breached.

I took Ken along the path to the cliffs, only he became more nervous with every step. Risk wasn't his natural habitat. He looked at the loose scree like a physicist, calculating friction. And the more marble-sized rocks underfoot, the greater the likelihood of a slip or a slide. From his perspective, every step seemed more precarious than the last. From mine, it was a simple trail I'd traversed hundreds of times without incident.

Ken's shoulders hunched in his leather jacket and he kept looking back along the footpath. I bounced over the boulders with practiced balance while he hung back. I'd suggest a place to hold on, but he'd wave me off, preferring to keep as far from the edge as possible. Even though it was only a hundred yards from the marked trail, it took us forever to reach the outcropping. And by the time we reached the cliff, Ken's face had transformed from pink and ruddy, to pale. I was exhilarated, while Ken was out of breath.

I stood balanced at the rock edge, gazing out at the lake. Ken, however, stayed as far away from me as he could. "Isn't this amazing? Look down."

Ken shook his head, as he wiped the sweat from his forehead with his green hat. I walked over to him and took his hand. "Come on. It's safe. Nothing's gonna happen."

"I don't like it up here." His words were rushed, as if they were trying to propel us back up the trail.

"You've gotta see the view from the edge. If you look down, it's all water and trees."

"That's okay. I've seen enough."

"Just get low. You won't fall in." I got down on my ass and showed him how to inch forward, one boulder at a time. "Come on."

Not wanting to be outdone by a girl, Ken slid toward me doing a tentative crab crawl. One hand, then a foot, then his bum would plant on the uneven rock and he'd move six inches. I lay on my stomach on the painted "76"—our height above the water—and waited for him to join me.

We gazed out at Lake Champlain in its full autumn splendor. Wherever there was land, there were trees in staggering shades of crimson and gold. The water was still, with only a few boats making creases in the surface. Ken's breathing was fast and nervous, as I pointed out all the local landmarks. "That's Shelburne Point, the very tip of Shelburne. The big piece of land over there is Juniper Island. It had the very first lighthouse on Lake Champlain. In the 1820s, the lake was actually a shipping route for lumber and ore. And do you see that little speck beside the island?"

I mistook Ken's silence for interest, so my monologue continued without pause. I was fifteen and clueless. "That's Rock Dunder. During the Revolutionary War, some Brit mistook it for a ship and blasted it with a cannon. When the fog cleared, he realized what he'd done. He's supposed to have said, 'It's a rock, by Dunder!' Can you imagine mistaking a chunk of slate for a ship? They sure were dumbasses back then." Ken grunted.

Oblivious, I chattered on. Talking seemed safer than silence, because silence was a void to be filled. "I like the Algonquin legend. They believe this region was created by a giant. He had no legs, and as he dragged himself from place to place he carved out the mountains and the rivers. Cool, eh? Right there, in Rock Dunder is where the Algonquin believe he rests."

It then dawned on me that Ken wasn't listening, so I rolled onto my side to look at him. Ken was frozen, and I had failed to notice his fear. I nudged him. "Wanna go back?" He nodded. Impulsively, I pulled him toward me. I'd been thinking about a kiss for weeks, and perhaps I thought a kiss would make him love the cliffs as much as I did.

Ken glued his thin body to mine as I traced his mouth with my fingers, and then followed up with my own lips. His pulse was fast, like a mouse, and his breathing shallow. I didn't let go of him as I rolled on top, pressing him down against the rough quartzite surface. He lay there, still, as I caressed his face and hair and gathered the courage to kiss him again. He moaned quietly as I pushed my lips down on his and explored his mouth with my tongue. He tasted of chocolate.

The sun had heated up the rocks, so I unzipped Ken's jacket and snuggled into his chest, listening to his heart race. Ken remained quiet as I nuzzled his neck and traced my tongue and teeth down toward his chest. I'd read that men had sensitive nipples, so I opened his shirt a few buttons and bit his. First his left, then his right, and I delighted when my experiment yielded positive results and his nipples hardened to my touch. Goosebumps formed on his exposed skin, but he made no effort to cover himself or to push me away.

I sat astride Ken, while he closed his eyes behind his wire-rimmed glasses and left his arms stuck passively to the sides of his body. Ken's faded jeans bulged beneath me. I undid the last of the buttons of his shirt, paused, and released the button at the front of his Levi's.

"Do you want me to stop?" Ken let out a small squeak that sounded like "no," but nothing further. The forest was silent. We were alone.

I was too embarrassed to say I'd never seen a boy's penis before, so I unzipped his pants and pushed aside his white briefs. His skin was a light cream, dappled with a few freckles, and the curly hairs around his hard, pale cock were the same red as the maple leaves surrounding us. As I touched the glistening head of his penis with the tip of my index finger, he ejaculated. Warm streams of cum pooled on his abdomen. Ken squirmed and turned his head away from me. Without thinking, I dipped that same index finger into the puddle and tasted it. He was briny-sweet, like an oyster.

In quick movements, Ken inched away from the edge, even as the rocks scratched his back. He grabbed a handful of the fallen leaves, and used them to wipe away the evidence of his arousal. In seconds, he had restored his clothing. We returned to the trail as if nothing had happened out on the ledge. It was easier than discussing what we'd done. But I'd liked that mix of fear and arousal. The moment imprinted on me.

I had the odd boyfriend in college and grad school, but nothing serious. I enjoyed the Harvard guys more than the Burlington guys, but it was hard to find the balance between work and play. There was always a goal demanding attention, making the commitment to a social life seem like an unattainable luxury.

First, I had to graduate. Then I had to get into the right graduate program. Then I had to launch my career. Every step required more commitment than I could muster for some boy or man.

CHAPTER 4

HUNTING AT THE GEORGE HOTEL

While working on my MBA, I found a "friend with benefits." Jean-Claude studied molecular biology at MIT, and he was brainy and beautiful, with a seductive French accent. I loved looking at his swimmer's body, but even that lost its charm when he started making plans for a postdoc in New York and talking about a future together. My male classmates had so many more paths to success than I did, and they were far more likely to find a partner who understood how consuming their work could be. Jean-Claude was a self-described feminist, but even he seemed baffled by my commitment to an eighty-hour work week.

I knew it couldn't last when he grew resentful of all my time with Jon. To rise in a male-dominated milieu like BFB was fraught, because there were obstacles everywhere and so many ways to fall off course, and yet ascension was my goal. "Jon's just using you. Are you sure it's worth it?" Jean-Claude would ask. He wasn't jealous of Jon, just exasperated that I was rarely there for him. And I couldn't answer "yes" or "no" with any certainty, but for a kid out of Vermont, the prospect of a salary big enough to cover my student loans and then some was even more seductive than the biologist. I'd seen people struggle financially, there are few secrets in a place like Burlington where everyone knew which families shivered throughout the winter because they couldn't afford to heat their homes. And because of my dad's work with the electric company, I'd even heard whispers about people who'd frozen to death. The prospect of feeling need frightened me. Money was freedom, and I craved both.

When I returned to the bank after my MBA, it took a while, but I figured out how to address my libido without having to bother with polite chatter with dull guys, or to wrestle out of relationships with men who wanted more from me than Jon or BFB would permit.

It didn't happen often, mostly just when the stress at work got so great that a pressure release valve was essential. After work, I'd get my hair blown out and my makeup freshened, and then I'd channel Erika and plant myself at a barstool at some hotel uptown. I tried the Four Seasons once or twice, but couldn't relax. I was constantly looking over my shoulder, fearful I'd run into someone from work.

Instead, I'd go twenty blocks further north, beyond an invisible border that kept my colleagues and my fears at bay. The George Hotel, with its quiet, elegant bar, served my needs. It had perfect stools and wonderful lighting. I'd bring a book, always something respectable, but not too serious, perch at the bar, and wait. At worst, I'd read a few chapters of whatever was at the top of the *New York Times* bestseller list. At best, an out-of-town executive might offer to buy me a drink, sometimes two, and then follow it up with some champagne from his minibar upstairs.

The first time I did it, it was terrifying. But it had been almost a year since I'd had sex, and it was becoming an unhealthy preoccupation. Was I turning ugly? Was I getting old? Would my pussy shrivel up from underuse?

I needed data, so I stood naked in front of the full-length mirror in my bathroom, where the light was harshest, and gave myself a thorough inspection.

My skin could have been clearer, so later that day, I made an appointment with Dr. Nygaard, my dermatologist. There were potions and lasers that could help. The solution only cost cash.

My hair seemed tired, so I consulted *Vogue* and booked a $500 appointment with Serge Normant for my Sunday off. It would be another five hundred for the highlights, but I was worth it, right? It takes a lot of money to look naturally polished and fresh.

My body was fine. I was five pounds above my ideal, but I could still wear the same size six since graduation, only the clothes were far, far better. My closet bulged with thousand-dollar Gucci dresses and Armani suits. It was possible to look cute on a budget, but the curatorial eye that personal shoppers and the best saleswomen bring to the table made a huge difference to my wardrobe. And since I didn't have time to wait for sales or to hunt through racks, I just bought whatever the saleswoman pulled that appealed. Grey Chanel trousers with tabs at the waist and the perfect taper to my ankles? Bring it on. Black silk Dior sweater with geometric details on the shoulders and cuffs? Magnificent, that's for me. I called it "speed shopping."

When I realized that my clothes either said "Corporate bitch" or "where's the spinning class," it took thumbing through a few fashion magazines to find something that said "seduce me." A quick trip to the Alexander McQueen store in the Meatpacking District solved my problem. That season, he'd designed a long-sleeved wool dress with a V-neck that caressed my collarbones, and where the fine black fabric skimmed my hips before it hit just above my knees. It was black, and from behind it looked almost demure, but from the front, it said Italian movie star.

From there, I moved on to the Hat Shop in Soho. I'd always loved their retro designs, even if I had no need for them. In a fit of whimsy, I found a little black cocktail hat with a single, elegant feather. Worn with the McQueen, I'd be someone mysterious—an actress, a fashion designer, a princess in exile.

Clothing has always felt like costume to me. Perhaps because I've never really felt like I belonged. As a kid, I balked at wearing jeans and T-shirts, the de facto uniform of my public schools. Instead, I'd dress like an English schoolgirl, wearing a red kilt and white shirt. As the smartest kid in every class, I was picked on incessantly. My fantasies centered around living in London and going to some posh school named St. Margaret's or Brimfield Academy, where my academic achievement would be celebrated and where I would get the title of "Head Girl." I wasn't one of those artsy kids who joined the drama club, but putting on that kilt felt like I was someone else, if only for seven hours, Monday through Friday.

I had that same feeling in college. When I arrived at Harvard, I felt like an alien. Sure, there were kids from North Dakota and New Mexico, but Vermont felt light years away from those students who'd attended elite prep schools and who had an instinctive way of signaling their belonging. Their shirts were frayed in the right way. Their Barbour jackets looked lived in, yet appropriate. Most of my clothes had been left behind in Burlington, replaced by things that were brand-new and purchased at Filene's. My jeans weren't right. My shoes were off. For four years, I'd inspect my classmates for clues on how to style and comport myself for their milieu. If I couldn't be them, I'd try to pass.

Dressing for work wasn't much different. I studied the few women at the bank who seemed to have a decent sense of style—they were scarce—and then ask for fashion advice. I didn't begin with my own fashion sense, but it was efficient to borrow theirs.

Over time, donning the navy, gray, or black ensembles that their personal shoppers picked out for me, I grew to understand the difference between an Armani suit and an Akris. I learned to like my wool with a bit of stretch, and to have the tailor nip in the waist of my jackets to accentuate the difference between my hips and my bust.

There was a similar learning curve with accessories. I began wearing Nine West, but my feet acquired a taste for Prada and Jimmy Choo. There was an elegance and a refinement to the shape of those shoes that my eye began to appreciate, and I loved how a 3 or 4-inch heel enabled me to tower over men. They might not have been comfortable, but I'd wear my highest heels whenever a slight boost in confidence was required.

My first "nice" purse was a mahogany brown Regina from Coach, a gift from my mother who recognized that I needed something with more polish than the canvas bag I'd used all through college. The Regina had a top handle that I could slide my entire arm into and then tuck the soft leather against my body when I was crushed on the subway. When I got my first raise, I splurged on a $1,500 Bottega Veneta tote in Black Nappa, because I'd learned that the woven *intrecciato* pattern was a subtle signifier of taste. The Regina got hidden away.

What started as a costume became a kind of armor. On an ordinary workday, I'd throw on a soft knit camisole by Hanro—it was creamy against my skin, like a gentle hug. When I wanted to feel more assertive and turbo-charged, I'd upgrade to something black silk and lace trimmed by Dolce & Gabbana. The Italians understand aggressive femininity. Next, was a slightly over the knee skirt, then my sculpted blazer. A peplum was my friend. I'd then apply my game face. Enough makeup to suggest refinement, but not so much as to suggest effort. The final touch was a pair of killer, patent Manolos. I never felt like I truly belonged at BFB, but I looked the part and that was enough.

My hunting trips at the bar of the George Hotel demanded a different camouflage. Sleek, tight, sexy, but not too overt. I wanted to look enticing, but not like a hooker. The first time I took my place on one of those red leather bar stools, it was mortifying. I was certain everyone in the place was sizing me up and recognizing a woman with carnal appetites. Since that time, I've learned people don't pay attention. I acted like I belonged, and so I did.

For me, the trick has always been looking like I'm a little busy, but open to interruption. I'd bring a novel or a magazine. Nothing too highbrow, but something that would serve as an easy conversation starter. I might struggle with idle chatter, but I know how to engineer my environment to make things easier. A copy of *The Economist* was verging on the edge of improper, but *Time* and *Newsweek* were great. They were a little light for my tastes, but they were nonthreatening, and they could help me consume the Zeitgeist.

I'd settle in at the bar with my reading material in front of me and order a glass of a Riesling or a Pinot Grigio. White wine has never been a favorite, but the calorie count is low and there'd be no inclination to empty the glass quickly because it was so delicious. My drink could be nursed for as long as was needed.

There was always the fear I'd see someone from work or grad school, although I never worried about running into someone from Burlington. Manhattan is actually a small town, and yet it never happened. In those dimly lit bars, it was possible to drink and hunt in anonymity.

Fit professionals in their forties and fifties were my preferred candidates. They all varied in height, hair color, and occupation. Some were lawyers, some executives in town for a meeting, even the odd consulting partner racking up miles on the client's dime. I liked them rakish, because that took the onus off me to do the heavy lifting.

The first time you do anything, it's always the most terrifying, but that's what makes it satisfying. That was true for my first serious job interview with Jon, even. Jon and some of his fellow investment bankers came on campus for an evening of schmoozing. We students all donned our fanciest corporate-costumes. I tried my best to look like one of the women I'd seen in *Fortune* magazine. Who wouldn't want to emulate "The Toughest Babe in Business"? The success she'd achieved through a combination of smarts, savvy, and sex-appeal made me aspire to be her. I even did my best to sound like her. The stakes felt real, and they were. Securing that initial offer from BFB brought me to where I am today.

The stakes were lower on that George Hotel barstool, although I still felt ridiculous in my McQueen dress and feather fascinator. I remember wondering if I was out of my mind. Who even wears a hat anymore? I toyed with heading back to my apartment and bingeing in shame on a thousand calories worth of creamy, rich Zabar's macaroni with goat cheese. Just as I was closing my copy of *Wallpaper* magazine, filled with the type of impossibly chic home I yearned to occupy someday, a tall gentleman in a gray suit sat down next to me.

"I hope you're not leaving. I was just mustering the nerve to come buy you a drink." He touched the back of my hand. "Can I get you another glass of..."

"Oh, hi." He didn't look like the kind of guy who had to work up the nerve to do anything. With the body of a runner, his fine wool suit draped his body perfectly. The buttons on his cuffs worked, with the last one open as a signal to the discerning eye he was wearing bespoke. His face was animated, and his eyes transmitted geniality and curiosity. For a split second, it occurred to me that a psychopath might transmit the same thing, even as I met his gaze. He seemed worth further evaluation. "Well, it's the Riesling."

"Great choice." He leaned in to the bartender. "Two glasses of the Riesling."

While the bartender poured, I probed further. There was no wedding ring visible, not that it mattered much. "What brings you here? Business? Family?"

He sat down on the stool next to me and unbuttoned his jacket. "Business. Working on a deal with HBO."

"How exciting. So, you're in entertainment?" A little flattery seemed in order. "Are you an actor?"

"No. Never." He leaned back, obviously tickled by the question. "How about you? Guest of the hotel?" His voice had a pleasing quality, with just a hint of a California lilt.

"No. I had a tough day, and something about hotel bars feels curative." I took a sip of the Riesling and smiled. "Yes, this is definitely helping. Thanks."

"You're welcome. It's hard to talk here. Sit with me over there." One of the dark tables in the corner of the bar was empty, and of course, I accepted. "What's your name?"

"Jennifer Smith." The name came to me without much thought. Jennifer was a girl in my kindergarten class who'd moved to California when her parents divorced. She disappeared after first grade, so she'd never learn I'd stolen her identity for the evening.

"Do you live in the neighborhood?"

My apartment was downtown, but he didn't need to know that. "Yeah." I decided to sell the lie. "It's actually really quiet at night. You think, Madison Avenue . . . all hustle and bustle, but it's very civilized."

"Great hat. Very ladylike. Do you like civilized?" His hand caressed mine, as it rested on the top of the table.

"Usually . . . but that lady over there," I pointed discreetly at a gray-haired woman sitting with her similarly gray-haired husband, "she likes it rough."

"Really, Jennifer? I had her pegged as only fucking once a month. And only with the lights out."

"Oh no. Look at her hair, the way it's brushed back so severely. She means business. And the lipstick she's wearing? That's not old-lady-coral. It's vixen red."

"Hmmmm . . . what about the husband?" We both looked at the seventy-something man in a navy double-breasted blazer and natty pocket square.

"Her bitch. She spanks him. He's very naughty."

"Wow. You never can tell, but I believe you. They look so normal." He took a sip of the Riesling and moved his hand to my thigh, where his fingers pressed into my flesh. "You're good. Now, what about me? Read me."

I leaned back, took hold of his navy silk Charvet tie, and pretended to examine it. After I had run my fingers along the fabric, I paused. "Oh, you're easy. You have a taste for actresses, but you'll settle for civilians when you're on the road."

"You're wrong. I never settle. And actresses are exhausting." Then he took hold of my hand and kissed my palm. While still gripping my fingers, he leaned in and placed them discreetly on the front of his pants. "I just wanted you to know the effect you're having on me."

I feigned shyness while fanning myself with my free hand. "Oh. My. You don't think your hard-on is my responsibility, do you?"

"Of course not. I just wanted you to know I find you appealing. Do you like champagne?"

"Of course."

"There's a bottle in my room. Join me."

I shook my head in a mix of disbelief and delight. He was attractive, appreciative, and game. He was ideal. But still, to accept his offer was to acknowledge something distasteful. I couldn't help but verbalize my reluctance. "What will people think of me? What will you think of me?"

"No one notices. No one cares. And I think you're sexy." He brought my hand to his lips. "I'd love it. And I promise, you'll have a good time, too. Come on, let's go." In a practiced move, he never let go of my hand as he helped me up from the banquette and guided me toward the elevator.

As we walked through the bar, I gripped his hand tightly, pantomiming familiarity. Of course he was right. No one cared.

As soon as the elevator doors shut behind us, he backed me against the wall and pushed his body into mine. The urgency of his erection could be felt through the wool. He probably tasted the need on my lips, as I kissed him back. His right hand clutched my breast, compressing it through the crepe. I let my head fall back as he lifted my chin with his left, exposing my neck. He inserted his thumb between my lips as he kissed my throat, eliciting a moan.

"You've done this before," I whispered in his ear. "I like experts."

The doors opened onto the eleventh floor and he led me down the thick, carpeted hall to his suite. A quick swipe of the keycard, and we were inside.

"I promised you champagne. Would you like some?" He went into the kitchen and pulled out a bottle of Taittinger. While he busied himself, I carefully removed my hat, and stowed it in a corner beside my purse.

"No. I'm good. But you're really bad." He returned the bottle to the fridge and put his arms around my waist. A trace of beard abraded the skin on my neck as his lips trailed down toward my chest. I gave his tie a yank. "This has to come off."

"Whatever you say, madam." He unknotted his tie, tossed his jacket on one of the lounge chairs in the living room, and began to unbutton his shirt. His erection caused the gray fabric of his pants strain and bulge.

"Let me help. My fingers are nimble." I made quick work of his belt, pushing the stiff leather through the buckle, and then unhooking the tab at the front of his pants, the button, and then the zipper. His pants rested on his hips, as I began to ease them down his legs.

"Oh, your shoes have to go!" I got down on the floor and untied his brown oxfords, maneuvering them off his feet along with his socks. "Socks have gotta go, too. A naked man wearing socks? It's a really bad look."

"I aim to please. Don't want to offend." He grinned, as his body became revealed.

"Are you a swimmer?" The suit had hidden how athletic he was. There was a bit of golden-brown fur on his chest and around his cock, but otherwise, his body was smooth, lean, and muscular.

"Close enough. I row. Do you like what you see?" He gave his hips a tilt, and his thick cock a swing.

"Yeah. A lot. This is a wonderful surprise."

"It's your turn. This dress has to go." He held me close to his chest, kissing my mouth and teasing my lips, as his hands unzipped me. He paused, to inch the dress off my shoulders. I stepped out of the McQueen. "Nice. You're hot. Let's leave this on," he played with the strap of my black lace bra. "It's really sexy."

"You have great taste. It's La Perla. What else would you like?"

"Leave the shoes on, too, but ditch the panties. You won't be needing them."

I appreciated his style. He knew what he wanted, and he wasn't afraid to ask for it. "Anything else, while I'm feeling accommodating?"

"Yeah, you can suck my cock. On your knees, princess." No one had ever called me princess before, and it enchanted me. Maybe I really was a princess in exile that day?

"Princess? You want a princess on her knees?" I sat on my haunches on the floor as he slouched opposite me on a large, blue velvet armchair.

"Yup. That's a good girl. Now tell me what you're going to do."

"What do you mean?" Instinctively, I pulled my long hair back from my face.

He brought his cock closer to my mouth. "Describe—in words—what you're going to do next. I like to hear it. It excites me."

My eyes rolled, as my embarrassment became visible on my cheeks. I had to stifle a nervous laugh. "You want me to *tell* you how I'm going to suck your cock?"

"Yes. But you can do better. I know you can." Now he was wearing a grin on his face, as he stroked my chin and neck, running his fingers along my skin and making me shiver. My face moved with his fingers, enjoying his touch and seeking more contact.

I looked into his gray eyes and began. "So, you want to hear how I'll lick your cock from the base to the tip?" He nodded. It felt ridiculous, but I gathered some steam. "You want to hear how I'll run my tongue over the head, tasting that tiny bit of precum?"

He nodded again. "That's exactly what I want to hear. You can do it, princess."

I inhaled, trying to decide if I should leave or give him what he wanted. It felt absurd yet transgressive, trying to improvise pornography in a suite at the George Hotel. He wanted oral sex and aural sex, and he seemed to enjoy my indecision, his face expressing doubt about my commitment or skill. His eyes smirked at me. It's a look I've faced for years, and it has always made me want to prove the man wrong.

"I'll first need to get my lips really moist so that they'll slide along your shaft. I'll want to caress your balls with my tongue, taking each into my mouth and rolling them back and forth. With my hand, I'll hold the base of your cock, as I work my mouth up and down, letting you fuck my face and use me. Don't be surprised when you feel the very tip of my tongue teasing that tiny little opening as I hunt for your precum."

At twelve, I found my dad's porn stash hidden in a box in his basement workshop. When my parents were away, I'd sneak down and extract a magazine or two, making note of where they'd been so the issues could be replaced perfectly. And then I'd read them curled up in bed.

The women's bodies fascinated me, with their full breasts and hips, and their large, expectant eyes. But my favorite thing was *Penthouse Letters*. "I never thought it would happen to me . . ." And how the writers launched into some improbably lurid encounter with some improbably gorgeous woman. Cocks thrust. Pussies dripped. Those words elicited that first whiff of arousal, that first clench of my cunt. They must have imprinted on me because their essence returned to me, as a smutty script while I knelt on the carpeted floor.

The man sat back, his eyes closed as he listened to my monologue. He wasn't pushing himself on me, making me feel unsafe, so I continued in a slow, quiet voice. "I'll bob my head, my lips tight against your shaft, so that your thrusts match my pace. I'll be merciless, working you over and stroking you as I move my tongue and mouth."

With every sentence, his penis hardened in front of my eyes. Soon, it was jutting straight out and pulsing subtly, along with his heartbeat. It was odd, knowing that it only took my words and imagination to elicit such a powerful response. I was spinning increasingly hardcore images, and all the while, he sat there quietly, his prick bobbing to my voice.

"Do you have the kind of cock that wants to hit the back of my mouth and make me gag?"

He moaned, but didn't move. His cock glistened and turned purple. Despite kneeling at his feet, I was totally in charge of his body.

"I'll find out when I take you deeply. Will you let me relax, and let me take you slowly and carefully, or will you push yourself in and forcefully take my throat?" I paused.

"Oh god. Don't stop."

"Don't stop? Maybe I'll gasp and sputter. Maybe you will. Because I won't stop, even when I feel you twitch. I'll lick you faster with my tongue as I anticipate those spasms. And then I'll taste you. Your cum will be salty and fresh, and I'll drink every last drop."

I sat back in silence, curious what he'd do or say. "You've got me so hard. Come here." I inched forward, within his arm's reach. He took his hands and ran his fingers through the back of my hair as he pulled me forward, so that my lips finally touched his cock. And then I did all the things I said I'd do. Teasing him, stroking him, licking him and finally, once his cock couldn't handle my mouth for another second, he spurted, his cum hitting the back of my throat and coating it with salty goo.

We moved into his bedroom, where, with a sharp movement of both his arms, he yanked the cover down to reveal the crisp white cotton sheets. I centered myself in the middle of the bed as he retrieved a condom from his shaving kit.

"Do you want me to describe how you're going to fuck me? Or is that your job?"

"We've gotten beyond talk, we're doing now."

"Is that so! Well, then, get on with it."

"Spread your legs, princess, 'cause I'm going to fuck you hard." Which is precisely what he did. Once the condom was on his erect cock, he plunged into me as he balanced above, his muscles flexing and his hips straining. I lay back, letting the pummeling of my cunt blot out any thoughts of work. With every thrust, my mind was filled with that feeling of ache and anticipation, and not the worries that had taken over my life. My mind was at peace, even as my body was being crushed into the mattress and my pussy was being battered. It was more than a fair trade.

After we'd both come, I waited a polite ten minutes before fetching my panties and my dress from the living room.

"Jennifer, you're not leaving, are you?"

It took a second, but then I remembered he was talking to me. "Yeah. I have an early morning, and I'm sure you do, too."

"Come here for a moment."

With my dress in hand, I wandered back into the bedroom and crawled on top of the bed, kneeling astride my host. "That was just what I needed. Thanks."

"Happy to help." He kissed me on the lips as he ran his hands down my back until they reached my bottom, where they paused. "I'd like to see you again." His fingers kneaded my flesh, as I kissed his chest and rested my cheek against his skin.

"I like the sound of that." I pulled myself up and climbed off him and the bed. In a second, my dress was back on, with any evidence of our assignation, smoothed away along with any creases. "Do you have a card? I'll call."

He bounced out of bed, and over to his pants, still crumpled on the floor. He pulled out a business card and handed it to me. "Yes, please call. You're spectacular."

I tucked the card into my purse without looking at it. "You'll hear from me." He wrapped himself in one of the plush terry robes hanging in the bathroom, and then walked me to the door.

"Your name isn't Jennifer, is it?" As he clutched the doorknob with his right, he held me close while nuzzling my neck with his lips and teeth.

The door swung open, and as I was leaving, I blew him a kiss. "I never asked for yours. . . ."

CHAPTER 5

CRUSHED BY THE DEATH STAR

Where 2005 had been filled with frantic activity and no deal could be done fast enough to satisfy the hunger of my customers, by 2006 things had begun to cool. By 2007, however, my nightmares were happening once a week, and there was nothing I could do to stop them. Some of my colleagues had upped their daily Macallan quotas, but scotch did nothing for me. Others were popping Prozac or Zoloft, but antidepressants left me cold. Tums were somewhat helpful, because my stomach roiled as much as my brain ruminated.

In January of 2007, everything began to unravel. Navia, named after the constellation named after a ship, was our first deal to collapse. The five hundred million invested in it was rendered worthless. This particular ship was hurtling us over a waterfall, and there was nothing we could do as successive offerings also crashed. Navia was followed by Sextans, which was followed by Cignis. One after another, the deals we'd underwritten, that Pulsar had sponsored, all failed in quick succession. All of those deals, with their fancy, starry names had turned into toxic crap.

We weren't alone. The problem was systemic and huge. By March, hedge funds were getting crushed by bad bets, and fear was starting to spread. It was horrifying and terrifying, seeing all the hard work we'd done, all the assurances we'd given our investors, be for naught. The risk-free investments we'd promised them had turned into something else. My nightmares were finally being realized.

By the summer of 2007, things had slowed to a stop. There were no new deals being made, and a huge portion of our old deals had gone bad. Jon and I just staggered around each day, trying to keep ourselves busy as we figured out what to do next. Every option was unpleasant. There were no obvious solutions.

And then the bottom fell out of the market, wiping out my personal portfolio in addition to my clients' holdings. I'd been saving for a condo for years, and that account was destroyed when the stock market dropped hundreds of points on successive days. The bonus pool went to zero. It wasn't just the shadow economy that was getting crushed, the daylight economy was getting creamed as well. Like everyone, I'd misjudged the risk, and my declining balances showed that miscalculation. It was clear we were teetering on the brink of something huge and grim.

For months, I went to bed anxious. My sleep was fitful, and the nightmares were frightening. I'd imagine living on the streets as a member of a gang of suit-clad panhandlers harassing those few people who'd managed to get out of the crisis intact. Sometimes, I dreamed I'd moved back in with my parents, only the prospect of waking up in my old bed in my pink-walled bedroom made my heart race.

Every day started with that same sense of dread. Where I used to jump out of bed as soon as the alarm sounded, my snooze button got pummeled in a feeble attempt to delay the inevitable. Eventually, my bladder—which didn't care about the S&P—would overrule my head. I'd turn on CNBC and get a blast of whatever fresh hell was about to befall us. Every day had new news of economic disaster. Of markets seizing up. Of billions lost.

I tried different things to distract myself. There were multiple trips to the George. Once I was Rachel, another time, Philippa. But that old trick didn't help. Flirting with strange guys offered no peace of mind when everyone wanted to talk about the stock market. Instead of Riesling, I'd taken to ordering bourbon and that wasn't healthy. I'd sit at the bar, fretting with some lawyer as we both worried about the state of our portfolios. The hotel's typical guest had tons of market exposure, so they were feeling the pain, too.

There was the attractive sales rep from Cleveland who managed to get me up to his room in a moment of weakness. Once there, instead of falling into bed, I made the mistake of mentioning the stock market and the moment passed immediately. I skulked out of his room, feeling like a loser who didn't know how to keep her mouth shut.

Another time, the president of a consulting company got me upstairs. There was a newspaper open on his bed, with one of those alarming headlines: "Crisis on Wall Street as Lehman Totters." He threw it off the bed as quickly as he could. That title was radioactive, a written anti-aphrodisiac.

The man was handsome, with closely cropped white hair and the body of a cyclist, and I was so ready. I'd started the evening wearing my McQueen dress and my best Manolo pumps. My feet were killing me and I wanted out of them. He was a gentleman as he unzipped my dress and lay me down on the bed. He went first, teasing my cunt with his tongue and mouth as he swirled his fingers inside me, applying that perfect pressure to just the right spot.

I did my best to relax. An orgasm would be my medicine. I needed to feel my body out of control as my head filled with pleasure and all my worries were obliterated, but the newspaper had wrecked it for me. He tried. His tongue spent minutes exploring every crevice and fold around my pussy as he inserted successive fingers into me. He knew where the nerves were, and he worked them over, but my head wasn't there, and my body didn't cooperate.

"Just fuck me."

"You sure? I'd like you to come first."

"I need your cock inside me. Now." I didn't have the heart to tell him that his tongue wouldn't get the job done, but his dick might do the trick. Always the planner, I'd stowed a condom inside my purse. "Here. Put this on."

He complied, and I watched as he carefully inserted his prick inside me. "Don't be gentle. Fucking use me."

He raised an eyebrow, but he did as he was told. Instead of using his cock as an instrument of pleasure, he transformed it into a battering ram.

I raised my legs, to find the right angle to get him as deep as possible.

Every time he hit my sensitive cervix, I yelped and urged him on. "Fuck me deeper."

He lifted my legs up and braced himself against the backs of my thighs as he pummeled me, pushing his cock into my body. "Is this how you want it?"

"Yes. Harder." I snarled. The ache filled me and squeezed aside any other feelings.

He reached around and grabbed my throat, his fingers compressing my neck. "You like this, slut?"

"Yes. Harder." Even with that hint of menace, my mind was empty and my cunt throbbed. A pressure was building.

With his right hand, he slapped my face. "You want this, bitch?"

"Yes. Harder." I could barely speak. The shock emptied me as my body responded. Finally, after so much work and so much frustration, that slap precipitated my orgasm. Before he could hit me again, I grabbed his hand, pushing it onto my pussy as he continued to pound me with his cock. My brain floated, my cunt flooded, my body twitched, and I relaxed into the void. Success.

After it was all over, I fled the hotel, horrified by what had happened, even as I made plans to return.

If I could have, I would have banished newspapers from the George. The headlines blared some new calamity every day: "Wall Street Worries Wreak Havoc on Markets," "Mounting Fears Shake World Markets," "New Phase in Financial Crisis as Investors Run to Safety," "Markets in Disarray as Lending Locks Up." There was no escape, not even in the cosseted suites of the George Hotel. I couldn't fuck my way out of despair. No orgasm could get my mind off the markets.

At the bank, my corner of the world was no different. By the time of the market meltdown, many looked at my group askance. We weren't patient zero of the financial crisis, but we were close. The toxic assets we'd been selling had tainted Jon and me. It's like we carried some terrible, infectious disease. Something worse than herpes, something teetering on the brink of Ebola.

Where my life had previously been phone calls and lunches, explaining deals with clever names like Cignis and Sextans to potential buyers, it became frantic meetings with higher-ups at the bank, or even more frantic encounters with buyers of our products, whose investments had become all but worthless. I appointed myself the person who'd take the calls from sad or angry investors. Somebody had to comfort them, and Jon balked at that unpleasant task. He was great closing deals on the golf course, but he was cowardly when it came to bad news, so he had no capacity to console. If one of those calls came through to him, he'd transfer it to me, immediately.

For hours at a time, I'd talk to these people, doing my best to communicate what we knew, and to try and nurture their relationship with the bank. At some point, I hoped the crisis would be behind us and there would be new business to sustain us.

For months, I consumed customer worries by the ton. What can you say to the chief investment officer of the Tennessee Teacher's Retirement Fund, except, "I'm sorry." What do you do when the representative of the Canadian Association of Public Employees starts to cry on the phone because the stuff you sold them was now valued at zero? All the free-floating anxiety had to land somewhere, and it arrived hourly on my desk.

For weeks, we'd all creep in to the office, wary of water-cooler chatter and the inevitable speculation about who was going to lose their job next. "Dave got crushed. They're gonna get rid of his seat." "That managing director lost four hundred million. No bonuses for his team this year, let alone jobs." "The reaper's coming, heads are gonna roll." "I'm going long on Xanax and short on hope."

CHAPTER 6

BEYOND WRETCHED

Jon and I took to reading anything and everything, looking for an angle or a clue about what to do next. What we had asserted was low risk, turned out to be pieces of shit. It felt so shameful that I didn't even want to look anyone in the eye, let alone talk to any of our customers who'd entrusted their money to us for a sliver of Sextans.

While Jon tried to mollify the twenty-eighth floor, I tried to understand what had happened. With the help of Tom Chen, one of our research analysts, we conducted autopsies on our failed deals. Chen had a Ph.D. in statistics from Penn, so he was the ideal person to help. He was also impossibly shy, so he'd be discreet. We spent hours in my tiny office, on nights and weekends, digging in to the specifics of each deal, trying to unearth what had happened.

Chen explained that the problems were all related to Pulsar and to Birch Advisors. The deals I'd thought were weird when we were doing them had turned out to be the worst. My suspicions had been founded, only I had failed to do more than worry. "Those stupid fuckers. How'd they do so badly?"

"It's like they had a knack for picking the nastiest possible investments." Chen shook his head in disgust as he described the contents. "The Pulsar deals were stuffed with liar loans, you know, where the borrower fabricates his income and nobody cares, and mortgages out of Nevada and Arizona, ground zero for dodgy real estate deals and defaults. They couldn't have made dumber choices or bought worst stuff if they'd tried." We both sat there stunned, unable to understand the depth of their incompetence.

"I hope the morons at Birch lose their jobs before we do."

"Is it that bad? Really?" Chen's voice got low.

"I don't see how we all make it out. I've cut way back. Haven't shopped in months. But man, my nut is major. How about you?"

"I'm being careful, but I live in Brooklyn, so my rent isn't too high."

"I shoulda stayed in Murray Hill, 'cause Soho is killing me." We both slouched in our seats, pondering the uncertain future we faced. I sighed. "All my fuck-you money has gone up in flames." Chen sat quietly opposite me, looking as helpless as I felt. "I'm gonna miss you, Chen, when we're all fired."

"Me, too, Amy … me, too." Chen slumped out of my office and wandered back into the maze of cubicles that filled the rest of the floor. He took his spot back at his desk and engaged in the busy work that was keeping pretty much every other member of the team occupied.

Jon was in a foul mood when he returned to his office after yet another meeting upstairs. I'd offered to go to the twenty-eighth floor with him for moral support, but he wanted to face the executives alone. I imagined him taking their abuse on behalf of all of us, even though it was unlikely the team was his first priority. Jon's top priority was always himself.

"Hey Jon, you got a minute?" Warily, I poked my head in his door.

"Sure, what's up?" He looked grim as he sat at his desk, his hands clenching and unclenching a sheath of papers. "Can you help me get my mind off upstairs?"

"I dunno about that. But I'd like to discuss an analysis Chen did. Our deals that went south first were almost all sponsored by Pulsar. And every last one of Pulsar's deals cratered. The relationship is solid. Pulsar's deals failed first, and no other deals did as badly."

"No shit. That's fucking awful. I need to give this some thought."

"Sure thing, boss. I realize we didn't select the bonds, Birch did, but something went wrong with 'em. Their contents are consistently awful. From way too many liar loans, to mortgages out of Nevada and Arizona. These deals are filled with foreclosures."

"Filled with foreclosures? I thought they were plain vanilla deals."

"Far from vanilla. What Birch did was beyond wretched. They seemed to find every bad mortgage in the Southwest, and then put 'em all into our deals. Did Birch do anything else for us? I hope not."

"I don't think so. They're a really small outfit."

"How'd they get the business, then? They're the worst I've ever encountered."

"Beats me. Pulsar wanted us to use them. Those San Fran guys were adamant."

"And what Pulsar wants, Pulsar gets? This stinks."

"For sure." John looked down at his desk and grabbed a massive document that he thrust at me. "But first, could you read this and let me know if you think there's something to this business that could save us? We need to prioritize our own professional future, and not think so much about the failures . . . Failures that weren't even our responsibility."

That night, it took an Ambien and a Benadryl to get to sleep, because my nightmares bounced between San Francisco and New York. The Transamerica Pyramid collapsed on top of Wall Street, leaving dusty piles of rubble throughout the city.

There was no point getting to the office particularly early. Nothing was happening, and no one was around at 7 a.m. anyway. For months, I'd been walking in circles around my apartment while CNBC blared on the TV. I'd come to hate those talking heads. I despised the big-haired women, announcing financial calamities in their chirpy, clipped voices. The men were no better. They projected authority, but they didn't know any more than the rest of us, and I felt like I knew nothing.

I'd stopped taking a cab to work, preferring to save the ten bucks by taking the subway. It was an exercise in denial and self-flagellation, but getting crushed in a car with all the other commuters seemed to validate my sour feelings. It was fitting and right that we should all be miserable as the economy fell off a cliff.

When I arrived at work, Jon wasn't around, so I hunkered down in my office. At 10 a.m., Jon buzzed and asked me to come into his office. It was an odd request since our offices were only thirty feet apart, but I hopped up, grabbed a notepad, and put my game face on. When I arrived at his office, there was an unfamiliar, blonde woman standing next to his desk. "Hi, I'm Amy Lefevre."

Jon glanced up from his desk. "This is Donna from HR." I looked from Donna to Jon, trying to make sense of the intruder.

Jon resumed. "Amy, sit down, please."

"Okay." I smiled as blandly as I could, even as I feared what would come next. It's never a good sign having HR in a meeting.

"I've got some bad news for you. This is your last day." Jon kept his face still. He could have been ordering a steak at Smith & Wollensky. "As you know, we've had our worst quarter ever, and I've got to reduce the headcount. HR will walk you through the separation agreement. Call me in a week. I'll have some ideas and contacts for you." With that brief conversation, I was fired. It was staggering. Certainly, the quarter had been devastating, but there had been no hint of anything amiss between Jon and me. I thought we were closer than this, and yet I was the first to go.

After Jon said his piece, Donna, the HR drone, escorted me to my office where some documents and two empty boxes awaited. I handed over my laptop, my phone, my keycard and all my company belongings. Donna the Drone, in her navy Ann Taylor dress, eyed me suspiciously as I gathered my personal items. There weren't many. A few books, a box of Blueberry Bliss Luna bars, a pair of Nikes, and a few dumb crystal deal toys, relics of various offerings.

The flotsam accumulated over eight years barely filled one box. I'd seen people escorted out of the building with multiple mail carts ferrying all their stuff, and yet all mine fit in a single brown cardboard box. This said something profound, only I had no idea what it was.

The light load did simplify things as Ms. Drone escorted me on my walk of shame. A few colleagues spotted me, but once they figured out what was happening, they quickly disappeared. Only Chen dared look me in the eye, although he kept his distance, too.

Defensively, I found a spot on the wall and just walked toward it. Staring at that little black blur helped me ignore the cubicles and everything going on around me, and it helped me to keep from crying. The last thing I wanted was for Jon and the trader-bros to see tears on my cheeks. I could even hear their chatter. "Hey, did you see Amy? She was bawling like a girl as she was escorted out of the building. *Like a little girl!*" They'd get no such satisfaction from me, so I kept my chin up and tuned everything out.

While making my way off the floor and out the building, I managed to stay steady, even as my world fractured. Jon's words had shaken me. I was the first team member to go. Why me? And who divorces his work wife this way?

That afternoon, I took stock of my finances and my future. Our competitors were laying off people like me by the hundreds. My bank account was fair, but my expenses were high. How badly damaged was my reputation? How long would this crisis persist? Did I need to rethink Wall Street? Did I need to get back on Prozac?

I had no answers and a gnawing sensation it could be a while before any sense of normalcy returned.

I took to bed, hoping to wake up and learn it was just another nightmare. I replayed my conversations with Jon repeatedly, but could find no further meaning. I tried to interpolate between his words, and extrapolate beyond them, but came up empty-handed.

Days passed, and I awoke to the same dreadful reality. I was unemployed in a sector that was tanking. No one had even called to see how I was doing. A week passed and my cell phone only buzzed once. Wrong number.

My personal email was marginally better. There was one message from HR asking me to return the signed documents, there was a message from Chen, checking in, and there were four emails from my friend Erika. Finally ready for some connection, I emailed her back. Maybe she had some good news to share.

CHAPTER 7

A GALLERY FILLED WITH TORTURE

Erika had parlayed her doctorate in art history into a gig at Larry Gagosian's gallery. Her research had been about the Impressionists, but her instincts led her to contemporary works because that was the natural habitat of wallets and whales. Within three years she had left Gagosian for her own gallery in Chelsea where she repped emerging artists and routinely sold hundred-thousand-dollar works.

It's awkward to admit, but I always had a crush on her. I'm not into girls, but there was something about Erika that was dazzling and seductive. Her long, dark hair and severe bangs evoked Bettie Page. Her body was lithe and toned from hours on a Pilates reformer. Her skin was perfect, her makeup was flawless, and her style was glamorous yet edgy. Just by entering a room, she changed its energy for the better. If she hadn't been a friend of fifteen years, I'd have hated her on principle.

Erika had always confused me. She broke every rule of business, but it never seemed to matter. She actually treated her customers like shit. At one of her shows, I witnessed her reprimand a customer for not buying an expensive painting. "I won't talk to you until you show me you're serious," she said to an older man in an impeccable gray suit. "You've earned this magnificent work, and it's time you realize you deserve it. Be a man, not some pathetic little wannabe. Buy this." He slunk away. I figured after being humiliated in front of a room filled with patrons, he'd disappear. To my amazement, he returned with his checkbook.

I sent Erika a brief email explaining that I was out of work and feeling fragile. Seconds after hitting "send," my phone rang.

"Erika here. Get over to my place. I've opened a bottle of Screaming Eagle."

"Screaming Eagle? Woah. That's serious stuff. You must really feel sorry for me."

"You need to taste it. I can't say it's cheaper than therapy, but it's more delicious."

There was no room for discussion or disagreement. This was wine that demanded respect. I didn't even want to consider how Erika had snagged a bottle, it was so elusive. If you could even get your hands on a bottle, it would retail for over a thousand bucks. "Yes, Erika. I'll be right over."

The prior week had been spent shuffling around in a succession of flannel nighties and pajamas. The thick fabric was my cocoon, protecting and warming me, but it was unfit for polite company. Since I couldn't go over to Erika's dressed like a mental patient, I found a purple knit dress in my closet and threw it on over a pair of black tights. It dawned on me that it could be months before I had to wear one of my suits again.

I took a cab to her place on 25th Street in Chelsea. Erika owned the small red brick building where her gallery comprised the first floor. She lived above the shop.

The door popped open seconds after I pressed the buzzer. It was after closing, but she'd left a few lights on, making it feel particularly indulgent and magical to be alone with the art. Erika had a knack for finding subversive works. Her current show was all oils, in the style of old masters, with very contemporary images of savagery and pain. I lingered, admiring the paintings.

While climbing the stairs, I called out. "Hey, it's Amy! Spectacular new artist. Love all the torture on your walls!"

Her apartment door was open, so I wandered in and sat down on the low-slung couch that was straight out of *Architectural Digest*. Erika's home was spare but exquisite. Everything was carefully curated and thoughtfully placed. The walls were a rich, textured gray, which served as a backdrop for the vintage pieces in sumptuous materials like velvet and leather. Her best artworks were displayed, and everything was perfectly lit.

I could hear Erika on the phone in her office. "Just buy the fucking painting. You will get down on your knees and thank me later. Do it. Now." She wandered into the living room, looking as sharp as always in a white turtleneck that clung to her body, a black miniskirt and a wide black patent leather belt that pulled the two halves of the outfit together. I was underdressed, as usual, standing there in my tights and a pair of Prada Mary Janes while she was sporting sheer black hose and an extraordinary pair of strappy Louboutins.

"Hey, Erika." I gave her a shy wave. The circumstances of my visit were mortifying—I had never been the subject of a pity party before. And Erika's fabulous ensemble only made me feel more frumpy.

"Amy, I'm so glad you're here, but I'm so sorry about your job. You deserve better." She poured me a glass of the red and gave me a huge hug.

The wine was graceful, velvety, the perfect lubricant. I told her everything, from Jon's abrupt handling of the firing, to my uncertain future. "I don't know what I'm going to do. I saved, but the crash wiped out my portfolio. I can get a cheaper apartment, of course, cut back, get a sane job, sell some things, but it's overwhelming. I've got enough to cover my rent for a few months, but then what? Those fuckers barely gave me severance."

"Darling, it's tough out there. My sales are down, too. Thankfully I own this place, or the rent would crush me. We both need a break." We sighed simultaneously.

"A break would be awesome. Of course, now that I have the time for a vacation, I don't have the money for one."

"They say change is as good as rest."

"Is unemployment the kind of change 'they' had in mind?"

"Good point." Erika wandered over to the kitchen, equipped with stainless steel counters and cabinets that glistened, as if she were a scientist in a fancy laboratory or a pathologist in a luxury morgue. She pulled out a second bottle of the red from her wine fridge and proceeded to open it with the smooth wrist motions of a sommelier. We'd already drained the first, sprawled on her enormous couch. "This needs to breathe. I want to show you something."

"Something good, I hope!"

Erika cocked her head and smiled mischievously. "Follow me."

We climbed down the stairs that led into Erika's private office. She unlocked a door leading to the basement when she paused. "A warning—you may be surprised by what you see."

"What do you mean, I love surprises." I shrugged nonchalantly, even as my curiosity was gaining in strength.

"Great. I don't show this often, so please don't jump to any conclusions." She looked at me gravely as she bit her lip.

I was perplexed, but I'd also known Erika for a long time. I'd seen her through affairs, jobs, engagements, exams. She had my trust and confidence, and yet she looked nervous. "I promise, Erika, I'll reserve judgment."

She flipped on some lights, and we descended the staircase. "Almost there."

"Your basement seems pretty ordinary, Erika. This is where your inventory lives, right?"

"You're mostly right. But there's more." There was another locked door. She put her fingers on a scanner, and the door opened quietly. "This is the vault."

Subtle lights came on, illuminating a room that was deco meets de Sade. It was a fully operational, incredibly chic dungeon. There was a chrome exam table, a wooden cross made of burled walnut, a cage that practically gleamed. The walls were covered in black leather. The floor was covered in soft, gray rugs. The room was as exquisite as her home.

Erika said nothing as she walked over to a magnificent Macassar cabinet, which she opened to reveal an array of devices I couldn't identify. "Is that French?" I asked, relieved something was familiar. She nodded.

The scent of leather filled the room, and I tried to imagine how everything was used. "Can I look around? Touch things?" Again, she nodded.

I kicked my shoes off and climbed onto the exam table. The surface was padded leather with eyebolts running its length. I stretched out and closed my eyes. Erika stood next to me, holding her breath. I spoke first. "What do you do to him? Her? Them? How often do you use this space? How long have you been doing this?"

Her breathing calmed. Erika had been nervous about my reaction. "I see a few clients a week. I have for years. Mostly men. Mostly senior executives because I'm very expensive." She paused, her face a pale white in the soft light of the dungeon. "It's how I got the building and the seed capital for my gallery."

I opened my eyes and sat up, while trying to take it all in, but Erika had caught me off guard. "To say I'm surprised would be an understatement." I hesitated, grasping for the correct words. "You've built an amazing business, and if you flog a few asses to keep it going and to keep things interesting, well, I'm impressed."

"Would you like a demonstration?"

"Oh, no. I don't think I want to be tied up. I'd rather tie the knots myself." The smile and color returned to Erika's face.

"I hoped you'd say that. Would you like to see a demo on someone else? I have a volunteer!"

Curious, I shrugged. Erika whipped out her phone and texted. While I poked around the room, exploring her stashes of handcuffs and blindfolds, there was a discreet knock on the door.

"Is that who you texted? That's awfully fast!"

"Oh, Michael was waiting outside. I wanted to be sure you were comfortable—or gone—before he entered."

I was stunned. "How long has he been out on the street?"

She looked at her watch. "Maybe an hour? But he'd have waited there all night."

CHAPTER 8

THE DUNGEON DEMO

Erika opened the door and ushered in a distinguished-looking gentleman of around sixty. He didn't seem like the kind of man who waited for anybody. "Michael, I'd like to introduce my friend, Amelia. She will be observing us, so you'd better demonstrate adequate devotion." Erika caressed his chest and arms as she removed his coat. She threw it on one of the Wassily chairs by the door.

She grabbed his face, pressing her fingers into his cheek firmly enough to leave small dents. Then she gazed into his clear blue eyes. "Don't you dare embarrass me. Do you understand?"

"Yes, mistress."

"Louder, so Amelia can hear you."

"Yes, MISTRESS." Still fully dressed in his pinstriped suit, he got down on his knees and kissed the tips of her black Louboutins. He looked up adoringly. "I won't disappoint you."

Erika crouched down so they were at eye level, and she ruffled his hair. "You're going to make me very happy today, aren't you Michael." She smiled as she grabbed his blue Zegna tie and forced him to crawl behind her on the floor. The navy pinstripe fabric contrasted with the gray carpeting as he moved forward.

I found a hook for his coat, and settled in on the leather chair, prepared to watch whatever Erika wanted to show.

It was a strange spectacle. At times gentle and nurturing, and at times cruel and vicious. She unbuttoned Michael's shirt and trousers with a practiced delicacy, almost as if she were undressing a child. Once he was naked, however, she grabbed his balls and led him forcefully to the padded table. He scurried behind her, desperate to keep up with his testicles.

She secured him to the table using black ropes. His body was crisscrossed in an artful pattern and his legs were splayed. He was utterly helpless to her every whim. While he suffered, she gave me a running commentary.

"And now I'll bind his cock. As he gets hard, his flesh will strain against the rope." "And now I'll flog the inside of his thighs. When he's chairing his partner's meeting tomorrow, he'll remember where he's been." "And now I'll put clamps on his nipples. Every time they brush up against his shirt, he'll remember tonight." She was precise and assured at every moment.

"Tell Amelia why you're here, Michael." She gripped his chin, positioning his head so he was looking at me. He inhaled and launched into an explanation.

"Well, Amelia, I've fantasized about submission since I was a teenager, but it took years before I had the courage to explore it. Erika changed my life." Erika stroked his chest as he spoke, gently coaxing him as his voice gathered strength. "I used to be ashamed of these urges—to be used, hurt, and humiliated by a woman. But now I realize it's just part of me. So long as I give these impulses a little oxygen, with the right woman, I have equilibrium."

Erika spoke up. "It's universal, Amelia. The urge to submit . . . to dominate . . . I've found pornography from the eighteenth century that depicts floggings. And those early Greeks and Romans? They were very twisted."

"Right, Erika. Suffering is universal. I didn't realize it could be, uh, eroticized quite so productively."

"Pleasure, pain . . . sometimes they're the same thing. Isn't that right, Michael?"

"Absolutely. They can blur together." Michael's voice transmitted the same certainty I heard in all the best boardrooms.

"Amelia, come here. Let me show you something."

Unsure what to do, I looked them both in the eye. Michael grinned at me as Erika summoned me with a finger. "Okay. What would you like?" Erika handed me a crop.

"Michael should suffer for you, too." I took the implement and waved it in the air. It vibrated in my hand. Erika pointed at the side of the rack. "Hit here."

I brought the crop down hard against the rack. It made a loud snap on impact, startling me. I giggled, instinctively. "Oh. I bet this hurts." I flicked it against my thigh, and the popper at the end of the crop seared my flesh for a second, before the sensation melted and faded into a warm, dull ache. I did it again, letting my hamstring bear the brunt of my experiment as the leather snapped against my knit dress.

Feeling bold, I ran the soft popper over Michael's skin. He flinched whenever I lifted it up as if to strike, and yet he never asked me to stop. I knew it could hurt, and yet he accepted whatever I cared to do.

My mood turned mischievous and I used the crop to caress his nipples. Michael's back arched invitingly. I then ran the leather along the sides of his face. Instead of turning away, he rubbed his cheek against the implement like a cat. When I got to his inner thighs, however, he twisted and wiggled against the bindings. "Are your thighs sensitive?"

"Yes, very!"

"That's good to know." My mind reeled at the absurdity of the tableau, and yet I couldn't help but explore the limits of such a willing victim. "How about here? Is this sensitive, too?" I drew the crop along the length of his erect cock. The ropes dug into his shaft, making the head purple and engorged.

"Extremely sensitive," Michael whispered as a large drop of pre-cum had collected on the tip of his cock. To my amazement, his eyes bulged when I used the end of the crop like a spoon and picked up the blob. The cum glistened against the matte leather surface as I brought the crop in front of his face and toward his mouth. His gaze never shifted from me.

"Stick your tongue out." He complied, and I deposited the salty drop between his lips. He cleaned the crop's surface with a broad swipe of his tongue, and then he licked his lips. I returned the crop to Erika, amused and yet baffled by such an eagerness to submit.

She nodded at me. "Would you like another demonstration?"

I rested my hand on Michael's chest, feeling it rise and fall. "I think I'll leave you two alone. Thank you for the privilege of letting me watch." I turned to Michael and ran my fingers along his jaw and lips. "It was very nice meeting you, Michael." He nuzzled me in return.

I retreated to Erika's apartment, unsure what happened between a dominatrix and her client as the service culminated, but certain I wasn't ready to watch. I dozed off on the couch.

Erika returned to the apartment thirty minutes later. She woke me up when she opened the fridge to retrieve some grapes.

"Erika, I've gotta ask," I grabbed a grape, "why'd you share this with me, now? We've known each other for ages, and yet I had no idea."

"This may sound crazy, but I think we can help each other."

"Help each other? How? I'm in finance, and you're . . . well, you've got a lot going on here."

"I really need a break. I haven't had time off in years and one of my best clients wants to put me up in Geneva."

"Geneva? That's a long way to go for a break. Wouldn't Costa Rica be easier?"

"It has to be Geneva, because that's where he is. He's promised me a butterfly painting by Damien Hirst if I come for a couple of months."

"A Hirst? Those things are valuable. That formaldehyde shark's worth millions . . ."

"I know. And get this, the butterfly paintings are made of actual butterflies!"

"Butterflies? So the painting's special."

"Yeah, it's really special. It's gorgeous and ghoulish and worth a ton of money. But I don't want to put all my other clients on hold and lose them while I'm gone. Submissives are so demanding. Why don't you take over my practice for a few months?"

"A few months? But I have a job hunt, a life, that sort of thing."

"Your lease is up soon, right?"

"Yeah."

"Don't renew it. Stay here. Save a few grand. I haven't told Edouard when I'm coming yet, but I have to tell him soon. And I'll be there at least two months, probably three."

"Three months? That's a lot of rope . . . A lot of cocks and asses."

"Work with as many clients as you like. There are files. This isn't rocket science, but it requires a certain sensibility."

I was astonished. This wasn't the kind of job offer I was accustomed to. Moreover, I had none of the technical skills required. My knot-knowledge was minimal. "Oh, Erika. I can't. I don't know what I'm doing, I might hurt someone. And besides, I'm a banker, not a dominatrix. What if someone I know shows up for a session? My people are your people!"

"I'll train you. Seriously, it's not that hard. You just have to convey authority, and you do that already."

"Then why was I just fired? I couldn't muster the authority to keep my job."

"Amy, the economy is in the tank. It's not you, it's them."

"I want to believe that. I do . . ." I took a large, soothing gulp of the Screaming Eagle. "You're special. You can do this. I'm not up to the task."

"Oh come on, you're hot, the men will fall all over themselves to serve you." Erika sat down beside me and pushed my mess of hair out of my eyes. "Seriously. In a latex dress, they'll kneel instinctively."

"Latex?" I rolled my eyes. "All I have in my closet is wool for work and spandex for the gym."

"Those are speed bumps, not roadblocks."

"Besides, I lack your expertise."

"You're really smart. You'll pick up what you need to know. Just read my files before you book a session."

"There are files?"

"Locked away, but yes. They're very complete. You'll see who he is and what he wants. If you don't want to oblige, just decline."

"What if I know him? What if he knows me? Aren't you afraid of these guys stalking you or, I don't know, calling the papers?"

"I promise you, Manhattan is a big city. My people are not your people."

She paused and lowered her voice conspiratorially. "Well, maybe two or three of them are, but you'll figure out your people before you accept an appointment."

"Okay, but still . . . how do you preserve your safety?"

"I've been doing this for a decade. Since I lived in Boston, even. I've never had a problem client. The trust and respect work both ways."

"That's incredible. Not one?"

"Not one. They're all perfect gentlemen, and the men you'd be dealing with all come pre-screened—by me. I can't think of a safer scenario for you."

I took a deep breath. "It's not for me . . . but I am curious what you get out of it. What do you earn?"

She laughed. "It figures you'd want the numbers. The pay is excellent. Usually cash. Sometimes, if they're really wealthy, they buy art." Then it dawned on me where I'd seen Michael before. He was the gallery client she'd humiliated at the opening, demanding he buy an expensive work.

"That makes sense. And what a great way to boost your sales."

"The sessions start at two thousand and escalate from there. One gentleman bought me this building."

"This building? What an extraordinary deal."

"Yeah. I see a few clients a week. Not so many that it interferes with the gallery, but enough to keep me solvent."

I slouched back on the couch, clutching my wine glass, trying to make sense of Erika's revelations. Even the nitty-gritty aspects of her life were a source of curiosity. "How long is a session?"

"It depends on what he wants. It could be as short as ten minutes, or as long as a weekend."

"A weekend sounds grueling. You must be really good at this stuff." The more I learned, the more perplexed I became.

"I am. I have the best practice and the best clients in the country. Michael is the name partner at a huge law firm, and he's par for the course. My practice is very discreet, but it's also extremely successful."

"I know you don't do anything second-rate, Erika. But my brain is still processing what you're telling me."

"Understood. So, let me be clear, whatever you earn, you keep. I don't expect a cut. I just want my clients content so they don't look for someone new."

"So, the fact I'd be returning to banking is actually an asset, not a liability."

"Now you understand. Seriously, this could be good for both of us."

I was amazed by the math and riveted. "How does an encounter end? Do you have sex with them?"

"God, no. That's part of the game."

"Like when we hustled dinners back in Boston?"

"A bit. Maybe? It's about the tease. I make them beg and then deny them the thing they're craving. We all know sex isn't on the menu."

"No sex, ever?"

"No. Not ever. Well, not unless I feel like it. And I never feel like it. What they want is immaterial."

"Fair enough. You're in charge."

"It's actually liberating. By emphasizing the dark and dirty, rather than the conventionally sexual, we can both cling to the illusion this is about satisfying some esoteric fetish."

"Well, do they get off? Do you?"

She laughed, as if my question were incredibly obtuse. "Sometimes. Them, I mean, not me. I find the work interesting, not arousing. Most often, I leave it in their own hands. Although, sometimes I help."

"You help? How naughty!"

"Yes, very naughty. But there are labor saving devices. You don't need to break a sweat unless you really feel like it."

"This is all news to me, Erika. You've blown my mind, but I don't think I can help you. I'm looking for real work."

"Oh Amy, this work is very real. And besides, the financial mess could take months to clean up. Even my clients are adjusting. You need a contingency plan. Think about it. Please."

"I'd love to learn more, but I can't take over your practice. Truly. I'm not able. I'm not ready."

Erika sighed. "Let me know if you change your mind, okay? I won't tell

Edouard I'm coming until I have someone lined up, and you're the only one I trust so far with my gentlemen."

As I put on my jacket, Erika kissed me on the cheek and gave me a hug. "I'll think about it, sure. How could I not? But I'm not your girl." I grabbed my purse and walked toward the door. "And thanks, by the way, for sharing your secret with me. I won't tell anyone."

I left Erika standing in her darkened kitchen, sipping the last of the Screaming Eagle.

CHAPTER 9

A ROGUE'S REFERENCE

It was late when I got back to my apartment. My evening with Erika and Michael lingered in my psyche and I drifted off to sleep with images of Michael writhing. He seemed happy to be there, but I responded violently.

My dream was vivid and nasty. I imagined tying a man up and seeing his flesh bulge while tightening the ropes around his arms, thighs, and cock. I dragged him by his balls down to his knees, as he begged for mercy. I beat his erection back with a flogger and I tortured his balls with a cane. His ass grew red from my paddle, as he pleaded for forgiveness. This display of anguish and agony left me breathless and excited. The violence and delight being surfaced by Erika in my subconscious left me disoriented and I woke up in a cold sweat. It was only after showering that it dawned on me that my sadistic fantasy had been about Jon.

The next week was a daze as I tried to figure out how to unsee the images from Erika's dungeon. For better or for worse, they were seared into my brain. Unfortunately, the markets were still frozen, and no one was returning my calls or emails. There were no meetings to distract my mind from prurient matters.

Erika was slammed at work as she prepared for an opening, so we weren't able to get together. Every time we spoke or emailed, she'd end things the same way, "Let me know when you're ready." I admired her persistence.

After being fired, I began to use my gym membership more diligently. I had the time and needed the stress release. I still did spinning classes, but my passion became kickboxing and real boxing, basically any class that involved hitting and the mimicry of brutality. I pictured Jon's face on the punching bag, and it improved my aim. With each blow and kick, all those late nights eating takeout at my desk were slowly being exorcised. My body was starting to feel hardened and tough, where it had felt soft and fragile for months. It was liberating to wear a size four again and I delighted in the random catcalls on the street.

During my unemployment downtime, I tried to get caught up on all the networking I should have been doing for years. I worked the phone, calling old classmates in the business, old colleagues who'd moved on, customers who hadn't gotten destroyed in any of the recent deals, anyone I could think of.

The calls were pleasant, but nonproductive. Many of us were also hunting for opportunities. There were the people like me—the Armani-clad canaries in the financial coal mine—who were the first to hit the street. There were others, whose finely tuned antennae had picked up vibrations that banking had shifted, and the future they had visualized was suddenly more precarious. We were like dogs at the park, all sniffing one another and the air, but uncertain where to plant our noses.

Over the years, I'd received queries from many headhunters. These conversations were always enjoyable—headhunters are a charming, pleasant lot as their job is to schmooze. They are experts at eliciting who's responsible for hiring decisions, who's looking for an opportunity, and how to angle themselves for the search. Every discreet chat with a headhunter felt like a date, only I was married. I had yoked my future to Jon's, so the conversations were flirtatious, but of no true significance.

Once my life was different, headhunters were no longer like secret dates, they were essential tools. I remembered who had been particularly solicitous in our sly coffee chats, and which headhunters had laughed the hardest at my jokes and who had been most enthusiastic about my prospects. I called several. Their jobs were at risk, too. No one was hiring, let alone searching.

Finally, after a month of checking in on a regular basis, I got a nibble. Zack

Miller, who headed the executive search practice at Humbert-Scholes, told me about a boutique bank that was specifically looking for a woman to head up their fixed income team. It was a small operation, the comp would be half what I'd been earning, but it was a job. Better still, I'd be the person in charge, and not some staffer. I'd been itching to take on more leadership within BFB, but Jon liked having me by his side. He even called me his "secret weapon," as if I should value being either a weapon or his own personal secret.

As always, I did my homework, analyzing the bank's current practices, and identifying areas in which growth might be possible once the markets settled down enough that stability and confidence were restored to the economy.

That morning, I put on my lucky suit, a crisp navy Alexander McQueen, where the tailored jacket nipped in at my waist and flared out at my hips. It came with the perfect pencil skirt, and I always felt particularly powerful and capable when I wore it. Beneath, I slipped on a grey silk tank and a simple pearl necklace. I splurged and had my hair pulled back into a neat chignon at my neighborhood blowout bar. It was a look that telegraphed cool competence, and not the sense of agitation that overcame me whenever I pondered my future.

The interview went like a dream. I met with the bank's president, and the conversation was somber but productive. The most challenging question was when he asked me about a time I'd failed, and how I responded.

"Well, that's why I'm here. Like most of us, I was stunned by the meltdown, and horrified that so many of the deals my team underwrote had become worthless. It was a staggering failure, and I continue to feel awful for it. But once I recognized the scope of the problem, I ordered an autopsy of the deals that blew up. If I were still in the group, I'd be looking more carefully at those early signs that something was amiss, and creating products and procedures that would acknowledge those lapses.

"The experience has taught me that sometimes you can't avoid failure, but you can mitigate its consequences. I'll always be honest with you, about what I'm seeing and what I'm fearing. I was with my prior boss, too. And if things should go south, I'll be there to help clean up the mess."

It was a serious time, and he appreciated the earnestness of my reply. The chief investment officer was just as generous with his time and enthusiasm. The head of human resources walked me through the compensation structure. She was blunt, telling me that it was down to me and one other person. For a change, when I got home, I opened a bottle of champagne. It was beginning to feel like my luck had improved.

After my glass of champagne, where the acidic bubbles had burst pleasurably against my palate, I gave Jon a call. I wasn't sure what I wanted from him, if anything, but it had bugged me that he hadn't kept in touch more diligently. It seemed unlikely, but if he was embarrassed by the firing, it was important to me that he know we were still okay.

He picked up right away. "Hey, you." For a second, I wondered if he'd confused me for one of his models.

"Hi, Jon. How are you?"

"Well, besides the world falling apart, you mean? I'm doin' alright."

"I know the feeling. I'm still afraid to open the newspaper in the morning. The headlines are so grim."

"Yeah, tell me about it. It's still dead here, although I've managed to hang in. I'll probably be axed soon enough."

"It really sucks, Jon. But at least it sucks a tiny bit less for me. I'd like your advice on something."

"Sure, Amy. It's not the same here without you. Whaddaya need?"

"I think I'm going to get an offer from Knight Partners."

"Oh wow, that's great. Knight, eh? So, you're considering a boutique operation?"

"Yeah, they're kinda tiny, but they did alright during the crash, and their investors are looking for similar deals. Flight to quality. Yadda, yadda, yadda."

"Dave Okafor's the founder. Good guy. He was ahead of me at Princeton, but I know him well."

"I thought that was the case. Well, I've never asked for a favor like this before, but a good word from you could close the deal."

"Yeah, sure," Jon paused. "But do you really want to stay in the industry?

Why not get that Ph.D. you were considering a few years back? Teach. Corrupt young minds."

"I dunno, Jon, are you trying to get me out of the business? I'm too old to go back to school."

"You're not that old! You're what, thirty-six, thirty-seven?"

"Ouch, Jon. I'm thirty-three. You sure know how to hurt a girl. Look at Chen. He's still in his twenties, and he's already got a Ph.D. I'd be pushing forty when I finished."

"Age is just a number. You'd be a great professor. You should think about it. Seriously."

"Seriously? Are you trying to tell me something? Get me out of banking?"

"No, no, no. Of course not." Jon's voice shifted as it went from playful to firm. "I'm just saying it could be grim for a while, and you could do worse than hole up in a university."

"You could be right, but I'm not that desperate yet." My mind turned to Chen. "Hey, did you ever talk to Chen about his analysis of the Pulsar deals and what went wrong with them? It's startling stuff."

"No. I haven't spoken to Chen about that. I'm thinking about what's next, not thinking about what happened. Who has the bandwidth for more?"

"I understand. But it's really bizarre, Jon, what he showed me. Pulsar's deals couldn't have done worse if they'd tried. They didn't just take a haircut. All their deals became worthless."

"I get it, Amy. When there's time, and I'm not fighting for my future, I'll check it out." Jon sounded depleted. "In the meantime, let's get you settled somewhere."

"Thanks, Jon. I appreciate it. You know what to say to make the magic happen." We both laughed, as a bit of levity seeped into the conversation.

"Speaking of magic, I've given up the last of my models." Jon was now purring into the phone.

"Impossible!"

"Can't say I'm practicing monogamy, but there's only one adjunct these days. Everyone's cutting back, like, everywhere."

"Sounds like a wise move, Jon. I hope she's treating you right. Is she one of those leggy Brazilians?"

"No! Believe it or not, Amy, she's petite and Chinese."

"You're stretching, Jon. I'm proud of you!"

"Hey, I took your advice."

"Jon, you know just what to say to get me all hot and bothered. Hang in there, man. And thanks."

"No prob, Amy. I'll call Dave tomorrow."

"Thanks again. And goodnight."

I went to bed and slept. Between the wine and the fifty-fifty shot at employment, my mind was calm.

The next morning, the group fitness classes at the Equinox were filled. All the people who used to shell out for private trainers were now taking group spinning or yoga instead. Paying a hundred bucks a month for access to gym facilities still made sense, but blowing hundreds more a week for some former model to count as I did crunches seemed insane. The club had doubled the spinning and yoga offerings. If the personal trainers were suffering, the group instructors were thriving.

At 7 a.m., I took my place on the last bike available and panted to Rihanna over the scratchy speakers. For fifty minutes, my thoughts focused on the countdown to the end of class, and whether I should have brought a second water bottle. It was a glorious state of empty.

When I was still working, the 6 a.m. class at SoulCycle was my bliss, but when the market puked, there would be no more designer spinning class, with motivational mantras and hot beats, at forty bucks a class. Instead, it was the sterile classes at Equinox. The instructors weren't as cute, the music wasn't as awesome, and the bikes weren't as new, but the cost was included in my monthly fee.

Not long after I got home and showered, my phone rang. It was Dave Okafor. "Amy, I just wanted to call you personally to let you know the job is yours if you want it."

"I want it, Dave. I want it!" I began to bounce and dance as he gave me a few additional details. The market might still be in the doldrums, but things were looking up for me. "Should I follow up with HR for all the onboarding details?"

"Yeah, I'll have Sondra call you later. Welcome to Knight."

"I like the sound of that, Dave. Thanks for the opportunity. Can't wait to get started."

"We're excited to have you as part of the team. We still have to finish off your reference check, of course. But we hope you can start next week."

"Perfect. Next week it is."

As soon as I got off the phone with Okafor, I reached out to Jon and got his voicemail. "Jon, thanks. Whatever you said to Dave did the trick. I just got an offer from Knight. I'll start next week."

A few hours later Sondra, the head of HR called. "Amy, I've got some bad news for you. We've surfaced some new candidates for the position, so we've put everything on hold."

"New candidates? I thought the search was down to two . . . And Dave phoned me this morning with the offer."

"Yes, that was a mistake." Her words lingered as I realized this kind of "mistake" was fatal to my prospects. "I'm very sorry. There are new candidates. We'll be in touch."

"Uh, thanks." Where I'd been joyful only hours before, I was anxious again. Dave Okafor was unavailable, and his assistant wouldn't put my call through. Zack Miller, my headhunter, had to know something, but his response was bafflement.

A few hours later, he called me back. "Amy, I don't know anything first-hand. It's all secondhand." He paused, as he lowered his voice.

"What's up, Zack? What happened? They didn't just open up the search again."

"No, that's not the impression I got. They're all clammed up and not talking. I had to call around to learn anything."

"What does that mean, 'not talking?' Don't they have to talk to you?"

"They were evasive, but someone—and I can't tell you who, so don't ask—said you had a rogue reference."

"A 'rogue reference'? Do you mean a really bad reference?"

"Exactly. Did somebody have it in for you at BFB?"

"No. I wasn't fired for cause. I was an "E" for crying out loud. I have the performance appraisals to prove it. I was laid off because my group was downsized."

"Well, somebody trashed you. You may want to revisit who you're using for references."

I sat there, stunned. There was only one person who knew about my interview at Knight, and there was only one person with the juice to undermine my offer. Jon was the most probable culprit, only it seemed inconceivable he'd do something like that to me. Sure, he took out competitors with a shocking frequency. On the squash courts, his swing was menacing, it was intentionally wild and broad, and he regularly drilled his opponents with balls. And if someone was a threat at BFB, it was astonishing what might happen to their career. One guy's sordid affair got leaked to the twenty-eighth floor and he was quietly asked to leave. Another guy's coke bender made it to *Page 6,* and he was gone, too. Jon was too subtle to leave fingerprints, but he benefited from each scandal. My wariness of Jon also held my personal ambitions in check. My success had to be the best idea he ever had, and he'd always viewed me as an ally. Could it be that he now saw me as a problem? Should I have just kept my mouth shut about Pulsar? It was confusing and dispiriting.

My day had started so well, and then it finished with another bodyblow. The news sickened me, leaving me feeling numb and lonely. Desperate for a diversion, I needed to get out of my apartment.

I rummaged through my closet and put on a tight Hervé Leger dress I hadn't worn in years. It fit, thanks to all those spinning classes. I put my hair in hot rollers and began to apply some makeup. I stabbed at my skin with the brushes, enjoying the sting of the bristles against my face.

Once finished primping, my hair fell in full, brown waves. And despite my wavering emotional state, I managed to draw the perfect little wings with my eyeliner.

CHAPTER 10

DOMINATION IMPERSONATION

The George Hotel was too far uptown for my state of mind; my mood was as manic as the stock market. The Thompson Hotel was only a few blocks away, and it would suffice. Its lobby bar was full of men in suits and women in tight dresses like mine. I planted myself on one of the barstools and ordered a scotch. White wine wasn't going to cut it.

While the bartender prepared my drink, a gentleman sat down beside me. He was a little awkward but very cute. He was tall, around forty, with floppy bangs. He looked uncomfortable in his navy suit, even though it fit him well. He even struggled to talk to me.

After my horrible day, I felt raw. And in turn, I became bold. In that instant, I decided to try my best friend's life on for size. I'd pretend to be the woman she thought me to be. "Hi, I'm Erika. What brings you here?"

"Conference . . ." He practically sighed with pleasure as he tugged at the sleeves on his jacket. "I'm here for a conference on cybersecurity. And you?"

"I live around the corner. I've had a tough day and thought some scotch might help."

"Sometimes it does. Sometimes a lot." He stammered a bit as he spoke.

"Do you have a name?"

"Sorry . . . yes, sorry . . . I have a name. Roy Patterson." Improbably, he blushed. His shyness was so sweet and disarming that I guided him through a conversation. I learned about his hobbies—dogs and kite surfing. I learned about his background—a Ph.D. in computer science from Berkeley. I learned about his work.

"I'm sorry . . . god, I need to stop saying that. But you're so beautiful and smart. You've got me tongue-tied."

"Pay off our tab, and let's go somewhere we can talk. I find you fascinating."

Roy looked startled, but he pulled out his wallet and took care of our drinks. "I have a room here. Is that okay?"

"Yes, that's okay, Roy. Let's go." I took his hand and walked him over to the elevator bank where an elevator was waiting. We went inside. In a clumsy move, Roy descended for a kiss. I grabbed his balls and gave them a hard squeeze. "How presumptuous. Did I say you could kiss me, Roy?"

"Uh, no you didn't. Sorry. It won't happen again." He looked chastened as we walked down the hall. "Here's my room."

"Give it to me." Roy looked puzzled. I pointed at the keycard. "Give it to me."

"Sure. Okay." He handed me the card.

The scotch had made me daring. Knowing I'd never see Roy again, I decided to channel Erika. "Do you want me to come in your room? Have you been fantasizing about fucking me?" I drew the card down his body and let it stop at the bulge in his pants. "Tell me."

"God, yes. I thought about fucking you as soon as I saw you downstairs."

"How badly do you want me?"

"Desperately. You have no idea."

"Prove it."

"How?"

"Get down on your knees and crawl into the room."

He looked at me, bit his lip, and then got down on his knees. He gazed up at me expectantly. I paused, letting him wonder if someone would walk by and see him there, begging. I lingered thirty seconds and he didn't budge. He just waited for my next instruction. I finally inserted the card.

He crawled inside the room while I issued commands. "Get the bathrobe." "Pull out your shaving kit." "Get me the hand lotion." He scurried around, complying with my requests.

"Take off your clothes. And call me mistress."

"Yes, mistress." Roy stood in front of me and began to unbutton his shirt. First the buttons on his sleeves, and then the white buttons down the front of his shirt. I could see the expectancy and nervousness in his fingers, as he pushed each successive button through the fabric. His fingers trembled, even as his eyes never left mine.

He peeled off his shirt, revealing broad shoulders and delts made strong from kitesurfing. I couldn't help but smile at the fine body that had been hiding beneath his suit. He hopped out of his shoes, and then he unfastened his navy pants. While they rested on his hips, he slid his fingers into his pink cotton boxers, and pushed both layers down together. In short order, he was completely naked, and it was a lovely sight that took my mind off my horrible day.

I remained dressed, even as I inspected my playmate. He stood in the middle of the suite, passively watching and waiting. I prowled around him, grabbing his muscular ass, round and firm. His nipples were brown and sensitive, and they hardened to my touch. And as his nipples stiffened, so did his cock. Without even touching his genitals, he had acquired an erection that turned his pink cock into a toy for my amusement. It was thick at the base, tapering to an engorged head, and I just wanted to hurt it.

"Now lie down on the bed. Spread eagle." Roy obeyed immediately, climbing onto the bed and arraying himself as instructed.

As he lay in the middle of the bed, I extracted the belt from the bathrobe and used it to secure his hands to the headboard. His cock was erect as he stared at me in wonderment. I played with his nipples, pinching and biting them. I parroted Erika. "Every time your nipples brush up against your shirt tomorrow, think of me."

"Yes, mistress."

A pair of binder clips from his briefcase went on his nipples. "Be grateful these aren't going on your cock," I noted dryly.

"Yes, mistress." He nodded.

I looped his leather belt through the buckle and then put his cock and balls inside the loop. With the belt tightened, it became a leash around his genitals. I lifted up Roy's head, and had him bite the tail end. If he so much as lowered his head, the belt would become a noose around his privates.

"If you let go of the belt, there will be consequences." Roy nodded, tugging at his testicles with every motion. He didn't unclench his jaw.

I became a cat playing with a mouse. I'd slap Roy's cock or his face, to see how he'd respond. He just kept staring at me with a hungry gaze. Neither his interest nor his dick flagged for an instant.

I was a scientist, conducting an experiment, and instinctively, I knew I could do whatever I wanted to Roy. Within limits, of course. I whispered in his ear, "Tonight, I'll only leave scars on your psyche." He moaned as I scratched my fingertips along the length of his body. He panted as I drew little circles into the head of his prick.

I grabbed his cock and gave it a few sharp strokes. He stiffened at my touch. I then slapped his organ, only to find him stiffen further. He purred. It was as if nothing I could say or do was wrong. We were strangers, yet we were tuned into one another in a way that was surprising.

Emboldened, I lifted up my skirt and straddled his chest. I released the belt from his teeth and looked into his eyes. "You'd love to eat me, wouldn't you? What would you give to taste me? To get me off?"

"Oh mistress, what do you want? I'd love that . . . "

"Sorry. No deal." Erika wouldn't let him, so I wasn't going to either. I put my hand down my panties and stuck a finger inside. My cunt was wet, and my finger became coated. I pulled my hand out and ran it beneath his nose. "This is as close as you get."

He whimpered. "Please. Whatever you want. Whatever I've got. Just take it."

"What do you want me to take, Roy?"

"Take it all and take me, too. Please, mistress."

He looked adorable, lying there, needing me so badly. I turned my body so I was facing his cock, while my pussy hovered a few inches above his face.

"I only want to feel your breath. If I so much as feel your tongue, I'll stop and you will suffer. Do you understand?"

"Yes, mistress."

"And one other thing, I'm going to untie your right hand. When I tell you to, you can jerk off. But you're not to come before I do. Do you understand?"

"Yes, mistress."

I released his hand and placed it alongside his body, and then I got astride Roy again. My hand went back inside my panties as I started playing with my clit. Roy's breath was warm and ragged on my inner thighs.

While closing my eyes, I pushed my fingers inside me, making them slick. My focus centered on that small bundle of nerve endings and the outrageous situation I'd engineered. Maybe Erika was on to something, because my body was responding, only I had to figure out how to finish the encounter her way.

"Start now, Roy. Fuck your hand. Hard. But don't come until I say so."

He pumped furiously, while my body twitched, and it only took a few seconds before I heard him say, "I'm close," which was my cue to dismount. Once out of the line of fire, he received my permission, and Roy ejaculated onto his belly, grunting with every thrust. A towel from the bathroom took care of the goo.

We nuzzled and held each other until that polite ten minutes had passed. While I was fixing my makeup in the bathroom, Roy came in holding a wad of cash. "I know we didn't discuss how much, but this is all I have. You're worth so much more."

My sense of astonishment must have registered on my face, because Roy put the money down on the sink and began to stammer. "Did I misjudge? You're a professional, right? Women like you don't just pick up guys like me in hotel bars . . ."

"Oh, Roy . . . You're amazing. If women aren't picking you up in bars, it's their loss! And no, I'm not a professional." I grabbed the bankroll and stuffed it in my purse. "But maybe I should be."

I watched as he put on his T-shirt and got ready for bed. I kissed him and thanked him for a memorable evening. He handed me his business card. "Call me. Please."

As I walked down the hall, curiosity overcame me. I opened my purse and began to count. The pile contained $730. If he'd had more, he would have given more. I was staggered.

I pulled out my phone and dialed. The call went straight to voicemail. "Erika, it's Amy. I'm ready."

PART TWO

CRISIS

———

Crisis [krahy-sis]

1. An unstable period, often involving risk and danger

2. Archaic slang for climax or orgasm

CHAPTER 11

GETTING DUNGEON-READY

Saying I was ready and being ready were two different things, for Erika and for me. I held out hope that one of the headhunters would call me with a great opportunity and help me escape the dungeon. I was prepared to go to London, Frankfurt, or even Qatar if required, but things remained dead. The S&P was down 25%, and no one was sure if it had bottomed out.

All eyes were on Lehman Brothers as it scrambled to avoid catastrophe. The firm had lost almost $3 billion in the same crisis that had eliminated my job, and with their workforce reduction, a further fifteen hundred people were out on the streets, looking for the same opportunities as I was. Death spirals are ugly, and this one was no different. My confidence in my professional future was eroding faster than investor confidence.

Men and women in sharp navy suits were swarming the city. I had been networking hard for months already, but through their sheer numbers, those Lehman cast-offs had overwhelmed the synapses of the financial sector brains.

It felt like everyone was holding their breath, waiting for a sign that the financial apocalypse had passed. Only no sign was forthcoming. It was a miserable state of limbo.

Amazingly, Erika's clients kept calling her for appointments. While the rest of the country was suffering involuntarily, they were paying through the nose for the privilege. I could be as busy as I wanted. I could earn as much cash as I cared to. I just had to show up and commit.

If I could have hit the pause button on my student loans, I would have, but that wasn't an option. Lots of money was going out of my checking account, while no money was coming in.

Erika's proposition still seemed theoretical and unreal. Even though I had accepted her offer, and I was going through the motions of getting up to speed, the prospect of being in the sex industry seemed preposterous. I could almost pretend that someone else had volunteered for service.

She'd given me a stack of books to read. From Krafft-Ebing's work on paraphilias, to Midori's on rope bondage, to Valerie Steele's on fetishwear. As always, with a massive pile of reading material, I just worked my way through it, consuming page after page as if preparing for a graduate seminar in perversion.

In my darkest moments, I visualized the headlines in the *New York Post* "Harvard MBA Turned Dominatrix Arrested," "From Harvard to the Dungeon." And even as I cringed at the thought, momentum kept me moving forward. There was something compelling about having an interesting secret for a change. Going against my programming was at once unsettling and thrilling.

Reluctantly, I gave notice to my landlord, and put my furniture in storage. Erika loaned me one of the strong guys who helped at her gallery, and together we packed boxes and began the process of cleaning out my old life as I prepared for something new. Whether it was working in a Chelsea dungeon or in a boring office in Abu Dhabi, I was ready.

Erika still needed to prepare for her Swiss sojourn. She would ship large crates of costumes and gear, and because the guy was a latex freak, all the items were made of rubber—from the body bags and gas masks to encase him, to the dresses and stockings to encase her. The crates practically squeaked as she filled them.

As part of my education, I helped her place layers of tissue paper between the fetish items so they wouldn't stick together or get damaged in transit. As we packed, Erika gave me a detailed assessment of each implement, as she identified the duplicates remaining in her basement. She was as thoughtful about her gear as she was about her art.

There's a difference between a normal pair of cuffs and a pair of suspension cuffs, I learned. Suspension cuffs are designed to distribute the tension evenly while the wrist cuff is being pulled from above or the ankle cuff is being tugged at from below. Erika's were lined in soft fleece, which gave her prisoners a little extra comfort. I marveled at the elegance of their design, even as their function mystified me.

"What's the point of suspension? Why do your guys want to dangle?"

Erika was patient. "Imagine standing in the middle of a room, with your hands tied above your head. You're flat on your feet, and you have options. If I want to touch you, you can still avoid me. Not by much, of course, but you still have a lot of control." She continued. "Now imagine I raise your arms by a few inches. In my dungeon, I just hit a button, and the winch winds a turn, and the submissive's arms get pulled up. What then? What can you do, if you're in that position?"

"Less than before, I guess. I can't fend you off as much. Is that what you're getting at?"

"Yes. Precisely. Every inch your wrists get raised represents a heightened sense of helplessness. If I keep lifting your wrists, soon you're on your tiptoes. What can you do then?"

"Even less. My sides are exposed. If I'm naked, my genitals."

"Right. If you want to protect yourself, you have few choices."

"So maybe I can spin a bit . . . kick?"

"Exactly. For every inch your hands go up, your options go down."

"So you're playing with the notion of inevitability?"

"Often. Yes. That sense of helplessness in the face of the inevitable can be thrilling. In my dungeon, helplessness is rewarded. Their trust turns into arousal. Their fears become pleasure."

"It's a mix of dread and anticipation?"

"Precisely. And different types of bondage evoke different feelings. Suspension is about feeling stretched, physically, and mentally. Of being exposed. Of being unable to stop the inevitable."

"What other types of bondage are there?"

"So many . . . rope, which we've tried, has a different energy. There's a rhythm to the task of wrapping hemp that makes it contemplative. And once your prisoner is helpless, each turn contorts the body to your liking. He becomes your work of art."

"You make it sound like a ritual."

"It is in the Shinto faith. They use ropes and knots to purify. Shibari was developed by the Japanese during the Edo period. You should see the art from that time. The intricacy of the ties, and the fiendish ways they humiliated prisoners is staggering. There were no jails. It's how the Samurai confined their prisoners."

"From prisoners to play?"

"Yes. That's a pretty typical trajectory. We're drawn to the things that terrify us. Kink offers a carefully calibrated dose of terror. In the dungeon, my clients get just enough terror to thrill, but not enough to harm."

"Like a roller coaster. Only sexual."

"Precisely. Adult fun for grownups."

"By the way, this rope bondage stuff seems way too intricate for me. I'm decent with knots, but there's no way I'll remember everything."

"Don't even try. Just get a few basics down, and you'll be fine. None of my rope bondage customers will expect you to do the fancy stuff. But you already know how to tie a karada, and that's a lot."

"A karada—that's the body harness, right? The one where the ropes crisscross the torso?"

"Yes. It's foundational. You can improvise around it for hours. You're going to do great."

CHAPTER 12

THE ESSENTIAL
LAB RAT

Michael was a willing victim, helping me acquire the fundamentals of the trade. Erika showed me how to tie somebody up with rope or leather to minimize the possibility of nerve damage, while simultaneously heightening the possibility of arousal. I'd read a lot of the theory, but the practice was bewildering.

Erika had spent years acquiring her specialized knowledge, and I was trying to pick it up in only a few days. At times the project seemed insane, but I launched myself into it with my typical single-mindedness. You solve one problem at a time, and then you solve as many of them as you can. As for the rest, you just try to fake it.

Secretly, I was hoping one of my old classmates or a headhunter would call with news of an opportunity, but there was nothing. There'd be no last-minute reprieve from the dungeon.

To prepare, I poured over technical books like *S&M 101* and *Different Loving*, each seeking to explain and describe Erika's demimonde. There was a beautiful book on Japanese-style rope bondage, and Erika gave me lessons on the intricacies of making harnesses. Michael was game. He became a regular presence at my evening tutorials, offering feedback with every twist and turn of the rope.

"That knot is a little close to my wrist and my fingers are tingling. Maybe move it a bit?" Erika agreed, and in an impromptu anatomy lesson, I learned the location of the radial nerve and the implications of its compression.

My fingers discovered a surprising fluency with rope. Just like there's a language and logic to finance, there's one to cord, as well. When you want to tie someone to something, a hitch is the right knot, either half or clove. A bowline works when you don't want things to slip or tighten. And when you're in a hurry, and style doesn't matter, the classic square knot can't be beat. Had I been a sailor in a prior life?

As someone running a small business, Erika knew how to allocate her time for maximum impact, and she approached my skills gap with the same practical eye. "When you're doing bondage scenes, stick to using the equipment and the gear. Don't do anything elaborate, but show some cleavage." Michael always concurred.

After I'd gotten the basics of bondage down, and I'd learned how to swing a flogger without hurting myself, only my victim, Erika announced it was almost time to meet some of her men. She would leave for Geneva and her rubber freak in a week, and she wanted to make the handover as smooth as possible.

My first task was finding something dungeon-appropriate to wear. She assigned that task to Michael. "Take her to DeMask. Get her a few things."

Michael immediately consulted his calendar. "What are you doing tomorrow afternoon?"

"Going shopping?" I replied.

"Meet me at 144 Orchard Street at 2."

"Got it." I scribbled down the address, curious what they had in mind.

Michael arrived at the DeMask storefront at precisely two o'clock. His driver let him out of his black town car and didn't seem to notice or care that his boss was going into a sex shop on a dodgy block on the Lower East Side. Merely standing in front of a store with mannequins tarted up in latex dresses and kinky body harnesses in its windows made me self-conscious, but I was still new to the scene.

The store interior was mostly red, with glossy surfaces and velvet curtains, and accented with the odd blast of purple. This background offered the perfect counterpoint to the shiny black latex that dominated the racks.

I held back, staggered by the array. Michael signaled the saleswoman and began rifling through the racks. He turned to me. "What size are you?"

"I'm a four in the real world. In Fetish Land? Who knows."

"Excuse me, miss. But could you help us pick out a few dresses."

The saleswoman, whose spiky hair was dyed blue and who had multiple piercings in her left ear, helped me remove my coat and gave me a quick glance. "The nice thing about rubber is how it stretches. The smallest things will fit you perfectly."

"Oh! I like the sound of that."

"Most do. Latex is embracing and very forgiving." Her look may have been harsh, but her attitude was very friendly.

"Well, I've never worn it before, so I don't even know what suits me. Could you pull a few different things you think will work?"

"For sure." Miss Blue Hair wandered through the racks grabbing dresses in different colors and styles. Some were simple, some had buckles and laces, but all reeked of fetish. She bundled a half dozen dresses on a hook in a change room and invited me to try them on. Michael relaxed on a large leather chair and began typing into his Blackberry.

I pulled the first dress off the hook. It was a complicated garment. The dress itself was black, but it had red straps crisscrossing the torso that buckled in place at the hips. And there were more shiny silver buckles on the straps that held up the molded bra cups.

Fortunately, the straps were more decorative than functional. There was a zipper at the back. I took off my clothes and bra and stepped into the latex dress. At first, the rubber felt cold and sticky against my skin, but I was able to rearrange my breasts to fit into the cups and then to inhale as the saleswoman zipped me in.

"Let me get you a pair of pumps. Don't move." She ran off to the back of the store and came back with a pair of black platform pumps that added almost six inches to my height. I sat down carefully, not wanting to injure the dress or myself as I strapped on the shoes for full effect.

It took a moment to get my balance, but Michael deserved a peek, so I opened the curtain and stepped into the store so he could see Erika's apprentice.

I cleared my throat and got Michael's attention immediately. "Wow, Amelia. That's stunning."

"Is it a little much?"

"All those belts and buckles? Maybe, but I like them. The latex really suits you. It shows off all your, uh, assets."

"Thanks. I feel a little silly with all this stuff." I blushed, while yanking at the belts and straps.

"From where I sit, the straps are hot. But if you don't feel comfortable, keep going."

I turned to the saleswoman, "Do you have anything simpler?"

She retrieved a plain sleeveless dress. "Try this. It's a very clean look."

I glanced at Michael while ducking back into the changing room. "I like clean!"

"You're probably the only one in this store who does. Give me dirty, any day." He chuckled at his own joke.

The saleswoman helped me out of the strappy dress and presented me with the simpler frock. It was in a rich purple latex with black edging around its deep V-neck. The zipper even went up the front of the dress, making it easy to put on and take off. As soon as I'd zipped it in place, I knew it was for me. The dress felt solid and secure. The rubber was thick. It felt like flexible armor; tough enough that everything would just slide right off.

I stood in the entrance to the dressing room and posed with one hand on my hip and the other extended along the doorframe. I cocked my head at Michael and gave my hair a toss. "What do you think?"

Michael looked up from his Blackberry and paused. He eyed me up and down as he nodded. "Spectacular."

"I could wear something like this to dinner. In a different fabric, of course." I played with my bust, shifting my breasts beneath the stretchy rubber. My flesh spilled out of the neckline. "Too much boob?"

Both Michael and Miss Blue said "no" in unison.

Michael spoke first. "Magnificent. You look ready to play."

"Would you play with me?" With as suggestive a waggle as I could muster with my index finger, I summoned Michael.

He got up off the lounge chair and positioned himself in front of me. "See, it's magic. The dress works. You made a man appear."

"Magic, eh." I grabbed his tie and yanked him forward, next to my body. He emitted a little gasp as his lips drew close to my throat, where his breath was warm and moist against my skin. I caressed the back of his head with my free hand, tugging at his short gray hair. "Could you submit to this?"

He whispered, "Yes, mistress." With my free hand, I caressed the side of his face, running my fingers from his ear, down across his jaw, over to his lips where he gave them a gentle kiss.

I released him and turned to the saleswoman. "Okay. We're taking this. What else do I want?"

Michael chimed in, "Gloves. Opera length. Black. And there's an incredible twelve strap garter belt that laces up the back that you've gotta try, mistress."

I shrugged and looked at the saleswoman. "He has a point. I gotta."

Michael then turned to the saleswoman. "Oh, and she'll need a catsuit. And how are your leather corsets?"

No one came into the store as I tried on things, eliciting a thumbs up or down from Michael and Miss Blue Hair. Business was as quiet on Orchard Street as it had been on Wall Street. But Michael whipped out a wad of hundred-dollar bills and paid for my dresses and accessories. I might not have felt like a dominatrix, but I was starting to look like one. My costume was coming together. With every step forward, what had begun as a whim, was turning real.

"There's a bar around the corner. Are you pressed for time, because I'd love a drink. That latex is toasty."

"Sure. I'd love one, too."

Although I lugged a big black shopping bag stuffed with oddities, in his tweed overcoat and my long gray wool coat, we looked like colleagues who'd snuck out of the office to gossip.

We took a small table in the back of Max Fish, next to the pinball machine. It may have been a dive bar, but it knew its clientele, and offered above-average liquor. I settled in with a Heineken to Michael's Jameson. "Thanks for everything. I mean it. You've been such a good sport about showing me the ropes."

"You're welcome. It's been fascinating . . . and not without its pleasures."

"I understand. But you've been extraordinarily generous with your time . . . your insights . . . well, with everything."

"Erika is a special woman."

"I agree. She was my first friend at Harvard, and she continues to surprise me."

"And she's an excellent judge of character. I'd like to see things work out for you and for her."

"Do you know anything about her Swiss adventure?"

"Not really. But I worry about her. I've known her a long time."

"Just how long? When did you first meet?"

"She was still working on her doctorate. She had a little studio in Cambridge, overflowing with equipment, and I'd read about her. I had to see her, so I manufactured an excuse to travel to Boston and she changed my life. I've hardly seen anyone, since."

"But you live here. Why would you see a dominatrix in Massachusetts?"

"I like the best. Whether it's wine, food, or kink. I've seen other dominant women, and Erika's top tier. I helped set her up with Madame Margot when she was on the verge of retiring. That made New York feasible. They worked together for a couple of months, and then Erika took over her clientele and got her own place."

"Erika's never told me any of this. But I've wondered how connections are made."

"The answer is 'carefully.' Over the years, I've visited a few women here in New York, but they weren't exceptional and I worried about discretion. There are houses and sleazy operators, but after a while, it's easy to know who's got class and staying power. I knew Erika was special from the moment

I met her. She's the total package. First, she's a lady. But she isn't afraid to take charge."

"The other women. What were they like?"

"Some were lovely. But they weren't special. I want to submit to someone I feel is worthy. It's more satisfying if I'm a little awed by the woman. Erika inspires that feeling."

"Yeah, she inspires that in me too. So why are you helping *me*?"

"You're impressive, Amelia."

"I'm not Erika." I took a sip of beer, tasting the hops and feeling the foam on my lip.

"True. But I see so much potential in you."

"Potential? Perhaps. But actual expertise? Hardly. Am I asking for trouble, taking this on?"

"Not from my perspective. Erika has been refining her clientele for over a decade. These are not men looking for problems. And they should find you sane and reassuring."

"Sane? That's a pretty low bar."

"Yes and no. These interests are on the periphery. You can find dangerous people lurking on the edges. The fact you have high standards and high stakes will be reassuring."

"High stakes. You mean, because I don't want to be found out any more than the clients do?"

"Exactly. It's mutually assured destruction. We're not just talking about nuclear warheads. It's also about reputation."

"Alright, that takes care of the clients, but what about the acts. Some of this stuff is dangerous. You've been warning me about nerve damage and how to avoid hitting kidneys at every session."

"True. So feel free to give the client only what you feel comfortable doing. You're not Erika, and they don't expect you to be. And besides, skills can be learned. Erika couldn't always hit a bullseye with a bullwhip."

"I worry that I can only do half of what they want. Or maybe even less."

"That's fine. If they're like me, they want safety first. And I mean physical and reputational safety. And then they want the erotic charge from digging into whatever brought them to Erika in the first place."

"That makes sense. They need to feel safe before they can embrace calculated danger."

"And don't forget, novelty is exciting." Michael emptied his glass and signaled the bartender for another round. "What you don't realize is how common your situation is. I've seen it many times. A beautiful woman loses her job, walks out on her man, something happens. The sex industry is filled with part-timers who never imagined they'd give it a shot."

"Just hearing the term 'sex industry' put a chill down my spine."

"I understand. But it's the oldest profession. And honorable, too. Despite what you may think."

"Prostitution is the oldest profession."

"Yes, but think about it more broadly. Prostitution is just helping clients see their sexual fantasies realized. Domination is the same."

"I'm not sure I want to be in the same boat as the hookers."

"I've known some lovely escorts over the years, but I prefer dominant women, they're more fun." The bartender returned with our drinks, and we both got quiet for a moment. Michael resumed, "But don't dismiss the prostitutes. I saw one for years who had a Ph.D. in English from Yale. A gorgeous girl. She finally finished her novel, and she's doing great. No one ever knew she'd been an escort."

"No kidding. How'd she keep it a secret?"

"Only her clients knew, and clients don't talk. I doubt she told many people in her life. I don't even know if she shared it with her husband, but she's got a great life. She got tenure last year. We still keep in touch."

"Even now? This is fascinating and a little reassuring."

"People keep secrets all the time. Even from family and friends. *Especially* from family and friends."

"Who else knows your secrets?"

"My therapist knows a few of them. Erika knows a few others. And now you know some, too. But I enjoy having a secret life. I find pleasure in the fact that no one knows the whole me."

"Don't you want to be known fully?"

"When I was young, probably. But now? Having a few secrets makes me more interesting. If someone looks at me they see a white-haired lawyer with a respectable business card. But I know I'm much more than that. And the person sitting opposite me at the negotiating table will make assumptions, but they'll never have the full picture."

"You're like a spy. You have your own, mysterious, agenda. People think you're one thing, but you're another. I must confess, all this makes me wonder what you're getting out of helping me?"

"Well, it is delightful, having two brilliant, gorgeous women treating me like an object to be used . . . That works . . ."

"I can see that. So you like being in the laboratory during the experiments."

"I'm not just in the lab, I am the lab rat. I am essential."

"Alright, Mr. Lab Rat. . . . What else are you taking from this?"

"Hmm . . . well, I've wondered whether dominant women are born or made."

"I think Erika was born that way. She's been bossing around people since college. Probably before."

"And how about you? Born or made?"

"Beats me. What do you think?"

"Born. But the labs are helping."

"Born? I feel like I'm being made. I wouldn't be here except for Erika . . . and for the fact that I suddenly have a lot of time on my hands."

"Very true. But you were open to the idea. Doesn't that suggest bravery, and a willingness to buck convention?"

"Possibly. But it doesn't say I was born to tie men up and beat them."

"True. But it doesn't exclude that possibility, either. I bet you were a very good investment banker."

"That's what all my evaluations said. Likewise, my clients and my colleagues. And yet here I am. I was the first person cut on my team."

"It's happening everywhere. Somebody's always the first. Your situation's not unique."

"I know, but I wasn't the person making the decisions about who stays and who goes. I submitted to my boss's axe. And here I am, 'exploring other options.'"

"Okay, then, you're a work in progress." He took a long sip of his Jameson and sat back against the black vinyl padding. "I'm enjoying your evolution."

"Thanks, I think."

"Maybe you're born and made."

CHAPTER 13

EXPLOITING TURBULENCE OF THE LIBIDO

I brought my haul over to Erika's and proudly displayed my collection of fetishwear. She nodded approvingly at each item. "Michael has great taste. You have a short black skirt, too, right?"

"Of course."

"You can always wear it with a bra or a bustier. Some clients, and this will be in my notes, don't need the full fetish mufti."

"That's good to know. Rubber clothes aren't exactly comfortable . . . I don't know how you're going to survive Geneva."

"I know. You're either too hot or too cold, and you're always compressed. But the look can't be beat. Did you get any polish?"

"Polish? Do I need some?"

"Let me show you where I keep the essentials." Erika had a small stockroom just outside the dungeon where she kept duplicates of everything she needed. She held up a matte white bottle, "This is Black Beauty latex polish. Have the client buff you. Most of them love rubbing out any smudges and making you shine."

"How useful, for those hard to reach spots."

"I'm bringing some clients here tomorrow for you to meet. That way, the handoff should go smoothly."

"You're kidding. Already? I don't know enough."

"Sure you do. I've seen you in action with Michael. This isn't rocket science."

"You keep saying that, but neither of us is a rocket scientist."

"The layoff must have really fucked with your brain. This isn't the Amy I know. The Amy I know is fearless and ferocious."

"This Amy doesn't want to hurt anybody, herself included. I don't want to trash my reputation."

"No one will know. The men are discreet."

"You keep saying that."

"What they want—to submit to a woman—could destroy their relationships and their work. They'd be mocked, and that's the worst fate imaginable when your egos are as big as theirs."

"I don't want to be on *Page 6* either."

"And you won't be. I've never been there, and I've been doing this for a decade. You didn't even know."

"Good point. Is this stuff even legal?"

"Maybe? It falls in a gray area. That's one of the reasons I never have sex with clients. Sex for pay is definitely considered prostitution. But is a spanking illegal? No. Is bondage? No. Is foot worship? No. Most of the things I do are not conventionally sexual, and they don't fall within the scope of prostitution. And by the way, those prostitution laws are yet another example of patriarchal bullshit. The laws pretend to protect women, and sure some sex workers are exploited and need protecting, but does arresting ladies really help their situations? And why should something that you can enjoy for free become illegal when there's money involved?"

"You have a point. It's just commerce. And I don't see any signs of exploitation here . . . Well, not unless you're the one doing the exploiting, Erika."

Erika laughed, "The only exploitation on these premises is strictly consensual." She continued, "Now, there are a few things, like touching a cock, or even tying one up with rope, that might be considered prostitution. But these are hypothetical concerns."

"How can you say they're hypothetical, when a plain reading of a prostitution statute would include hand jobs?"

"It's hypothetical because these laws aren't enforced against professional dominants. There are far easier cases to be made with actual hookers. In New York and New Jersey, there's about one arrest of a dominatrix per year. And usually, it's because the neighbors noticed and they complained. Look it up for yourself. You won't find much, because there isn't much."

"One a year doesn't seem like a lot. But who wants to be that one? Do you talk to the other women in your business?"

"I did at first. It's how I got set up here. I apprenticed to a very experienced, very discreet domina. I'd been in the business before, but her guidance showed me how to take things to the highest level. I bought her book."

"Her book?"

"Yes. Her customer list. As she was retiring, she introduced me to all her clients. Michael was one of them. She had the best practice in the country. I took it over, and then I expanded it very carefully."

"There's a market in these lists? I thought I'd heard of everything!"

"Not really. It's not like there were other bidders. But she liked me, and we worked together with some of her clients—like I'm doing with you. And she knew they'd be in good hands. A book like hers—a thoroughly vetted list of top-tier clients? That's almost priceless."

"Your business fascinates me, I must confess. It's a market unlike any I've seen."

"In some ways, this is the ultimate luxury. It's personal, attentive, and completely for the client. Some people only buy things so that others know they own them. I see that all the time with the gallery. Anyone who owns one of those oversized balloon dogs by Koons is just screaming to his friends, 'Look at how much money I have to blow on shiny nonsense.' Our kind of consumption is special. The only people who know about the experience are me and the client. What could be more exclusive?"

"It's like an expert performance for an audience of one."

"Yes, but the audience is also part of the performance. It's a unique art form. It's personal, intuitive, interactive, adaptive, and utterly ephemeral."

"It's the ultimate, hands-on improvisation for two. You're the director and the lead actress, and he's the lead actor and the audience."

"Something like that. It's erotic performance art."

"I'm even more fascinated, but the safety issue still troubles me. You don't know any of your colleagues, and they don't know you?"

"Not anymore. I used to, but once I got my practice where I wanted it to be, I stopped reaching out to the other women. It was better for me to fly far below the radar."

"What do you gain by being so invisible? What about referrals?"

"Secrets are powerful. If they're not sure I exist, the possibility of mischief is moot. This practice is very quiet."

"Your clients know. Your employees know. That seems like a lot of people right there."

"I found my employees through the scene. They understand the importance of discretion, too. And if I need a spare pair of hands in the dungeon, they can help. But mostly, they run the gallery."

"So that guy who packed my stuff is kinky?"

"Yes. Josh is a bottom. If I'm feeling generous, I'll give him a caning. He's very sweet."

"So they can run interference if anyone unwelcome stops by. Like the cops."

"Absolutely. Notice how I don't have any neighbors? This means zero-risk from nosy neighbors. And as I've mentioned, all my clients are thoroughly vetted. They are not cops. They will not call the cops. You will not be arrested. And if you want to talk to a lawyer about this, I have Samuel Edelson, one of the top criminal defense attorneys on retainer, and he loves talking to bad girls."

"Okay, so I probably won't be arrested."

"If you're arrested, something truly unprecedented has happened. And if it happens, I will cover your defense."

"So I'm unlikely to be arrested and even less likely to go to jail. What else can I do to protect myself?"

"Well, let's give you a new name. You're not Amy anymore. Who do you want to be?"

I grimaced, even as my mind flitted back to all the pseudonyms I'd used at the George Hotel. "Who do you think I am?"

"You're tall, you're smart, you're regal. You should be named for a queen."

"Elizabeth? Mary?"

"No," Erika paused. "Catherine. Cat for short."

"An empress. How fancy. Didn't she fuck a horse?"

"That's a myth. But what an amazing legend. It says she's fearless in the face of a stallion and all his sexual energy."

"Oh my…" I fanned myself. "I don't want to make promises I can't keep."

"Don't be silly. It's just a name. But the guys will like it. A lot."

"Okay, I'm Catherine. Do I need a last name?"

"It's better if you have one. That way, if you leave a message with an assistant or on voicemail, you just identify yourself. But your pseudonym must sound real. There are some ladies in this business who have crazy names—like the Marquise de Sade or I.M. Stern. Can you imagine choosing that?"

"Yeah, those are really subtle."

"And then there are the stripper names, like Minx, Steele, Brutal. So trashy. So déclassé. My clients wouldn't want to have anything to do with those vulgar women." Erika's contempt for her competition was obvious.

"I had no idea you were such a snob! I like Steele. The name sounds solid. And Minx sounds like someone who'd be really fun. Let me think about it. Maybe something French?"

"Just not de Sade! You can do better."

"Understood." We sat there, carefully packing her gear so the rubber wouldn't snag or tear. "Why isn't this business suffering? How do your clients justify the expense of seeing you? You're the ultimate luxury."

"Well, not everyone is hurting right now. One of my clients, a real bondage freak, cashed out a year ago. He knew something was going to happen, and now he's just watching and waiting."

"That was prescient. I wish I'd had his foresight."

"Don't we all? You're only seeing the losers in this crisis. But there are winners. They're out there. And some of them come here, cash in hand."

"But that must be a minority of your clients."

"True. And some are hurting. And I won't hear from most of them … They'll just drift away until the need to submit becomes acute and they have to call me. Or maybe they'll see one of those cut-rate mistresses, in one of those trashy McDungeons, and get scared. Those guys will be back, too."

"You make it sound like an addiction."

"Not exactly. But having a fetish can involve compulsion. Every hobby's like that. There are golfers who can't keep away from the driving range, even when they've got a back injury. Kink isn't any different."

"I believe you. I'm just stunned the financial crisis hasn't ruined your business. Everyone I know is saving every penny."

"You're not paying attention, Amy. Haven't you noticed that some bars and restaurants are buzzing. For everyone who gets tight-fisted, there's someone else who says 'there's no time like the present.'"

"I guess. It's hard for me to get my head around what you're saying."

"The same thing happened after 9/11. Some guys stopped visiting. They wanted to nest, spend time with their families. But others doubled down. More sessions, more often. The terrorist attack was devastating to the city, but it also inspired turbulence of the libido. Business was quiet for the first couple of weeks after, but then it was up for months. The art world was dead, but I was selling tons of spankings."

"Kink as the perfect hedge? When art goes down, perversion goes up. And vice versa."

"It's not perfect, but I'm still afloat, and that's saying a lot. I just heard another one of my neighbors is closing his gallery. He couldn't cover his rent."

"Fuck."

"Yeah. Fuck. So please keep the guys engaged while I'm gone. Call me with any questions, or if anything happens, because I always want a hedge. Seeing a few clients a week is my safety net. But if I can score this Hirst, I'll be set for years."

"I don't need a Hirst. I just need a job."

"This mess could drag on for a while. You need a hedge, too."

"Bondage as a hedge against banking? That's an unusual strategy."

"Stick with me, baby. You ain't seen nothing, yet."

"You mean it gets weirder?"

"Only as weird as you want it to go. It takes two, and your consent and comfort are just as important as the client's."

"I've been reading about limits. It's usually the submissive's that come in to play. The red line beyond which they don't want to go."

"Sure. Some clients hate humiliation. Others don't want pain. We all have limits. I don't have sex with clients. That's a hard limit. Some dommes draw the line in other places."

"I get it. I'm still struggling with the prospect of their arousal."

"It takes some adjustment. But after a few sessions, their erections will become unremarkable."

"Ho, hum . . . Just another hard-on at the office?"

"Exactly. I'm really glad you're here. You get it." Erika gave me her most seductive smile.

"I hope so. I still worry I'm going to get caught."

"If you don't talk, they won't talk. So keep this to yourself, and you'll be fine."

"That's what Michael said, too. And I haven't told anyone. Not that there's anyone to tell."

"When you see my files, you'll understand. No one wants to air their dirty laundry. And this stuff is out there. If I didn't think you were discreet, I would never have brought you downstairs."

"I have no intention of talking. About you or the guys."

"That's great, because my privacy and security are now in your hands. If you tell the wrong person, you can hurt me, too. We are all in this together, now."

"Michael called it 'mutually assured destruction.'"

"He would and he's right. But as outrageous as the work may seem, peo-ple try it all the time. I've known women who worked in a dungeon for only a few days. Others do it for decades. And none of us talks. We kinksters understand that our safety depends on the silence of others. We respect that. It's a code of honor."

"I don't know what to say. I want to believe you, that everyone is as serious and as upstanding as you are."

"This can be the best part-time job ever because you have complete control over your time. It only takes two or three sessions to make a great week. So, if you need to travel out of town for a job interview, just don't book any sessions those days. That's how I balanced the needs of the gallery with the needs of my clients."

"You make it sound easy. Part of me can't believe what you're proposing, and the other part of me can't believe I'm giving it a shot."

"Yes, I understand. You aren't coming to the work from the usual place. I've been dabbling in S&M since high school. The work evolved organically from the interest."

"You were a teenager, and you knew you liked this stuff?"

"I'd read *Story of O* and thought that gothic embrace of pain and pleasure was for me."

"It's on my reading list, but I haven't gotten to it yet."

"It's a very decadent love story. Did I give you a copy of *Venus in Furs*, too? It's the flip side of *O*."

"It's also in my pile."

"Great. So that takes care of the fiction of dominance and submission. And then you'll see my files, which are the nitty-gritty nonfiction. They'll give you roadmaps to successful sessions."

"I need all the guidance I can get."

"Tomorrow, I'll introduce you to a few of my regulars. And what you'll see is they're very clear about what they want and need. You just need to pay attention."

"That's one step closer to making this real." I paused, still incredulous that I was inching towards sex work. But there were more immediate, practical matters to consider. "What should I wear?"

"That short black skirt we were just talking about. And something revealing up top. You don't need to go full fetish. Well, except for your hose and shoes. Wear fishnets or a pair of back seamed hose. And very high heels. You want to look commanding."

"Back seamed hose? I don't have anything like that in my closet. Let alone fishnets."

"You'll have to get some. 'Art is in the details.' But I have some spares until you get your own."

CHAPTER 14

NOM DE GUERRE

My apartment had been emptied of almost all my belongings, leaving me with only an air mattress, a couple of boxes stacked nearly in a corner, and my suitcases—the essential cargo for my detour. In only a few days, I'd be moving into Erika's apartment, and it was imperative that I should have the right ensembles for the next couple of months. Clothing had always been a costume, and Chelsea required something different from Wall Street. I'd packed accordingly.

Even though most thought the crisis would linger another six to twelve months, I still wanted a few sharp business suits at the ready. I remained desperate for an interview, with anyone, anywhere, from Miami to São Paulo. Unfortunately, no one was calling me for a job, and all of my calls were going unreturned.

Beyond the obligatory Armani suits, I packed anything from my old life that had a whiff of fetish about it. Every short skirt I owned, a couple of kinky bras, and any pump with a heel above four inches. There weren't many shoes that would work at Erika's, but there were a few pairs, purchased in those frantic after-Xmas sales at Bergdorf's where the women swoop down on half-price Manolos like vultures attacking carrion.

My parents were staggered and alarmed when they learned I was giving up my lease. My mother immediately told me to consider a return to Burlington. She was sure I could find a great job back in Vermont, and a man, of course. "Bob Huntley's single. Did you know his veterinary hospital has six vets, and he's planning on expanding further?"

"No, Mom. Wasn't Bob the guy who called me a lesbian? Like a gazillion times. He made my life hell."

"Oh, right . . . Well, that was high school. You're both older now."

Talking to my mother was rarely easy, but this conversation was particularly excruciating. I could hardly tell her that hooking up with Bob wouldn't happen because I was going to be busy torturing wealthy New Yorkers.

My father was much more sympathetic. He wanted to know if I was going to use the layoff, which he delicately called a "hiatus," to do something fun. Try yoga at an ashram in Bali? Take pasta-making in Tuscany? Go trekking in Nepal? Even though he was born and raised in Burlington, he read *National Geographic* diligently. His curiosity extended far beyond my mother's, whose preferences for the safe and familiar always trumped his desires.

I didn't like answering too many of their queries, because doing so reminded me that I was keeping more and bigger secrets. It was also humiliating to tell my dad that running off to go trekking was beyond my means. My portfolio had been filled with risk, and my holdings had been pummeled. If Citibank had offered me a spot in their Karachi office, the proposal would have merited serious consideration.

To allay their misgivings, I promised to visit once settled at Erika's. This seemed to placate my mother, which was its intended effect. In the short term, I wouldn't have to answer questions about what I was doing. Instead, I'd get to answer questions about when I was coming to Vermont.

Once I'd finished being deceptive to my parents, it was time to formalize a different lie. While I sat alone in my empty apartment, sipping one of three remaining Diet Cokes in my fridge, it was time to find a last name for Catherine.

My initial instinct was "Lemieux." I was searching my brain for French names, and it was the first one that popped to mind thanks to the hockey player, Mario. It took only a second to dismiss it. *Le mieux* meant "the best," and that level of expertise was far beyond mine. It was also masculine. Catherine deserved a name beginning with "la."

I scanned Google for ideas. "Lacroix" sounded fashionable, but too religious. The prospect of dealing with real penitents unnerved me. My Catholicism was so lapsed that crosses scared me. "Laguerre" was intriguing, because I often thought of the war between the sexes, but it seemed awfully martial. "Laflamme" was a no-go, because my hair was brown, not red. And then I spotted "Lachance," which was a reference to luck. There hadn't been much luck in the past year, so it was a name that dripped with irony, even as it exuded hope. I called Erika immediately with my decision. I would be Catherine Lachance. She approved.

At lunchtime, I presented myself for duty in Chelsea wearing a black skirt I'd bought online in an Ambien-fueled shopping frenzy. It had been too short for the office, coming only halfway down my thighs and revealing my gap. It had lurked, unworn, in my closet for a year waiting for its chance to be seen.

I had a single black longline bra that I'd picked up to wear at some highbrow charity event the bank was supporting. To play my part in the bank's theater of community engagement, I owned a black strapless dress by Ralph Lauren. The dress had a dusting of beads and a tiny bit of tulle, but it was otherwise simple and clean. It made me look like a patron of the arts, without requiring any knowledge of opera or ballet. The bra itself was a feat of engineering. It squeezed my ribcage as it thrust my breasts upward and outward. In it, my average C-cups looked like they belonged to a pinup. Jon gave me a wolf whistle whenever I wore it, making it ideal for the looming introductions.

The crazy black patent pumps that Michael had picked out for me at De-Mask would be carried to Chelsea, not worn. With their platform base and 5-inch stiletto heels, they were strictly indoor shoes, and ideally, to be worn only while seated.

Before we'd parted company, Erika had handed me a package of Victoria's Secret fishnet thigh highs. It was almost underwhelming. If I'd thought about it at all, I would have imagined she'd wear some fetishy, esoteric brand.

But no, Victoria's Secret was the mainstay of Erika's hosiery wardrobe. The pros know what it takes to get the job done, and Victoria, with all her secrets, was up to the task.

The specifics of meeting clients would require coaching. I brought my makeup bag with me, unsure if a look that said "day" or "night" was preferable in the dim lighting of the dungeon. Or if there was some other factor that needed consideration.

When I arrived at her apartment, Erika took one look at me and guided me to her bathroom, which had an enormous vanity with a mirror that would not have looked out of place backstage at a burlesque. In that unforgiving light, she sized me up. "You're on the right track. You want to look like an amplified version of yourself, but not a caricature. Think Paris, by way of Pigalle."

"Where the streetwalkers worked?"

"Yes, but they were the most chic streetwalkers ever. Just start with a little foundation to even out your skin." Erika wiped her face clean and we did our makeup together. I had the tools, but lacked the knowledge.

"Now, you need to play up your eyes. During scenes, the men want to stare into them, and feel like you're understanding their suffering. The eyes are key. I go with gray shadows, for a subtle smoky look." She gave me a hard stare. "I think you're better served with browns. Use the dark shadows closest to your eyelashes, and then this vanilla on your brow ridge. And use black eyeliner on your waterline. It adds drama." It took a few tries, but I finally got it done to Erika's specifications.

"You have gorgeous cheekbones. They're French, *n'est ce pas?*"

"*Oui, madame.* French Canadian, actually."

"Make them more pronounced without being cartoonish." Erika took a brush, dabbed it in some contour powder, and showed me where and how to apply the powder. It felt ridiculous getting a tutorial about something most girls master at fifteen, and yet I knew the limits of my expertise.

"And lastly, the lips. What colors have you got?"

I poured out my lipsticks onto her counter, and she inspected the tubes. "Too neutral." "Too invisible." "Too pink." She turned to me, fished out a

Chanel tube from her stash. "Use this. You want deep red lips. They say you mean business." It was like we were back in Boston, as she applied the blood red cream. "Check yourself out. You look stunning."

Reflexively, I grimaced. Mirrors show me all my flaws and failures, so it was a surprise when I checked my reflection and barely recognized the person looking back. Erika had done little, but she had done it artfully. There was dungeon-ready drama, but it was mostly polish.

"Leave your hair down. It's so pretty today." I gave my hair a brush so that it fell in long, smooth waves. Erika pulled her tresses back into a severe bun, while her bangs framed her face.

"Read this. This is what Arnim enjoys. He's our first appointment." She handed me a file folder with his name, "Arnim Schmidt" printed formally on the tab.

"Who's your secretary for this stuff?"

"Me. I keep all my own files, and my standards are high. Read it, and you'll understand."

I sat down with Arnim's file open in my lap, and it had multiple pages inside, each describing prior scenes, and what had worked and what hadn't. She was as detailed as she had promised.

Visit #3: We undertook a role play where he was a boss who had sexually assaulted me, a female subordinate. I threatened to complain to HR unless he showed he had changed. He looked ashen, and asked how we might keep this between us. I suggested a spanking. Over my knee. He agreed. I began with my hand and then escalated to a hairbrush and a tawse. Arnim howled, and promised he'd be a good boy and he'd treat women at work better. I said that wasn't enough. That he needed a more brutal kind of punishment. He pleaded for mercy, but I offered none. He shook when he saw the cane.

Even as Arnim was shrieking, his erection was visible. This was highly arousing. I bent him over the spanking horse, leaving his hands/arms free. Then I chastised him for his deplorable behavior.

He groveled, desperate to avoid the cane. I brought it down hard on the horse, and he'd jump. But when I told him to assume the position, he did so, with his chest on the horse and his buttocks presented for punishment. As I was stroking him with the cane, I reminded him that bad behavior begets bad consequences, and if he wants to avoid being punished in future, he must treat women better. He agreed to do so. As a conciliatory gesture, I invited him to masturbate while I gave him the final strokes of the cane. I indicated that it would enmesh pleasure and pain together, and every time he jerks off, he would be reminded of his worst behavior and this would challenge him to be a better boss. This precipitated an orgasm onto the floor.

NB don't forget to put down a large towel prior to commencing the scene.

The biographic information was succinct yet helpful:

Arnim Schmidt

Born: August 21, 1952.

5'9", 160lbs. Athletic.

Software company CEO.

Lives in Minneapolis, comes to NYC often on business.

Hobbies: flying and golf.

Referred by Madame Margot.

1st session May 8, 2002. Visits monthly.

Feels overwhelmed by the stress and responsibility of his job and uses erotic spankings as a release. Has been active in the scene for twenty years, but due to family commitments, he can only pursue release on an infrequent basis.

Interests centers on discipline. Likes formalized correction. Bondage not required unless he squirms. Have tied face down to rack and across the spanking horse. Backs of thighs are particularly sensitive—use broad paddle to avoid bruising. Hairbrush, strap, cane, belt have produced positive results. Discreet marking is acceptable, but nothing his underwear can't conceal. Chastise like a naughty schoolboy. Release permitted, but only after he "earns" it.

CHAPTER 15

A CEO CHASTENED

Erika was busy readying the gear for Arnim's visit, while I read through her extensive notes on prior sessions. I was beginning to understand why she was so confident her files offered a roadmap. Being dressed down verbally for his sexist misdeeds seemed just as critical to Arnim as the actual discipline, and while I could talk the sexism, the notes seemed intended for someone with greater familiarity with the language of kink. "What's a tawse?"

Erika held up a leather implement with a long split in the leather. It looked like a belt, cut lengthwise, so that two long tails flapped independently. "*This* is a tawse." She brought it down, like a whip, against the spanking horse where it made a loud snap. "It's what the Scots used to keep misbehaving school children in line. It's a classic tool for corporal punishment. We'll be using it today."

"And Arnim likes that?"

"'Like' might not be the right word. He *appreciates* the tawse. And tomorrow, the memory of the tawse will excite him."

"Hit me with it." If I was going to use the implement, it was critical to know how it felt.

"Are you sure? It's going to sting."

"Just do it."

"Well, if you want to do it right, raise your skirt. This works best on bare skin."

I inched up my skirt and bent over, putting my hands firmly on the surface of the rack. "Okay. I'm ready."

"No you're not. Spread your feet. Assume the position." Erika abruptly moved my legs back and apart with her knee, in one powerful motion. Then, she applied force on my back, lowering my shoulders and exposing my bottom more fully.

"Oh." I inhaled sharply, as my blood pressure spiked. "This position." I immediately felt more vulnerable.

"Yes. Do you feel the difference between how you stand instinctively, and how I placed you?"

"Yes. Everything feels more stretched and pronounced. I liked the way you seized control and the upper hand. Now what?"

"Now I discipline you. You can back out, of course. This would be a good time to talk about safewords. Do you have one?"

"Uh, no. I've never needed one before."

"Most people like colors—'red' for stop, and sometimes 'yellow' for slow down. A few oddballs like words, like 'banana' or 'aardvark,' things you'd never say otherwise."

"The colors are easier to remember. I get 'red,' but when does 'yellow' come into play. Isn't that putting a lot of control in the hands of someone who wants to cede power?"

"You've captured the paradox of domination. The bottom is in control. To a degree, anyway. My goal is to make them never want to use a safeword, and to never burst the illusion that I'm in charge. The trick is to skate up to a limit, to get them close to using a safeword, but never actually compelling them to use it."

"You weaponize empathy?"

"That sounds sinister. But the best tops tune in to the bottom's suffering, and then play with it. I'll show you how it's done with Arnim. We're going to be hands-on, if that's okay with you."

"In for a penny, right? Just tell me what to do."

"That's the right attitude. I'll be presenting you as my trainee and giving him the opportunity to help with your education. Only do as much as you feel like, but don't be afraid, either. You did great with Michael. This should be straightforward. No knots, only swats!"

"A little domination humor!"

"And why not? This stuff is supposed to be fun. We're not curing cancer here."

While we prepared the room for Arnim's arrival, Erika demonstrated the various implements on me. The hairbrush left me unimpressed, as did the ruler. The paddle pushed me into the bench, but it was otherwise benign. The tawse was sharp and memorable. And then she lightly tapped my bottom with a cane. Very little force produced maximum sensation. An acute pain began in my ass and then radiated through my body, and I wanted to surrender to it. "Do it again. Harder, please."

Erika didn't hesitate. She drew back her arm and sliced the rattan through the air and across the backs of my thighs. The cane whistled and made a loud crack as it hit my skin. The searing sensation made me grab the rack, as my fingers dug into the leather. I howled. "Again, please."

Once again, Erika brought the cane down across my bottom, making me gasp. The sensation filled my head, and I couldn't think of anything else. The ache was encompassing. It wasn't pleasurable, but it emptied me of my worries. I hadn't felt that delicious nullity since the George, but I'd also had enough. "No more, thanks. Christ, that hurt."

"Let me rub a little aloe vera into your skin. It'll help." As Erika applied some gel to my sensitized skin, the soothing sensation of the cool lotion overcame the heat of the cane. I sighed with relief as a different emptiness took over.

"That's part of the game, isn't it? You make them ache, and then you make them better?"

"It can be. Absolutely. Some guys like it when you toggle between stern and sensual. It keeps them off balance." Just then, the buzzer sounded. "Arnim's here. I'll go get him."

While Erika was fetching her willing victim, I played with the implements. The cane balanced in my hand, and it made a slicing noise when whipped through the air. The paddles had more substance. They felt solid and sturdy as I swung them, like weighted tennis racquets. Erika and Arnim arrived just as I was flicking the crop against the spanking horse. They caught me mid-strike.

"Arnim, the gorgeous woman wielding the crop is my trainee, Catherine." I walked over to Arnim and extended my hand, just as if it were a business meeting, and he responded in kind. The start of the encounter was extraordinary only in its banality.

Schmidt was stocky. His muscular body was covered with a thick layer of padding. He looked like a guy who could take a serious beating, or dish one out if required. When Erika instructed him to stand in the middle of the room, I could see a slight grin on his face. He was having fun.

He was still fully clothed as Erika circled him. Arnim stood at attention as she removed his jacket, a move I'd seen her perform with Michael. Undressing the gentleman was done in stages, with a theatrical flourish. She handed the jacket to me, and I placed it on an elegant rosewood valet in the corner of her dungeon.

"Undo Arnim's belt and hand it to me, Catherine."

"Yes, Erika." Like an obedient deputy, I flipped the buckle open and extracted Arnim's belt with a quick jerk. Arnim adjusted his body, as his weight shifted from the applied force. I folded the belt in half, lay it on my outstretched palms, and presented it with a flourish to the woman in charge. If I was going to be there in the dungeon, it was essential to embrace the camp inherent in my role. I'd never met Arnim before, and it was up to me if I'd ever see him again.

Erika proceeded to dress him down. "You've been naughty, I can tell. Your behavior has not been up to my high standards, has it?"

Arnim muttered quietly, "No, Mistress Erika."

"I didn't think so. I can see the guilt on your face. And I'm going to see the stripes on your ass in a moment. Take off your clothes and hand them to Catherine." Arnim hung his head like a schoolboy caught peeking at another student's test. He unbuttoned his shirt, removed his pants, shoes and socks, handing me each article as he stepped out of it. Only his white boxers remained, as he stood with his hands clasped in front of him.

"Are you ready to serve as target practice for Catherine? You both need remedial instruction."

"Yes, Mistress Erika. Catherine can practice on my ass." He barely whispered his acquiescence.

"Thanks, Arnim. I still have a lot to learn. Which of these should I try first?" I held the wooden paddle and the leather tawse in front of Arnim, who looked at each implement in turn. He pursed his lips and said nothing.

Erika paused, shifting her weight from one foot to the other as she tested each tool against her hand. "The paddle will really hurt today." She whacked it against her hand, making a loud thump. Then she returned the paddle to me and grabbed the tawse. In front of Arnim, she brought it down in a sharp move against her palm. "Ouch." She yanked her fingers back and gave her hand a quick shake. Arnim's breathing deepened as he watched Erika abuse her own hand. "The tawse always hurts. Let's practice with it today." She handed the leather whip to me.

"Excellent. I wanted to try the tawse." I gave Arnim a slight smile. "It looks painful."

"It isn't just painful, is it Arnim? It's excruciating." Arnim nodded slowly, his jowly face having turned resolute and ready. "Bend over. Grab the bench." Erika pointed at the spanking bench, with its broad leather surface.

"Yes, Mistress Erika." Bent over the padded bench, Arnim's fingers turned white, as they squeezed the edges.

I walked up beside him, noting his outstretched arms, and his bottom, still covered with his boxers. It felt surreal, treating a 55-year-old man like a youthful miscreant, and yet that was the task at hand. With my left hand, I pushed down on his back while nudging his feet further away from the bench with my knee. I could see the changes to Arnim's breathing, as his broad chest expanded and contracted more slowly.

Stepping back from his body, I positioned myself to ensure the tawse would fall centered on his bottom. In a practice motion, I slowly brought my arm through an arc, as if the tawse were a badminton racquet. Arnim must have been watching me, because when the tawse touched his skin, he jumped, even though the strike was as gentle as a caress.

Once confident my aim was accurate, I brought my hand through that same motion, only at a much faster pace. And when the leather impacted Arnim's ass, it let out a serious crack, followed by a serious yelp. I looked over at Erika, and she nodded, so I did it again. And again. And again.

And once Arnim was collapsed onto the bench, I told him to drop his boxers so that I could hit his bare skin. "Oh please, Miss. My bum is so sore. Please."

"Your bum is going to be even more sore when I'm done with it. You've been bad, haven't you?" The prospect of improvising disciplinary patter was daunting. Erika routinely filled hours of session time with her monologues about the consequences of bad behavior, and after only a few sentences, I was grasping for ideas that didn't seem ridiculous. It was a relief when I remembered a sentence in Erika's notes, where Arnim had been taken to task for being a pig of a boss. Feeling perverse, I asked a business question. "What percentage of your senior management team is women? Tell me?"

"Uh, seriously?"

"Do I seem un-serious to you?" I felt un-serious, but there were hours to fill, and it was the only topic that occurred to me.

"No, Miss. It's, I dunno, 15%."

Clearly, he'd never bothered to tally, and that was genuinely irritating. "Liar. In software, I've never seen over ten."

"I'm sorry, Miss. I don't know the number. I was guessing. It's hard to think right now."

"I understand. But that's not good enough. Does that seem good enough to you?" I'd learned from Erika that a client's behavior is rarely sufficient to avoid painful consequences.

"No, Miss. I've been remiss. I'm sorry." I gave his bare ass a solid hit with the tawse.

"I don't want to hear apologies. I want to hear a plan."

"I'll do better." He readied himself for another blow with the tawse, and I obliged.

"That's idle talk. Tell me one thing you'll do tomorrow. Something verifiable." His skin was striped and it was making me worry about marks.

"Seriously? One thing? Shit." His voice flipped from naughty schoolboy to corporate CEO. I gave him another blow with the tawse.

"Do I need to hit you harder to focus your attention?" We were eating up minutes, without destroying his body, and that felt like a victory. I brought the tawse down against the bench, so that it struck in front of his face and I left it lying in front of his eyes. Erika shrugged her shoulders with indifference when I discreetly pointed at the angry red welts. It was a clear signal to proceed.

"No, Miss. I'll talk to HR. Maybe I need a diversity committee?"

"That's a start. Mistress Erika, could you hand me the cane, please?"

Erika wandered over to a leather umbrella stand filled with canes of different lengths, thicknesses and shapes. She pulled out an assortment. "Which do you prefer, *Mistress* Catherine?"

Her use of the dungeon honorific didn't go unnoticed to me or to Arnim. "The one with the red handle, please." I took it in my hand and felt its balance as the air further deflated from Arnim's lungs.

"You do realize there are consequences for such shoddy performance?" I tapped the tip of the cane across the raised stripes that crisscrossed Arnim's bottom.

"Yes, *Mistress* Catherine. I'll talk to HR tomorrow and see what I can do."

"I want you to taste what will happen if you fail to impress me next time. Are you ready for your caning?" Arnim said nothing at first. So I repeated myself. "Are you ready for your caning, Arnim?"

"Yes, Mistress Catherine." His body shifted and his legs stiffened. I tapped him a few times, teasing him with the rattan. But once his body relaxed, I brought the cane down sharply across his ass. Arnim grunted in response.

Erika caught my eye and waved a towel at me. I nodded at her, and she placed it on the ground by Arnim's feet. "Arnim, I realize these lessons are painful. But a tough guy like you needs strong medicine."

"Yes, Mistress Catherine. I need a painful caning to correct my bad behavior."

"That's exactly right. So, I'm going to cane you now. Slowly. And I want you to jerk off as I'm doing it."

"Yes, Mistress."

"And this way, every time you masturbate—and I know you do it often, you naughty boy—you're going to be reminded that your behavior has consequences."

"Yes, Mistress. Serious consequences."

"I'll give you a head start. Begin stroking your cock. And I'll begin caning you in a moment."

"Yes, Mistress. I'm jerking off now. Jerking off for you and Mistress Erika." A sing-song quality appeared in his voice. He was saying his lines and performing the fantasy that had been rattling around in his head.

"Very good. You're a very good boy. But you can be so much better." I paused and gave him a whack. "You're going to HR tomorrow. And you're going to hire more women. You have work to do."

"Yes, Mistress."

Arnim proceeded to pump his cock furiously, and every ten or twelve strokes, I'd bring the cane down on his ass. I didn't do it with any particular force, but more as a reminder to stay focused. And as he jerked off, I continued my monologue of women's empowerment in the executive suite. It felt ridiculous, but if I was going to chastise this man for his inadequate behavior, it might as well be for an important cause.

Arnim soon upped the pace of his fist, as he stood on his tiptoes and stretched his body. He grunted, then emptied his cock into the towel Erika had positioned on the floor. Within seconds of his orgasm, Erika had Arnim wrapped in a large bathrobe. Her attention to customer service was extraordinary. And once he'd gotten his comeuppance, Arnim seemed looser and more relaxed than when we first met.

"Well, that was something . . . Catherine. I'm going to feel this for days."

"I hope so." I smiled, unsure what the right response was. "I may need some ibuprofen for my arm. You took a lot."

"Yeah." He turned to Erika and grinned. "Your trainee is talented. Diabolical. I thought she was serious for a minute."

Erika nodded at me. "Catherine was very serious. If you don't want to be savaged next time, you'd better have a plan for more diversity at your company."

I shrugged at Arnim. "I'm very passionate about closing the gender gap." It wasn't something that had animated me much before, but in the moment and in the dungeon, it seemed appropriate.

"Shit. You're not joking." Arnim breathed in deeply. "Alright. You have a point. And maybe I'm a little scared of you."

"You say the nicest things, Arnim. I like inspiring fear." I had no idea if Arnim would talk to HR, or if he was truly frightened of me, but it felt strangely empowering to plant the idea that he needed more women in his midst. Even if he did nothing, I could pretend I was doing something. And should he return for another session, this conversation would give me something to discuss in greater depth.

Erika brought him a glass of fresh orange juice. "This should perk you up. Sit down. Catch your breath. I'm impressed. You really endured."

"Yeah, I did, didn't I!" Arnim looked pleased, as he plopped himself on top of the rack, and stretched.

"Your ass doesn't hurt when you sit on it?" It seemed extraordinary that just minutes after he'd taken a caning, he was seated so comfortably.

"Not really. But you sure dished it out, Catherine. How long have you been doing this?"

I looked at Erika, who shrugged. "A couple of weeks?"

"You're shitting me." Arnim turned to Erika. "This chick's a natural."

"I knew you'd like her." Erika resumed tidying up, and I delighted the compliment. "I'm going on a scouting trip to Europe and I'll be gone for a month or two. Catherine's taking over for me. I hope you'll take advantage of her arm in my absence, otherwise your behavior may lapse."

"Absolutely. Catherine, I'll be in touch. I have my marching orders."

"You know just what to say, Arnim. You're a real gentleman." I doubted he'd do anything specific at work, but it pleased me to hear him say he would.

Then Erika walked Arnim over to a private restroom where he took a shower and put on his clothes. Ten minutes later, he emerged looking like he'd just had a meeting. "That was excellent. I'll be in touch. Thank you, ladies."

Erika kissed him on each cheek, and then she escorted him out of the gallery. When she returned, she retrieved a fat envelope that Arnim had left behind in the restroom. In front of me, she divvied up the money. We each got half—a thousand for her, and a thousand for me—in crisp hundred-dollar bills. "You did good, Amy. Next, it's Peter at four. Let's clean up."

Erika showed me how to clean the surfaces of all the equipment we'd used—Lysol wipes on the metal and sealed wood surfaces, saddle soap on the leather implements. "You have to do this right after every encounter. The equipment will still be out, so you'll know exactly what you used. You just need to wipe it all down. If you have any questions, ask Josh upstairs."

"Got it. So what's Peter's thing?"

"Let me get his file, and you'll understand." Erika disappeared into her office and returned with another fat file containing meticulous descriptions of every visit Peter had made to her Chelsea basement. I sat down and consumed it. Once again, to my great relief, I didn't know him. Peter Frank was an orthopedic surgeon whose specialty was performing hip replacements. Like Arnim, Peter was not someone I'd cross paths with under normal circumstances. It felt safe to transgress with him.

CHAPTER 16

THE ULTIMATE PERFORMANCE ART

While I got busy learning the ins and outs of Peter's psychosexual makeup, Erika got ready to exploit it. She wandered around the dungeon, pulling items out of drawers and cupboards, and placing them on the padded leather surface above the cage. There were paddles, whips, knives, hoods, electrodes, anal plugs of varying sizes, clamps, clothespins, candles, and even some medical implements.

The assortment of toys baffled me. "Are we going to use all this today?" I waved my hand over the arsenal.

"Perhaps. That's up to you. And Peter." Erika smirked as she spoke. "Do you know Marina Abramović's work 'Rhythm 0'?"

"No." Erika was the art expert, not me. "What's it about?"

"It's a performance art piece where she put a bunch of objects on a table. She lay there passively, and the audience was invited to use them on her. Some of the objects were about pleasure, while others were about pain. She even had a gun and a bullet available."

"Christ, that's crazy. Who does that?" I looked at the bench again to see if there was a pistol I'd missed, when my eyes landed on the anal toys. "She had butt plugs in her piece?"

"No. That's my own *special* variation. I'm going to have Peter lie down, unbound, like Marina. And then what happens will be up to you and his safe-word."

"Oh, that sounds intense."

"It should be. The term of art for this kind of scene is 'mindfuck.'"

"Whose mind is being fucked, his or mine?"

"Yes." Erika paused for dramatic effect. "You understand."

At precisely 4 p.m., there was a knock on the dungeon door. Peter had ar-rived for his session. He was a tall, lanky man with thinning brown hair and a friendly smile. As soon as he entered the dungeon, Erika pointed at a spot in the middle of the floor with a good view of the assortment, and with her other hand, she held her index finger up to her mouth, to signal silence. Peter took his spot and didn't say a word.

"Welcome, Peter. This is my trainee, Catherine. Today, we are going to test your will to submit. You can use your safeword at any time, but once you do, you have to get dressed and leave. You are not to speak unless it's to say your safeword. Nod if you understand."

Peter nodded, and reflexively, so did I. Erika had that effect on me, too.

"Catherine, Peter's safeword is 'Red.' If you hear it, stop whatever you're doing immediately."

"I understand. If Peter says 'Red,' I drop everything."

"Excellent. Now Peter, I want you to take a good look at these things. Catherine will be using them on you today. She'll select something, show it to you, and it's up to you to decide if you want her to continue. I'm not going to tie you down. Your submission is all on you. Do you understand?"

Peter nodded again.

"Catherine, help Peter with his clothes."

In a slow and deliberate way, I peeled each layer off Peter, beginning with his olive suit jacket. He stood there motionless, except for a subtle tilting of his head, as I extracted his necktie, teasing the knot open with my fingers, and then slowly drawing the silk tail out from beneath his collar. I toyed with each button while undoing it, from the buttons on the front of his shirt, to the ones on his sleeves, to the one at the front of his pants. It was flattering and emboldening, to observe his excitement at my hands.

Soon, he was standing in the middle of the floor wearing only his white briefs, which offered a stark contrast to his tanned body. I walked over to the table and picked up a pair of scissors. With the metal tool balanced on my hands, he had a proper view of the gleaming blades. I waited a few beats while he saw and processed what was in front of him.

Silence.

I took the scissors in my right hand, and drew the sharp points down his body, scratching at his skin. Peter looked over at Erika, who nodded encouragingly in response. When the scissors reached his shorts, I pulled the fabric and inserted one of the blades close to his skin. I paused again, to give him a chance to react. More silence, but his cock stiffened noticeably, despite or because of its proximity to menace.

"Do you find this arousing?" I wiggled the scissors a bit, as the blade teased his skin. He inhaled sharply, in what was clearly an affirmative response.

With a quick snip from the waistband down to the bottom, I released one leg. I stepped back, tracing patterns on his abdomen and chest with the sharp tips, careful not to pierce his skin, but curious if he'd ask me to stop. Silence once again, but then he smiled, just like Jon would when he'd uncover some flawed assumption in a model by a junior employee. I hated that smug, self-confident smirk. It had always pissed me off.

This time, I put the blade alongside his cock and tightened my grip slowly, so that the fabric of his underwear sheared a millimeter at a time. I gave a real time narration. "Gee, Peter, one slip of my hand and I could cut some skin. A bigger slip, and I could cut your cock." He twitched, and his smile faltered. "Oh, you realize the stakes are real now, right? You don't know me at all. I could be your biggest nightmare. Don't you think it's crazy to trust a stranger with a sharp object so close to your nuts. Aren't you worried?" His smile disappeared. I was getting to him. "I might not plan to cut you, but things happen."

I shot Erika a quick glance, and her face remained neutral. Peter was standing statue-still and holding his breath. In tiny snipping motions, I destroyed the white cotton protecting his genitals. His cock emerged, shooting out perpendicular to his body. It had begun flaccid, but now it was rock hard and jutting. The threat of the scissors had produced an erection, no further contact required.

"Bend at the waist and put your hands on the table." Peter complied and found himself staring at the array of tools and devices that Erika had selected for his torment. "Don't blame me for anything that happens today." I ran my hands over his body and then lifted his chin, so he was looking into my eyes. "Erika picked them out for you. I'm just helping." Peter's cock bobbed as I grabbed an enormous butt plug and held it in front of his face. "How much work would it take to get this into you?" I tossed it down on the table in front of him. I picked up the container of clothespins. "Hey, Erika, I can put all these on his cock, right?" Peter and I both looked over at Erika.

"Sure. If they'll fit. I think his cock's just big enough. I bet he could take a dozen."

"That's what I thought. I'll keep that in mind."

I held up a black leather hood. "If I zip this closed, he can't see, right?"

"Yes. Blind as a bat."

"But where's the fun in that? Maybe it's better if he knows what's going to happen."

"It's all up to you, Catherine."

I grabbed a pair of nipple clamps and put them on Peter's chest as tightly as I could. "Did you hear that, Peter? It's all up to me." Peter nodded. "Then lie down on the table. It's time you got tested." I moved the toys and tools aside and Peter took his place, stretched out on the table, in a position very similar to the one Abramović adopted during her performance.

From whips to paddles to clamps, I tried every implement in an effort to get Peter to say "Red." My lungs mirrored his, as we inhaled and exhaled in unison. I could feel his anticipation in my body, and the tension thrilled me. There were a few moments where I was sure he might break, our breaths had become sharp and quick, but he retained his composure and persevered. It was almost hypnotic, watching the electricity form purple arcs between the violet wand and his skin as I zapped his cock and sensed the ache that satisfied his body. A few more jolts was all it took, before he ejaculated. Peter then squealed "Red! Red! Red!" I regained my focus and turned the machine off, as Erika swooped in to address its aftermath.

Erika whispered in his ear, "You may speak now, Peter."

"Holy shit, that was intense, Erika. I thought she was going to cut off my cock for a second. Where'd you find this one?"

"Catherine's great, isn't she?"

"Fucking awesome. She has that gleam in her eye that makes you wonder. Fuck."

"I knew you'd like her."

"Hell, yeah."

"I'm going away for a month or two, and if the urge to play overcomes you, call my office. Catherine's around."

Peter had a towel wrapped around his waist, and he jumped up and pumped my hand. "You'll be hearing from me. Great to meet you, Cat." He disappeared into the shower, leaving Erika and me alone in the dungeon.

"You did great, Amy. You found the flow. You pulled back when he was getting close to his limits, and you pushed forward when he had an endorphin rush."

"Seriously? I was just watching his jaw clench and unclench."

"Well, your instinct is phenomenal. The jaw can say a lot. You're a natural."

"The jaw tells all?"

"No. Some people show in their toes. Others, their brow. You just need to find the 'tell' that shows how close they are to the edge. My clients want you to understand them. You just need to pay attention."

"You make it sound simple."

"Like everything, it starts hard, but it becomes simple. You spotted how Peter communicates stress with his body. I didn't tell you to look at his jaw. You figured it out."

Once again, we undertook the ritual of sanitizing every surface and object we had touched. By the time we'd finished, Peter had emerged from the shower, restored to his prior self.

"Cat, I'm going to call you. See you soon."

"Looking forward to it."

"Bye, gorgeous. Hope your trip goes great. Gimme a call if you have a moment, you know I love hearing your voice."

"You're the best, Peter. I love hearing yours, too. But what I'll really want to hear is all about what Catherine's done to you. And I hope it's awful."

"Me too."

I gave him a little finger wave goodbye before entering the bathroom to clean it, as well. On the ledge by the bathroom sink, he'd left an envelope addressed to Erika.

"Hey, is this where they leave the 'tribute'? That's two for two today."

"Yes. I never ask for money, personally. They've been instructed to leave it behind. It's more civilized and the clients like that I trust them."

"Do they always pay?"

"Well, one guy didn't realize he'd forgotten his wallet until after. But he couriered over the envelope the next day. If they want to return, they have to pay. It's as simple as that. No freebies. Got it?"

"Got it." I handed over the envelope to her, and she pulled out another thick stack of hundred-dollar bills. There were $3,000 in total, and she divided the spoils evenly.

"So, things have been bumped up. I'm leaving the day after tomorrow. Do you understand the routine?"

"Yes and no. This still seems insane to me. You're trusting me with their safety and your revenue stream!"

"'My revenue stream'? I love it. And yes, I am. You're phenomenal. Both Arnim and Peter will be back in a couple of weeks. You don't need a lot of sessions to keep busy and make money, you just need enough."

"Right. A few a week."

"Follow me. I'll show you my files. But please, please, PLEASE don't lose them, show them to anyone, or do anything that will undermine the privacy of my clients. PLEASE. You can add your own notes—I'd like it if you did—but please respect the seriousness of the information at your fingertips."

I followed Erika into a small office in the basement that had a single four door file cabinet inside. "This is it, and here's the key. It's alphabetized by last name." She opened the top drawer to show me. "This is where my secrets live. Don't share this key with anyone."

"No, absolutely not." I took the key from Erika and promptly locked the drawer shut. "I don't need to look inside until I get a call."

"Precisely. It's better that way."

As Erika finished up her packing and planning for her Swiss adventure, I finished up packing and planning for my Chelsea adventure. It still seemed unreal or surreal that I was moving forward and taking over for Erika, but she had a way of bending people to her will. It was true of her clients, and it was true of me, too. She asks, the rest of us say "yes." It was easier than the alternative. And what else was I doing, anyway?

CHAPTER 17

MASTERING THE DUNGEON GRIND

The day after Erika left for Switzerland was the day I moved into her apartment, and the day I stepped into her life. Erika had put the contents of her bedroom closets into storage, likewise her personal effects, leaving me with a clean slate I could dump my own belongings into. It felt like staying in a movie set with the most exquisite furnishings. From the Nakashima table to the Jacobsen Egg chair, each item had been selected and placed with intention and style. Since couch surfing would be part of my immediate future, it might as well be near an Edward Wormley upholstered in the richest silk velvet.

Even though I had committed to seeing the odd client, I reminded myself daily, it was always possible to decline. There was just the matter of no in-flow of money, and a constant out-flow, from my student loans to my credit card bills. Everybody wanted a piece of my depleted checking account.

When the first call came in from one of Erika's clients, as much as I wanted to refuse immediately, the money beckoned. Two grand was too enticing, even if it required me to spank an ass or tie up a pair of balls. Staying on top of my financial commitments was far more worrying than dealing with some rich guy's perversions.

The first solo client was a harmless foot fetishist, who wanted nothing more complicated than to kneel at my feet as he nuzzled my toes. At the end of the session, I let him use my foot to jerk himself off. In just over an hour, I was $2,000 more solvent. A quick shower took care of any lingering saliva or cum on my insole. For all the transgression in the room, it was an alarmingly ordinary transaction. I felt no different afterward than following a seminar on interest rate modeling.

My second solo client was into cock and ball torment. It required some study online to grasp the full extent of what he wanted, but truly, it wasn't complicated. If the client says cock and ball torture, that's all you have to do. I tied him down and went to work on his testicles. From clamps, to crops, to crushers, Erika had an assortment of devices. Her gear was inventoried, labeled, and stowed specifically, and each device was designed to apply some fiendish amount of pain and pressure.

While deploying Erika's arsenal, the man's toes curled when confronted by a particularly evil contraption with screws that could be tightened a turn at a time to slowly ratchet up the pain. Once I noticed that "tell," I knew I had him. It was staggering to see the agony of his ball crushing turn into ecstasy, as his cock responded favorably to every incremental increase in misery. By the time I'd put the clothespins around the head of his cock, he was ready to explode. And when the clamp that was pinching the head of his penis shut was released, the cum just gushed out. Another happy customer, and another envelope with $2,000 in the bathroom.

I didn't see clients every day, but as I gathered steam and confidence, the frequency of sessions increased. And besides, there wasn't much else going on. I went to the HBS alumni mixers, called my fellow classmates, did as much networking as I could stand, but there were no job leads. Beyond reading back issues of *Institutional Investor*, or the latest sizzling white paper from the Federal Reserve, there wasn't much to do. The markets remained seized.

Lehman had collapsed, and the bankruptcy had kicked thousands of bankers onto the streets. I may have had a head start in networking, but there were so many unemployed MBAs that they overwhelmed the industry. My calls and emails were drowned out by the roar of their desperate voices.

I wasn't completely forgotten. My favorite statistician, Chen, called in every few weeks to gossip about who had been cut and who was still going. Jon never rang, but he continued to survive. I tried to suppress my painful suspicion that he'd been my "rogue reference." While replaying our conversation about my impending job offer, I grew convinced that he'd hesitated on the phone when I asked him to speak favorably on my behalf. I even wondered if he'd found himself another work wife.

Jon's actual wife, Susan, continued to leave me messages, which went directly to voicemail. I wasn't ready to face Susan, with her look of gentle concern, and a nod that communicated the perfect amount of empathy and encouragement. After all, the conversation would veer to Jon, and I'd have to hear about his successes, even as I was still expected to lie about his sleazy habits. Whenever the phone rang, I had to steel myself for something I wasn't fully prepared to encounter.

A perfect example was a call I received in my third week. It was from one of Erika's thickest files. I read page after page of Erika's session notes, and they revealed a man with a very narrow and specific set of needs and desires. He liked to be bound and left in a darkened room. There would be no pain, just isolation and immobilization, with the odd bit of erotic stimulation thrown in to keep things interesting. There were notes where Erika had tried different things, like introducing electrodes or a vibrator, but he wanted none of that. The human touch, a voice in the darkness, but nothing else. The bondage had to be inescapable, the room had to be dark, and he had to be left like that for hours.

The file was scant on identifying information. The client was a 47-year-old named Dan Levine, but beyond that, and his profound fondness for captivity, there wasn't much else. I googled the name, and found a few Dan Levines in medicine and accounting, but otherwise drew a blank. It seemed like a simple enough assignment, and he wasn't familiar, so I accepted.

The next day, a trim man with close-cropped dark hair appeared at my door. He was one of those in-between heights, not tall or short. In my Louboutin stilettos, I loomed over him.

"I understand you like very restrictive bondage. How do you feel about body bags?" Erika had a leather body bag that could turn a human into a leather-encased sausage, with only his head sticking out at the end.

"The bags aren't my thing. Leather cuffs. That's all I want."

I went to the drawer and pulled out Erika's wrist and ankle cuffs. "Any other wrinkles I should know about?"

"Lock the cuffs on me and lock me to something that can't move."

"The bondage will be inescapable." I'd read that some people preferred knowing that they could wriggle their way out of bondage—that that knowledge added to their experience. While others needed to understand that the bondage exceeded their capacity for escape. Somehow, knowing resistance was futile added to their enjoyment. They could just lie back and submit to the experience without wondering how they might flee.

"Right. Completely inescapable. And I want it dark. Turn the lights out."

"Okay. That's what Erika told me. Thanks for confirming the details. We'll get right to it once you're undressed."

Dan stood up and I helped him remove his clothes. It wasn't a playful exercise in disrobing as it had been with other men, instead, it was a means to an end. He handed me his khaki pants and black cashmere sweater as soon as he'd taken them off, and then he hopped up on the rack, waiting for me to put him into leather, chains, and rope.

While I was down on my knees on the floor and fastening the leather cuffs to his ankles, I ran my fingers along the soles of his feet.

He yanked his feet away. "Don't do that. I don't like it."

"Sorry." I was worried that we'd gotten off to a bad start. "I must say, you've got excellent reflexes." I looked up at him and we both smiled.

"Yeah. I'm a little jumpy. Don't worry about it." He held his foot out as I buckled the cuff in place. He then held out each wrist to be entrapped.

"Outstretched or arms by your side?"

"By my side, thanks." I took padlocks and secured the cuffs to some chain, which was then fastened to eyebolts on each side of his hips. I repeated the procedure with his ankles, locking them to the chain which was in turn, locked to the bondage bed. He could sit up, but he couldn't leave.

"You're not going anywhere now. Any other points of confinement you'd like?"

"A collar, please, so I have to lie still." His voice became quiet. Asking for a collar seemed to embarrass him, and yet he persisted with his mission.

I found a soft leather collar with metal D-rings in one of Erika's drawers. I held it up for him. "Will this do?"

"Yes." He tilted his head back, exposing his Adam's apple and throat to me as I carefully buckled it in place.

"I'm going to fasten this to the rack so you can't sit up. If you make any sudden moves, you could be injured. Do you understand?"

"Yes." He exhaled as I took some cord and tied the collar to the rack, leaving enough slack so he could twitch and move without hurting himself.

"Are you comfortable? Do I need to tweak anything? I'm going to turn out the light in a second."

"I'm okay." His breathing accelerated as his voice became little more than a whisper.

One by one, the lights went out and the dungeon became darker. Just before turning the last light out, I moved the Wassily chair over beside the rack and set the timer on my phone to vibrate in three hours. I grabbed a couple of bottles of water from the fridge, and then the room went black.

It took a few seconds for me to find the chair, but Erika warned me about the pitfalls of leaving someone like Dan unattended. He was vulnerable, and that demanded close supervision. Once I focused on his breath, he became easy to monitor. His breathing was deep and consistent, almost meditative in its pace.

At first, he lay there motionlessly, but after an hour he began to test his bonds. The chains rattled, he fidgeted and adjusted himself, there were even a few sharp, violent moves, but he settled back immediately and grew quiet again. He wasn't asleep, but he wasn't fully present either. I wondered if being a captive was a fantasy he'd been exploring in his head for decades. Erika had taught me that many fetishes take root early, even in childhood, and they can be very specific. But these yearnings seemed different.

I got up from the chair and found his body in the dark. My fingers ran up along his chest and neck, until I found his head. "Are you trying to get away from me?"

"No. I'm sorry." His voice sounded panicked. "I won't do that again."

"Good. I want you right where I left you."

"I'll do whatever you want."

I sat back down, wondering what his fantasy was. Erika's notes described acts they'd done. Her notes didn't describe what was propelling him. And there were few details about what Dan wanted.

While he lay there, I rested my hands lightly on his body. I was curious if this would be welcome, or if it would undermine his compulsion. He said nothing and his breathing deepened. I moved my right hand up to his face, tracing my fingers along his jaw. He moved his head like a cat and nuzzled me. I stepped back, abruptly removing my hands from his body. His back arched and strained, as he searched for my fingertips with his chest.

He remained quiet, and so did I, but his breathing had become more audible. It was odd, standing in that darkened dungeon, trying to figure out what he wanted and needed from the encounter. I didn't want to undermine the experience he'd so carefully engineered, but boredom seemed like a risk, too.

I began to play with his skin. He remained still as my fingertips made contact with his feet and ankles. I didn't linger down there, preferring to migrate upward, along his shins, and then up his thighs. His knees rolled open to accommodate my touch. The hairs on his legs were standing straight out of his body, as goosebumps formed. I slowed my hands as they approached his genitals. Dan's breathing slowed down as well. When I paused, so did his lungs. He was holding his breath while I decided what to do next.

Erika's notes had been very thorough about describing the extent of his bondage, but they had been vague about what else he was seeking. I assumed, since he was visiting a sex worker, that the underlying impulse was sexual, and yet he'd said nothing about arousal.

My fingers crept toward his cock, as I listened for any changes in his lungs that would indicate retreat. His hips flexed subtly, as he tilted toward my hands, a sign of acquiescence, or at least of interest. My fingers then found his organ. One quick breath in, as I grasped him, followed by a long breath out when I released him immediately.

My phone served as a flashlight while I tracked down some lube. A quick squirt onto my hands, and they became slick. My fingertips crept forward and reclaimed their spot on his shaft. He moved his hips up and down, pushing into my fist, so I opened my hand and pulled it away.

"Everything that happens to you is because I want it to happen. Do you understand?" I dragged my fingernails along the taut skin of his cock.

"Yes. Do whatever you want to do. I can't stop you." His voice was soft but even, almost as if he'd said that line before. Perhaps he had, to Erika?

"That's right. You can't stop me. If I want you to suffer, you will." I groped around and found his nipples and gave them a hard tweak. "But for now, I want you to feel pleasure." My hands returned to his cock and I began stroking him rhythmically.

It was an odd experience, being leisurely and deliberate in orchestrating his arousal. His breath was my signal to stop or proceed. I had no visual cues, just that one, simple audio cue and whatever my hands identified.

"I'd like you to let me go." Dan's voice pierced the darkness.

"No. I'm not done with you." It was an odd request, especially since it didn't involve a safe word. I decided part of his fantasy had to be trying to negotiate his release.

"Please. I'll give you whatever you want."

"What do you think I want?" Was he going to offer me his tongue or cock? I hoped he wouldn't be so vain or silly.

"Money . . . I can arrange it. Just for you. No one else. How does a million sound?" His fantasy involved the exchange of money, even when his reality did so, by design. He had my attention, even as I knew I wouldn't release him until his time was up.

"Sorry. You're not going anywhere. I've got other plans for your body."

"Oh really." His voice subtly challenged my assertion. It was odd of someone in such a vulnerable spot to suggest even a whiff of contempt. I'd meet his bet and raise him.

"Yeah, the stakes aren't high enough yet."

"Oh." He exhaled loudly as he lay still.

"You're going to pay. I hope you're ready to suffer." I grabbed his cock again and began to stroke it. Perhaps my definition of suffering was atypical, but at least it put an end to an odd conversation.

While sitting in the darkened dungeon, slowly stroking my prisoner's dick, I had one of those out-of-body moments. My fancy degrees and professional experiences had brought me to a pitch-black basement where my hands were covered with lube, and where they'd likely be covered in cum, soon, too. And yet, there was a perverse thrill in pursuing perverse thrills. I'd never rebelled as a kid. My trajectory had been utterly straight. Taking this detour was head-spinning. It wasn't a vacation, the money served as proof of labor, and yet it was so unlike my "regular" life that different neurons and muscles were being activated. The client was just another puzzle to be solved.

Feeling bold and slightly bored, I climbed up on the table, and knelt astride Dan's legs, all the while stroking him at a pace designed to turn him mad.

Dan began to moan and flex. I increased my frequency and was rewarded with heavier breathing.

"You realize I could stop any second," I whispered.

"Please don't."

"I'll think about it." His cock stiffened in my hands.

"Please keep thinking . . . I'll give you whatever you want." He was back to offering me "whatever."

"This is all I want." I leaned forward and put my fingers on his mouth to silence him. "Be quiet while I take care of you."

Dan nodded and remained silent as I began to pump his cock more forcefully. After enduring so much teasing, it wasn't long before he neared the edge.

"Tell me when you're close. It's important." My hand kept going, and his breathing became shallower and more ragged. Soon, his prick was fully engorged and his body was straining along with his genitals.

His voice came out in a loud whisper, "I'm really close. Please let me come."

I slowed down a bit, and then began a monologue. "You're so used to being in charge, aren't you? Well, you're not in charge here. You don't have an orgasm until I let you. I can stop, and you'll be stuck there, waiting for whatever's next." My hand paused to emphasize the point. "Men like you are used to getting whatever you want. Well, today, you're getting what I want. And I'm not ready for you to finish." He squeaked. "But maybe, in a minute, I'll feel differently." His body collapsed a bit into the rack, although my hand continued with its fast strokes. "I'm almost ready. Are you?"

"Oh yeah. Please." His voice had strengthened. "Whatever you want."

"This is what I want. I want you to come." And with those words, his cock exploded and he ejaculated all over my hand and his chest. I left him tied down, still lying in the darkness, as I went in search of a fresh towel.

After dabbing away the blobs of lube and semen that had landed on his chest, Dan asked, "Are you going to untie me?"

"No."

"Erika unties me after I've come."

"That's her prerogative. I don't feel like it."

"You're new at this, aren't you?"

"How'd you guess?" I sat down next to his head and began to run my fingers through his short hair. As unusual as our encounter had been, it had also felt intimate. He rubbed his scalp into my hand.

"Most women would take my orgasm as their cue to untie me. To let me go." His voice suggested humor mixed with a large dose of intelligence.

"Is that so? Well, I hope you're not disappointed. Did you want to get up?" My fingers drifted down from his scalp to his face.

"No. This is nice." I caressed his mouth as he spoke, and he kissed my fingertips.

"Nice? That's not the word I'd have chosen. I think it's brave. You've put your body at risk in the company of a stranger. I can do anything to you, and there's nothing you can do to stop me. It's gutsy." I stuck a finger in his collar and gave it a gentle tug. He lifted his chin in response.

"That's right. I'm at your mercy, only it doesn't feel like bravery to me. More like compulsion." The room felt still. I stroked his face and chest as we spoke.

"What's this about? There's something here, that you're poking at. What does the darkness and the bondage mean to you?" There were lots of books and articles about kink, but none of them really explained the whys, only the hows. The mechanics were straightforward, but the metaphysics were elusive. Why would someone like Dan be compelled to put himself at risk this way? He just teased me with his answer.

"It's a long story. I'll tell you some other time." Dan inhaled. "So, what are you doing next Tuesday afternoon?"

"Tying you up?" He was friendly, appreciative, and what he wanted wasn't too taxing, technically or physically. He was my kind of client. Square knots were within my skill set, so was fastening padlocks.

"Perfect." His body shifted with my touch, accepting my hand and appreciating it. He responded like a dog being pet.

"When will someone notice you've gone missing?" I couldn't resist playing a bit with anxiety, even though I liked him.

"Hard to say. Maybe an hour or two. Did you want to test that?" His voice remained level, even though his body betrayed heightened tension—his shoulders squared themselves to the rack and his breathing became tighter and faster.

"I'm not sure. Just establishing the facts. But what would happen if I kept you locked up overnight?"

"My colleagues would notice. They're used to me emailing them at 3 a.m." His body remained tense, even though his voice flowed naturally. This was something he worried about. It surprised me when he didn't mention a wife noticing that he was missing.

"I know your type. For you, sleep is optional. It must be hard finding people who'll keep up." His chest relaxed a bit when the subject shifted to something business-related.

"It takes time to assemble a good team. But I like where I'm at. And because they're good, I have time for my compulsions." His breathing steadied as he answered. He must have figured out that I was only messing with him.

"Selfishly, I applaud your compulsions. And if there's anything I should know or try, please tell me." I removed my hands from his body and turned on a low light. Some visibility restored, I released the cord fastened to his collar, pulled out the key and proceeded to unlock all the cuffs. Dan was free, again. He sat up and stretched. I handed him another towel. "You need a shower. And probably some yoga, too."

"A sun salutation is exactly what I need. But a shower, first. I'll be right back."

"Take your time. Can I get you some juice, or something a little stronger?"

"What have you got?"

"OJ in the fridge. Diet Coke. And some vodka in the freezer. Does any of that appeal?"

"I'll take a glass of the juice. I still need to think today. But thanks." He walked toward the bathroom as I retrieved a glass of orange juice. His body would welcome the sugar and fluids. "I'll join you in a minute. Just keep it there." I put his clothes on a stool in the bathroom, and after a few minutes, he emerged, dressed and ready.

We relaxed in a pair of leather lounge chairs. "So, what keeps you busy when you're not working and when you're not all tied up?"

"I work a lot." He paused, leaning forward in the chair as he sipped his juice. He looked up impishly. "I should probably lie and make up a hobby, but I love what I do."

"What do you do?" Erika's notes had been uncharacteristically remiss in this area.

"I buy and sell things."

"Big things? Little things?"

"Both. Whatever captures my imagination, and wherever I can find an upside."

"Fair enough. It can be consuming, this search for things. There's always another deal on the horizon, right?"

"It works like that. Yes. My shrink says I should chill out, but that's not advice I find helpful."

"Does your shrink say anything about the bondage?"

"I don't discuss it with her. I'm working that shit out here, with you. It's called repetition compulsion. I don't need a doctor's help for that."

"Oh? Happy to be of service, Dan. I'm really glad our paths crossed. Whatever you're working out is fascinating."

He snorted. "Yeah, fascinating. It's like a loop in my head, that I keep replaying. Same bondage, same acts, same fucking loop. The only thing that changes is the voice."

"That's quite the loop. How long have you had it? Since you were a kid?"

"No, it's more recent." He paused for the time necessary to do a quick mental calculus. "Four years."

"I thought most people picked up their fetishes pretty young. You're an anomaly." I wanted to know what happened four years ago, but it wasn't my place to ask.

"Yeah, I'm a fucking anomaly. And here we are." He put his hands on his thighs and raised himself up out of the chair. He was finished. "So, next Tuesday, are we on?"

"Absolutely. I'll clear my afternoon. Any ideas you'd like to plant in my head? Anything you'd like to try more or less of?"

"I liked it when you talked to me, in the dark. And I really liked it when you touched me. You brought a lump to my throat."

"Good to know. I'll get that lump back next week."

He left abruptly, and I set about cleaning every surface and toy we'd used, as well as the bathroom. Left behind in the bathroom, there was a bulging envelope. Unable to contain my curiosity, I counted out the bills on the counter. He'd left $5,000 behind for three hours of my time. My Tuesday would be his Tuesday. He could return as often as he cared to.

CHAPTER 18

LEARNING TO SEE

As I lay awake, stretched out in Erika's serene bedroom, atop her gray velvet platform bed, I tried to make sense of my day. It had started checking my emails and voicemail messages for the nonexistent queries from headhunters or banks. It had veered into the bizarre, as I babysat and fondled a bondage freak. The pile of cash from the various scenes had gotten pretty tall. It had only been a week of living in Erika's place and helping Erika's clients, but I had already earned over $10,000.

My ego balked at doing sex work piecework when it wanted to be collecting a salary plus bonus, but my bank account was delighted to be fed. If I were somehow able to sustain this pace, a safety deposit box or a strategy for handling the money would be necessary soon. Large cash transactions send up flares in retail banks. Cash is preferred by terrorists and traffickers, and I was neither. But a conversation with the IRS because someone had filed a Suspicious Activity Report on me would be a disaster. That kind of blemish could harm my real career, which was another compelling reason this kinky adventure was insane. It wasn't just the risk of arrest or accident, there was enormous risk just doing something prosaic, like depositing money.

I got in the habit of calling Erika every other day, to debrief on any sessions I'd undertaken or to prepare for any imminent encounters. Her quest for the butterfly painting was going slowly, but her benefactor remained enchanted by her company, so she remained committed to staying in Switzerland.

I asked her about Dan. "I saw Levine, the bondage freak, what's his story? How'd he find you?"

"He was a referral, so I don't know much about him. He's just a great client. He shows up, pays well. You know what he wants, and he's happy with what he gets."

"Yeah, that was my experience, too. But why the cuffs in the dark? Don't most men want to be able to see themselves, or at least be seen?"

"Yes, that's why I have mirrors all over the place. So they can see me work, and so they can see themselves squirm. I don't know why Levine likes the dark. Did you ask him?"

"Not really. It seemed personal."

"Every fetish is personal. I guess I'm just not that interested in where it originates. Everybody has a story or a theory, but it's rarely actionable. It's enough to know what the guy's button is, and then you just have to push it."

"You make it sound so simple."

"It is. Find the button. Often, they'll tell you what that button is about — and then push it. And once you've pushed it gently, you hammer it. You just need to pay attention."

"Right—look for the signals."

"Precisely. Their mouths may be incapable of saying what they want, but their bodies scream it. So pay attention."

Erika's words became my mantra. "Pay attention." Instead of just taking people literally, I started really looking at them. It was shocking how much information they revealed, without even realizing it. For instance, Erika's gallery assistants were feeling out of sorts. They dragged themselves in and took endless Starbucks breaks. Certainly, the foot traffic was slow to nonexistent, but there were things they could do to cultivate existing clients and to ready the gallery for an economic turnaround.

We explored which art bloggers covered works by artists similar to our own. Free coverage felt smart and appropriate. I also spent hours with Josh, as we figured out seductive ways to re-engage past clients. We started a blog in Erika's voice, calling out images and artists that aligned with what we had in inventory. It wasn't much, but at least it gave them something to do. Erika's Swiss client may have been covering her overhead, but her employees were lacking direction.

I went online, too, but for other reasons. I was scouring the trade news for any whiff of opportunity. If an old classmate got any press, they got a handwritten congratulatory note. If an old colleague popped up as a conference speaker, I followed up immediately. I was working every angle to find that next job, but all those notes and queries received only polite responses in return. The universe was telling me to spank ass.

Every few days, it was a new client and a new adventure. Erika's men were feeling the economic slowdown, but it hadn't diminished their appetite for kink. There was the law partner into cross-dressing, the CEO into paddling, the movie producer with a fetish for stockings. It was a regular parade of weird, and it challenged me in many ways.

Instead of reading endless reports and encouraging the analysts to construct better models, I was working with my hands and thinking on my feet. Improvisation and empathy became essential tools. In the space of the first fifteen minutes of a session, I had to transform Erika's notes into practical, tactile knowledge. It was a constant stream of unspoken questions about where to touch, whether to be playful or strict, whether to be knowing or innocent, whether to hit hard or harder.

The men gave clues. I was starting to observe the signals that Erika mentioned, the way their shoulders relaxed when the crop landed in just the right spot, or that look of exquisite anguish when I taunted them about their longings. It was staggering to realize just how much I'd missed before. There was so much information that had gone unnoticed, but thanks to the strangest classroom ever, I was learning to see.

The days flew by, and my Tuesday with Dan arrived. He was prompt, although he was muttering into his phone as he entered the dungeon. "See if they'll go for a toxic convertible deal. They seem desperate. Who knows when they'll hit bottom, but I think they're pretty fucking close." He nodded, and then he ended the conversation. "Going into a meeting and turning off my phone. Talk to you tonight. Tell me how they respond."

The snippet of conversation had my attention. He was negotiating to buy a distressed company when everyone else was holding tight or bleeding. I gave him a harder look, but he was oblivious to my curiosity. Without coaxing, he undressed, putting his khakis and black cashmere sweater in a tidy pile. He hopped up on the rack and stretched out, ready to be locked in place.

"Somebody's eager today." I smiled while surveying my victim.

"No point delaying the desirable. Lock me up, please."

"You'll be my captive in a minute." One cuff and padlock at a time, I set about securing him to the rack. "You're not going anywhere. I've got you." I slid the collar underneath his neck and buckled it in place before fastening it to the rack. His breathing changed as soon as that last knot was tied. I grabbed my phone and turned out the lights.

Neither of us said anything for a half hour as we settled into the rhythm of his confinement. I'd reach over and stroke an arm or run my fingertips along his jaw, then snatch them back quickly. His face or limb would reach, but find nothing there. He'd let out a low sigh every time as his breathing deepened.

I placed my hand on his chest and told Dan the truth. "I was thinking about you. I even asked Erika about you." His breathing remained steady.

"Oh? And what did you learn?"

"Not much, actually. I was curious how you came to this particular scenario, but she had no idea. So . . . how'd you wind up liking being bound in the dark?"

"It happened to me once, that's all. And now I'm just sort of reliving those moments."

"That was some girlfriend."

"Not exactly. I'll tell you about it some other time." His body stiffened, his breathing became measured. Worried I had overstepped and turned him off, it was a relief when he asked me to stroke his cock.

"You think it's that easy? Just ask me to stroke your cock and I will? Maybe I'd like to tie your balls up first, and then maybe, I'll *choose* to stroke your cock."

"You're the boss." His breathing returned to normal.

I slapped his inner thigh. He yelped. "Not what you were hoping for?"

"Not exactly. But you're in charge."

"Now how about this?" My hand grasped his genitals.

"That's an acceptable alternative." His body melted into the rack as his prick became hard in my hand. I found a comfortable position, squeezed some lube onto his shaft, and got to work. It astonished me how quickly the sleazy, gooey aspects of Erika's business had become banal. Instead of concentrating on Dan's penis, I was mulling the snippets of conversation I'd overhead. Dan had said he bought and sold things, but toxic convertibles were used to buy pieces of public companies in dire shape, that needed a rapid infusion of cash. He wasn't buying little things, he was buying substantial pieces of large publicly traded firms, which also meant he had the cash to do so. He had to be a major player, only there was nothing in Erika's notes suggesting he was a big deal.

After we had finished our session and Dan was getting ready for his shower, I couldn't help myself while handing him a towel. "Dan, what's up with the toxic convertibles? You must have a taste for risk."

"They make sense right now. I don't know where the bottom is. They give me protection."

"Isn't that what Jonsson thought before he got crushed by WeMu?" Sven Jonsson had lost over a billion dollars using toxic convertibles to buy a piece of Wellington Mutual. "That was a classic death spiral."

"You got that right. WeMu was a horrible deal. It spiraled all the way into insolvency." Dan snorted. "Jonsson got complacent. He believed his own press. If he'd done better due diligence, he'd have recognized the bank's losses would demolish the bank's capital and corrode investor confidence. It was clear to me that would happen when I looked at the deal."

"Orange juice when you're out?" The complexity and sophistication of Dan's analysis was staggering.

"Perfect. I'll be a few minutes."

I put Dan's clothes in the bathroom and poured both of us a glass of orange juice. He emerged from the bathroom promptly, towel-drying his hair. He looked at me, his eyes narrowed. "Who are you?"

"The woman who ties you up?" I tried not to betray my nervousness. "Who are you? Who's doing deals with toxic converts these days? That takes *cajones*. You're not just a masochist in here. You're a masochist out there, too!"

"No, seriously, what's your story? What are you doing here?"

"It's nice of you to ask, but I'm just helping out Erika. She's my best friend."

"Erika's your best friend? Did you guys go to school together?"

"Yeah."

"I know she went to Harvard. So you did, too?"

"Guilty as charged. Please tell me we're not fellow alums? I don't recognize you."

"You wouldn't. I was in school just down the street, only I didn't get off campus much."

"You went to MIT? Nice! I've always enjoyed the company of fellow nerds."

"You're no nerd, Catherine. Nerds don't wear latex."

"They don't begin wearing latex, but you never know what they'll put on when they grow up."

"Good point." Dan pulled out his phone and turned it back on. "Well, I have to run. What are you doing next Tuesday afternoon?"

"I'm tying you up."

"Perfect." This time, as he left, he hugged me and gave me a kiss on the cheek.

After cleaning up the dungeon, I changed and went to work on Google. Who was "Dan Levine"? Some preliminary searches on his name, including words like "deal," "toxic," "finance," went nowhere. I broadened the search to "Daniel Levine" but still had no useful hits. Baffled, I decided to go backward, with the type of deal and see if that helped. Toxic convertibles had gone out of favor in the '90s. I hadn't heard about them in years.

The most recent hit on "toxic convertibles" was a small article in *Bloomberg Markets* about the reemergence of this type of deal. It quoted Sven Jonsson and Daniel Levin. Erika's notes had been off by one letter, and that "e" had mattered to Google. My client was Levin, not Levine, and I knew exactly who he was.

Dan Levin was one of the most successful private equity players. He had a knack for finding distressed companies and then cleaning house. Fraud and incompetence were his preferred habitats. His uncanny ability for turning around ailing corporations had resulted in scores of column inches dedicated to his work, but he was notoriously shy, so there were very few pictures of him. I wasn't surprised I hadn't made the connection because, like most people, I had no idea what he looked like.

Levin had a reputation for brilliance. He'd studied math at MIT and he'd been accepted into a doctoral program at Princeton. Only he'd spent the summer of his junior year at Goldman Sachs where he'd impressed top guy, Greg Rubel, with his work doing risk arbitrage. At twenty-one, Goldman had offered him such a lucrative package, that he gleefully opted for application over theory. A few years later, on the verge of becoming the youngest partner at Goldman, Levin had bailed and founded his own fund, Inflection Investments. He had quietly, and steadily, become one of the most successful people in a very rarefied business. He had billions under management, and some of those billions belonged to him.

The downside of genius, however, was that Levin was rumored to be troubled, and possibly a drug addict. He was skittish, press-shy, and he'd disappear for days at a time. Was it to rehab or to a psych hospital? Anyone who knew had been sworn to secrecy and that secrecy was enforced with ironclad nondisclosure agreements. I'd heard stories about how jumpy and twitchy he was, but they seemed at odds with the calm, confident man I'd spent two afternoons entertaining.

It seemed implausible that his hobby was bondage, and that I hadn't been asked to sign something, and yet this was where things stood. Perhaps he thought his fetish for secrecy would contain his fetish? Perhaps he trusted in the integrity of perverts to keep his perversions to themselves? I had no interest in revealing his peculiar enthusiasms to the public, but I had to decide if I should tell Dan himself that I'd figured out his secret. He might be unnerved, and never return. In which case, I'd have hurt a consistently excellent revenue stream. As before, he'd left behind an envelope containing $5,000. That was money I'd hate to lose, and that Erika would miss if her extraordinarily generous and longstanding client chose to move on.

When I spoke with Erika that evening, and told her of my discovery, she was unimpressed. He wasn't the only billionaire she'd seen, and he was far from the most deviant. She thought his bondage fetish practically pedestrian. And as to whether I should share that I'd figured out his identity, she was unsure. As expected, she absolutely didn't want to lose Levin as a client. He was one of her most reliable and deep-pocketed gentlemen. She begged me to be cautious. She implored me to pay attention to any signs of hesitation or anxiety.

I didn't have to wait long. The next afternoon while researching Islamic banking, Dan called. "What are you doing tonight?"

I debated creating some artful lie, but opted to tell him the truth. "Reading *The Economist* and watching *Real Housewives*. Why do you ask?"

"Can I see you? At nine?"

"That's a little late."

"I know, I'm sorry, but I have an early dinner and you've been on my mind."

"How tight would you like the ropes tonight? Going to bed early is overrated." It didn't sound like he was asking me out for a late drink, but I wanted to be sure he knew this was business.

"As tight as can be." He chuckled, his voice whispering into the phone. "I'll be there at nine sharp."

He hung up the phone immediately, while I sat there pondering what to share and what to withhold. He was a fucking genius, he had to know I could make connections about his identity. And I had to know, if he were curious and so inclined, he could make connections about mine.

CHAPTER 19

A BILLIONAIRE
IN THE DARK

I spent extra time getting ready for Dan's arrival. It was one thing to prepare for some anonymous client, it was quite another to prepare for one of the most successful billionaires in private equity. He'd get the full kitten-with-a-whip experience. My hot rollers got called into action, there was an extra coat of mascara on my eyelashes, and my lips became the deepest shade of crimson available in my makeup kit.

At nine o'clock, Dan arrived. He embraced me, as my body conformed to his for a second. My black lace bustier compressed against his black sweater as his hands pulled me into him. I enjoyed the warmth of the cashmere before righting myself. He grabbed his briefcase and pulled out a box wrapped in extravagant purple and gold paper, with a large gilt bow balanced on top. "Would you like me to open this now, or should we do it later?"

"Let's do it after we've played." The box got placed on top of the lounge chair where it would remain safe from the fray.

This was the third time I'd locked him to the rack, and he positioned himself for maximum efficiency. He held each leg up toward me as I was putting on the cuffs and securing them to the table with padlocks. He did the same with his hands. He even lifted up his neck, to let me slide the leather collar in place behind his head and lock it in place. A few twists of rope later and we were seated in the dark.

"I like what you did with your hair." Dan's voice filled the room.

"Thanks. Hot rollers. I wanted to be a bit glam for you, since you saved me from an evening of reality TV."

"Happy to help. At your service." I put my hand over his mouth, and he quieted immediately. I then rested my hand on his chest, listening to his breathing slow and his pulse calm. We stayed motionless, for several long minutes.

I squeezed some lube into my hand and began to slowly stroke his cock. "You understand this is mine." I gave his penis a firm squeeze. "Any pleasure you feel is up to me. Any pain you feel is up to me, too. Your fate is entirely up to me."

"Yes, you can do whatever you want, and there's nothing I can do about it." He whispered to me, his voice staying low and barely audible.

"You are correct. It would be so easy for me to see you suffer." I brought my hand down on his thigh. The hard slap made him flinch and whimper. "But I can bring you pleasure, too." I resumed the slow strokes. His breathing was measured as it deepened. Although tied up and taunted, he had relaxed into the hardware.

"I think you like being stuck here. Being trapped with me."

The room was dark. The stillness made our games more audible and obvious. I could feel him begin to tremble. In a quiet voice, Dan said, "Please don't hurt me."

"Why would I hurt you? I like my toys intact." He wasn't acting frightened, rather, he seemed to be reliving something.

"Please. I'll give you whatever you want. Just don't hurt me." His body strained against the rack.

Amused by his plea—I was merely his dominatrix, not his murderer—I brought my mouth to his earlobe and bit it. Hard. He yelped, tempting me to bite it again. "I don't want to lose my toy. What's in it for me?"

"I've got money. My office can arrange the payoff."

"Intriguing, but not what I have in mind. I'm just going to leave you here for a while. You need to learn some manners." My fingers found his cheeks and gave his face a firm squeeze.

His breath warmed my palm as he whispered, "Did I offend you? I didn't mean to."

Still gripping his cheeks, I forced his face toward mine, only inches away. I whispered back. "No offense taken. But you can't buy me like that. Is that the kind of woman you think I am?" As I said the words, my brain buzzed, knowing that he could buy and sell ten of me.

"I'm sorry. I'll be quiet. Just don't leave, please."

I wouldn't leave him, but I wasn't going to touch him or offer any reassuring contact. I moved my chair back from the rack and remained as still as possible. We both stayed quiet for long, empty minutes. Dan spoke first. "When are you going to let me go?"

"Not until I'm ready." The answer seemed vague, and yet also, quite true.

"What would that take? Tell me, I'll make it happen."

"You're not going to offer me your tongue, are you?"

"Would you like that? I'd do a good job. You'd just have to loosen the chains a bit so I could raise my head."

"Not a chance."

"About my tongue or about the chains?"

"Both. You're staying right where you are. And so is your tongue."

"Can't blame a guy for trying. I thought it might persuade you to let me go."

"You think eating me out will make me want to release you? If you're any good, it might make me want to keep you."

"Good point. It wasn't a wise negotiating tactic."

"You can say that again. Unless you want to be stuck down here forever while your tongue falls off due to exhaustion."

"When you put it that way, I might be persuaded."

"You're pretty funny for a guy who's bound. Maybe I should gag you, too."

"No, no, no . . ." His voice took on a desperate edge. "That won't be necessary. I'll keep my mouth to myself."

"That's much better. Except I find you fascinating. Surprise me. Tell me something interesting." I was practically daring him to reveal something personal.

"Surprise you? You seem pretty hard to surprise."

"Oh? I can be stunned. It happens all the time. Come on, I know you can do it."

"I don't know where to start."

"Okay. Do you have any hobbies?"

"Not really. Do you?"

"Me neither. Okay, that was a bad example." I searched my mind, looking for some other form of small talk. "Have you read anything decent lately?"

"I just got through *Lords of Finance*."

"I've read that one, too." He probably heard my smirk.

"You're not saving it for the beach?"

"Nope. It's too timely, since it's about the central bankers who cratered economies, caused the depression and set the stage for World War Two." I was in my element, and finally feeling competent.

"Yes! It's hard not to think about economic chaos and decline these days. It's in the air. Your turn. What have you been reading?"

"Okay." I went from feeling capable to feeling coy. "I just finished *Story of O*."

"The classic of deviance." He paused. "Did you really? Or are you shitting me?"

"Seriously. I thought it was time to read the kinky cannon. I've been remiss."

"That's not what I would have predicted."

"I trust your crystal ball more than mine at the moment. It's so dark in here, I can't even see it. What's going to happen next?" I reached down and resumed stroking Dan's cock. "I predict arousal, followed by orgasm. You succeeded in surprising me, and now you've earned a reward." It took only a few strokes before the perfect rhythm became apparent. Dan's body was clear, and it was only a few minutes later, with the tease prolonged just because I could, that he had an orgasm. His balls twitched, just before the warm cum exploded from his body. His body tensed up, straining against his bonds, and then he relaxed. The chains and padlocks didn't move, as he lay there, completely still.

"That was great. Thanks." I could have given him a haircut or handed him a report, he reverted immediately to a polite kind of formality even after we had done something so weirdly intimate. After being released, Dan remained stretched out and languid.

"Can I get you something to drink? Would you like to take a shower?"

"I'm fine, thanks. Do you have a few minutes?"

"Of course. What's up?" I toyed with mentioning what I'd learned about his identity, but worried it might spook him.

"You shocked me yesterday, so I called Erika today." He looked me in the eye. "I wanted to know what kind of dominatrix knows the ins and outs of toxic convertibles. Who reads books on finance for fun?"

"Oh." I paused, wondering if my fear of discovery would be realized. "What did she tell you?"

"That you were her best friend from Harvard. That you are absolutely trustworthy, and that you're an unemployed banker. I figured the rest out myself. Nice to meet you, Amy Lefevre." He stuck out his hand, and by instinct, I extended mine. He had me, and though unnerved, I wasn't freaked out, especially since I had a card to play.

"While we're engaging in confessions, I figured out who you are, too." I retrieved my hand and sat back next to the man. "Erika had your name wrong in her file. I had no idea you were *that* Dan Levin."

"Yeah, I'm *that* one." His shoulders betrayed fresh tension. He'd gone from loose to tight in only a few seconds. The power in the room had shifted once again. He was off-balance even as I was regaining my footing.

"You should definitely avoid talking about toxic convertibles when you want to be discreet. You never know who might be listening. I had your full bio inside of two minutes."

"I could have found me in one."

"Probably right, Dan. My synapses aren't built for speed."

"You did good work at BFB. What happened?"

"The crash happened. I'm looking for my next gig, but it's dead out there."

"True. There's almost no movement. I think we're approaching a buying opportunity, but the misery hasn't maxed. The Dow's down five thousand

and there's worse to come." He cocked his head. "How are you finding this work?"

"Honestly? I don't know. I feel weird watching my old industry from the sidelines. But I am getting off on being an outlaw. And the clothes are awesome."

Levin looked me up and down. "They suit you. But it can't be just about the stockings."

"No, of course not. I've always done the expected and the correct, and this feels refreshingly bad." My pride kept me from telling him I needed the money.

"It's definitely edgy. You're not like most of the women in this business. There are a lot of actresses and artists. Like Erika. They love the drama."

"Erika's the only woman in the business I know. I'm learning lots about risk in here, but I'm not sure the knowledge can be put to use outside these walls."

"I bet you're learning very useful skills. You sure know how to ring my bell."

"Thanks, I guess. I just never thought I'd be working with my hands."

"This is hardly manual labor. Your hands are involved, but your brain is the weapon. You only just started, right?"

"Yup. I'm a rookie. Just a baby dominatrix."

"I've been with other dommes, and you're a natural. There aren't many who can dial in the way you do. You're dangerous now. You could become devastating."

"I don't know what to say. But maybe you'll tell me about some of your experiences some time? Or, if you want to get cleaned up, we could go upstairs and sit down on a proper couch and have a proper conversation. I have stronger stuff if you're thirsty."

"I'd like that. Give me a minute."

He didn't dawdle in the shower and minutes later he emerged in his khakis and sweater. I led him upstairs to the apartment and pointed him at the sofa. "Do you mind if I slip into something more comfortable? I can only stand these shoes for so long."

"Sure. You've put in your time in stilettos. Put on some slippers."

"You read my mind." I left the door to the bedroom ajar so that I could observe Dan while removing my battle gear. In the soft light of Erika's living room, his brown hair looked speckled with gold, and his face exuded a charm I'd missed in the dungeon—he had a deep dimple that invited attention. I quickly found an oversized gray cashmere sweater and a pair of black yoga pants.

"This feels so much better." I stretched. "I hope you're not underwhelmed after so much artifice and skin."

"Not at all. You're a beautiful woman. Not everyone can wear Lululemon so well."

"Why does no one have a fetish for yoga pants? Now that's a kink I could get behind!"

I offered him two bottles of wine and a corkscrew. He chose the red, and as we sat down, his phone let off a shrill alarm that made me jump. "Shit, I gotta take this." The conversation was quiet and brief. After he put the phone down, he shrugged. "Sorry, that was just my staff checking in."

"They must keep you on a short leash. It's after eleven. Don't they sleep?"

I poured us each some of the Pinot Noir and handed him a large glass. He swirled it, and then took a substantial gulp. As soon as his lips were off the glass, a hint of a smile emerged. "What can I say, it's an occupational hazard."

"So, what's your story? Google tells me you were married years ago, but that ended. No kids. No angry exes. How do you keep such a low profile?" His body relaxed into the sofa. I positioned myself at the opposite end, not wanting to seem too cozy or familiar.

"It's hard work, but it's worth it. And frankly, I'm pretty boring. I love what I do, and right now, that's enough." He let out a sigh and took another drink of the wine.

I nursed my glass, mulling how much interest to express with every sip. "You've been at it for a while. It doesn't get old?" I wanted to know more about him and his work. He was unusual, and he had my attention.

"Not at all. Every deal is different—they have personalities and quirks. To get 'em done right, you have to be part shrink, part financial engineer."

"Are you working on anything particularly neurotic these days? Got any deals on your couch?" I was curious about his plans, but didn't want to seem nosy. He was navigating the crisis well, and that made him an exception and someone I wanted to learn from.

"Not that I can talk about. But you get the idea. When you're buying a company outright, or even a piece of one, you come up against ego issues in addition to financial ones. CEOs are a sensitive bunch. They don't take direction well."

"A call from you might be the best and the worse thing the CEO gets that week. Their life's gonna change, like, soon."

"Indeed. Not everyone understands that." I went to pour him a little more wine, but he held his hand over the top of his glass. "No more. Gotta be sharp tomorrow."

His discipline was admirable, but it only made me more puzzled by his fondness for bondage, where he explored being out of control. "How about your interest in this? Where'd it come from?"

"It's relatively recent." He put down his wine glass and pulled at his sweater. His fingers gripped the yarn, as if to shred it. But just as quickly as he'd grown tense, he relaxed again. "But I gotta go. My driver's waiting." I wondered if he'd try to kiss me or make some move, but he gave me a half hug, half handshake. My body registered my disappointment, so I kicked myself for not being more forward myself. What kind of wannabe dominatrix was I?

"Good night, then." As we walked downstairs to the front door of the gallery, he turned and gave me a proper kiss. His lips felt soft against mine, and without thinking, I kissed him back. My fingers of my left hand grabbed at his hair, and with my right, I stroked his chin. He pulled me tight to his body. "Well, Dan, you just did a number on my blood pressure. Thanks!"

"You just did a number on all of me. When can I see you again?"

"You're a priority." I played with my hair, unsure how much of my interest to reveal. "When do you want to come back?"

"I'm going to London in a couple of days for some meetings. Wanna join me? You're the first woman I've met who's bilingual in bondage and finance."

"So tempting, but I have meetings of my own." There was nothing in my calendar. Lehman's bankruptcy had dumped thousands of people just like me into a job market that wasn't hiring, but I didn't want to seem too available. "So, when you get back we can play again. I like the way you squirm."

"Roger that. See you in about five days. Tuesday still works?"

"Tuesday's perfect, Dan."

"No, you're perfect, Amy."

"You say that to all the girls, don't you?"

"No, you're the first." He looked out at the street, where his car was waiting and a large man stood silhouetted by the car's rear door. "But shit, now I really have to go." He gave me a quick kiss on the lips and bolted out the door. As I peeked out onto the street, I could see the light come on in a black Mercedes. The driver remained in the front while the other man, whose sharp suit barely contained his muscular physique, held the door open for Dan.

As soon as the two men were in the car, it sped off. As the taillights disappeared, I slumped against the door frame, wondering if Erika had ever necked with any of her clients. Impulsively, I grabbed my phone to ask her. Her mobile rang a few times before she picked up. "Hey, Amy, what's up? Is everything okay?" Her yawn was audible. "It's, like, 6 a.m. here."

"Shit, I'm sorry . . . I just figured you were the only one I could talk to. I fucked up with Dan."

"Did you injure him? Is he in the hospital?"

"No. Nothing like that. I kissed him. Or he kissed me . . ."

"Is that all?"

"Well, yeah. It's not like I had sex with him. But the kiss was nice."

"Google 'girlfriend experience' and see what those escorts do with their clients. They'll have a big glass of wine, talk about their day, stick a tongue down the guy's throat and then fuck the client stupid. The amount of emotional labor those girls undertake is extraordinary. They are goddamned warriors."

"Isn't it against the rules, or something?"

"Rules? You make the rules, although I wouldn't make a habit of kissing the clients. They'll want more. They always want more. And you have to know where to draw the line."

"What line? He knows who I am, Erika. He knows everything."

"Oh, I wondered if he'd connect the dots. He called me, to see if you were safe. I said you were, and that you'd been my best friend since freshman year. He must have figured things out from there."

"I feel naked. Like my reputation could evaporate in a millisecond."

"Don't. He knows who I am, and he's never fucked with me. They're all too smart to mess with the woman who knows their dirty secrets."

"Christ, I hope you're right. It just felt weird . . ."

"It's mutually assured destruction, and they all think they have way more to lose than you. Hubris, you know."

"Men."

"But you like him, don't you?"

"Yes." I sighed. "Maybe a little? He's interesting, and impressive. But I don't want to fuck things up for you. Or for me."

"You won't. You couldn't be safer with him. But don't accept any trips. They all want to bring you along on business trips, and you'll find yourself bored out of your mind during the day, and then working your ass off every night. It's not worth it."

"He asked me to come to London."

"What did you say?"

"That I had meetings."

"The perfect answer. You're busy. Those foreign adventures just aren't worth the trouble. Well, not unless they're paying you in Hirsts."

"That's a very particular currency. How's your project going, by the way?"

"Fuck if I know. I violated every one of my rules, but the upside is huge. He's dangled that butterfly painting in front of me, and I want it bad. Unfortunately, he knows it."

"That's gotta shift the power dynamic."

"For sure, darling, for sure. These rich guys fantasize about ceding control even as they refuse to give it up. So now it's a negotiation, where I wield a cane and he takes as much as he can. We'll see who lasts longer."

"I'd put money on you, Erika. Hang in there. Stay strong!"

"Thanks, darling. Gotta get some shut eye. We were up 'til 3 this morning, and I am beat. Hah, I mean, he's beat and I'm exhausted."

"Goodnight."

"You'll be fine, Amy. You're doing great."

I hung up the phone and slumped into the couch. The wine had transformed from nectar to need, and all I could think of was how much I sucked as Erika's surrogate; how I'd fire me if I were her. That she was encouraging me instead of excoriating me could only mean one thing. She must truly crave that Hirst.

It took me hours to get to sleep. I kept replaying the encounter. Around 3 a.m., I staggered to the basement to clean up. It seemed ridiculous to be awake, and not get that minor task taken care of. I wiped down the surfaces we'd touched, put all the towels and ropes in the wash. It wasn't until I was about to clean the bathroom, that I found Dan's wrapped box.

The gilt ribbon untied readily, and then I slid my fingers beneath the tape holding the heavy, handmade gold and purple paper together. It occurred to me that he must have had it wrapped, the packaging was so exquisite. Inside was a first edition of *Histoire d'O*, in the original French. Also inside the box, was an envelope containing a handwritten note saying little more than, "I hope you understand French. Thanks for everything, Dan," and a tall stack of hundreds totaling $5,000.

A perfect copy of such an iconic book was undoubtedly worth more than the cash it had been packed with. I tried not to be impressed by how elegantly and thoughtfully a billionaire could spend his money, but it was hard not to be moved. When you don't have to worry about paying off your student loans or finding a job, your mind has the space to come up with the perfect gift. Reciprocation in kind was impossible.

The phone woke me up at 10 a.m. I'd somehow slept through my alarm—probably thanks to the Pinot Noir. It was Dan.

"Hey, Amy. Dan, here. Have I caught you at a good time?" His voice jolted me awake.

"Oh, hiiiieee. Yes, this is an excellent time." I stifled a yawn.

"I just wanted to let you know I really enjoyed last night. It was great seeing some of the real you."

"Thanks. I enjoyed our conversation, too. And I'm sorry we forgot about your gift. I hope you don't mind, but I opened it. You are full of surprises."

"I don't mind at all. I hope you like surprises."

"Of course!" I paused, trying to figure out how much enthusiasm to transmit. The gesture had touched me, so I opted for sincerity. "The book is amazing. What a coincidence that we were just talking about it, too."

"I know. When you mentioned you'd been reading *Story of O*, I resisted the urge to say more. But this version is different, obviously."

"Of course. Good thing I have some French, so I'll be able to enjoy it. I can't believe you tracked down a copy."

"I asked my dealer for help. You're not mad, are you?"

"No, of course not. I'm moved. It's an extraordinary gesture. I'm almost afraid to touch it. But don't worry, it'll wind up snuggled in my lap, being read. So thank you. Hey, aren't you heading off to London, today?"

"Yes, but not for a few more hours. I just wanted to follow up and let you know that you're unlike any woman I've met. I'd really like to get to know you better."

"Let's discuss when you get back. It's a lot to take in. I'm still not sure what to make of things."

"Tell me about it. But you're special. You really made an impression on me, Amy."

"You made an impression on me, too. But this could be complicated. And unprecedented, for me, anyway."

"For me, too. But we have so much in common. We are people who thrive on complications, who love challenges, who understand risk. I'll call you when I have a chance."

I almost recognized myself in his statements, but I sure wanted to be that woman. "Bye, Dan."

"Bye, Amy. And I mean it. You're exceptional." After hanging up the phone, I lay still, trying to figure out if he was playing me, or if he meant everything he'd said. He seemed sincere, but we'd met under the weirdest circumstances possible, where I'd been his sex worker and he'd pleaded with me for release. Maybe it was some kind of post-kink spillover, and he still wasn't thinking clearly; the endorphins had scrambled his brain. Or maybe he made sport of seducing his servants. My mind didn't like where it was going, when it really wanted to believe that he was legit and sincerely intrigued by me. Because I was sincerely interested in him, whatever that meant.

CHAPTER 20

THE PERVY SHERPA

Still baffled by my close encounter with Dan, I checked my schedule for the day to see how much more weirdness was in my immediate future. There would be a follow-up session with Arnim, the software CEO and corporal punishment freak. At a minimum, he'd help me keep my mind off the bondage freak in my life. I returned to the basement, and pulled out all the disciplinary tools, from the tawse to the wooden hairbrush, from a leather paddle to an assortment of rattan canes. Arnim would receive a beating.

Not long after I'd changed into my sexy corporate attire, Arnim presented himself for his punishment. I picked up a cane as he walked into the dungeon, and then I cracked it down hard, to make him flinch.

Arnim stood up a little straighter. "I got your message loud and clear, Mistress Catherine, I just wanted to let you know that."

"What message was that?"

"The one about the percentage of women at my company. I formed a diversity committee."

I tried not to let my surprise show. To me, it had merely been a riff during the scene, an opportunity to chew up time as I took him to task for his company's performance at hiring and promoting women, and yet he'd taken me seriously. Maybe this wasn't just a forum for role play, but also for advocacy. Stranger things had happened, so why not embrace his initiative?

"Wonderful, Arnim, but that won't cut you any slack in here. I need to hear of actual improvement. Now take off your belt and hand it to me."

"Yes, Mistress Catherine." He threaded his brown leather belt from his wool pants and deposited it in my hands. "But we're getting closer. Baby steps, right? Baby steps."

"I'm pleased. But I won't be satisfied until you've doubled the percentage of women. Then, we can celebrate."

"Yes, Mistress."

"Now take off your clothes and I'll give you all the punishment you deserve."

"Yes, Mistress!"

I laughed all afternoon, once Arnim had gone. He had left me surprised and charmed with his embrace of feminism, and he had left me the same $2,000 tribute as before. Even though there was little action in the broader market, there was plenty of action in my tiny corner of it. My stack of hundred-dollar bills was growing tall. Soon, I'd have to think like a drug dealer or a money launderer and identify a strategy for dealing with all my cash. I was deliriously happy, trying to work my way through this problem. Finally, there was some financial peace and the feeling that my life was on a more even keel.

That calm was shattered, only a few days later, when Michael—my pervy Sherpa and the man who dressed me at DeMask—had a heart attack in the dungeon.

He was stretched on the rack. I was applying clothes pins to his nipples, and then knocking them off with a crop. He was howling and he was hard. Our games were going great until he suddenly began to sweat profusely. "Amelia, stop. I'm not feeling good."

I undid the clips holding his wrists in place and sat next to him for a moment. "Are you feeling better?"

"No. This is serious. I need to get to a hospital." He slid his hands out of the cuffs and threw on his pants and his crisp white shirt. He left it unbuttoned and hanging off his shoulders. He clutched his side. "Do you have any aspirin?"

"Yes. Keep going and I'll follow with some." I kicked off my pumps and darted for the bathroom where there was a bottle. I came back to find him slowly climbing the stairs. "Should I call 911?"

"My driver can take me to St. Vincent's."

"Are you sure? Should I come with you?" I tucked myself behind him. His gait was so wobbly, he looked likely to collapse. As we reached the top of the stairs, I handed him a pill. "Here, take this right now." And just like he did earlier, he obeyed immediately. We struggled together toward the front door, while I grabbed a coat for myself.

"Just walk me to the car. I'll be fine once I'm inside." He'd straightened up a bit, even as he stood there only half-clothed. Beads of sweat pooled around his face, and yet he maintained his composure. It was a gorgeous fall day, and we were a strange sight, both of us panting and only partially dressed, but it was Chelsea, so nobody gave a damn. His driver saw us coming and joined me in helping Michael into the car.

"I think he's having a heart attack. The closest emergency room is St. Vincent's."

"Got it. Thanks." The driver gently placed Michael into the back of the black Mercedes and he sped off with his boss. He had looked so tiny, slumped against the tan leather, and the thought of his helplessness made me feel weak, too. I had been enfeebled in sympathy with his condition. He could have died in my dungeon or needed a paramedic. The prospect that our little adventure might have contributed to his situation terrified me.

The stakes of play seemed intolerably high, all of a sudden. This wasn't the job I'd signed up for. I went back inside, stunned, my mind racing on adrenaline and panic. All I knew was that some distance from the dungeon was essential.

Erika wasn't picking up, so Josh and I discussed the close call. And then I called my parents, and announced I was coming home for a few days. Burlington seemed like the opposite of Chelsea, and the prospect of having someone to take care of me for a change was comforting. JetBlue had an open seat to Burlington the next day. I just wanted to sleep in my old bed, eat my favorite foods, and ponder the fucked-up mess I'd created for myself. Someone had almost died under my watch, and that was a level of responsibility I couldn't stomach. I needed my mommy.

CHAPTER 21

THERE'S NO PLACE LIKE HOME

The fall is a glorious time to be in Burlington. And as I flew in to the airport, I got a view of the maples changing color. The entire plane was filled with leaf peepers, those out-of-towners who make a pilgrimage to Vermont to see the gorgeous spectacle. Some might even forget that there was a presidential election happening, and that the stock market had plummeted. The national tumult seemed far removed from this local quest for nature. As for me, I'd almost killed a client, and I was desperate to think about something else. I hadn't come to be filled with beauty. I'd come to be emptied.

Mom fetched me and my small carry-on at the airport in her green Subaru wagon. There was no point bringing many changes of clothes to Burlington, all anyone wore was denim and wool, or maybe khakis and a sweatshirt, if they wanted to mix things up. The black jeans I was wearing put me at the far edge of fashion in my hometown, but NYC is filled with chic ghouls dressed as if for mourning, and I'd been assimilated.

I spotted the car and climbed in before Mom had a chance to get out. My goal was to get home and hide. And maybe binge on some of her lasagna.

My face must have betrayed me, because Mom didn't even ask why I'd returned. As we rode in silence, she would reach over and stroke my shoulder from time to time. It was a relief, because I didn't want to explain what had happened to Michael, even if I could omit some of the damning details, and I really didn't want to lie, either. She probably figured it was job related, and she'd have been right. But she would have been thinking about the wrong job.

Mercifully, Mom didn't say anything until we were walking up the steps to the house. "Dad's at work, today. Can I make you some lunch, dear?"

"I'm not feeling right. I think I'll take a nap, if that's okay?" I looked around, the place was basically unchanged since I had left at eighteen. The brown leather sofa looked a bit more worn, and my dad's recliner—the same one I used to tease him about mercilessly—was in the correct position with a perfect view of the television set.

"Sure. I made up your bed with fresh sheets. You look exhausted." She straightened her gray hair with her fingers, as she adjusted the tortoise shell hair clip that held in place her ponytail. "I'm thinking of making lasagna. Would you be up for that for dinner?"

"Yes, Mom. That's my favorite." She gave me an enormous hug, and I was transported back to childhood. She knew how to comfort an ailing child, and I was sick. I clutched her back, and then retreated immediately to my small bedroom. I worried that if I stayed next to her any longer, the tears would gush, and I really didn't want my mother to see me out of control. Cool competence was my preferred state, and I didn't want to shatter that image, even if the cracks were becoming obvious.

There was an old pair of my pajamas still lurking in the back of my shaker bureau, so I put on the red flannel, and climbed beneath the quilts. My body instinctively went into a fetal position, and I slept all afternoon. It was the hushed tones of my parents speaking with each other that finally got me to sit up and take notice. They seemed quite worried, which meant I had to listen in.

"The job search must be going really badly. She hardly spoke in the car."

"Do you think she's depressed? There was an article about Prozac in *Time* magazine the other week, and it's supposed to be very effective. Maybe the doctors here are better."

"Oh, I think she's got good doctors in New York. What she needs is a job and some stability."

"I wonder if they're hiring at Merchant Bank here in Burlington. Or even at one of the banks in Boston. I know they're local, but a job's a job, right?"

"Dunno. But we can mention it to her."

Each idea was more painful than the next. Antidepressants, working at some retail bank, living back in Burlington. Yes, I needed a job, that was beyond dispute. But at BFB, there'd been an extraordinary level of challenge and opportunity. Unless they wanted me sucking back Prozacs by the handful at some shitty Burlington bank while helping small business owners get tiny loans, that wasn't going to cut it. I threw on a robe and wandered out into the living room where my dad was enjoying a bottle of beer.

"Hey, what's that you're drinking?"

"It's called Circus Boy, a local Hefeweizen. Wanna try some?" He handed me the bottle and I took a swig.

"That's not bad. Do you have more in the fridge?"

"Sure, in the usual place." One of the vegetable crispers had been designated my dad's beer drawer, and it was filled with eccentric brews. Although his body didn't travel much, his palate did. I fished out a brown bottle of Magic Hat with a cute yellow label and found the bottle opener in the cutlery drawer.

I returned to the sofa with my beer and we all got caught up.

"Yeah, I'm still consulting for Erika. That business she had in Europe is taking a lot longer than planned, so I've been overseeing her gallery for the past month or so."

"Oh great." My dad took another sip of his beer, and he held the bottle to his lips for a very long second. "Does this signal the end of banking?"

"No. God, I hope not. It's just that no one's hiring right now." The cold beer bottle dripped down my hands. "I heard you guys talking about the local banks. They're not hiring, either. And the work isn't my cup of tea. It's better if I just ride this out."

My mother nodded as the little creases between her eyebrows became deeper and more pronounced. "We understand, dear. Selfishly, we'd like to see more of you. That's all."

"I'd like that too. And here I am."

"Do you want to have some dinner, now?" It was 6:25 p.m. If this had been New York, dinner would still be hours away. We didn't dine as late as the

Spaniards or the Argentines, but we certainly dined later than the folks in Vermont. But having skipped lunch, I was ravenous.

"Oh, I'd love to eat. Thanks. Let me set the table." As I went into the kitchen to get the plates and the cutlery, my mother leaned into my father and whispered something in his ear. I immediately turned back into the kitchen, their secret conversation would go unacknowledged.

As I positioned the plates and the knives and forks beside them, my dad sat heavily in the wooden spindle chair at the head of the table. Mom deposited a fresh bottle of Circus Boy by his side, we weren't the type of family who'd dirty a glass unnecessarily. Bottles were perfectly fine.

Mom looked like something out of a home ec movie, as she brought the steaming lasagna to the table, wearing a pair of red and white dotted oven mitts. I got the knife and carved it up, giving my dad a corner piece because he liked the crunchy bits. I took a corner piece for myself, because we shared this quirky preference, and Mom got her usual small piece. A little green salad filled up the other half of our plates, and we were set.

When Mom looked at me after her first mouthful of pasta, I had a feeling it was going to be about whatever they had been whispering about. "I ran into Sharon Huntley yesterday."

"How's Mrs. Huntley? Is she still teaching?" She'd been one of my high school science teachers, but I knew that wasn't why my mother had brought her up.

"No, she's retired. But I told her all about you, and Harvard, and your work."

"Oh? Does she have a thing for finance?"

"No, but she told me something interesting about Bob. You remember her son, don't you?"

My mother had already mentioned the possibility of setting me up with Bob Huntley, and I had shot her down. He'd been a horror in high school. He'd been two years ahead of me, and yet he still took the time to harass and hassle me. When I was in ninth grade, he'd called me a lesbian, and other boys followed his example. It was mortifying, to be taunted about something that I was not, and something that seemed so taboo, adult, and sexual.

It was one of the reasons I rarely dated—so many of the boys at school were willing to be cruel to me. And because I didn't date, there was no way to prove I wasn't a lesbian. It was a nasty game that was impossible to win. And when you're fourteen or fifteen, you just want to be like everyone else. Conformity was security, and I was already being called out for being different.

"I remember Bob really well. And not favorably." I stabbed at my lasagna, finishing off the serving in record time. I heaped another chunk on my plate. "I can't believe he's a vet. I'd have thought he was too cruel to help anything living."

"People change. I've talked with him recently, and he's always been perfectly lovely to me. And he always asks about you."

"Always?" I snorted.

"Seriously. Always. I think there's a part of him that wishes he'd left the area. But he took over his dad's practice, and now he's got a half dozen vets working for him. He's even thinking about expanding."

"Well, good for him, but that's got nothing to do with me."

"His mother told me he's been talking to a private equity firm about selling the practice."

"That's unusual. I wonder what a PE firm is doing out here?"

"Bob thinks it's strange, too. He's intrigued, the offer's decent, but the Huntleys wonder if this would be bad for the clients and employees."

"Those PE guys are usually great at wringing costs out of operations . . . and that usually means firing people."

"Exactly. So, I thought maybe you could talk to Bob. You know people in private equity, you know finance, maybe you could help him think through the offer."

"Oh! I was afraid you were trying to set me up."

Mom rolled her eyes. "I know you better than that. You'll do the opposite of what I ask. But maybe you can help the Huntleys. Jack and Sharon still own a piece of the practice. They'd appreciate your take."

"Well, okay. It's not really my thing, but I can help them think about it a bit, and maybe point them toward a real expert, if it comes to that."

"Perfect. I'll call Sharon after dinner with the news."

And that was how, the next evening, I found myself having a working dinner with my ninth-grade nemesis. He'd reserved us a table at Leunig's, a cute bistro in downtown Burlington next to City Hall. It was as close to fine dining as Burlington got. The place had white tablecloths and votive candles flickering in the center of every table. The walls may have been painted an odd shade of sienna, and there were mock stained glass accents every ten feet, but I tried to put aside my inner snob and enjoy the place. I retrieved my trusty HP12C, in case any calculations were required, and my parents' Subaru keys were ready, in case Bob offended me.

My Blackberry had some news from New York. Michael was fine. The heart attack had been mild, and the prompt response had gotten him the necessary treatment. I hadn't killed or injured the man. He was back to normal. This elevated my mood and I flagged down the bored blonde waitress for a glass of wine. She recommended the house cabernet sauvignon.

My glass was almost finished when Bob arrived. I was taken aback. He looked different from the teenaged bully I remembered. He was broad and strong. His shoulders filled out his brown leather jacket, and he wore his flat-front khakis tight across lean hips. He rushed into the restaurant and gave me an enormous bear hug, compressing me against his chest. I could feel his muscular pecs through the thick leather of his coat. "I'm so sorry you had to wait. We had an emergency, and it took longer than expected to get everything stabilized."

"What happened?"

"A calving went wrong. I mean, everything was bizarre with this pregnancy. Spring is calving season around here, and yet we're already in the middle of fall."

"Hmm, very odd. Do they know what happened?"

"The farmer fucked up, I guess. Who knows. Usually the farmers can take care of things, but this was a full breech." He unzipped his jacket and put it on the back of his chair as he sat down.

"Full? Yikes! That's where they're coming out tail first, right?"

"Yes, and the back legs are pointed forward. If we don't intervene, the calf dies, and the cow probably gets injured in the process. Childbirth is dangerous for every species."

It was a bit gruesome, but also fascinating, hearing about the intricacies of large animal care. And his eyes really lit up as he described the scene in the stall. "What an afternoon. You earned your pay today!"

"Yeah, it got really messy. But I feel great because the momma and the baby are fine."

"That sounds intense. You have to reach in, right?" When you live in dairy country, even the town-dwellers understand the basics of bovine husbandry.

"You got it. It's very delicate, but also very physical. You have to reposition the calf." He demonstrated some of the motions to me, highlighting his athletic shoulders and physical grace. "But they have hooves, and you don't want to tear the uterus. There's so much that can go wrong. But today? Everything went right. It just took time. And then I had to shower and change. You would not have enjoyed me an hour ago."

"It's cool. I've only been here ten minutes, so you're hardly late at all." And then I gave him a proper look. He was different than I remembered, sturdier and more serious. His dark brown hair was cut military short, revealing a square jaw and highlighting his brown eyes. "I hardly recognized you. It's been, what, ten years?"

"Maybe longer. And longer still since we were in high school."

"Oh, I prefer to forget about that. You were horrible to me!"

"I was?" He stroked his chin with his big hands. "You know, I'm sorry about that. I could be a real shit then, and I was always awed by you. You were the smartest cute girl on campus." He put his hand on top of mine for a second and looked me in the eyes with great sincerity. "So thanks for taking the time to talk to an ignorant knucklehead. I know what I'm good at, and it's treating animals, not making financial decisions."

"You don't seem ignorant to me. Can I reserve judgment on the knuckle-head part?" I laughed. "You need a drink!"

Bob waved over the waitress. "Can I have one of those?" He pointed to my wine, and we started talking again. "You know, I don't like to think about what a jerk I was in those years. Fortunately, jerks grow up. People change. You've changed."

The meeting wasn't going as I had expected. I had been prepared to hate him, and yet he had been disarming and sweet. Bob pulled out the term sheet the PE firm had given him, and we went through it as he ate his filet and I enjoyed my beef bourguignon. "It seems wrong to be eating beef today, after your close encounter with some cows."

"Not at all. And I suggest we have some cheese for dessert. Just to be complete." I nodded approvingly. After all, I had nothing better to do, and his attention was delighting me. For the first time in months, the interaction was flirtatious and yet utterly conventional. The flavor vanilla was suddenly very appealing.

"I have a question. Your hospital . . . do you think their valuation is correct? I'm surprised by the number."

"The number seems surprising to me, too. It's maybe 40% too low."

"Seriously? What kind of facility do you have?"

"It's like a human hospital, only for patients that can be huge." He shrugged his fireman-strong shoulders, and then he leaned his body in toward mine. "Have you ever been inside one?"

"No. And thankfully, I've never had to spend much time in human hospitals, either. But I'm curious." It was clear where this was going, and I was game. "Could you give me a tour?"

"What are you doing after dinner? It's only fifteen minutes away." He leaned back in his chair and crossed his beefy arms across his chest. "Although I have a confession, I'm an equipment junkie. I like to work with the best tools, so my hospital is a bit over the top. There isn't another one like it in Vermont."

"Seriously? Let's check it out." I admired how forthright he was, and how he went straight for the kill. He could have worked on Wall Street.

"Deal." Bob then motioned to our waitress, and had her take our orders for a cheese plate. We ate the delicious local cheddar and camembrie with gusto. Bob paid the tab, and then he eased my thin wool coat over my shoulders and put an arm around me as we walked outside.

"Let me drive. It's close, and I have to come back anyway, 'cause my place is in town."

"Are you sure? I don't want you inconvenienced."

"No, it's totally cool. And you've been away for a long time. I could probably drive there in my sleep."

"Ah, stay awake this evening, okay?"

"How could I doze when I'm with you. You're not like the women who live here, that's for sure. Why do all the gorgeous, smart women go away?"

"Thanks. Well, you're not what I remember, either. I was prepared to hate you, and here you are, kind of hot and hunky."

"'Kind of'? Geesh . . . I still ski race to avoid any qualifications on 'hot and hunky.'" He smiled at me rakishly, as his dark eyes twinkled from behind the steering wheel of his green Range Rover. And then he reached over and grabbed my hand to kiss it. I may even have blushed as his lips connected with my fingers. It all felt so nice and regular, without any buzzkill whiff of kink or transaction. My fingers lingered on his cheek, stroking the slight stubble on his skin, before I returned my hand to my lap. I enjoyed sinking into the plush leather seat and feeling the heat of his attention.

Throughout the fifteen-minute drive, he let his hand rest on my thigh, as he gently stroked my leg. It was distracting, but enticing, and I couldn't help but ponder my emotional flexibility. I'd gone from skepticism and distaste, to curiosity and arousal, in a mere two hours. That had to be a record.

We pulled into the driveway, and his headlights revealed a long, low-slung building. "Here we are. This is my office."

The words "Huntley Veterinary Hospital" were written above the main door. "Nice signage."

"It's better inside. Let me show you." And after unlocking the front door and flipping on some light switches, Bob proceeded to give me a tour. He had a large surgical suite, complete with hydraulic table, EKG, full anesthetic set up, blood gas monitoring equipment, and all the things you'd expect in an operating room for humans. Only, everything was scaled large. There was a smaller suite adjacent to the big one, scaled for use with smaller animals. There was a padded recovery room, multiple stalls, a room for ophthalmic appointments, and cameras everywhere so the animals could be monitored in real time. The hospital offered endoscopy, dentistry, and digital radiology. I was stunned by the extensive nature of his practice, and the sophistication of his facility, and I told him so.

"Well, I had a head start because of Dad. But I really invested. My team is very busy. All this equipment gets used."

"You must have spent hundreds of thousands . . . millions on this place."

"Yup. What can I say, I anticipated the demand for a state of the art hospital, and here we are. Business is good. And now investors are knocking." Bob tugged at the sides of my wool coat and pulled me into his chest. His meaty arms enveloped me, even as he tilted my head up to connect with his lips. I closed my eyes and returned his kiss, it had been so long since I'd been with someone I hadn't first met in a hotel bar or who hadn't been a kinky client. My body relaxed into his as the kiss deepened.

He was muscular and eager. His hands moved rhythmically down my back, until they were grabbing my ass. My body responded to his touch when Bob pulled my hips closer to him. I could feel his erection, trapped beneath the khaki. He had gone from zero to fully aroused in only a matter of seconds, which startled me. When he grabbed my right hand and pushed it into his crotch, I was even more surprised. And when he unzipped his pants, I was staggered and pulled back a bit. The kissing felt great, but further escalation was unwelcome.

He grabbed my hair and pulled my head back, exposing my throat in a move filled with force and menace. He kissed my neck, even as I squeaked with displeasure. "Hey. Let go." Bob ignored me and pulled my hair harder. His rough movements dragged me down until I was forced to my knees on the floor with my legs splayed. With his right hand, he lowered his pants and underwear, revealing his cock.

"You know you want it. I saw the way you were looking at me at dinner." Bob's fist kept the tension on my hair, even as he pulled my face into his crotch.

I was frozen for a second. He was very strong, probably two hundred pounds and well over six feet tall, and my nerves took over. No one had ever forced themselves on me like this. "Please, Bob, that hurts." My words had no effect on him, as he yanked my hair even harder. "Let's just go back to kissing," I pleaded. It was beyond my comprehension that the threat of assault I faced calmly in the dungeon, where I met strange men in a highly sexualized environment, was actually playing out in a Vermont veterinary clinic with someone so familiar.

He ignored me and used both hands to manipulate my head as his cock sought my mouth. His moist, engorged flesh squished into my cheeks, poking at my face, trying to find an orifice to violate. My scalp ached from the strain, as my eyes watered. It took every ounce of self-restraint not to bite him, because that would have been a disaster for my health. Bob was still the cruel jerk I remembered from high school. He'd just learned to mask it better.

Finally, I found an opening and used my hands to push myself away from him. I landed on my ass at his feet. I used my firmest Catherine voice. "No. I'm not going to fuck you, so keep your hands off me."

Bob looked at me with disgust. "You're still a lesbian. I knew it."

I grabbed my purse and jacket and ran out the door. Bob followed behind me. "Fuck off, asshole. Get away from me. Don't you dare touch me again or I'll call the cops." I had no intention of calling the police, I worried that my adventures as a sex worker might somehow become known, undermining the credibility of my allegations and my future career prospects, but Bob had no idea I was bluffing.

Bob's voice changed immediately. "Hey, it was all a misunderstanding. I'm sorry. Look, let me drive you back to town. I'll buy you a drink, and maybe we can laugh about this in an hour."

I pulled out my phone. "No, I'm calling my mother. I don't ever want to see you again." I gathered some steam and hurled the only insults my MBA brain could conjure up. "And I hope your hospital goes under because of all that debt. I can't believe your revenues are what you're claiming. You don't have the capacity for that many dogs and cows."

"Fuck you, you arrogant slut."

"Fuck you, you wannabe rapist. Now leave me alone." I turned and walked out to the road and dialed the family home. My dad picked up. "Hey, it's me. I need a ride." And then I began to sob. I'd once read that for women, crying was anger turned inward, and my rage was intense. It even angered me that I was sobbing in Bob's aftermath, because he did not deserve to elicit such strong emotions.

CHAPTER 22

A GULFSTREAM TO THE RESCUE

As the surge of adrenaline that had helped me flee Bob dissipated, a soft, grassy patch by the stop sign at the corner of Essex and Mountain View beckoned. I sat down and leaned against the signpost, feeling ridiculous and praying no one I knew would spot me there.

The roads were empty. The odd dog barked, but otherwise the countryside was still, at least until my Blackberry buzzed. The caller was Dan Levin, the last person I wanted to hear me snivel. I answered it anyway.

"Hi Amy, it's Dan." I tried to stifle my lingering whimpers. "Do you have a moment? Did I catch you at a good time?"

I barely squeaked out a yes.

"I just got back from London and wanted to confirm we're on for Tuesday."

I took a deep breath and steadied myself. "Dan, Tuesday's not gonna work."

"What's up. Is there a problem?"

"No, no problem. I'm in Vermont for a few days, at my parents' place." Despite my efforts, my voice still trembled.

"You sound strained. Are your parents alright? Are you in trouble?"

"Everything's fine."

"Amy, are you okay? Seriously, you can tell me." Hearing his voice and sensing his kindness just set me off, and I couldn't hold my emotions in check any longer.

"Oh, Dan. It's been the worst week, and it's gotten worse still."

"What happened. Are you alright?" I said nothing. Dan continued, "Why are you in Vermont?"

"I needed to get out of New York. But I didn't escape the bad. A guy from high school just tried to rape me. Can you believe that? What was I thinking, coming home?" I leaned back against the stop sign and poured out the entire pathetic saga of Michael's heart attack, Bob, and sleeping in my parents' house. "And as much as I was looking forward to seeing you on Tuesday, I can't be Erika anymore."

"I don't want Erika, it's Amy who fascinates me. The only thing that matters is that you're okay."

"You caught me at the worst moment ever. I am such a fraud."

"You were assaulted, Amy. It was not your fault." He paused for a moment. "Where are you?"

"Burlington," I snorted.

"Where in Burlington?" I gave him my parents' address. "I'll see you tomorrow morning, now get some sleep."

"You can't be serious. Please. I don't want you to see me like this."

"You're debating the wrong person. I'm coming. And you're gorgeous. I bet you even cry pretty."

I had to laugh, even as I half-sobbed. "Okay, fine. But you can change your mind. And if you do, I'll understand."

"You're important to me, Amy. I won't change my mind. See you at 11."

"My dad's truck is pulling up. But don't worry if you can't come tomorrow."

"See you in the morning, because nothing will come up."

I hung up as I climbed into my dad's Tacoma, pushing aside the piles of rags and cups that littered the seat and floor. "Hi, Daddy." I sniffled at the sight of my father.

"Hi, baby. It's gonna be alright." He took his right arm and gave my shoulders a firm squeeze.

"I hope so. Bob's still an evil asswipe." I fished in my purse for some Kleenex and dabbed it at my eyes. "Don't ask me what happened in his fucking hospital. I never want to think about him and his wretched family again."

"You won't, baby. We won't mention him again." A silent minute passed, and my dad couldn't help himself. "So who was that you were just talking to?"

My dad's question caught me off guard, even though it was utterly predictable. How should I describe Dan? Was he a friend? A colleague? Could I say the word "client" without betraying my deep, dark secret? He wasn't a lover . . . But he was an intimate. I decided to be vague. "Dan's someone important to me."

"He must be, if he's coming tomorrow."

"I don't know how he's going to do that. He's very busy, and we just don't know each other that well." I paused, because my explanation seemed inadequate. My father looked at me, expecting more information, so I settled on a tiny corner of the truth. "It's all very new."

This seemed to satisfy him, so he continued, "Well, whatever happens, just know you can stay with us for as long as you like. We love having you home. We'd love it if you stayed awhile."

"I know, Daddy. It's great to be home. Except when it involves the Bobs. . . ."

"Well then, no more Bobs."

"Yeah, I can't take another Bob."

"Kiddo, you're gonna be alright."

Once I got back to the house, I took an Ambien and tried to empty my head.

Bob's assault had shaken me. And not just because of the act. I wondered if my work in the dungeon had somehow contributed to my attempted victimization. Had being a sex worker changed the way I moved through the world, making men like Bob think they could use me? Did my stint as a dominatrix somehow permeate by manner, making assaults more possible? Had spending a couple of months selling sexual fantasies tainted me in ways I hadn't yet realized? These prospects were terrifying. My little adventure could have terrible long-term ramifications that had never even occurred to me. My mind raced and refused to be stilled.

I didn't manage to sleep until 4 a.m. My night was dreamless and deep. I didn't wake up until my mom came into my bedroom. "Amy... Amy..." She shook my body. It took me a few seconds for her presence to register. "You have a visitor." My grogginess dissipated instantly, replaced by angst.

"A visitor? Who?"

"Your friend from New York. Dan. You know, the one who said he'd visit today."

"Holy shit. What time is it?"

Mom looked at her silver Timex. "11."

"Seriously, it's 11?"

My mother sat down on the edge of the bed. "I could hear you tossing and turning when I got up around two, so I didn't want to wake you this morning."

"I look like hell. Could you tell him I'll be out in a minute? I need to brush my teeth and put on some clothes."

"Sure, honey." It took me only about five minutes to put on a pair of low-slung, gray McQueen jeans and a tight black turtleneck sweater, to pull my hair back in a tidy ponytail and to get the plaque off my teeth. I didn't want to keep him waiting. I imagined Dan and my parents all staring at one another.

When I got into the living room, my dad was deep into an explanation of the plant overhaul he was overseeing, with detailed descriptions of the plant's new emissions reduction system. Dan was drilling into its intricacies, and my father was enjoying showing his stuff. I waved at them. Dan waved back. "You made it." He sprung off the sofa and gave me a hearty embrace.

"I said I would, and I'm a man of my word!" Out of any other mouth, that would have sounded pretentious, but Dan's delivery was filled with the right mix of irony and humor. My mother could barely conceal her swoon.

"Please forgive me, but you got here when I was still in bed. I'll just be a moment." When I joined my mother in the kitchen, I couldn't help but look back into the living room through a billionaire's eyes. What had seemed cozy and familiar to me yesterday, suddenly appeared small and shabby. The edges of the sofa cushions were worn. You could see where a dog had chewed on a chair leg, only we hadn't had a dog since I graduated. The rag rug beneath the simple wooden coffee table looked like something made of rags. And yet, every tinge of embarrassment was accompanied by a whiff of shame. It was a fine house. It had served our family well for decades, and yet it suddenly seemed homely instead of homey.

"Amy, I asked Dan if he'd join us for lunch. He said he'd love to." My stomach lurched into my throat at the prospect of us all sitting together eating beef stew, or whatever she had planned. "He's great. How long have you been seeing him?"

"Uh, it's still really new. I'm kind of stunned he's here, to be honest."

"He was worried about you, so he flew here."

I tried to process those details. When he announced he'd be in Burlington, I didn't believe it would happen. Men make promises they don't keep all the time. Why should this particular bondage freak be any different? I replied to my mother, "When he said he was coming, I didn't take him seriously. And yet here he is."

My mother whispered to me. "Amy, I think he flew here on his own plane."

I nodded and whispered back. "Probably. He's very successful."

"He's nice looking. Smart. Why didn't you tell us about him?"

I kept my voice down. "With guys like him, you never really know where you stand. I guess I didn't want to get too far out ahead of things? And it still might be nothing."

"Of course, but it's so thoughtful. You know, he thinks the world of you."

"Seriously?"

"Absolutely. I can see it in his face. The way he speaks about you . . . He told us that you are the smartest and most beautiful woman he's ever met. That you're one of a kind."

"No kidding. He hasn't told me that."

My mother patted me on the back. "It sometimes works that way."

"What's for lunch, anyway?"

"Do you think he'd like spaghetti?" I nodded. Everybody enthused about my mother's meat sauce. A Tuscan wouldn't have recognized it, but who cares about authenticity? She pulled a large tub out of the freezer and began to heat it up in the microwave. I wondered when Dan had last eaten something that had been nuked.

"Yeah. That'll hit the spot. Thanks."

I stuck my head into the living room. "Can I get either of you something to drink? We have coffee, tea, Diet Coke."

Dan spoke up. "Let me get some water. That's all I need."

He followed me into the kitchen where I got him a tall glass and motioned to the tap. "Is Burlington's finest acceptable?"

"You bet." I poured him a glass, got a Diet Coke for myself, and brought him into my bedroom where we'd have some privacy. It was mortifying when he spotted my bulletin board filled with academic ribbons and postcards and polaroids from vacations twenty years in the past. He fingered a picture of me at twelve, standing in my pale green one-piece bathing suit at the edge of the cliff at Red Rocks Park. "I'm not surprised, but you were a really cute kid."

We both sat down on the edge of my bed, on top of the blue and white log cabin quilt my mother had made in a crafty phase when she was pregnant. Dan took my hands. "I hope this isn't an intrusion, but I was worried about you."

"Last night was horrible. But I shouldn't have let you come here. I was out of my mind."

"I'm glad we spoke. I'd been thinking about you—a lot—and I needed to see your face." I leaned back on my pillow, incredulous that a billionaire had somehow made his way into my tiny childhood bedroom. Dan moved his body alongside mine, so that we were both stretched out on my single bed.

"Are you having flashbacks to your college dorm? I am." I took his hand and put it around my waist, so that he was embracing me. With his free hand, he stroked my hair as he balanced on his side.

"I loved college. But I didn't spend time in bed with a beautiful woman very often."

"I loved college, too. And I didn't spend much time with exciting men, either." Dan rolled toward me and pulled my body tight into his. He drew his fingertips gently along my jaw, and nudged my mouth up toward his. His tongue touched me even before his lips. It was a gentle darting, not a hard thrusting. It was a tease, not an attack. And I accepted his overture.

We lay there for long minutes, necking like teenagers. The innocence of the encounter was thrilling, even as I wondered what would happen next. His hands cupped my face and straightened my hair, while his mouth played with mine. I nuzzled his neck and chest, deliberately avoiding his genitals, in an effort to keep further physical progress in check. Dan must have felt my reticence.

"I could do this all day, but maybe we should take a breather."

"Maybe. It feels odd to be kissing you in my old bedroom, lying in my old bed, with my parents only about fifteen feet away."

"That makes us outlaws. Sneaking affection behind their backs."

"I like that. We're outlaws," I drawled. And then I remembered why he'd come, and my smile evaporated. My head crushed the pillow. "Outlaws with secret lives. . . ."

Dan sensed the change in my mood. "You've had a rough week. What do your parents know?"

"They know about Bob, obviously. But they can't know anything about Michael or how we met." It dawned on me that Dan had sat with my parents while I got dressed. "What did you tell them?"

"I just said we are friends from New York, and that I was worried about you." His eyes softened, and he gave my forehead a kiss as he cupped his hands around my face, tucking my hair back and touching my cheek. "Don't worry, I didn't tell them anything. Why would I? We both have things we don't discuss with outsiders."

"Of course . . . of course. I'm out of my mind. They're my parents, you know."

"I know. I feel the same about mine." He lay back, placing his hands under his head, his elbows braced against the pine headboard. With his right arm, he pulled me up against his chest. "After lunch, let me get you outta here."

"Oh? What did you have in mind? Take the ferry across Lake Champlain? Do some leaf peeping?"

Dan laughed. "I know a better way of leaf peeping. Let's go somewhere. My plane's here."

"Oh? What's its range? How far can we get?" I was just being silly. Playing along with his outrageous offer as I rested my head on his body, enjoying the warmth and the connection.

"Europe. Mexico. The Caribbean. Where do you wanna go?" Dan called my bluff.

"I don't know what to say."

"Just pick a place. It'll get your mind off what's happened. We'll spend a couple of nights. Two hotel rooms, I insist, no obligations. Let me do this for you."

The generosity of his offer staggered me. His time was invaluable, and yet he wanted to spend it with me. But dark thoughts kept intruding, that he was interested in spending time with my alter-ego, Catherine, and not me, Amy. That he had some freaky agenda that might manifest itself once we were alone in a strange place. And yet, I wanted to get to know him better. He was unlike any man I'd ever encountered before, and not just because he wanted to be bound and isolated for hours at a time.

"Montreal? It might be fun to get my French in shape for that book you gave me."

"Why not Paris, then?"

"Let's just keep this low-key. Paris might be too reality distorting, and I need a clear head when I deal with you." And that was basically true. I had decided to keep my "ask" modest to minimize any feelings of indebtedness, and so that he would have no justification in expecting much from me. And besides, if our time together was a fiasco, the flight back to NYC from Montreal would be cheap. I wasn't sure when my next payday would come, but it could be a while. My willingness to do Erika's work had diminished, because risking a client heart attack to pay off my student loans simply did not appeal.

"Montreal it is. I'll make the arrangements. We can leave after lunch." Dan grabbed his phone and outlined our plans to one of his employees. He was terse, so it was quick. "The crew's on stand-by, so let's shoot for wheels-up at 1:30. That should put us into Montreal around 2:15, if not earlier."

"That fast? Just what are you flying?"

"Oh, you'll see. You have a passport with you, right?"

"Of course, it's an occupational habit. Otherwise, I'd have suggested Chicago."

At noon we emerged from my bedroom into the dining room where my mother had placed our best dinnerware—a pretty Limoges china edged in gold that my grandmother had received when she married—on the table. Mom stood ready, with a large bowl of pasta mixed with a classic red sauce and a few ounces of grated parmesan. I grabbed the salad and brought it to the table. Dan took hold of the garlic bread.

My father had already planted himself at the head of the table, so I sat on his left, and Dan on his right. And then we had a perfectly normal conversation. Dan liked hockey, so the men debated the Islanders versus the Bruins. The chatter segued to the imminent election. My parents were also curious about Dan, and they elicited information that I had not. From his favorite book as a kid, to his preferred place to holiday as an adult. Dan was behaving like a suitor, trying to win over his girlfriend's parents, and they were treating him accordingly. I was tickled to see the human side of such a mysterious figure, but his presence was disorienting. I was attracted to him, certainly, but was it possible for a relationship that began in such a bizarre way to ever become normal?

After we had cleared the table, I retreated to my room and stuffed my clothes into my carry-on. Once done, I rolled my bag into the living room and kissed my parents goodbye. Dan shook my father's hand and then kissed my mother on the cheek. It was an excellent performance. I felt his sincerity, even as I wondered if it was sincere. Dan grabbed my black bag and bounced it a bit in his hand. "Your daughter sure knows how to pack, Mr. Lefevre."

"She knows lots, Dan. I hope we see you again. Soon." My dad gave me a bear hug and a big kiss. He whispered in my ear. "He's a good guy. I like him." I squeezed my dad's shoulder in response, wondering how much he'd like the guy if he had an inkling about the strangeness of Dan's obsession.

And then we were outside. The obligatory black SUV took us to Burlington International.

CHAPTER 23

THE BEN FRANKLIN EFFECT

As we pulled up by a large hangar, Dan gathered my passport and the body-guard's, and handed them over to a white-haired gentleman in a sharp navy suit. "This is Jack, my pilot. He has to log these into the passenger manifest."

"So I'll get it back, right?" I grinned at Dan, even as I had the crazed thought it might be some sex trafficking scheme. I remained out of my mind.

"Of course. In five minutes. We just wait here, and then we'll drive out to the plane." I pretended not to care, but my curiosity was intense. What did he fly? Was it his own plane? Probably. He called Jack "my pilot," but beyond that, I had no clue, except it had great range. I couldn't see the ramp from the SUV, and I tried to peek. Discreetly.

Someone waved us forward, a chain link gate opened, and we drove toward the apron in front of the open hangar. There were three private jets parked in front, but only one with a carpet in front of the stairs. It was long and sleek, with pale green trim on white paint, and seven small circular windows running the length. I knew what it was immediately, and it was hard not to be impressed. He had a Gulfstream 550, a plane that sold new for about $50 million, not that I was counting.

I turned to Dan. "Nice ride."

"Thanks. Got it last year from a guy whose fund cratered." Dan shrugged his shoulders. Somebody's losses had resulted in his big gain. "I acquired his crew, too. Fortunately, he was better at picking staff than he was at picking deals. Come." Dan led me up the stairs and inside the jet.

The interior was subtle and plush. The seats were a cream leather, and the wooden paneling was in a dark, textured ebony. There was a sofa, decorated with Hermès pillows, a worktable that could seat four, and two pairs of seats on opposite sides of the aisle. Dan took a spot in the most forward seat and motioned to me to sit across the aisle from him. As I was buckling myself in, a male flight attendant wearing pressed navy slacks, a crisp white shirt, and red tie appeared. We both ordered Diet Cokes.

Dan leaned over the aisle as he buckled himself in. "Buffett called his jet 'The Indefensible.' I call mine 'The Unconscionable.' I love it, but it's killing my carbon footprint."

"Yeah, with all your travel, you're going to have to plant a whole forest in Brazil or something to atone for your sins."

"I've doubled my donations to the Sierra Club. Maybe I'll start planting trees, too. I like how your mind works."

"Happy to be of service. It's a gorgeous plane."

"Not my doing. It came this way. But it is awfully pretty. And I think it'll turn a profit when the economy recovers."

"You wouldn't want to keep it? It's easy to get used to."

"I know. Really easy. And my partners and investors prefer the security." The beefy bodyguard entered at that precise moment, and he whispered a few words to Dan, who just nodded. The bodyguard then retreated to the front of the plane, and the door slid closed, leaving Dan and me alone in the cabin.

"Your security guy follows you everywhere these days? Your funds are doing great—your investors must be ecstatic. What's up—a hostile ex? Do you have a stalker?"

"No, nothing like that. It's just a precaution. There are crazy people out there."

I nodded, a bit flummoxed. It seemed odd that someone so anonymous would have that kind of security, and yet Dan wasn't frivolous, nor did he seem paranoid. He was confident enough to come into Erika's basement, and he was strong enough to explore some very intense things with me, a mere substitute. There had to be a sensible explanation, and I wondered if he'd trust me enough to share it someday.

We barely had time to get comfortable in our seats before we were accelerating down the runway. The nose lifted up, we were pressed into our exquisite leather seats, and we were in the air.

Flying privately was not unfamiliar, there were odd instances when a gang of bankers would get on the company Lear to go visit a client *en masse*. We'd arrive at the airport at 8 a.m. in the morning, squeeze together, every seat in the BFB jet filled. And then at 7 p.m., we'd climb back in the bus, and get the fuck out of whatever crappy town we were visiting that day. The bank had rules governing these flights—and it was only permissible if we were going to some minor city that didn't have a direct flight to New York.

A few times a year I'd be a guest on a client's jet. My favorites were the Gulfstreams like Dan's; they were the most spacious and comfortable of the biz jets. Unfortunately, I'd spend the entire flight sitting next to Jon as we explained the minutiae of some deal to our prospective wallet. The planes should have inspired lust and orgasms, but there was no time to enjoy the luxury. We were the help, and we were treated accordingly. The flights were invariably one way, and always at the client's convenience. After we landed, Jon and I would wind up heading back to Manhattan via Delta. Since these arrangements were often very last minute, we'd usually get stuck in coach. It's one thing to fly private to places like Aspen and Nantucket. Getting back was always a nuisance.

The worst was a client with a home at the Yellowstone Club in Montana. We'd fly with him into Bozeman, arrive in the evening and he'd take a helicopter to the club so he could start skiing on the club's private powder first thing in the morning. He liked to boast about waiting for the chairlift with Bill Gates. And while he was snuggled into his seven thousand square foot log home with gray stone accents, I was retiring to the local Holiday Inn, with its ugly blue curtains and tired gray carpeting.

Some people love Bozeman. *Outside* magazine always puts it on the list of great places to live. But I found it a lot like Burlington, only colder, and with a grim cowboy energy. Invariably, I'd be stuck in that boring little town over-night, because the commercial flights back to NYC didn't leave until midday. If I'd been partial to fly-fishing, I might have enjoyed the place more, but I came to loathe it because it always involved getting jammed into coach for the four-hour flight back to civilization.

We barely got to cruising altitude when it was time to descend again. Flying international in a private jet is exquisite. After the Gulfstream taxied to the VIP Terminal at Trudeau, we were boarded by a bouncy immigration officer who glanced at our passports briefly, smiled, and gave a hearty, "*Bienvenue au Canada.*" Another black SUV was waiting, and the bodyguard ushered us into the backseat and even retrieved our bags from the back of the plane. I might not have known exactly where we were going, but the way we were getting there was exceptional.

It was just as simple when we arrived at the Ritz-Carlton. Dan flashed his black AmEx card, and we were immediately brought upstairs to a large suite where the attendant completed the check-in process in the room, as we sat on a dark amethyst velvet couch. She handed us each a card-key, and then she showed me to a room adjacent to Dan's. I was surprised. In the hierarchy of hotel rooms, mine was better. My suite had a large living room with a massive sectional upholstered in a demure, taupe mohair. There was also a dining room, with a sleek table for four, in the unlikely event there was an urge to entertain. There was even a fireplace. Dan had assigned himself the junior suite, where the sofa abutted the foot of the bed. The furniture might have been elegant, with its carved wood and dreamy upholstery, but it was still a small room for a billionaire.

As soon as I realized what had happened, I knocked on Dan's door. "Please take the other room, you'll make better use of all the space."

He was already unpacking his shaving kit on the white marble counter in his bathroom. "No, I wanted you to have the suite. I don't need much space."

"Why are you being so kind to me?"

"Because you deserve it. And you've been kind to me, too."

"Maybe at dinner you'll tell me a bit more about what brought you to Erika?"

"That story might take a couple of stiff drinks, more so than a meal."

"Whatever it takes, Dan. I want to understand you better. And if you change your mind about the suite, don't be shy." I walked up next to him in the bathroom and put my arm around his waist. We exchanged a chaste hug, rather than the steamy kisses we'd enjoyed on my childhood bed.

"Dinner at 8?"

"Great. I'm going to take a shower and maybe lie down for a bit." I paused, wondering if he'd suggest joining me in bed or in the shower. Dan didn't bite. So I extracted myself from his room and returned to mine, thoroughly baffled.

As I was unpacking my Tumi, it dawned on me it contained only Burlington clothes, and nothing that was even slightly sexy. Flannel, denim, merino wool . . . I didn't even have pretty underwear, and I wanted to be ready, just in case the mood struck again. Instead of a nap, the cute, gay concierge gave me a shopping recommendation to the nearby Holt Renfrew. There was little time to browse, I had even less money, and yet I had a mission.

I made a beeline for the Prada boutique, but the dresses were all too coy, with their high necks and guipure lace accents. But more significantly, their expense was staggering. Who was buying this stuff, at the height of a financial crisis, I wondered. There was no point looking at YSL or Chanel. And then I found the Max Mara collection, and hit pay dirt. They had a pony skin skirt in black, that looked dark and dangerous. It fell about four inches above my knee, so it showed some leg without being garish. And it fit me perfectly. It wasn't cheap, but it wasn't mortgage-my-future expensive, either. I then found a short-sleeved cashmere turtleneck, also in black. It was sumptuous against my skin and tight against my body. And since I didn't already own one like it, the $600 expenditure could almost be rationalized. I picked up a pair of plain black suede Stuart Weitzman boots with a spiky 4-inch heel, to complete the outfit without destroying my bank account. I wasn't sure if the ensemble made me look like a dominatrix in search of a victim or a witch in search of a coven, but the look perked me up. I wanted to impress Dan, but confidence had faltered, leaving me unsure if I still possessed the skills to do so outside of a room filled with instruments of erotic misery and torment.

The lingerie department beckoned me, but a glance in the section told me to return to my hotel room immediately. If Dan were lucky enough to see me in my underwear, he was in no position to complain about my boring Chantelle bra with its lace trim.

When I got back to our corner of the Ritz-Carlton, the noise must have rousted Dan's bodyguard. The door to the room opposite me opened as I was inserting my key card, and he poked his head out. "Oh, hi." I waved as the bodyguard nodded back and quietly shut the door again.

After a stint in the gym and some artful primping, my watch said it was 6:30. It was still early, and yet I was ready for the evening. I left my hair down, so that it fell across my shoulders. My lips were a shade of crimson that Erika had selected, and my black eyeliner made perfect wings at the corners of my eyes. I smoothed the pony skirt, in an impossible effort to get the hairs to orient in the same direct direction. The light scattered off the fur, giving the skirt a faint luster. Unsure if I should wait or knock on his door. I decided to call, instead. "Hey, it's Amy. Do you wanna have a drink before dinner?"

"Sure. Let me know when you're ready."

"Does 'right now' sound too eager?"

"Not at all. I need a few more minutes. I'll knock when I'm ready."

"See you shortly!" I imagined him closing deals or buying countries, as I sat down in my living room and checked my emails for the twentieth time that day. Erika had written, but she didn't have much to say. My former boss Jon was in touch. And to my surprise, Jon's wife Susan had sent me a message, too. It had been over a month since we'd last discussed getting together for lunch after my firing, so I wondered if their messages were related.

While waiting for the knock on the door, I enjoyed the same sense of anticipation as in high school, when one of the rare boys weird or brave enough to ask me out on a date would stop by the house to pick me up. I was never sure how ready I was supposed to be, and my dad liked to intercept those knocks and invite the fellow into our living room for a brief chat anyway, so there was no point rushing from the bedroom to answer the doorbell. I'd listen for the door to open, inspect myself in the mirror, and then I'd count to twenty before rescuing my classmate from my father's gentle interrogation.

This time, I scrolled through the messages on my Blackberry while waiting solo for the rap. After about ten minutes, Dan appeared in his uniform—khaki pants, black cashmere sweater. Only this time he wore a black suede blazer over top. "You look nice. Welcome to my humble hotel room." I held the door for him and made a sweeping motion with my arm to usher him in.

"Oh, this is a good suite. Maybe I should have claimed it for myself!"

"It's not too late. We can still switch."

"I'm not serious. You look fantastic, by the way." Dan walked up to me and held me close to his body. I ran my fingers through his wavy hair and then along his jawline. My tongue met his lips, and they parted for me, inviting me in. He tasted like peppermint, so I probed further. His hands migrated up my back and knotted into my hair. He pulled my mouth closer still to his. Our tongues touched and teased, as I lowered my hands and tugged at his sweater. I wanted to feel his skin against mine, to smell the fresh scent of the Asprey body wash he'd used in the shower. And he felt the same way because his hands snuck up under my sweater as he eased it over my head.

"Is this okay?" He whispered in my ear. I was moved that he was so concerned about my well-being.

"Yes. Absolutely. I want more." I began to remove his clothes. I tossed his jacket aside, and then made quick work of his shirt and pants. He had to hustle to kick off his shoes and socks, I was so determined to strip him down quickly. It took only a few more seconds, and I stripped down to my plain black underwear. But what was supposed to be a thrilling moment of discovery turned into a moment of fear. I'd spoken too soon. I was not okay.

Dan stood tall in front of me, with his penis bulging behind his boxers, right at my eye level. My heart began to race as I visualized Bob in that same position, when he tried to force his cock into my face. And then my blood pressure dropped, and I had to sit down because my head was spinning. At first, I felt faint, and then I felt like a fool. I had wanted to impress Dan, only he was seeing me in a weakened state. My willpower was insufficient to stanch my tears. Sobbing was becoming a bad habit.

Dan looked on as I began to shake. "Amy, I'm so sorry. I should have known better." His voice was quiet and filled with sympathy. It only made me feel worse.

"I'm sorry. I am such a jerk." The words came out as sputters between sobs. Dan wrapped his arms around me, as I buried my face in his chest. "You've been great. This is so exceptional…And here I am, blubbering away."

"Amy. Please. Don't think twice about it. Can I get you anything? Do you want to be alone?"

"This is so embarrassing. And no, I don't want to be alone, but I don't want you to see me like this. Oh shit, I don't know what I want. . . ."

Dan retreated to the bathroom and pulled out the heavy terry robe. "Here, put this on. When you're hungry, let's call room service. And maybe, we need some booze. What's your poison?"

My breathing calmed at the prospect of strong liquor. My voice must have sounded meek as I bleated out, "Is there any bourbon in the minibar?"

Dan explored the cabinet. "No, but there's a bottle of Canadian whiskey. How do you feel about Crown Royal?"

"It'll do." I bundled myself in the robe and lay down on the top of my bed, just like I did when I was feeling rotten as a child. A few moments later, Dan appeared with a tumbler filled with the brown fluid and handed it to me. I took a big gulp and relished the way it burned my tongue and throat as I swallowed.

Dan had restored his clothes, and he lay down next to me. "Is this alright?"

"Yes. I'm not normally so fragile, but these past few months have been really disorienting." He lay there quietly, stroking my face with his fingertips and gently pushing my hair back out of my eyes. It was calming, which prompted me to explain how I'd transformed from the woman who'd tied him up to the woman who'd fallen to pieces. "I wonder if I'm on overdrive from overstimulation. And then Bob happened." My sadness had morphed into rage—it pained me that my high-school nemesis should continue to interfere with my life, especially when I was in the company of someone so intriguing.

"You're not weak. You took a serious shock to the system. And a crisis can make the most unlikely things seem reasonable."

"Yeah, like me becoming a dominatrix." I snorted, while reliving my improbable journey into the dungeon.

"And me, trying to get tied up in knots." Dan lay back and let out a large sigh. He'd been holding something back from me, and it seemed like he was trying to bring it forward.

I rolled onto my side, propped my head on my hand, and gave him a hard look. Dan's mouth was strained, and his hands clenched in tight fists that rested on his chest. I grabbed one of his hands. "What happened? You're not like most of Erika's clients. That became obvious, pretty fast. What are you working out?" If I could change the subject, he might forget about my moment of frailty.

"You've met Mark. The guy next door."

"Right, your bodyguard."

"That's relatively recent." I cocked my head and rested my cheek on his chest. He wrapped an arm around me and pulled me to his body. "I don't suppose you remember my investor meeting a few years ago."

"You mean the meeting where you famously didn't show up? There were rumors you were in rehab, or something."

"I wasn't in rehab. I've never even tried coke." His breathing stabilized, but his chest remained tight.

"So where were you? Your absence made CNBC. '*Where's Dan Levin*?' Nobody blows off those meetings."

"I know. There were a hundred people waiting to hear me speak. I had interviews lined up with the *FT* and the *Journal* afterward."

"Yeah. It was quite scandalous in our incestuous little world. I think you even made *DealBook* the next day."

Dan inhaled deeply. "Yeah, well, I was kidnapped. They held me for four days." His words stunned me. In two brief sentences, he had conveyed a personal horror that I couldn't even begin to understand.

"Oh fuck, that's awful." I pulled my face up to his and kissed him. The sadness of our mutual memories deepened the moment, and I hated to pull myself off his lips, but I wanted to learn more about my mysterious client. "Is that where the bondage thing comes from?"

"Exactly. They kept me tied up in a dark room, and one of them—*the only woman*—would sometimes keep me company."

"Ah. And I guess you tried negotiating with her? Tried talking your way to freedom?"

"Yup. What choice did I have? I'm just grateful they didn't gag me." We both let out a little snort. What a rookie mistake, I thought, even though I was barely not-a-rookie myself, where bondage was concerned.

"So, how'd you get out?"

"I made her think if she let me go, we could go to the bank together, and I'd give her millions."

"Seriously? That worked? She believed you?"

"She wasn't the brightest, and I think she wanted to believe. We, uh, spent a lot of time together in the dark. I had her look up Stockholm Syndrome. She thought I loved her too much to turn her in."

"You must be very persuasive."

"I think she wanted to be persuaded. The kidnapping was her boyfriend's idea, or rather, her *ex*-boyfriend's idea. She was no criminal. She was exploited by her man. He even assigned her to take care of me."

"'Take care'? Do you mean what I think you mean?"

"Yup. They figured if I was getting off every few hours, I'd be more complacent. It was easier than drugging me, I suppose. And she was dim enough to go along with it." His voice became clinical and detached. He was describing a profound violation of his body in utterly dispassionate terms.

"Those moments of pleasure, mixed in with the terror, must have been bizarre."

"They did a number on me, that's for sure. My therapist called it sexual assault, but I got off every time. And I even asked for it. I had the idea that if I asked her to do easy things for me, she might be able to do something really difficult for me later."

"The Ben Franklin effect! If someone does you a favor, they're more likely to do you another."

"Exactly. I had some time to be alone with my thoughts, and to strategize."

"But if there were arrests, how come they never made the press?"

"The prosecutor understood these morons might inspire similar acts, so the courtroom was closed and the kidnappers all pled guilty. Once we had one of 'em, we had 'em all. The FBI really performed. But man, those were four awful days."

Dan's story took my mind off my own distress, and maybe that was his intention. But learning about his time in captivity gave me insight into his role-play. He was trying to reframe some of the most horrifying moments of his life as something erotic. And he was engineering scenarios where he was in control, and not his kidnappers. The sheer gutsiness and resilience of his kinky scenarios moved me, and I found myself relaxing into his torso. I wanted to comfort him in the same way he wanted to comfort me, only my means were different.

He'd been lying on his back, sometimes looking at me as he described his ordeal, but just as often, he stared at the ceiling. The story required emotional momentum, before it came spilling out. But once it had, he lay passively on my hotel bed, his hands tucked beneath his head. He was still fully clothed, his obligatory cashmere sweater in place, and likewise, his khakis.

I nuzzled his soft sweater, and then brought my mouth up to his throat and then to his lips. Dan remained still, so I kissed him more deeply. Parting my lips and nudging his open, so that I could feel his tongue against mine. My tiny licks were soon met with something more forceful, although his body remained immobile. I ran my fingers over his mouth, while my mouth migrated down his body. I lifted up his sweater, and swirled and bit each nipple. They stiffened in my mouth, but his response was strictly physiological. Still no movement.

With my fingers, I positioned his face so that we had eye contact. His gaze didn't waver as I began to unzip his pants and eased them down toward his thighs and ankles, and then off his body. I was in control, and the growing erection and the deepening breath indicated that he approved.

Just as I had in the dark, I began to tease his meaty cock. This time, I could see every twitch of his balls, and the emergence of a single, perfect bead of precum on the head. I could see his face and look into his eyes and confirm consent with every stroke.

"Dan. Is this okay?" I teased the head of his cock with my fingertips, massaging into the sensitive skin that little blob of moisture. I swirled my finger over the ridge encircling his glans.

"Yes, Amy." His breathing slowed, but he left his hands beneath his head as I worked on his prick.

"You say the word, and I'll stop." I slowed my hand and brought it to a halt, although I continued to apply pressure to the shaft.

"You can keep going." He let out a deep, strangled sigh.

"Good to know. I want your consent. Nothing's going to happen without it." We were playing a different kind of game, and I was curious if it was to his liking. Certainly, the involuntary spasms suggested he was enjoying what was going on. "Did your female friend ever fuck you, while you were tied up?"

"No." He answered quickly, as he exhaled. The word was barely audible.

"Did you want her to?"

"Yes." Dan rolled his eyes and looked away from me. His elbows flexed and tensed, as they pushed down into the pillow.

"Of course you did. I mean, what else did you have to do? There are worse ways to kill time." I climbed astride him, watching him for any signs of reluctance. His hips lifted up as he prodded my panties with his cock. I wondered if he could sense how wet I'd become? I also wondered if he thought me bipolar and off my lithium. Only a crazy person could have shifted gears so thoroughly in the space of a couple of hours—from despondency to depravity. "Now, don't move."

Dan positioned his head on the pillow so that he was looking straight at me. His eyes gleamed with longing. "Yes, ma'am." Without any further tease, I extended my tongue, and brought it to his cockhead, swirling around and lapping at his organ. I stared at him the whole time and saw only a heightening of interest as I carefully took his entire organ in my mouth and paused once my lips reached the base of his shaft. I stifled a gag, and relaxed my throat, permitting him to enter me as deeply as possible, my lips applying pressure as I slowly brought my mouth back to the head.

I remembered that I'd stashed a condom in the nightstand, and quickly put it in place. Where my mouth had been only a minute earlier, my pussy took over, and I rode him. His hands remained tucked under his head, as if glued in place, as I balanced on his hips, grinding my body into his, and enjoying the sensation of being filled. I pushed down on his elbows, pinning him to the bed. His back arched in response.

I let my hips swirl, as I lifted and lowered them, my fingers then digging into his pecs as I balanced and steadied myself. He became increasingly rigid, his prick pulsed along with his heart. He was pinned beneath me, and I needed to accelerate and to tease. With a slight shift of my pelvis, he impaled me as deeply as I dared permit. As my arousal heightened, I spread my legs wider and shoved my fingers onto my clit, grinding my cunt into them even as I ground into him. It took only moments, but I began to feel that giddy lightheadedness that precedes an orgasm.

Dan must have felt it too, because he began to tilt his hips, and strain beneath my body. His thrusts were hard, piercing my body and causing my brain to shatter. The nerve endings fired throughout my pussy, making me tingle and throb. As my cunt clenched him, he began to shudder, too. I could feel my orgasm roll from my clit outward, even as I felt him burst inside me. I collapsed onto his chest. Finally, he moved his arms, putting them across my back, and crushing my torso into his.

We lay there quietly and unmoving for several minutes. I was relishing the contact, but unsure what to say. What's the correct protocol after you've fucked a client? What does a "real" dominatrix do when she's breached one "ethical" line after another? What does a woman attracted to a man say when she's fucked him, right after seeking solace for a near rape? What does it mean when a kinky client transforms himself into a kinky lover? And was this relationship just a fantasy or a folly, or was it something real?

Dan finally spoke up. "I could get used to this." It was one of those ambiguous statements I'd heard many a trader-bro utter. It implied an interest in a prolonged relationship, but it also telegraphed uncertainty. He "could" get used to it; he wasn't saying he "wanted" to. I knew the difference. As Jon used to say, "It's that enormous gap between a cup of coffee and a certified check."

He wasn't the only master of ambiguity. "Yes, so could I." As much as I wanted to nudge things forward, he was the most exciting man I'd met in years—we spoke the same language, we appreciated the same things. Clarity would be elusive. I couldn't shake the notion that he had a lot in common with the traders at BFB. Dan might not seem steeped in entitlement and privilege, but maybe he was just too subtle to show it.

I rolled off him and explored the nightstand for the room service menu. The cool-girl-vixen mode I'd perfected at the George Hotel seemed like a safe disguise. "Man, after what you just did to me, I need some nourishment."

Dan reached for me, and tugged me back next to him on the bed. "Don't leave me."

"I'm not going anywhere. The food's gonna come to us. What do you want?"

Dan paused, and then grabbed the menu. He held it close to his eyes, the one bedside lamp didn't offer much wattage. "I'll take the *hambourgeois de boeuf Angus*. Even a hamburger sounds exotic when you say it in French."

I wasn't exactly hungry, but the menu contained the correct reply. Fun girls eat food. Preferably red meat, or raw oysters. "I'll do the veal filet. I'll save the oysters for the next time we're together."

Dan reached over and grabbed my thigh and gave it a shake. "I like how your mind works." And even as I grinned back at him, my stomach tightened. It was the fantasy girl he'd responded to, not the real woman by his side. And that woman was feeling less and less like herself.

The room service waiter set up our plates and food on the dining table at one end of my suite. I signed the bill with a flourish and tipped him generously. It was all being paid by Dan, so why not? As I sat in front of my veal, I let my bathrobe fall open just the perfect amount. Dan would see my cleavage in the soft pink light, and then he'd watch me devour my meal with the same gusto I went down on him. I wanted to obliterate those moments where my face was blotchy and tear stained. The stuff of fantasy doesn't include a woman sobbing in her bra and panties.

Being together didn't feel completely organic. All our encounters had been tainted by artifice or context. I wondered if a man like Dan could ever fall for the "real" me, or if Catherine, and her capacity to conjure fantasy would always overshadow Amy. And yet, I didn't want to have that conversation with Dan. The "What are we doing here? Is there a future?" questions were impossible to ask. It was too early to wonder, and they would dispel whatever lingering aura I might have of having my shit together. Only whiny wannabes ask if there's a future when they're with a guy like Dan Levin, and he had to know it. It's like the Heisenberg uncertainty principle of dating, where the mere act of asking fundamentally undermines the trajectory of the relationship.

After dinner, I invited Dan to join me in my bed. The room was cool, so I wore an oversized Harvard T-shirt, and he retrieved a thin white T-shirt from his room. We lay together, sandwiched between the Egyptian cotton sheets. Dan clutched me to his body, and I lay there still against his body, listening to his heartbeat as my ear pressed against his chest. He stroked my hair over and over, hypnotizing me to sleep.

CHAPTER 24

DOWNGRADE FROM BUY TO HOLD

It was noon before I woke up, alone. The room service trolley had been removed, Dan had departed, and I had slept through everything. Fortunately, Dan had left a note:

> "Going to gym. Back at 1. Got a cool lunch idea—
> save your appetite."

A quick shower and the hotel blow dryer helped me to restore a whiff of glamor, but I had to resort to my Vermont clothes, which took the look down a dozen notches. Gray denim and a bulky cream J. Crew turtleneck are not the most fashion forward choices, but my bag offered me few options. I was putting in a pair of discreet, white gold Cartier hoop earrings when Dan knocked.

Dan eyed me up and down and smiled broadly. "Good morning, er, I mean good afternoon, gorgeous!" He pulled me into his body and gave me an enthusiastic smooch on the lips.

"Good afternoon to you, too! So, what have you got planned?"

"We're going to eat like the natives. I've got it all figured out. We'll go to Schwartz's Deli for smoked meat sandwiches." I cocked my head. "You know smoked meat, right? It's a lot like pastrami, only better."

"I thought that's what you said. You must educate me."

"Then you're overdue. Let's go!" Dan grabbed my jacket from the closet, and like a gentleman, he helped me put it on. He then held the door to the suite open for me, and we joined Mark, who had been waiting for us outside my door. Fifteen minutes later, the black SUV arrived at a gritty deli whose sign, "*charcuterie hebraique*" accurately described the entire menu. Once inside, we were ushered into a small corner table by the owner, at a restaurant where there was no reserved seating. The signs plastered on the wall said "first-come, first-served." I was impressed by Dan's advance team, wherever they were and whatever they had done to secure us that spot.

"So, what are you going to have—smoked meat sandwich, smoked meat poutine, or perhaps the smoked meat platter?"

"I could go crazy, and get the turkey." Dan looked at me in mock horror.

"You are such a deviant. That would be heresy."

"I might have to walk back to the hotel, right?"

"You might have to walk back to New York."

"A smoked meat sandwich with a side of fries, then. I don't think these shoes could get me back to Burlington, let alone back to New York."

"Forget your walking shoes. I don't want to lose sight of you. You're coming back with me." I pretended to mop my forehead with relief. Dan continued, "Speaking of New York, what are you plans? What are you considering?"

"I just don't know. I'd like my old life back, but it's not on offer right now. I've interviewed at a few places, I've networked like crazy, but nothing seems to be connecting."

"I'm still not seeing much deal flow either. Everyone's sphincter is clenched. I'm hoping things will loosen up after the election."

"Me too. So, realistically, that puts us into 2009. I don't think there's going to be much activity at the end of the year. If I didn't have ugly student loans every month, I'd just go to Thailand and learn to scuba dive or something. You know, punt for a quarter."

"Can I join you?" Dan took my hand and gripped it tightly on the Formica tabletop. "Let's both punt. It's going to be ugly for a while."

"I'd love to. God, I'd love to. But I can't." I wanted to convey how tenuous my financial status was, but it might sound like I was asking him for money, or perhaps he'd think I was a financial fuckup. How could someone earn two hundred thousand a year plus a bonus, and still be broke? I was living proof it was possible.

When our thick sandwiches arrived, we both dug in. The meat was pink and juicy, the mustard added some necessary tang to cut through the fatty flesh, and the rye bread added an essential heft to the experience. We chewed mostly in silence.

After lunch, I proposed walking back to the hotel. Dan was game, and Mark trailed behind us at a discreet distance. Boulevard Saint-Laurent was filled with low-slung brick buildings. The street was tree-lined, but most of the trees had lost their leaves already, leaving the branches gray and nude, and poking angrily at the sky.

When we turned down Sherbrooke Street, the neighborhood became livelier, especially as we crossed through the *Université du Quebec*, and then McGill University. The city transformed in only a few blocks, going from dirty brick to handsome stone. A few more blocks, and we hit the high rises and the fancy storefronts. Just as in New York, many of the storefronts were empty, because the victims of the financial crisis were far-flung. The pain was shared broadly, across industries and nations. The consequences were impossible to miss.

As we were walking toward our hotel rooms, Dan put his arm around my waist and steered me towards his room. "Come join me." And so I did.

Afterwards, it was my turn to speak. "I could get used to this."

"Yeah. So could I."

The afternoon turned into evening, which turned into dinner at Joe Beef, Montreal's most celebrated new restaurant. With its chalkboard menu and low-key ambiance, I was overdressed in my black Max Mara pony skin skirt, but Dan seemed enchanted. He gazed at me through the entire meal, playing with my fingers on the wooden table, staring at me over his glass of ruby red *Barbera d'Alba*.

Dan dared me to order the horse, but I opted for the lamb. He got the filet, and we both devoured every luscious bite and every last drop of wine. Mark's presence felt useful, instead of intrusive, as we staggered down the hallway and I fumbled with the card key to my room. The cocktails had tortured my fine motor skills, so Mark took over and opened the door for me. I waved at Mark and slurred, "Thanks . . . and goodnight! We won't be coming back out 'til morning, so get some sleep."

I giggled as Dan gestured at Mark. "I just do as I'm told, so you might as well, too." We left Mark standing outside my hotel room door as the door clicked shut. We were both a little too drunk to do much more than cuddle in the bed, and that was fine by me. My pussy remained exhausted from all the action earlier. We both passed out, tired and silly from our wonderful evening.

Around 3 a.m. I jolted awake. Dan was snoring contentedly, tucked against my body, but my mind had begun to race again. I hadn't felt this kind of comfort from a man in a long time, and it unnerved me. What was Dan's agenda? Was he sincere? Was I just another trophy for him to screw?

I snuck into the bathroom and called Erika. It was already morning in Geneva. "Erika, it's Amy here. I fucked up. Or rather, I fucked Dan."

"Oh darling . . . how are you? What happened?"

"I lost my mind in Burlington and Dan swooped in with his Gulfstream. Those things cast enchantment spells. We're in Montreal now, and I feel like I totally messed up. I think I lost you a client."

Erika paused. I imagined her cringing or fuming, but if she was upset, her voice didn't betray her irritation. "Oh, don't worry about that. Clients are like fish, there's always another one." She sighed into the phone. "I know how to address the supply issue. Tell me what happened?" I proceeded to tell her about the attempted rape by the cow doctor, and the romance of the suite at the Ritz, and all the extraordinary and seductive things that Dan had at his disposal.

When I reminded her that it started with Michael's near-death experience in the dungeon, she said, "I've been talking to him every day. He's going to have a full recovery."

"Seriously?" I was mortified that such a simple thing had eluded me. After all our time together, in the dungeon and outside, I had grown very fond of Michael. But seeing him look so helpless had thrown me off. I should have been checking on him and making sure he was on the mend. "I need to call him. He must hate me."

"Don't be a drama queen, Amy. He adores you. He thinks you saved his life."

"The heart attack must have messed with his head."

"Amy, darling, no. The heart attack messed with your head."

"I can't argue with that. It did, which is why I can't work for you anymore. I'm not safe."

"Amy. You are the most responsible, most careful person I know. I wouldn't trust my business and my life to someone who wasn't. If I could, I'd come right back and pick up where I left off, but I'm closing in on the Hirst. Just a couple more weeks. Only do the easy clients. No one's going to die of a spanking."

"Erika, I just can't."

"Amy, you can't afford not to. I know your situation. I'm offering you a lifeline and you'd be a fool not to take it. Just do the easy clients, the ones you already know, and keep things together for me and for you."

"But what about Dan?"

"What about him? Only time will tell if he's sincere. In the meantime, you need to think about Amy. And Amy has debts. Amy needs to earn some money."

"Don't remind me." It was almost the start of the month and the due date for yet another student loan payment. My bank account was fuller than it had been in months, but my Harvard debts would require another decade before they were paid in full.

"Just the easy clients, fine, Erika. Do you always get your way?"

"Pretty much. But our needs are complementary, and that's my trick. I try to know what my counterpart craves most, and then I offer it to him, or *her*. You need money. The clients need attention. I need help. We can all serve each other. Tops and bottoms all need each other equally. It's not even clear who's in charge."

"As soon as I get a job, this has to stop. You understand that, right?"

"Of course. But I don't see things improving until next year. The view here in Switzerland isn't much different from New York. Everything has stalled; everyone's holding their breath."

"Dan and I were just saying the same thing. When will this fucking economy recover?"

"We were all screwed by those reckless bankers, so it'll be a while. Downgrade Dan from buy to hold. Okay? I need you. You're my best friend and my secret weapon. I don't know what I'd do without you."

And that settled it. I'd go back to New York and just get on with the work. If things happened with Dan, that would be fine, an unexpected upside to my Chelsea adventure. But otherwise, I'd continue with my job hunt and try to relaunch my career.

For someone asserting domination in the dungeon, it sure felt like I was submitting elsewhere. The irony was not lost on me. The economy was a bigger, badder top than I was, and like everyone, I just had to bend over and take it.

PART THREE

CONSENT

———

Consent [*kuh* n-sent]

1. The means of establishing boundaries and limits

2. Approval for what is done or proposed by another

CHAPTER 25

SOLDIERING ON IN SYREN LATEX

Lehman's collapse had a ripple effect throughout the economy. AIG got nailed. Investors from Hong Kong to Canada all got strangled when the bank defaulted. Dick Fuld personally got heckled by protesters when he testified to Congress about the horror show he'd overseen at Lehman. The blood wasn't just running in the streets, it was gushing.

Waking up in the morning and having something to do other than see how far the Dow had collapsed seemed like a gift, so I continued to tie knots and spank ass. Whatever happened on the stock market, a wild swing upward or a painful lurch downward, the demand for rope held steady.

Although Michael wasn't up for a visit—he was working from home and my presence would have prompted more questions than comfort—he was up for conversation. I gave him a brief shout every few days, regaling him with tales from the dungeon. He wasn't supposed to exert, but he was allowed to laugh, and it was reassuring to hear his voice and libido strengthen. The guilt and panic I'd felt when he first took ill was diminishing in tandem with his recovery. And every time I called, he kept stressing how meaningful our chats were. Ours was a real relationship, admittedly platonic.

Obama won his run for president, causing a slight upturn in national sentiment. Like everyone, I was riveted to CNN. Dan was on the road, traveling from city to city to speak with his investors. We put our phones on speaker and watched the results come in together. It was as close to a "date" as we could get.

I was thankful the economy would be the top priority of the new administration. The auto industry looked like it would follow banking down the tubes. It was going to be ugly for months, if not longer, and yet I had a survival strategy. My bills were getting paid.

Although we spoke almost daily, I didn't dare think of Dan as my boyfriend, and yet he was acting like one. All that familiarity preceded an intimacy. My job was a complication. I often wondered how much to tell him about my day. If he expressed curiosity, I'd answer as casually as possible and say things like, "Oh, my hand's still sore from a morning spanking." Or, "Man, I used yards of rope today." Otherwise, I'd say nothing about my sessions. Mostly, we talked shop. Discussing deals with one of the best minds in the business was a way to keep my investment muscles honed. If it weren't for the fact I had tied him up and jerked him off, and that he had paid me dearly for the privilege, we had a perfectly normal relationship.

There were periodic deliveries of extravagant flower arrangements. One week it was roses, the next, the vase was bursting with peonies. Dan was single-handedly keeping Banchet Flowers afloat. I got the odd box from Hermès, too. A pink gold bracelet that looked like a dog collar, a white gold necklace with diamonds, that looked like a sparkly bit gag. The boxes came in elaborate bags and the cards were signed by some saleswoman. The baubles were gorgeous, and even though they stirred feelings whenever I looked at them—diamonds may be hardwired to exhilarate—I tried to think practically. I decided not to get too attached to them because if my finances ever got tight, there were luxury pawn shops on 47th Street where treasures could be transformed into cash. And whether it was jewelry or flowers, the cards always said the same thing, "Thinking about you. Dan XOX."

Everything about our interactions signaled that Dan took my sideline in stride, and that he wanted me. But I struggled to reconcile Dan's affection with my own ambivalence toward the work. It seemed inconceivable that a guy like that wouldn't hold such an obscene part-time job against me, but there was no one else offering to pay my bills, so I soldiered on in Syren latex and 5-inch stilettos. And maybe I liked the look of admiration and gratitude the clients gave me? It was a relief relative to the indifference I was receiving in the job market.

With all the distractions and the grind of keeping Erika's businesses going, and despite my weird personal life, I was almost happy. Or at least I wasn't despairing. That changed when I finally returned Susan's call. She'd been leaving messages for weeks. I didn't know what to say —about me, my future, or about Jon—so I had ignored them. Covering for my old boss had become tiresome. Frankly, I wasn't sure if he'd been on the level with me either. In a moment of weakness, I made a lunch date with Susan. Her treat, of course.

We agreed to meet at Florent, in the Meatpacking District, a grungy little diner with exceptional food. It was punk rock meets Cordon Bleu. Susan and I arrived at Gansevoort Street at the same time, only to see a "CLOSED" sign in the window, and layers of dust on the restaurant's contents. It had been shut for months.

Susan waved at me with her black Chanel bag. "Hi! Hi! Hi! So sorry about this." She pointed to the sad storefront. "I could have sworn it was open the last time I was here. Let's just go to Fig & Olive."

"Perfect. Susan, you look great. How've you been?" Months had passed since we'd last seen each other but it felt good to reconnect. I'd always enjoyed her, and I had always hated lying about the misadventures of Jon's zipper.

We walked around the corner to the near empty restaurant where two bored waitresses were gossiping in a back corner. The financial crisis was helpful in one way, it made getting a table much easier. The hostess sat us right away.

Susan looked elegant and together. Her hair was always a perfect blonde, that sunny shade requiring hours of upkeep every three weeks by William Howe. Her hair signaled that she hadn't let the crisis change her grooming habits; the John Barrett salon at Bergdorf Goodman was still getting her money. And in a look that telegraphed "What financial crisis?" She was sporting sleek brown velvet pants, a matching turtleneck, and a red wool coat with a broad black stripe around the base. It was all by Gucci, and it was all current season, lifted straight from the pages of *Vogue*.

All the same, Susan looked uncomfortable. She crushed her Chanel purse in her hands, with her fingers digging into the quilted lambskin. She gripped the silver chain as if she were sure someone would rip it away.

"Susan, is everything okay? How's Jon? How are the kids?"

"Kids are fine. School's fine. Jon's fine. He got promoted. Did he tell you?" The words came out rushed, and yet she looked at me innocently. For a trained actress, she wasn't communicating equanimity.

"No. I haven't spoken to Jon in a month or two." I wanted to ask Susan if Jon had been bad-mouthing me, but if she didn't know of our breach, it seemed likely he hadn't been trashing me to her. I was slightly reassured, but the prospect of Jon getting a promotion left me staggered. "When did the promotion happen? What are his new responsibilities?"

"Oh, it hasn't been announced yet, but he's moving upstairs."

"To twenty-eight?"

"Yeah. He'll be heading global operations. François got pulled back to Brussels, so it'll be the same, just *more*." She paused, still playing with the purse balanced on her lap. "I thought you guys spoke regularly?" I began to wonder if she was thinking of bolting, because everything about her seemed poised for flight.

"It's been a while. When did the promotion happen?" The ponytailed waitress ambled over with menus and stacked them on the table. We both ignored her.

"Oh, it was only last week. It's so new, it almost doesn't feel real. That must be why he hasn't told you." I nodded, thinking there were surely ten other reasons he hadn't been in touch. But the prospect of him being rewarded with a promotion when he had overseen a fiasco was galling. You could lose millions at BFB, be a Grade A asshole, even, but if you had a penis and a squash buddy in the CEO's suite you could still get promoted. BFB remained a confederacy of bros. We women had no margin for error, but Jon's was hundreds of millions wide. Sitting opposite Susan, with her sleek hair and $3,000 coat, and being reminded of this fundamental inequity was making me cranky and impatient.

"Susan, is there something on your mind?"

Her lips formed a thin line as her fingers fumbled for the clasp of the Chanel bag. She reached in and pulled out a wad of papers. "These are recent expense reports. He left them on the printer by mistake." She handed them to me and pointed at several highlighted entries.

I flipped through the pages, unsure what she was getting at. Susan reached across the table and stabbed at an entry as she read it aloud. "River Café—client dinner. Alex Liu. There are three more entries just like that. Does that seem odd?"

"Odd, sure, but not that strange. Jon takes clients out all the time. Often more than once."

"The River Café is in fucking Brooklyn. Jon's no hipster. What's he doing in *fucking Brooklyn*?"

I hadn't recognized the restaurant right away. It was this ridiculously romantic place located beneath the Brooklyn Bridge. All the tables looked out onto the East River and across to the New York City skyline. At night, the view was breathtaking. There was a pianist on site quietly playing show tunes, a serious menu, and enormous flower arrangements, which all added to the magic. The one time I'd been there on some pointless date, two couples had gotten engaged.

"You're right. It's odd. Jon usually takes people to Smith & Wollensky. And I never heard of him going to Brooklyn."

"I know . . . *Brooklyn*."

"Who's Alex Liu?"

"I was hoping you knew."

I shrugged. The name was unfamiliar. "New client?"

"New girlfriend?"

I sat still and remained mute. Continuing to be complicit in Jon's secrets when he was no longer my boss seemed insane, but remaining silent was an old habit. My outrage, however, overruled my practice. I had never consented to be his permanent alibi. "Could be. And Alex wouldn't be the first."

"I thought so. Fuck."

"I'm sorry, Susan. But he's been a dog as long as I've known him."

"Fuck. Fuck. Fuck." She stared at me as her gray eyes began to glisten and water. "Why didn't you say something?"

"One—because you never asked. And two—because he was my boss. With Jon, you're either on his team or you're the enemy to be crushed, and I was on his team. You'd better be careful, because your husband is dangerous when provoked. Frankly, I think he kept secrets from both of us."

Susan pushed her chair back from the table and stood up. "I'm not feeling well. I need to go. Sorry to bring you down here for nothing."

I gave Susan a hug, but her body stiffened, as if to propel me away. "I'll wrap things up here. Go home. And if I learn anything about Alex Liu, I'll let you know."

Susan rushed out of the restaurant, leaving Jon's expense reports forgotten on the table. I sat back down, tucked the reports into my purse, and wondered if I could leave as well. We hadn't ordered anything, and the extra outlay for a solo lunch didn't appeal. I retrieved my coat and headed to the door. I tipped the hostess five bucks and apologized, muttering something about my friend having a family emergency as I hustled out into the cold November air.

As soon as I got back to my laptop, I set about researching Alex Liu. Jon was up to something, and I wanted to understand his game. It didn't take long before I found a reference to Alexandra Liu, Stanford MBA class of 1999. A few more keyboard strokes uncovered a picture of a petite Chinese woman. Alex had shoulder length black hair with wispy bangs, enormous almond eyes, full lips that formed a perfect cupid's bow, and a barely visible smattering of freckles across her nose and cheeks. She didn't look like one of Jon's models, but her appeal was obvious. Although her face seemed serious and her suit was a conservative navy, there was a slight twist on the right side of her mouth, suggesting a subtle smirk, as if she had a secret. Alex was sexy as hell.

An industry database revealed she was a financial advisor. But when her entry said she worked at "Birch Advisors," I almost spilled my Diet Coke.

That was the same firm that had picked and packaged the bonds in our most wretched deals. It was staggering. Jon's cock often made bad decisions, but this one had cost billions. Something weird had happened, but it wasn't clear if Jon was guilty of stupidity or something more insidious. This matter needed to be investigated further.

CHAPTER 26

WORK WIFE 2.0

Dan finally returned to New York. For the first time, he invited me to his apartment on Fifth Avenue. His sudden openness to me made me feel even more strongly about him. I wanted to understand him better, as he occupied so much of my imagination. All the same, he made me wary. His wealth and the ease of his life created a reality distortion field, and it was hard not to be seduced. It took him minimal effort to dazzle with an exceptional bauble or a ride on his jet. And despite knowing how the conjurer's tricks worked, I was still succumbing to their magic.

The man was a professional shark and a practiced acquirer, accustomed to getting what he wanted when he wanted it. Would I be just another possession, in fetishwear, wielding rope?

Despite my concerns, I could feel that emotional tug, where I was like a magnet, being dragged into his life by stronger forces than I would seek to overpower.

The Sherry-Netherland is a place I'd admired many times while walking along Fifth Avenue, but I'd never been in the tower, close to its gargoyles. Dan's apartment occupied the entire 36th floor. The elevator opened into a grand vestibule where Dan stood waiting for me. The black and white marble floors were an elaborate stage for a man dressed in his typical khakis and black cashmere sweater.

"Please, come in." The rooms were gorgeous, but not what I was expecting. The library walls were lacquered and deep green. The shelves were overflowing with books with leather covers. The desk was a grand antique, with carved wood and an enormous brown ink blotter on the top. The living room was a riot of art deco, with shiny woods and rich upholstery. The dining room had an enormous rosewood table with seating for ten. And the bedroom featured even more furniture that looked like it had been airlifted from somewhere else and deposited inside Dan's apartment.

The saving grace was the view. The apartment looked out onto Central Park from half its windows. From the other half, you could see a sparkling cityscape all the way down to the Empire State Building.

"What do you think?"

"It's spectacular." I wandered over to the window. "It must be amazing to look out at this whenever you want." Dan walked up behind me and put his arms around me, as we both gazed out at Central Park at dusk. "I must confess, the place doesn't feel like you."

"Oh, it isn't. I bought it a month ago. All this is Dennis Roberts' doing." Dan smirked. "He was the prior owner. The guy had a liquidity crisis, and I always liked the place, so I bought it from him."

"Dennis Roberts of Knarr Capital? Hasn't he partnered with you on some deals?"

"Yeah, but not recently. He's a real asshole." Contempt seeped from his voice. "I got the apartment and all its contents for fifty cents on the dollar. He needed a quiet, fast sale, and I was happy to help." Dan turned my body so that I was facing him, his hands still rested on my hips. "Hey, I ordered some food from downstairs—Harry Cipriani. Hope you like it."

He went into the kitchen to retrieve some aluminum containers. There were three types of pasta in the warming oven, and three types of salad in the fridge. There was even a small pizza layered with prosciutto sitting on the counter. "I won't reheat this until we're ready." It was a dizzying turn of pace. He'd gone from hungry vulture, attacking the assets of a rival, to mother hen, as he fussed about making sure the pizza didn't get overcooked.

Dan had already set the table for us. He held out my chair and helped me into position. My seat had me staring out at the city, from an expansive and expensive view. Dan brought out the salads and offered them to me, as he held the bowls. The apartment had even come with serving forks and spoons. Roberts had left the apartment well-equipped.

"What are you going to do with the place?"

"I don't know. I'm tired of living in Connecticut, so this seemed like a good first step. I don't think it's big enough, but the opportunity was hard to ignore." His voice, which at first seemed all business, suddenly became playful. "What do you think I should do with it?"

"Well, a place like this demands some drama. The question for you, is the drama inside or outside?"

"Good point. I'll mention it to my architect. To be frank, I'm on the fence about how much work I want to put into it. I expect to flip it in a few years, once the market has recovered."

"Yeah, that makes sense. You sure do have a taste for distressed assets." As the words came out, I wondered if Dan viewed me as just another distressed asset. It was a fleeting thought, but because it was so dark and cynical, I didn't dare let it linger in my brain. Defensively, I launched the conversation back at him. "Do you really want to live in Dennis Roberts' home surrounded by Dennis Roberts' stuff?"

'You're right." He grimaced as he heard the name. "It definitely needs something." We continued with our meal. Dan jogged into the kitchen and returned with serving bowls filled with potato gnocchi in a gorgonzola sauce, tortellini in a cream and prosciutto sauce, and even a classic spaghetti.

I switched back into girlfriend mode and made small talk. "Do you think we've got enough to eat? You went a little overboard."

"Well, I wasn't sure what you liked, so I got some of everything."

It was disarming, seeing Dan so solicitous. Only minutes previously, he had been reveling in his rival's downfall. His ability to shift gears was unnerving and giving me qualms about his earnestness, even as I hoped he felt the same way about me as I did about him. Just hearing the phone ring and knowing it was him had an effect on my pulse. Coming up on the elevator had heightened my senses, and every signal he gave suggested reciprocation.

"You didn't need to do that, but I'm glad you did."

He served himself some pasta and sat down next to me. As we ate, we discussed several deals he was evaluating. Dan nodded enthusiastically to many of my points, and then he grabbed my hand and kissed the palm.

"Who am I kidding? I can barely keep my hands off you." Dan stood up, and held me close to his body as he kissed my lips. His tongue probed my mouth as my breathing deepened. I pushed my body into his in return.

"Now that's more like it. Deal talk only gets me so excited. You push me over the edge." His passion aroused me. Despite my best efforts, I'd been fantasizing about Dan for weeks. That evening, as I looked out the windows of the thirty-sixth floor, my heart overruled my head.

"I'm not feeling the tortellini. I'm feeling you. Come." Dan released my back and took my hand and pulled me into the master bedroom. The room was dimly lit, with an enormous four poster bed serving as the centerpiece to the room.

Dan unzipped the back of my favorite McQueen dress, the one that had brought me so much attention at the George Hotel. He rested his fingertips on my collarbone, where he found the diamond encrusted "filet d'or" necklace he'd given me. "You like this?"

"A bit gag covered in diamonds. What's not to love? You have great taste."

"In women, too," he whispered in my ear. My heart raced with his words, and I practically melted when his fingers migrated from the necklace and eased the dress off my shoulders and down onto the floor. I'd been feeling playful when I dressed for the evening. I was wearing a matching bra and panty set in a textured red lace from Aubade. The engineering was phenomenal—it made my bust thrust upward, like the breasts of a teenage cheerleader. Black thigh-high stockings completed the outfit.

After stepping out of my dress, I gave Dan a slow twirl, while putting my weight onto one pump, and then the other. The only parts of his body that moved were his eyes, he was stuck in place for several seconds. Erika's dungeon had turned me into an expert in male attention, and his every response said he was rapt.

Once he got his bearings again, Dan undressed himself and lay down in the middle of the bed, almost as if he were lying on the rack in Erika's dungeon. Instinctively, I slipped into performance mode. My alter-ego, Catherine, emerged as I did a slow strip tease and removed the Aubade bra. A flirty push of the straps, and then a seductive unhooking of the back, I held the front of the bra up across my chest while crawling onto Dan's lap.

"Take it off! All off!" Dan reached for the bra and gave it a twirl as he tossed it on the floor. I knelt above his face, and he grabbed the fabric of the panties in his teeth. "This needs to come off, too."

It took a shimmy and the thong was off my body. It landed next to my dress. "Is this how you want me? I can tie you up?"

"Nah, not today. Just get on top of me." And to prove it, he grabbed my hips and thrust inside me with his cock. He then let me do all the work, as he lay still. Ropes weren't necessary to keep him passive.

My hip flexors exerted until finally, Dan exploded. A few more thrusts might have taken care of me, but he was done, and I was tired. He rolled me to his side, where I nestled into his body, resting my head on his chest and draping a leg over his. We'd been building toward a moment like this, and I was desperate to nurture a feeling of growing closeness. His arms drew me into him. "I've missed you so much."

"I've missed you, too, Amy. A month apart is too long."

"No argument from me. I thought about you every night." I ran my fingers lightly over his chest, watching goosebumps form in the wake of my touch.

"I thought about you, too. Those phone calls just left me wanting more." He squeezed my shoulders and gave me a gentle kiss.

I'd been afraid to articulate my thoughts, worried that if they were uttered aloud, it would somehow make them less likely to be realized. That the act of saying what I wanted would ruin things. But here we were, lying in bed, wanting more of each other. It thrilled me that we were on the same page, thinking about the same things. We might even be enough for each other. Maybe I'd hit an age where I was finally ready to consider a future with someone? Or, maybe all the risk and uncertainty in my life had made me value stability and predictability more? Anything was possible.

"Once a month isn't enough for me, Dan. I adore your company. So maybe once a week isn't really enough, either."

"How about every day?" His comment staggered me. Was he suggesting something serious and real? I paused, trying to figure out the correct response. Dan then reached into his nightstand and pulled out a large tan envelope. "This goes into what I'm proposing."

"Do you want me to read this now?" I was startled, but curious. What kind of proposition was this? What relationship requires a document?

Dan nodded, as he looked at me expectantly. I grabbed a pillow and pushed it behind my head. "This will be a minute."

"Of course. Take your time. And let me know if you have any questions."

"Of course." I opened the large envelope and almost dropped it when I read the heading on the document "EMPLOYMENT AGREEMENT." Somehow, I managed to keep my face still while scanning the four pages.

The document laid out a very specific offer. I'd be his firm's Director of Research, with a starting salary of three hundred thousand plus an annual bonus contingent upon my performance and the firm's returns. It was the kind of offer I'd been looking for elsewhere. "Dan, I don't know what to say."

"Say yes. I have an office for you, right next to mine. Think of what we could do together."

"I can't say yes." I was mortified that I had believed his interest in me was romantic, that he might even love me. And although the position offered more upside than my job at BFB, it would have been a disaster. Not only would it put me next to Dan, where his life would unfold in front of me daily, but it would put me in a service role, helping another guy refine and execute his vision all the while subsuming my own. My feelings for Dan were already complicated, and this would make them utterly bizarre.

"Why not?"

"I thought our relationship was personal, not professional. You've given me jewelry." I ran my fingers over the necklace, even as I felt ridiculous for making the connection between his gift and my misunderstanding.

"You don't like it?" Dan cocked his head, seemingly oblivious to the implications of the Hermès bling.

"Of course, I like it. It's spectacular." Did I really need to explain to him that only a man in hot pursuit sends a woman diamonds? He had to understand their effect, unless his wealth and privilege had somehow insulated him from the laws of physics, and he'd forgotten how actions beget reactions. I tried a different approach. "You flew to Burlington, for crying out loud. You've even met my parents!"

"You were in trouble, and I thought I could help. You're important to me." He reached over and gripped my fingers. It was an act of sincerity, but not of love.

"Right, but not important in the way you are to me. To me, swooping into Burlington felt like the extravagant move of an eager suitor. That you might even see a future for us, because I can see one." Dan remained silent, so I continued. There was no point keeping my thoughts to myself, I had progressed far beyond emotional circumspection. "I don't want to be your employee anymore. I thought we'd moved past that."

"There isn't much distance for me between the personal and the professional. You're brilliant, you're available, and you can't be tying up strange men every day. Doesn't this solve both our problems?"

"I'm not just another asset you can buy."

"Absolutely not. I'm not buying you, Amy. I'm hiring you. You'd be doing important work for me."

"For you, not with you. I can't work *for* you. I can't be just another one of your employees."

"You wouldn't be *just* another employee. We have an understanding. There's no one I trust more. There's no one I listen to more closely. You're unique."

"I wouldn't be unique, sitting in an office next to you, in a building filled with people all working for you." The prospect of being yet another man's work wife was devastating, although I did my best to keep my face impassive. Jon had taught me to handle sharks with extreme care. "I'm grateful for the offer, but I can't accept it. And quite frankly, I can't stay here any longer." I'd been trying so hard to retain my cool, and to keep my emotions in check. He'd already seen me bawling once, and the prospect of giving Dan a second glimpse of me at my most vulnerable was horrifying. How had I misread the situation so badly? How had I opened myself to someone who just wanted another distressed asset in his personal portfolio?

I climbed out of bed, retrieved the clothes that were strewn about the room and put them back on. Though my chin was quivering, I managed to maintain some sliver of self-respect. Dan walked me to the door, seemingly indifferent to my state. He gave me a chaste hug as we waited in his foyer. When the elevator doors opened, Dan said, "I'll call you tomorrow." I nodded, unsure if I'd even want to hear from him.

My night was restless and wrecked. I hated that I had fallen for someone, and that I had so badly misjudged the situation. How many women expect a romantic offer and get an employment contract instead? I only knew of one. Me.

CHAPTER 27

CONFLICTS
AND HEDGES

It wouldn't be easy, but I resolved to get Dan out of my heart. I wanted to analyze and think, to be back on my home turf, and to be preoccupied by a big, messy problem. Understanding what Jon and Alexandra had been up to, when they selected all those crappy investments for Pulsar, would be curative. I'd been afraid to look too hard, but it was time to get serious, and to get inside Jon's head.

I began with the San Francisco guys. The hedge fund was far too clever. The founders had named it Pulsar, after the kind of neutron star that forms when an enormous star runs out of fuel and collapses in on itself. This stellar death produces a supernova, a catastrophic explosion that kicks off most of the star's mass, leaving only a neutron star. Of course, not all of these explosions create pulsars. Some form black holes, which seemed like an apt metaphor for the meltdown.

Seth Volkov, the founder, was impressive. He graduated with distinction from Stanford in physics, and then launched into an astrophysics Ph.D. at Caltech. After graduation, he put aside astronomy and went to work as a hedge fund number cruncher. His results were exceptional. By 2004, Volkov had begun his own fund, where he continued to excel.

The guy might have gone into finance, but he remained an astronomy freak. In his spare time from Pulsar, he also founded SpaceGo, a company whose mission was to revolutionize interplanetary transportation. The launch party had been lavish, with live music and an army of NASA astronauts in attendance. There had even been an on-site photo studio where attendees could model the sleek grey and black SpaceGo space suits. While everyone else was clutching their wallets, he was opening his wide and money was flowing out. *Alpha Magazine*, the essential tabloid of the hedge fund set, said he'd made $250 million in 2007. The country was getting creamed, and he was making bank. It was astonishing. Pulsar wasn't bottom quartile of the hedge fund universe as Jon had claimed, they were at the top. Volkov had found an angle that everybody else had missed.

I called Chen to see if he knew anything about Pulsar. He pointed me toward *The Wall Street Journal* article that mentioned the firm had actively hedged their investments with a type of insurance that paid out only if their deals failed. As the Pulsar investments plummeted in value, their insurance would have soared.

Of course, if the value of the insurance exceeded the value of the underlying asset, when the Pulsar investments went up in flames, they would still stand to profit handsomely. It was a fiendish strategy, and completely legal. It would explain the donations to the planetarium. But it smelled rotten.

By my calculations, Pulsar had lost over a billion dollars in the deals it had sponsored with BFB. But the other BFB clients, who had bought alongside them, had lost even more. BFB itself had been on the hook for hundreds of millions. Jon had believed those slices were completely safe and he'd invested BFB's own money in them, only he had bet wrong.

Birch Advisors, which had picked the bonds for inclusion in the Pulsar deals, had been guilty of ignorance or malfeasance. To have consistently chosen the worse bonds was staggering. Somebody's always the bottom performer, but how did Birch earn such a dubious honor? My attention turned to Alex Liu.

Birch was such a small operation that it barely had a website, and there was no "about us" page with pictures of the key employees. There had to be some other way to learn about Ms. Liu.

I searched my database of contacts to see who I knew from the Stanford MBA class of '99. There were three hits. The first was a name I didn't even recognize, from a deal I barely remembered. The second name, Peter Smith, seemed more promising. We'd met at a conference five years ago, only his contact information must have been out of date because his email bounced back. Google was of little help, either. His name was common enough that there were several Peter Smiths, including one that might have been him, now living in Singapore. I sent that Smith a friendly email but didn't expect much to come of it.

Unfortunately, the third Stanford MBA '99 was one of the many guys Susan had tried to set me up with, one Rafael Ortiz, a vice president at Goldman Sachs. He'd followed up after the dinner party to try and schedule a date, only I had punted, so that second dinner never happened. It was a bit awkward, but I decided to try him anyway and sent a brief email, "Are you still around? How about that dinner?"

He replied immediately. "Would love that. How does tomorrow night at 8 p.m. sound? I can get us into Momofuku Ko." I accepted immediately. Momofuku Ko had only twelve seats, and it was the hottest restaurant in town. It was virtually impossible to get a reservation. Rafael was trying to impress, and it was working.

Since I was telling everyone I was running Erika's gallery while she was on leave, I decided to outfit myself like some artworld gangster-girl. It required a pitstop at INA, a consignment store in Soho. There, I found a black sleeveless dress, with darts that made it fall close to the body. It was so tight it could have been latex, the way it squeezed my curves. When I asked the saleswoman if there was something in a larger size, she gave me a look of horror. "It's perfect. Are you crazy?" The dress was by Lanvin, current season, and it still had its tags. Some fashionista must have ordered it last year direct from the designer, and when the crisis hit, she had to unload it for the cash. I picked up a $2,000 dress for only four hundred bucks.

I was the only person browsing, so the sleek brunette saleswoman played dress up with me as we tried to find the perfect *gallerista* accessories. "I've only got another two hundred to spend, and I want maximum sizzle. What have ya got?"

She pulled out a stack of enamel Hermès bracelets. "Two years ago, I'd have gotten two hundred for one of these bracelets. I'll give you these three for that same amount."

I slid them over my wrist and admired the colorful enamel and the bright gold "H." "I think they're too proper, but you're right, it's a steal."

She rummaged through a drawer and pulled out a black crystal bracelet by Tom Binns. It had a silver skull encircled by crystal tendrils. "Is this edgy enough for you?"

I tried it and had to laugh. "I don't think I'm goth enough, and my date works at Goldman."

"Oh, so now you tell me." She opened another drawer and pulled out a substantial gold cuff threaded with black leather pieces. "Try this one."

The bracelet fit my wrist perfectly. I twisted it around and delighted in the weight of the faux gold and the unexpected leather accents. "This is gorgeous."

"It should be. It's Chanel."

I handed it back to her. "It's beyond my price range." I'd been in the Chanel boutique before, so I knew how expensive everything was. Unless you were buying makeup or a key chain, it was impossible to get out of there without spending at least a grand.

"I'll give it to you for one fifty." The store tag was still attached. It had last sold for $1,050. I retrieved my wallet where there was a small stash of hundred-dollar bills earned as Catherine, and I peeled off enough for the dress and bracelet. My ill-gotten gains were being depleted.

Thanks to Erika and my work as her substitute, glamming myself up had become second nature. I could give myself the perfect smoky eye in a minute. My lipstick never smeared. And my breasts seemed to defy gravity, even though it was just the result of a serious investment in the best lingerie. I was ready for Rafael, and I hoped he'd be ready for me.

I arrived a few minutes early at Momofuku Ko, and handed my wool coat to the hostess. I wanted to look as bare and as glossy as possible. She led me to our spots at the counter, where I perched on the edge of my stool, letting my laser cut Alaïa stiletto balance on the footrest. The position elongated my leg, and I'd learned the effect that could have on men.

Fortunately, my date arrived soon after me. He swept in, rushed over, and gave me the Spanish air kiss on both cheeks as he clutched my bare arms. "Amy. You look amazing! Better, even, than I remembered."

"Thanks, Rafa. You look great, too. You still doing triathlons?" Rafael had wavy hair that had gone prematurely grey. His eyes were a bright blue, his body was lean from daily workouts, and his skin had a faint tan. He threw his long frame into the seat beside mine, and we launched into recaps of what we'd been up to. I had learned to speak *gallerista*, as I edited and embellished my time at Erika's gallery into something that resembled an actual job.

"So, you left BFB and now you're in a gallery in Chelsea? That's quite a shift." Rafael touched my hand as I nursed a glass of red. He'd ordered our eight-course meal to come with a wine pairing, so it wasn't even necessary to think.

"Yep. I've taken over the Grieg Gallery. But it's strictly temporary." I shifted my body closer to his. "I'm waiting out the crisis and helping out a friend."

"Grieg—that's contemporary works, right?"

"Yes, so you know it! Emerging artists, mostly. Do you collect?"

"I love art, and I have some pieces, but I wouldn't call myself a collector." He slouched a little as his hand grazed my thigh. "I'll stop by sometime and you can educate my eye."

"I'd like that . . . I'll show you our stuff." I cocked my head and gave him a half smile. "We've got a show coming up. A young woman who just got her MFA from Yale. Her paintings are incredibly lush, with just the right amount of eroticism. I bet they're right up your alley."

"Sounds great. Count me in."

At that moment, the chef put our first course down in front of us—an English muffin soaked in pork fat, topped with fluke. "Oh my. This looks insane. You'll tell me if any of the poppy seeds get stuck in my teeth, right?"

"Deal, but only if you tell me if there are any in mine."

That first bite was delicate and luscious, and set the stage for the rest of the meal. We made our way through several savory courses, from shaved *foie gras* to a soft-boiled egg topped with caviar, when slices of short rib cooked *sous-vide*, and then deep fried landed in front of us. The combination of tender meat and a crispy exterior was almost more than either of us could handle. "I think this could be better than sex," I whispered to Rafael.

"Then you're doing it wrong, Amy." He leaned forward on his stool and kissed my neck, letting his tongue and soft lips linger on my skin.

"Or I'm not keeping the right company. How'd you get this reservation, anyway? Isn't this impossible?"

"Not impossible, just very, very hard. I had one of my analysts hack into the Momofuku reservation system a month ago."

"You were just waiting for me to email?"

"Well, not exactly. But I can recognize an opportunity. And I'm so glad I did. I really enjoyed our dinner together when Jon introduced us, but you've changed. You seem different now. More curious and self-assured. More fun, even."

"Was I that bad two years ago?"

"You weren't bad at all. Just focused. Mostly on business."

"That sounds about right. And I must admit, Jon's introductions usually left me cold."

"Now you tell me! Well, I like a challenge. How is Jon, anyway?"

It was a relief that Rafael and Jon didn't seem to be in touch. I didn't want Jon to know that I'd been seeking background on Birch and the characters surrounding our deals. "He got a promotion. He's on the BFB twenty-eighth floor now."

"No kidding. Well, at least someone seems to be coming through this crisis upright."

"Oh yeah, Jon's a survivor. He looks out for Jon. But enough about him. Tell me something surprising. How are you still single?"

"I was engaged. A violinist at the Met. But we just couldn't figure things out."

"I'm sorry. That's tough. But her loss is my gain. I'm so glad this dinner worked out."

"Me too. I must confess, you didn't reveal this playful side the first time we went out. Or at least you didn't show it to me. If you had, I would have pushed harder for a second dinner."

"Was I a bit of a prig? I think I overcompensated when I was at BFB. I'm sorry if it made me insufferable."

"No, no, no . . . I found you intriguing then, but I find you incredibly sexy now. When we're done here, why don't we go back to my place for a nightcap?"

"Let me muse on that enticing offer through dessert, okay?"

"Okay. And if not tonight, then I'd like to see you again next week. I'm going to San Francisco for a few days, but I'll be back on Thursday."

San Francisco was my opening and I took it. "San Francisco? For business? Or is this something Stanford related?"

"You remembered! Not Stanford. There's a tech meeting out there. But I'll be seeing some of my old classmates, as usual."

"Yeah, I know how that is. I can't shake the Harvard crowd . . . Say, I ran into one of your old classmates. Alexandra Liu. Did you know her?"

"Alex? Yeah. But I lost touch. She's here? In NYC? She doesn't come to any of the alumni events."

"Alex Liu picked the bonds that went into the BFB deals."

"Really? How odd. I thought she'd drifted a bit. She was looking for a score, but just couldn't make one happen. She was hungry, that's for sure, but not the sharpest student in the class." He took a sip of his wine and scratched behind his ear. "It was strange, she'd been super serious as an undergrad. Finished with honors and everything, but she just couldn't connect at the GSB. She was one of only four students my year who graduated without a job offer. I'd heard she was even doing penny stocks."

"No kidding. Penny stocks?" It was a staggering prospect—that was the sleaziest corner of the investment universe, filled with speculators and manipulators. "Well, she seems pretty busy now, and kinda legit. Or at least she was before the crisis struck." I shrugged. "Oh, while we're talking Stanford, can I ask about another classmate?"

"Sure."

"Did you know Seth Volkov?"

"A bit, when we were undergrads. He was a couple years ahead of me, but we were both in the Judo club. Now that guy connected with everything he touched. Even then, he was a fucking genius. And now? Did you see the killing he made last year with Pulsar?"

"Yeah. Some of those deals were mine."

"No shit." He drummed the fingers of his left hand on the countertop as he rubbed his chin with his right. "You know, Alex and Seth dated . . . I'm not 100% sure, but I think when she was a freshman and he was a senior, he was really taken by her. She used to come watch our Judo matches. She was around all the time."

It was my turn to be surprised. "You don't say. Well, he's married with three kids now, so that particular relationship must have ended."

"Very true." Rafael adjusted his jacket and squared his shoulders. "Tell me, do you ever think about kids?"

"Sometimes. But I'd need to find the father first, of course. And you?"

"Sometimes. But I'd need to find the mother first, of course." We both smiled at each other from atop our stools. "We get one more morsel. Dessert is supposed to be worth the wait. Christina Tosi, the pastry chef, is a bigger genius than Volkov. The things she does with sugar. . . . "

One of the chefs prepared delicate deep-fried squares and garnished them with a dollop of pale white soft-serve ice cream and a swirl of caramel-colored miso. The chef put a plate in front of each of us. "Apple pie. Enjoy."

"This doesn't look like any apple pie I've ever seen." I dug my fork into a corner of the square. A large, elegant flake fell onto the plate as the hot filling oozed out of the ravioli. The scent of cinnamon wafted up. "But it sure smells like pie." I took my fork and fed the piece to Rafael, who gobbled it back, and then returned the favor.

"Here, some for you. But look, I'm giving you ice cream with your bite. You didn't give me any." He scooped a tiny amount of the soft serve onto the fork and transferred the warm pie and the cool ice cream to my mouth, as he held one hand beneath the fork, to catch any stray dribbles or drips.

I looked him in the eyes as I bit down on the fork, drawing my lips along the tynes, and cleaning every stray crumb from the fork with delicate flicks of my tongue. "Oh my god, that was so good." Rafael reached over and put his hand in the hair at the back of my head and pulled me to his face. His mouth still tasted of cinnamon. I closed my eyes and leaned into the kiss. It was refreshing, having such an uncomplicated encounter. It wasn't a transaction or a trade. It wasn't fraught with kink or need. It was just two people enjoying each other. "I really dropped the ball with you. You're something special."

"I won't let you drop the ball this time. I want more. Come home with me." He had the same look in his eyes as my clients did in the dungeon—eager and hungry.

It was tempting to accept. I glanced over at him, and in the soft light of the restaurant, he was especially handsome. I could practically visualize his toned shoulders and the muscular ripples in his lean abdomen. His lips were full and suggested an exuberant passion. "Next time?" I gazed up at him, and almost felt coy doing so. I laid my hand on top of his and gave him a squeeze of my fingers. He lifted my hand and kissed my knuckle.

"Next time. And I'll hold you to that."

After we left the restaurant, Rafael flagged down a cab and gave me an enthusiastic kiss goodnight. I couldn't help but look out the taxi window and wave back at him, as he stood balanced on the curb. It all felt so normal, like the calendar had turned back ten years, and I'd never met Jon in the first place, or accepted Erika's job offer.

When I woke up in the morning, I didn't have any great ideas for my investigation. Sure, Alex and Jon were tight, and certainly Alex and Seth might have been close a dozen years ago, but it was all just circumstantial. There was nothing concrete that supported fraud, or even, anything strongly suggesting collusion. What was clear, however, is that what the Pulsar guys in San Francisco had engineered had been wrong. It might have been legal, but it reeked.

A pleasant surprise arrived at the gallery from Rafael. A gorgeous, minimalist flower arrangement was delivered from Ovando. Lily grass was looped inside a long rectangular vase, and a perfect spray of purple orchids was captured inside.

The card was short and to the point.

Looking forward to next time. Rafa

I held the message to my chin, while considering my surreal life. I'd never had so many interesting offers, and yet I'd never felt so exposed and at risk. It was time for Erika to come back, and it was time for me to get serious about my future and move on.

CHAPTER 28

A BOMBSHELL AT SMITH & WOLLENSKY

It wasn't enough to probe what went wrong with Birch and Pulsar, I needed to learn what went wrong with BFB, too. I sent Jon an email, congratulating him on his promotion and suggesting we get together for lunch. To my astonishment, he replied right away, saying he was open at 1. Since there were no beatings or meetings in my calendar, I agreed immediately to visit our usual place, Smith & Wollensky. As the person who'd asked for the meeting, his terms were acceptable.

One of the things I'd learned from Erika was the power of clothes. Dressing in the correct banker-costume, adopting their dark colors and proper tailoring had worked for me at BFB. But clothes were more than just something to help you fit in. The right dress communicated class, curiosity, power, attraction. I wanted to wear something that conveyed a message I'd never sent to Jon before—sex.

I pulled out a dress from the back of my closet—a tight, red Gucci, with a neckline that plunged one inch too far. I rarely wore it, I'm not even sure why I bought it, it was so out of character. I arranged the neckline so that a bit of black lace bra peeked out from behind the fabric. Instead of my 3-inch-high banker Manolos, I put on my kinkiest Alaïas, all straps and laser cutouts. The 5-inch heel put me over six feet tall. I did my makeup in a way that Erika would approve. Still daytime appropriate, but with an extra dose of glamor in the lip and the eye. Jon had never seen me this way, and I wanted his undivided attention.

I splurged on a cab to midtown and arrived at the restaurant at 1:05. Jon hewed punctual; it seemed fitting that he should wait for me this time. After ceding my coat to the bubbly Hispanic hostess, I followed her to Jon's table. The energy in the room shifted. A dozen men stared at me in my crimson dress, so I slowed my pace.

Jon peered up from his Blackberry and seemed startled as I sauntered over. He'd rarely seen me in something other than a dark suit, and he'd certainly never seen me trying to channel my inner bombshell. I'd styled my hair so that it fell in lush waves. And between the stilettos and the décolletage, this was not the Amy he remembered.

He jumped to his feet and gave me an enthusiastic hug. It was almost sincere, even though I was certain he'd been the reason the job at Knight Partners had fallen through. I kept myself in Catherine-mode and returned his hug with enthusiasm. I even gave him a couple of showy air kisses, just to make him look like the big man I knew he wanted to be.

"Holy shit, Amy … What happened? You're a fucking knockout!" I slid in next to Jon, into the seat that gave me the best view of the room, and the room the best view of the two of us.

"Oh, thanks. I've had some time away from our old grind, as you know, so I've tried to use it well. I've taken up spinning."

"That's not all you're doing. But whatever it is, you need to keep it up." Jon stared at me, taking in Amy 2.0.

"Thanks. I've been running an art gallery for a friend. It's interesting work, but it gives me a lot of downtime."

"I'd heard you were at a gallery. Do you love it? It really suits you." He took a sip of vodka. "I dream of doing something completely different."

"It's a good diversion, but it's not the solution. I'm still looking for the right gig." I looked at Jon carefully. "I was really devastated when Knight Partners didn't come through, but I haven't given up." Jon's jaw flexed and his brow knotted when Knight was mentioned. I was following Erika's playbook, paying attention, and he was displaying plenty of anxiety and stress. Jon had no poker face with me, and if there'd been any lingering doubt about what had happened, his body language cleared it up. He'd been the rogue reference that had gotten the job offer rescinded. He was not a friend.

"Oh yeah, that Knight deal. What the fuck happened, there? I said great things about you to my buddy Dave Okafor, really extolled your virtues." Jon touched the side of his mouth with his index finger, and then moved on to adjust his tie. More classic signs of dishonesty. "It sucks when these things go sideways."

"Of course." I hadn't come to unmask his deceit, only to garner information. "And once the crisis is behind us, there'll be a ton of opportunities. I'm just so grateful you're on my side. You've been an amazing mentor. I wouldn't be where I am without you." Jon received my most adoring gaze.

"Aw thanks, Amy. I just wish that we were hiring at BFB. But we took such a hit in the first and second quarters that we're basically fucked until mid-2009 at the earliest."

"Yeah, we had a big piece of those Pulsar deals, didn't we?"

"Yup. We kept some of the 'safest' pieces for ourselves. And when those goddamned deals blew up, we lost almost a billion."

"It was that bad, eh?" Jon nodded, so I continued. "Well, I'm not here to discuss our mutual nightmare. I heard from Susan last week."

"Oh? She hasn't said anything about you."

"I'm not surprised. She invited me to lunch and she asked me about Alex Liu. She'd found some of your expense reports."

Jon's face blanched. Susan had clearly kept our conversation to herself, probably deciding to consult with a lawyer before she confronted her husband with evidence of an affair. "Oh, fuck."

"Yeah. Oh, fuck. I covered for you, as always, but geesh, Jon. What were you doing taking her to the River Café four times? Who goes there on a business dinner?"

"I'm a fucking moron. An absolute fucking moron. . . . Alex loved the oysters and the peanut butter soufflé. She couldn't get enough of that fucking soufflé."

"But Brooklyn? Nobody goes to Brooklyn."

"Not 'nobody.' But hardly anybody, which is a plus, if you know what I mean." Jon took another sip of vodka, his fingers clutching the glass. "What can I say, it was convenient. Alex's place is in Dumbo. A converted loft. Super cool. She works out of her home."

"Makes sense. Well, you'd better be ready for Susan, because she knows something's up."

"Thanks for the warning, Amy. You're the best."

"How'd you meet this one, anyway, Jon. She's not like your usual models."

"Business, that's all."

"Oh? I thought you usually kept business and pleasure far apart."

"I know. I usually do. But this one was all over me, right from the introduction. And, well, she's something else. I've never met anyone quite like her."

"I never heard you talk this way about your beauty queens."

"Well, she's smart and savvy. She reminds me a lot of you, actually." Jon smiled at me coyly.

"Thanks, I guess. So, this has been going on for some time. How'd I miss her? Did she come to the office?"

"It's been going on a couple of years." Jon relaxed at the table. The conversation was simple, and as always, I made an effort not to make him feel judged. "Things heated up at our first meeting. I thought I'd leave you out of it. You got enough of my girlfriend drama."

"This really is something different. Are you going to leave Susan?"

"Fuck no. But Alex really rings my bell. What can I say?"

"I hear you. She sounds unique. Here's my question for you . . . How'd Alex and Birch wind up picking the bonds for the Pulsar deals?"

Jon looked startled. It was the first time I'd made the connection between Birch and the woman he was having an affair with. "The San Francisco guys recommended Birch. And, uh, she sealed the deal."

"So, Seth suggested we use Birch to structure the deals Pulsar was sponsoring?"

"Yeah. I'd heard the Pulsar guys were difficult, and if it made Seth happy, it made me happy. Why not use Birch? They're fungible."

"Yeah, why not use Birch? Did you even talk to any other possible managers for the Pulsar deals?"

"There was no point. Seth was impossible. He liked things done a particular way, and he liked Birch. The ratings agencies all backed up his strategy. Fitch, Moody's, Standard and Poor's all rated the Pulsar deals the same as every other deal, and Birch built 'em."

"But there was so much risk built into the Pulsar deals."

"We see that now. Hindsight's twenty-twenty. But at the time, we were supposed to second-guess the analysts at Moody's? Those fuckers really screwed the pooch."

"Did Alex ever mention Pulsar or Seth Volkov to you?"

"No, why would she? I mean, she picked the Pulsar bonds, but that's not pillow talk. We had better things to discuss." Jon sat back in his chair.

"I'm surprised."

"Why?"

"They dated as undergrads at Stanford, and they remain tight." I was bluffing that the Alex-Seth relationship was still solid, but it had to be if he were throwing business her way. Jon became quiet. He stared at me without blinking. It was dawning on him that Alex and Birch had not been independent arbiters. "I have no idea how knowledgeable Alex was about Seth's plans . . . But it almost doesn't matter. She filled the Pulsar deals with trash designed to crash. Was she a dupe, or was she a coconspirator? Beats me. It wasn't even illegal what Pulsar did, just really, really dodgy. But she sure as hell wasn't independent. Of you or Seth."

"I did everything I was supposed to. BFB did no worse than its peers. A few deals failed on our watch, but they failed everywhere. We had deals rated AAA by Moody's for chrissakes. You didn't see a fucking problem at the time, and neither did I."

"But I did. You kept me out of all the deal talk, I never even looked at the Pulsar guys—you kept them and Birch to yourself. I asked you about those deals for months before they went south because they seemed off to me."

"You were involved in everything. We were inseparable, constructing every deal, including Pulsar's. How can you forget that? And you now say you inquired about the Pulsar deals for months before they went south? That's not how I recall things. If my good friend Dave Okafor ever offers you another job, you'd better not malign me with this crap. I talk to everyone, and I'll know . . . So, if you ever wanna work in this industry again, our memories had better be the same."

His threat was clear and unmistakable. His eyes squinted as he said it. "I understand. . . . Water under the bridge, right?"

"Right."

I shook my head in disbelief, unsure what to say next. "Moody's sure fucked up. Their lust for fees was as bad as yours."

"Yeah. Moody's sure fucked up." His voice remained hard. He looked at his oversized Panerai watch. "You know, I need to run. My day got crazy after we booked lunch. I'll pay on my way out."

"No prob." Though I tried to keep my voice as bland and as friendly as possible, I could threaten back. "Say 'hi' to Susan for me."

"Of course." Jon put his phone in his jacket pocket and exited the restaurant quickly. I remained seated at the empty table. We hadn't even ordered. The meal had been as satisfying as the one I hadn't eaten with his wife.

CHAPTER 29

HITTING SEND

As soon as I got back to Erika's apartment after my non-lunch, I created an anonymous email account. Thanks to Chen, I knew the name and email address of *The Wall Street Journal* reporter who had covered the mess with the most intelligence and care—Suneeta Singh. I tapped out a quick note:

> Hi. I see you've been covering the financial crisis very carefully,
> and you've touched on the fact that some investors had hedged their
> losses, earning billions while others lost. I was involved in some of
> the deals that blew up first, and I have evidence those deals were
> engineered to fail, so that their sponsor could make real money
> with the insurance. Let me know when you would be available for
> a conversation. BFB made some dreadful moves over the past
> couple of years, and they still haven't acknowledged their role in
> the ensuing calamity.

I hit "send," and wondered how long it would be before she replied. I was pissed, and I wanted Jon to pay. It felt crummy, selling out Susan, but she was the inevitable collateral damage in Jon's misadventures with Birch and Pulsar. She'd ridden Jon's stock up, oblivious or indifferent to the personal and professional risk he was overseeing. She might not have liked hearing the truth about Jon's zipper, but she deserved to know. A reversal in his circumstances could be imminent.

Unlike Jon, there were still some men who wanted to hear my voice. Rafael called as soon as he landed in San Francisco, and he positively trilled when proposing another gastronomic adventure, this time in Tribeca, at Corton. The prospect of atmospheric lighting with a playful partner appealed. It would be an uncomplicated evening, since Rafael didn't expect to be tied up and tortured at the end of it.

Michael also called. He wanted to know if I was available for dinner. Eager to see for myself that he was alive and well, I agreed to meet him that evening at Park Avenue Winter. At least with Michael, I'd get fed.

While primping for my sort-of date, I checked my fresh email account for any replies from Suneeta Singh. It had only been a few hours, but my impatience was growing. From my time in banking to my time in the dungeon, I had become accustomed to things happening fast and at my command. Journalism clearly happened at a different pace. I decided to add a little more to the original message, and resend it:

> Suneeta—You're one of the only journalists who can explain
> these complicated transactions in a way the public can understand.
> You are the ideal person to explain how BFB lost its way with its deals.
> They did not adhere to their internal standards. They did not comply
> with their usual rules. Multiple people were conflicted in these deals,
> which is why they wound up blowing up so spectacularly and losing
> billions. Happy to discuss. Please forward a number where I can
> reach you. Thanks.

I put on my new black Lanvin dress. No one would know it had been worn two nights in a row. But instead of the Chanel cuff from INA, I put on the white gold and diamond necklace that Dan had given me. The Hermès store was only two blocks from the restaurant, and it seemed like the perfect accessory for the Upper East Side and one of the most peculiar men in my life.

Michael was waiting for me when I got to the restaurant. He looked thinner than when I'd last seen him, slumped in the back of his Mercedes, but otherwise, he looked like himself.

"Amelia. Thanks for joining me tonight. I've missed you."

"I've missed you, too. You look great. Have you been working out?"

"Yes!" He grinned. "With a physical therapist. Can you believe it—that vicious little minx even has me lifting weights."

I squeezed his bicep. "I believe it. How great that some woman is cracking the whip and putting you through your paces."

"Yes, exactly. I just show up and do as I'm told. The suffering is a perk."

"I owe you an apology. I should have followed up with you sooner. It's just that the sight of you looking so sick freaked me out. It's embarrassing to admit, but I actually ran home to see my mommy."

"Please, don't think twice about it. I owe you my life. Your quick thinking got me out the door and into the hospital faster than I would have managed on my own. And that aspirin? The doctors and nurses at the hospital were ecstatic that I came pre-medicated. I'm here today because of you and my driver."

"You are too kind, but really, it's what anyone would have done. I'm just so glad you're upright again, because I was terrified I'd damaged you. I've hardly done any sessions since."

"I'm sorry to hear that. Erika said you'd been shaken. I brought something for you. I hope it helps." Michael reached into his jacket and pulled out an envelope and laid it on the table in front of me. "I know you'll put this to good use and it's the only way I can express my gratitude."

The waiter stopped by to take our drink order. Michael got seltzer, and I asked for a glass of Sancerre. The interruption gave me a moment to take in Michael's generosity. It was such an extraordinary token from a man who'd been like a fairy godmother, helping me get equipped for the dungeon, and then teaching me what to do once there.

"Michael. You don't need to do this." I wasn't going to turn his gift down, but I did want to state the obvious—the gift was entirely optional. I'd changed a lot since I'd adopted Erika's life, and I'd learned that money was not just for trade, it also had a symbolic nature. This gift was something he'd thought about, and it was something he wanted to do. And just like I embraced people's kinks while trying not to judge, I embraced his manner of expressing appreciation.

"I know, I don't need to. I want to. You're a very important figure in my life and I don't want crass, commercial concerns to influence the next decisions you make. You need to do what's right for Amelia."

I sat there, sipping the flinty white wine, and marveling at his generosity. The envelope was slipped, unopened, into my purse. "Thanks. I just wish I knew what was right for Amelia. Maybe you can offer some advice?"

As the waiter brought our appetizers, I launched into my newfound understanding of BFB and the deals that had failed. Michael nodded, interrupting only to get more detail and clarity from my convoluted story.

"So, Jon, your boss, was screwing the woman who was picking the bonds for your deals."

"Exactly. He kept her and all those wretched deals away from me. I didn't even know about them until things started going south. I'm friends with his wife, so I think he didn't want me knowing about Alex, and by shielding me from the Pulsar deals, he could fuck her without getting a lifted eyebrow from me."

"And the woman picking the bonds had a prior relationship with the firm who was sponsoring the deals."

"Yes, Alex and Seth had been close at Stanford. They'd dated. I don't know how corrupt their thing was—it could have been anywhere on a scale from 'she's a piker, and she didn't know any better' to 'she's a guilty cunt who was in on the whole shebang and she knew exactly what she was doing when she loaded the Pulsar deals with shit.'"

"It could be either. But really, the failure was Jon's. He should have been more astute when he was structuring those deals and hiring managers to select the bonds. He got greedy, saw huge fees, and cut corners. He got rolled by Pulsar. You're lucky the fiasco wasn't bigger."

"That's my take on things, too. But now what? I had lunch with Jon today, and he blew me off. Said the way I remembered things was at odds with the way he remembered things. And then he threatened me."

Michael raised his eyebrows. "What did he say?"

"He said I'd never work in banking again unless our memories were aligned. And his memories are exculpatory. He blames Moody's, and Moody's definitely fucked up. But if those deals hadn't been so compromised to begin with, they wouldn't have all failed. Every last Pulsar deal we oversaw blew up. *Every one.*"

"Has he threatened you before?"

"Not to my face, no. But he made sure I didn't get a job once. When my almost-employer was doing the reference check, one of the references came back bad. It was him. And scandals often landed on the guys who got in his way at BFB. His elbows are dagger-sharp." I finished my Sancerre in one hard gulp. Michael leaned back in his seat, his hands clasped in front of him on the white table cloth. "Do you have any advice for me? I just don't think I can forgive and forget, even though I'm supposed to. But the cost of confrontation is really, REALLY high."

"Yes, Emerson had it right. When you strike the king, you must kill him."

"Jon's no king, but I hear what you're saying. I even reached out to a journalist who covers this shit today, but she hasn't gotten back yet. That was probably a mistake, but I'm seething."

"Your anger is righteous, Amelia. Jon fucked with you. I'm going to tell you what I'd tell anyone important to me."

"Turn the other cheek?"

"No. You need to crush the motherfucker." I was staggered. Michael had never used profanity in my presence before, let alone with such passion. "Forgiveness is overrated. And it doesn't get you where you need to be." I sat back, my jaw slightly agape.

Michael continued, "Reach out to that journalist again, and tell her exactly what you told me today. That Jon and Seth and Alex had all fucked one another at some point in time, and that there's no way this didn't influence the oversight of the deals. BFB and its clients were victimized by three sleazy operators who were all taking shortcuts. Jon even had the gall to harm your livelihood. These people deserve to be punished."

"Seriously?" It was a relief to hear Michael put into words the very ideas I had been considering. My outrage had been suppressed for far too long.

"Yes, seriously." The waiter delivered our entrees. I stabbed at my lamb shank, imagining it was my old boss. Michael calmly cut into his fluke. "My doctor wants me to eat more fish. Of course, this means I'm craving steak."

"Well, at least he doesn't have you on one of those awful Ornish diets."

"My cardiologist knows better." Michael brought a tiny portion of the fish to his mouth, gave it a sniff, and then inserted the fork between his teeth. "Not bad. But not satisfying. So, tell me, Amelia, is there a gentleman? Someone special in your life?"

I brought my hands up to the sides of my head, in mock exasperation. "Until a week or so ago, I thought there was. But boy, was I wrong. Like your fish, it's not very satisfying."

"What happened? That seems implausible. If I were twenty years younger, and single, I'd be all over you."

"You say the nicest things, Michael. But you know men, they're complicated."

"How'd you meet this man?"

"That's what's complicated about it. I met him, you know, at *work*."

"I take it you mean, not at BFB?" I nodded. "Yes, that could be complicated. So, what's his story?"

"Well, I hadn't intended to let things get personal, but after your health crisis, I wound up back in Vermont where I faced a crisis of my own, and this guy really stepped up. We became very close, and even when he was away on business for a few weeks, we spoke every night on the phone. So, when he got back, and every signal said accelerating romance, I started to feel it. I was trying not to, but I fell for him."

"How do you know he doesn't feel the same way?"

"Because we were in bed. We'd just had sex and we were making all those lovey-dovey noises about making the connection happen on a daily basis. And then he pulled out an employment contract and offered me a job."

Michel put down his fork. "Oh god. How awful. He should have gotten down on his hands and knees and proposed."

"It would have been early for a proposal, but I wasn't expecting a job offer. Who does that?"

"What's his business?"

"Private equity, specializing in distressed assets. He'd just finished showing me the apartment he bought from a rival for pennies on the dollar."

"Ah." Michael shook his head. "Was it a rich offer?"

"Not especially. He likes a bargain. And besides, I couldn't be his employee after all we'd shared and done. And I don't know how he thought it could work out, either."

Michael nodded. "How'd he take your refusal?"

"We haven't spoken since. He said he'd call, but he hasn't. It couldn't be more over."

"Yes, that does sound final. And, how are you?"

"Fine, I guess. I had a date the other day, and it felt refreshingly normal. He's just this guy I've known for a few years."

"Promising?"

"Who knows. But he's fun. And I like that he's unaware of my alter ego. Having Catherine's shadow looming over that last relationship was unnerving. I didn't know if he liked me, or if he liked how I got him off."

"They're not necessarily in opposition."

"I know. But it's hard to shake that nagging doubt. That's why it's time to reenter polite society. To kill off Catherine and become Amy again on a full-time basis."

"Amelia, Catherine is part of you. You're not schizophrenic and she's not some alternate personality. Just because you only met Catherine a few months ago doesn't mean she's not real."

"I'm grateful to Catherine. She's taught me lots of things. Men seem a whole lot less mysterious because of her, although certain recent events suggest I don't know quite as much as I thought. But I definitely understand power more clearly."

"I can imagine." Michael cleaned his glasses, and then gave me his full attention. "You can pretend you never met Catherine. She's a figment. But I see a different woman next to me than the one I first met. You're more present, more aware. You see and feel things more clearly. Whatever you do next, you will be spectacular." He grabbed my hand and gave it a firm squeeze. In turn, I slid over and gave him a hug.

"You're the best, Michael. Can we do this on a regular basis?"

"I'd love that. I want only the best for you, Amelia. And not just because you saved my life."

CHAPTER 30

VERY DEEP BACKGROUND

Still buzzing from my fabulous evening, when I got back to Erika's place the first thing I did was check my fake email account. There was a terse email message from Singh waiting for me:

> Hi. Thanks so much for your emails. I've shared your thoughts with
> my editor, and we'll get back to you if there's a story.

It was almost midnight, but the glass of port with my *crème brûlée* had left me disinhibited. My fury could not be squelched.

> Suneeta,
>
> The lady who picked the bonds for the deals was fucking the guy
> who created and sold the deals. And she got the job because she'd
> fucked the guy who'd sponsored those deals. I have evidence. Is that
> enough conflict of interest for you and your editor?

I fired off the email, and then went to bed. There was still plenty of righteous anger in my system when the Ambien finally kicked in. When I woke up at 7, there was an email from *The Wall Street Journal* waiting for me. Suneeta had risen early.

> Would love to discuss at your earliest convenience. Are you
> available for coffee this afternoon?

There was nothing on my calendar, not even a spanking, so my reply was immediate.

> You're downtown, so why don't we meet at Edward's in Tribeca at
> 2 p.m.

Moments after sending, I got a reply.

> Perfect. How will I recognize you?

> I'll find you. Don't worry. :-) See you at 2.

It took an hour to walk from Chelsea down to Tribeca, but I wanted to clear my head. I arrived just before two, only to find that Suneeta had beaten me to Edward's. She was easy to spot—her long black hair was pulled back into a ponytail, her dark eyes shone through her horn-rimmed glasses, and her caramel skin gave her a dose of glamor, despite the jeans and burgundy wool turtleneck she was wearing.

Suneeta had staked out a booth in the back, littered it with reading materials, and she was halfway through a grilled cheese sandwich, when I found her. "Excuse me, Suneeta?" She nodded. "Hi, I sent those emails."

"Oh great. Join me." She waved her hand at the seat opposite her, as she cleared away some of the newspapers and file folders that had taken over the surface of the table. "Sorry. I didn't have breakfast today." She gobbled back a few French fries.

"No problem. Eat away." The waitress spotted the newcomer to the booth, and she came to my side, notepad poised. "A Diet Coke, please." She nodded and went back into the kitchen, leaving us alone as I slid across the banquette.

"I shared with my editor that email you sent last night. He was really excited."

"Yeah, I imagine. It's all so insane. You know, I don't even know if what they did was illegal. But it was wrong, and billions were lost in the process."

"Do you mind if I take some notes?" Suneeta pulled a yellow legal notepad out of the pile on the table and wrote the date in the upper right corner.

"Of course not. This stuff is complicated, which is how Pulsar got away with it. Seth Volkov flouted the rules. And you have to admit, the guy is a fucking genius, because he found the weak point. But just so you know, I don't want to be named in any of your pieces. I want this to be confidential."

"Confidential or anonymous?"

"Confidential. I need your protection before I give you what I've got. I want those assholes to pay for what they did, but I don't want them to know who was responsible. I'd like to work again, and I still have student loans to pay off."

"Do you mind if we revisit this?"

"We can revisit, but I won't change my mind. So, am I a confidential source? You'll want what I've got."

Suneeta reluctantly promised confidentiality, which would keep my name out of her articles. It felt odd, yet cathartic, to launch into the ridiculous tale. I sketched out the deals we'd sold and that Pulsar had sponsored, and how Pulsar had specified who should pick the bonds that went in. And how that manager was a second-rater, with deep ties to Seth, and who then got in deep with Jon at BFB. Suneeta scribbled furiously. "How do you know the deals were engineered to fail?"

"I know Seth specified bonds with a lot of risk. His foresight was anticipating which markets and which types of securities would be the first to blow up, and that was what he prioritized. Like, mortgages out of Nevada, Arizona, and Michigan, and lots of liar loans. He had a nose for foreclosures. He was too smart to put it in writing, exactly, but he went through a bunch of firms before he threw our business to Alex Liu and Birch. Most managers wouldn't accommodate the risk profile he wanted, for reasons we understand in hindsight, but Alex didn't understand or didn't care about the securities she was including, per Pulsar's guidance." I pulled out the documents Chen had prepared for me about our most serious losses. "See, these deals are all sponsored by Pulsar and picked by Birch, and every last one of them failed . . . and failed fast. This was calculated."

"Okay. I see what you're saying. But why build the deals to fail? How do you monetize that?"

"By insuring them, of course. *Alpha Magazine* said Seth earned $250 million in 2007. That was all from credit default swaps, the insurance—the hedge—these guys buy in the event their deal goes kaput."

"I still don't see the problem."

"Alright. You're a real estate developer and you're building a subdivision. It's in a fire zone. You build the houses to code of course, but you build with untreated pine. It's legal to do so, but you choose that material because untreated pine is your most flammable—legal—choice. You also make sure you get a complacent building inspector, who rubber stamps the deal. Next, you go and insure every house for ten times its value. Lloyd's knows you followed the building code, that your development passed inspection, and they don't look too hard at what you're up to, because this seems like every other housing development they've ever seen and they've seen thousands. In the meantime, you rent out the houses, so they're generating income. Sooner or later, however, your subdivision is going to go up in flames because it's *in a fucking fire zone.* Is this bad for you? Absolutely not. You've insured these houses for ten times what they're worth. And it's not like you started the fire, you just anticipated it. It was the insurance company's fool move that let you over-insure this ridiculous and impermanent asset in the first place. And so what if a bunch of homeowners are screwed? They're just collateral damage from your financial engineering."

Suneeta put down her pen and looked at me. "Shit. That's some sleazy stuff."

"Tell me about it. It was happening all around me. I raised alarms at the time, but not loudly enough. I didn't understand the depth and the stakes of what was going on. My boss kept that from me so he could fuck Alex Liu in peace." I handed the reporter Jon's expense reports. "You'll see lots of expensive, romantic dinners between Jon Brenner and Alex Liu. BFB won't like it, but they won't be able to deny it happened."

"What else have you got?"

"No more documents, but some facts and names. Alex had some career ups and downs, but mostly downs. She went from picking penny stocks to picking bonds. As if that's a logical trajectory?"

Suneeta made a face. She knew that penny stocks were for hucksters and criminals. "Is there a record of this?"

"Yeah. It's findable. Before she became Birch, Alex was at TOK Capital, penny stock speculators." Suneeta scribbled furiously. "You should talk to people from either Alex or Seth's Stanford undergrad classes to confirm his relationship with Alex. She used to watch him do Judo, that sort of thing. They were boyfriend-girlfriend for a year. It shouldn't be hard to report that, but it's not like I have pictures."

"How'd you hear about it?"

"From someone who's a friend of Jon's, so you don't want to go that route."

"Got it. Yeah, I should be able to pin that down independently. So, Judo, eh?"

"That's the story I heard. But I'm sure there's more. Freshman girls tend to follow their senior boyfriends around like puppy dogs. Isn't that how it usually works?"

"That's how it worked for me!"

"I was too busy studying at the library, so that unique experience eluded me. But it was common enough."

"You've given me a ton today. Do you mind if I go over it with my editor, and then circle back with any questions?"

"No problem. Just keep my name out of it. I'll share what I know, and I'll tell you if I learn anything more."

CHAPTER 31

MORE THAN A
ROUNDING ERROR

As I was walking back to Chelsea, still processing the conversation, I reached into my purse for my phone and pulled out the envelope from Michael. Somehow, this unexpected gesture had slipped my mind. A taxi honked loudly as I peered inside the envelope and found a cashier's check for $100K. I looked over my shoulder and panicked, because it dawned on me that I'd been walking around the city with a small fortune in my purse.

I needed to get to a bank right away, and I needed to call Michael to thank him. He had just changed my life.

Suneeta emailed a couple more times to verify facts and details, but there wasn't much further I could offer her. She was also making progress on her own. I had helped launch the missile at Jon, but Suneeta controlled its trajectory. When or where it would land was no longer in my control.

I still got elaborate flowers from Dan, a situation that was downright puzzling. I'd email him a perfunctory thank you, but there was never a reply. It seemed like either he'd arranged with Banchet Flowers to send me something every week and he'd forgotten about it since the cost amounted to little more than a rounding error. Perhaps his secretary was on flower duty, and he couldn't be bothered, or didn't want to let her know that there was a change in status. Or maybe the flowers were a passive investment; a low-effort way of keeping the channel open, and the only resource this required of him was money. The latter seemed most likely. Keeping in touch with me was just another hedge for him. By spending a few hundred bucks a week on tulips, roses and orchids, he was improving the odds that I might take his calls, or even tie him up, at some point in the future. The arrangements were pretty, so I always accepted them. It was too much drama to turn them back.

Christmas was looming and my parents were urging me to come home to Burlington for the holidays. Worried that if I ran into Bob Huntley I might do something awful, I opted to remain in New York. Mom sent an enormous box filled with my favorite cookies. Dad froze a couple of his *tourtières*, so that I could have a traditional meat pie on Christmas Eve, and I warmed to the idea of doing nothing, all alone.

I began an apartment hunt and refreshed my resume so that it was ready for the New Year. Somebody had to be hiring in 2009. I also needed to get out of Erika's place. She'd finally gotten custody of her butterfly Hirst. The timing of her return from Geneva was perfect, because I'd stopped seeing her clients, and there's nothing more needy than a hundred submissive men all clamoring for their comeuppance. The routine exposure to male indulgence and privilege was depleting, even if it came disguised as submission, crawling and begging in my presence.

Rafael became a frequent fixture in my life. He took me to Tribeca's most romantic and exquisite restaurant, Corton, and over the torchon of *foie gras*, we nestled together in our corner table, where the sides of our bodies practically adhered to each other. When Rafa gripped my hand, there was an electric charge. Frankly, I'd worried that all those random men in Erika's dungeon had dulled my appetites, but Rafael had heightened my senses. Feeling that jolt of desire and anticipation was a relief to me; it signaled that I remained capable of passion. It was also a delight that I was feeling passion for someone who was clearly feeling it for me. The ambiguity and uncertainty that Dan had demonstrated was not in evidence in Rafa. He wanted me, and when I invited him back to Erika's apartment for a nightcap after the caramel brioche, he accepted with enthusiasm. My body appreciated his attentions.

After Corton, Rafael took me to Dovetail, Matsugen, and Allegretti. We were eating our way around the city, and I was feeling adored and sated. Our sex life was refreshingly normal. In Erika's apartment, it was a second-floor adventure, only. The gizmos and gimmicks of the basement were not required to get either of us off. And unlike most men I'd known, Rafael would happily think ahead and imagine things we could do together, next month or even next year. He spoke concretely about his plans and our relationship. It was startling when it dawned on me that imagining a future with someone brought me pleasure instead of angst.

Things were coming together professionally, too. When I told Rafa I was leaving the gallery, he suggested working with one of his tech companies. And even though banking was my first choice, there were meetings and interviews on my schedule, again. My career muscles were staying taut and toned.

I signed a lease on a small one bedroom in Hell's Kitchen for $2,400 a month starting January 1. It was a far cry from my Soho place, further still from Erika's, but it was affordable, thanks to Michael and the crash. It was a newish building on West 33rd, where the developer had been forced to discount the rent substantially. The meltdown on Wall Street had even reached the mid-Manhattan real estate market.

CHAPTER 32

TABLOID
TREATMENT

A week before Christmas, Rafael called and caught me still in bed after a busy weekend. "Have you seen today's *Journal*? Check out the front page! Oh, and see you tonight...."

The move had left me so distracted that I'd almost forgotten about Suneeta. She'd had my information for weeks without a peep.

The headline was delicious "Lust Amid the Ruins: Investment Stars Flame-out." It began:

> It's hard to find sizzle in swaps, and yet Pulsar managed to do just that. Seth Volkov, the renowned founder of Pulsar, liked to name his deals after constellations, only his stars burned out faster and harder than their peers. The Pulsar-sponsored deals lost $12 billion, but through the extensive use of Credit Default Swaps, Pulsar had a stellar year.
>
> Does this kind of success happen naturally, is it in the stars? No. It requires careful engineering and the help of dealmakers like Jon Brenner of *Banque Fédérale de Belgique* who looked the other way when the deals created under his watch were filled with the riskiest

mortgage-backed securities at the urging of Pulsar. And it required the romantic entanglements of Alexandra Liu, the founder of Birch Advisors, who loaded the Pulsar deals with securities that were picked precisely because their odds of failure were high. It also required the ratings agencies to drop the ball and rate these atypical deals by their typical metrics.

The piece went on to describe Alex, Seth, and Jon in ways that none of them would enjoy, down to the wreckage of the deals they had touched together. Suneeta had even pinned down the college romance that had kicked off the entanglement and found the pictures to back it up. A 19-year-old Alex gazed lovingly at Seth in his judogi, as he held aloft an enormous trophy. Clearly, somebody with a grudge against her or Seth had shared that information. The piece was gruesome in its salacious details.

As I was finishing off the article, Chen called. "Oh my god, did you see the *Journal*?" We chuckled over the wicked details, like Alex's love of the River Café, and Jon's wayward cock.

"How long before he's out the door?" I mused.

"I bet he's gone already, BFB doesn't mess around. But I'll call you if he shows up. I'm at work, watching!"

"It's great having a spy on the floor."

"James Bond, at your service. What's gonna happen to the stock price?"

"It's going down, buddy. But who cares? Your options have been underwater for over a year."

"Thanks, Amy, you really know how to cheer a guy up."

"Keep a lookout, and report back. Chen, you're the best."

I turned on CNBC to see pictures of my old boss, Alex, and Seth on the screen. "Wall Street Love Triangle" It was rare that banking got the tabloid treatment, and CNBC was exalting in the opportunity. I fired off a note to Suneeta congratulating her on her front-page scoop while the talking heads discussed the dirty conflicts of interest in the case. *The Wall Street Journal*'s PR department had clearly primed the pump for their story, putting Suneeta on *Morning Joe* where she got into the naughty specifics of the love triangle and all the financial chaos that stemmed from it. The executives in Brussels had to be crazed when their stock price opened 8% lower on the news.

The finance love triangle was the lead story at the top of every hour. Like clockwork, Jon, Seth, and Alex's faces would appear on CNBC, as the story got repeated, giving the anchors an opportunity to shake their heads in mock disappointment. Viewers might not understand these complicated deals, but they certainly understood sex and sleaze. The intersection of commerce and coitus was irresistible.

By afternoon, there was footage of Jon leaving the BFB offices being hounded by tabloid photographers. He looked harried, and by Christmas, he'd probably be crushed. It was hard to imagine how he'd survive this professionally, and the paper trail led back to him. He might try to blame others, like me, but the *Journal* had set the stage for skepticism, and the stories of his affair made him seem particularly untrustworthy. Chen called me that afternoon with gory details of Jon's last moments on the floor.

"They had two security guards watching him, and they only let him take a few things from his office. They patted Jon down. It was intense. I thought he was gonna puke."

"No way. Not Jon. But here's my question. Have you seen the ticker lately? If the news is so devastating, how come the stock is up after its initial fall?"

"Oh, you'll like this . . . A mystery buyer just started accumulating BFB stock. And get this, there's even a rumor that our toxic little division is in play."

"You're kidding, Chen. Well, our nasty little corner is probably a really cheap date. I could buy the division for pocket change."

"Hah, you're dreaming. I asked a friend in the CFO's office what she knew, and she told me the stock purchase came through a Turks and Caicos shell."

"No shit. Isn't that how Al-Waleed does his deals? What are the odds it's Saudi money? Those guys have more dollars than sense." I hung up on Chen thinking the world had gone mad.

The Pulsar team was more fortunate than BFB. Since they were in San Francisco, they were mostly out of reach of the New York tabloid apparatus, but they were not out of reach of the SEC. In response to all the suggestions of impropriety, they put out a press release:

> Pulsar's investments were market neutral, and undertaken in good faith with *Banque Fédérale de Belgique*. Following news reports and an inquiry from the Securities and Exchange Commission, Pulsar management has retained outside counsel to review allegations of a conflict. The board has asked Seth Volkov to step back from his duties as Chief Investment Officer while the investigation is underway.

Reading between the lines, Pulsar was blaming BFB and Birch, while acknowledging Seth might have some culpability in this mess. All the same, this had to further complicate Jon's life. It wasn't going to happen overnight, but the bomb I'd set off had worked. Jon was being punished, and I could speak honestly and openly about how I'd questioned the Pulsar deals early and often.

CHAPTER 33

THE BUTTERFLY ALIGHTS

That night, Erika finally arrived home from her latex adventure. My clothes had been extracted from her closet because Rafael was letting me stay at his place until my apartment was ready.

Erika looked ecstatic when she reached the top of the stairs. "Amy! I'm so glad you're here. We've got so much to discuss. BFBs up in flames, and I have my painting." Erika held up a small, perfectly wrapped parcel she had hand-carried from Switzerland.

"Erika, it feels like ages. I'm so glad you're back." I pointed at the box. "Is that your prize?" She nodded. "Can you show it to me?"

"Let me get out of my coat first." Erika returned wearing a pair of loose-fitting tan trousers, a gray cashmere sweater, and holding a pair of white cotton gloves. With exaggerated care, she cut open the tape keeping the case shut. She then donned the soft gloves and began to remove the various layers that had protected the piece in transit—egg crate foam, Kraft paper, tissue paper.

When she got down to the Hirst, she carefully retrieved the painting from its protective nest. It was smaller than I had imagined. The background was a glossy black, and there were three iridescent butterflies of varying sizes and species, placed randomly on the canvas along with some sparkly glass beads, a few pins, and even a small cross.

"Spectacular, isn't it?" Erika looked at me, her pupils dilated with arousal.

I wasn't sure what to say. I'd expected something larger and more intricate, and maybe something with more butterflies. But if Erika thought it was special, she had earned the benefit of the doubt. "Very nice. You earned it. Where will it go?"

Erika pointed at her mantle, and walked over to the wall, carefully holding the work out in front of her. She centered the painting. "Here, I think. That way I can see it whenever I'm having coffee in the kitchen. Or whenever I'm watching the tube."

"Perfect. Something that significant should be enjoyed all the time."

"That's how I feel, too. We should make pleasure a priority."

"Speaking of pleasure, when things have quieted down, I'll go over my session notes for the clients. I started strong, but after Michael's heart attack, I didn't have the stomach for many more. I'm sorry about that."

"Please, don't worry about it. Once I knew I had the Hirst, I worked the phones, and I've got lots of scenes lined up. I even spoke with Arnim. He wants you to know he's added a woman to his board."

"No kidding! Good for him. So, I guess you won't take much of a revenue hit?"

"You were an enormous help. This is a business with lulls and spikes, just like yours, and when you've been at it as long as I have, you know how to accommodate the collective ID."

"The collective ID has taken a nonconsensual, financial beating, so it's long overdue for something consensual and recreational."

"I hope you're right. And if you ever change your mind, and you'd like to do a session or two, just let me know. You might want some extra cash, or a few bonus thrills. Whatever."

"Thanks, but Catherine has retired from the arena. Amy is back to doing her own thing. Don't get me wrong, I'm grateful for the opportunity. But it wasn't my cup of tea. The risk to me and to them seemed too daunting."

"You don't need to explain. It's not for everyone. But my offer stands, if the urge strikes."

I chuckled. "Maybe I'll want a whipping boy!"

"Exactly. Now, what's the deal with Rafael?"

"He's normal. I met him years ago through Jon and Susan."

"He has no idea, does he?"

"Absolutely not. And I'd like to keep it that way."

"Your secret is safe with me. The only person who might tell him is you! So, no talking in your sleep. Understood? And if you feel the urge to unburden yourself, think hard about the implications. Secrets can be the special sauce of any relationship."

"Understood. Well, let me give you your apartment back. I've put a few boxes in your basement for my move, and I've already sent my suitcase over to Rafa's downtown." I returned Erika's keys to her while grabbing my coat. "I'm grateful for everything. Thanks."

Erika clutched me to her body. "Not everyone could do what you did. The men will be talking about you for years. You're lucky my ego is healthy!"

"You're the expert, Erika. I was merely the substitute."

CHAPTER 34

TAKING TURNS

After I gave Erika's hard-won butterflies a final, admiring look, a taxi took me to Rafael's apartment on William Street. Since Rafael had always slept over at Erika's, it wasn't clear if I should turn left or right out of the elevator on the twentieth floor. Before I had a chance to walk in the wrong direction, Rafael had popped into the hall to lead me into his condo.

"Follow me to my humble abode!" Rafa held the door open, with a flourish. The apartment was compact and tidy. The shiny white kitchen occupied the left wall upon entry, and the right had an alcove with a desk and a closet, but then the room opened up to large windows and a living room. Rafael had gone for a masculine vibe in decorating the place. There was a substantial brown leather couch with roll arms and a tufted back. It looked like it had been stolen from an Eton library. The chair was upholstered in a vivid, emerald green, and a gray shag rug tied the room together. He had several small photographs in an array on his wall, and like all men of his vintage, he had an enormous television tuned to sports.

Rafael took me in his arms and gave me a deep kiss. His tongue probed my mouth, teasing my lips and tasting my enthusiasm. I tightened my grip on his body and matched his passion with my excitement. My hands snuck up into his sweater, and with his help, it was on the floor in a matter of seconds. He pulled me into the bedroom. "It'll be more comfortable in here." The room was compact, but the queen size bed was perfectly made up with crisp white sheets and pillows, and a large, heavy duvet.

It was Rafael's turn to undress me. First, he eased my sweater off, as he trailed his fingers over my shoulders and arms, causing me to shiver. He then eased my jeans off my body. I helped him by wriggling. "Oh, do that some more. Dance for me, Amy." I gave him a twirl as I hopped out of my tight black denim.

Rafael pushed me down onto the bed and straddled my body. His jeans remained balanced on his lean hips, so I pushed them down and off. He wore nothing but a pair of plaid flannel boxers in navy and green. I tried not to marvel at his six pack again, but it was impossible. I'd seen many naked men in the prior months, but none had abs so perfect. I caressed the muscles with my fingertips in awe. "Oh my god, Rafael, you're gorgeous. I just can't say that enough."

"No, you're gorgeous, Amy." He brought his chest to mine and kissed me again, until I was panting and breathless. His hands cupped my face as his fingers twirled and knotted my hair. I closed my eyes and let my lips find his mouth.

His tongue teased mine, but then it began exploring my throat, my neck and then both of my nipples. His teeth scraped at them until they were erect and sensitive. I wanted his lips to be back within reach of mine, but he waved me off, as he roamed lower.

Rafa slid off the bed and with his broad shoulders he got in between my legs and spread them wide. His tongue found my clit and the attack began. Between the gentle sucks and the flicking of his tongue, it was impossible to lie still, but his arms held me down against the bed, and made sure I remained open to him as he methodically made my heart race.

The tension built in my body, my nerves were under assault and I was thrilling to his onslaught. It wasn't long before I had to grab his hands to steady myself as my body shook and the orgasm tore through me. "Please fuck me now."

Rafael looked up at me from between my legs with a mischievous look. "Are you asking me to fuck you, or are you telling me to fuck you?"

I was grateful for a moment to catch my breath. "Does it matter?"

"Absolutely. To me. So, which is it?"

He was playing with me, spontaneously and deliciously. It took me a second to decide whether I wanted to ask or tell, since both options seemed like winners. "I'm asking?"

Rafael nodded, and burrowed back between my legs, his tongue resuming on my sensitive pussy. "I'm declining your request." Within a minute, he had me on edge again. I grabbed his hair as my hips began to shake against his face. He looked up at me again and grinned. I threw my head back in exasperation as my body convulsed with a second orgasm.

I lay flopped on the bed, my legs dangling off the edge, while Rafael remained kneeling between my thighs. The game he'd initiated captivated me, with its inherent give and take. I could be in charge, or not. Catherine was not an essential part of the moment. "Please fuck me now? And I'm asking, not telling."

Rafael shook his head, and his tongue returned to my clit and he inserted a couple of fingers inside my pussy to add to the pressure. I could barely stand the sensation, but I took it, and my body responded accordingly. My breathing had become so shallow from excitement that my lip was tingling. I was feeling lightheaded, and yet I let Rafael continue until he was satisfied and I had enjoyed my third climax.

This time, I lay on the bed in silence, as my body grew calm and my pulse returned to normal. Rafa lay on his side, next to me, lightly caressing my skin and saying nothing. It was pure pleasure to feel his fingers and to see such an exceptional man outstretched next to me, thinking about nothing but my arousal.

I straddled him, pinning him down to the bed. "Now I'm telling. You're going to fuck me. And you'd better do it right." It was his turn to submit, and I happily took charge and it didn't feel like a job or a chore.

"Yes, ma'am!" Rafael's cock was hard and ready, and I lowered myself onto it. He filled and stretched my pussy, as he guided my hips up and down along his organ. "You like this, don't you, Amy?"

"Hell, yes. Now faster." I hovered over Rafael and let him do the work of getting off. He'd arch his back and thrust, pushing his cock deeper into me every time. I reached down and played with his nipples with my left hand, as I dug my fingernails into his ass with my right. His eyes shut tightly, and his jaw strained. He let out a loud grunt, and then he convulsed. He had more than earned his orgasm.

As we lay there, depleted and delighted, Rafael brought me to his chest and took a deep breath. "Amy, you've amazed me in every way, but I have a really big test for you. Can you survive my family for a few days?"

"What did you have in mind?"

"Christmas is a command performance with my mom. She takes it very seriously, so we all come. There's a big tree, lots of eggnog, Christmas Eve Mass. Oh, and there may be, wait for it, singing." He looked at me sheepishly.

"Uh, is your singing any good? Like, I suck. Can hardly hold a tune."

"Oh, that's par for the course. We all suck, but we do it anyway. I know Buffalo has few charms, but it's only two nights. Can you take it?"

"I can take it, but can you? I don't want to make this a bigger deal than it is, but your mother will be there!"

"Oh, my mom is great. It's my sister Isabelle you need to worry about. She's a consultant at McKinsey, so she's even more impossible now than when she was twelve."

"You'll need to give me briefing notes on everyone. I don't do anything half-assed. Least of all go to Buffalo."

CHAPTER 35

FLOGGING THE BEAST

Two days later, Chen called again. "It's either the Saudis or one of those activist investors like Icahn."

"I'm so sorry for you. Either way, it can't be good. Where do things stand?"

"The buyer has 4.9% of BFB, so he doesn't need to declare, and I haven't heard anything more besides the rumors."

"Spill, Chen. Make my day."

"The rumor I'm tracking most closely is the one that says our division is in play. Despite the bad news, I think there's a future if we had better management. These deals aren't going away."

"You're right of course. We're going to be flogging this beast for years. Or at least until the next great security is invented."

CHAPTER 36

TYING UP AN
APEX PREDATOR

On Friday morning, as I was still lying in Rafael's bed, my Blackberry rang. Thinking it might be Chen with more gossip, I pounced on the phone. It was Dan. "Hey, Amy. How are you?"

"Fine, thanks. And you?" It was so staggering to hear from him after so many weeks of silence, that it became a struggle to keep my voice neutral.

"Good." Dan was never one for small talk, so that's where it stopped. "Can we meet today? There's something I need to discuss."

"Sure. Where?"

"The Metropolitan Club, right around the corner from my place. I'll be in the top floor dining room. Does 9 work for you?"

"Make it 9:30, unless you want to come downtown."

"It's more private at my club. 9:30 it is."

I pulled out my sharpest business suit, a rich pinstripe in black and gray with a bit of stretch by Dolce & Gabbana. It was fitted, so it hugged my waist and flared at my hips, and I always felt ready for anything when I wore it. The wool might as well have been Kevlar. The matching pencil skirt exaggerated my legs, and when coupled with a pair of bright red Louboutins, the look became frisky. I put on Dan's necklace to complete the outfit. It was a beautiful accessory, and one he'd surely notice.

While my suit said banking bitch, my makeup said vixen. I gave myself a classic, smoky eye, complete with eyeliner. And although I kept my lipstick muted, I lined my lips carefully, so they'd appear fuller. We'd be meeting at the Metropolitan Club, one of the city's oldest and most respected establishments. The place had a dress code—ties for men, skirts for women. There was a push to allow women to wear pants, but the club moved slowly, and I wasn't going there to rock the boat. I just wanted to rock Dan.

I pulled my hair back into a severe bun and eyed the completed look in the mirror. For once, I liked my reflection. I was ready for whatever Dan had in mind. After the fiasco of our last get together, it was a relief to be meeting fully clothed somewhere quasi-public.

The fastest way uptown was by subway, so I hopped on the 6 in my Dolce-combat-gear, while playing out various scenarios. I didn't want to work for Dan, and dating him was too complicated, the way his personal and his professional merged. I practiced saying different variations of, "I'm flattered by your interest, but I cannot accept your offer," so it would be at the tip of my tongue.

The courtyard in front of the Metropolitan had an enormous Christmas tree, festooned in lights and oversized red ribbons. The interior was similarly tarted up, with glittery white fairy lights covering the shiny wooden bannisters. It reeked of the holidays. I checked my coat and was pointed toward the top floor dining room by one of the liveried workers. Between the stone floors and the soaring ceilings, it mimicked Buckingham Palace.

The ancient *maître d'* ushered me to Dan's table. I almost didn't recognize him in his slick navy Kiton suit and contrasting gray tie. When I got to the table, Dan kissed me on both cheeks and motioned for me to sit down. His eyes lingered on the Hermès necklace. I touched the gold, out of instinct.

"Thanks for joining me. I'm sorry it's on such short notice."

"I was surprised to get your call, but I know you don't make idle invitations. What's up?"

"I'm closing on a big deal, and I'd like you to be part of it."

"You already offered me a job, and I already turned you down. I can't work for you."

"It's your old division at BFB. I took a stake in the bank, and I'm liberating it from the broader operation. Thanks to you, I realized the place was badly run, and with your help, there's a lot of upside." He slid another tan envelope to me.

"So the buyer of the 5% was you? Everyone figured it was Saudi money." I inhaled deeply, as my brain processed the news. "Is this greenmail? Is BFB giving you the division to get you to go away?"

"Nobody gives anything away."

"Of course. But still, the Belgians are probably grateful to offload such a controversial asset, and to get you off their backs in the process." I pulled the document out of its envelope but made a point not to look at it.

"I can't argue with that assessment."

"I have to hand it to you, you are tenacious."

"I know opportunity when I see it."

I opened my purse and pulled out my glasses because the type was tiny. Magnification was barely necessary because the deal was so straightforward. Dan was offering me a huge piece of my old division—49%. In exchange, I would receive a nominal salary while working to rebuild profits and revenues. I couldn't stifle a sigh as I placed the document on the table in front of me. For a split second, he had me. But then reality set in. He might have been subservient in the dungeon, but business was his real life, and in business, he was an apex predator. There was no question about who was in charge in this scenario.

"Dan, it's a generous offer, but no. I'd be working for you, and you baffle me. I thought we had something romantic, and then you sprung a job offer on me. It's too hard for me to keep those threads separate if I'm working for you."

"We'd be partners. You're getting a ton of equity. More than anyone else would give you."

"I understand that. But the equity is from you. I'd be working for you, not with you."

"You're getting hung up on trivialities. We're essentially equal partners."

"No. You'd have veto power." A twisted thought entered my head, as I flashed back to Erika's dungeon. "I'd be submissive to you. I'd be just another asset in your portfolio. You could trade me away or shut me down on a whim."

"This is a once in a lifetime offer. I don't do anything on a whim."

Suddenly it hit me. "WWDD"—What Would Dan Do? "I tell you what, I'll take the job if you give me 51%. Then we'd really be partners, and I'd feel solid."

Dan grimaced as he grabbed the document. He retrieved a purple marker from his jacket and crossed out the 49% and replaced it with 51%, which he then initialed.

"51% is yours." He applied the marker to the document again and wrote, "plus 6% interest, compounded annually" to the clause requiring repayment of the purchase price.

Dan was giving me difficult terms, but I believed in the asset and in myself, so I swallowed hard. That same delicious rush I'd felt as a girl came over me. Taking on the bank was a lot like running off the cliff and plunging into the cold waters of Lake Champlain. I felt empty and full at the same time. There was no need to weigh and evaluate, the answer was obvious. "Deal."

We signed at the bottom.

"Dan, when does the fun begin?"

"Monday. You won't be able to get into the BFB offices right away, but there's a lot you can do from my place in preparation for the close. I've set aside the office next to mine for you."

"The office next to you, eh?" I could barely stifle my smile. It was the office he'd proposed when he first offered me a job. "That'll be a good interim place. I'll start talking to real estate consultants to find some empty space for the team. With the crash, there are a ton of vacancies and subleases we can take on the cheap. I'll hit your numbers."

"Amy, I'm so glad you're on board. When I saw this deal, I only wanted to do it with you. You were the first person who came to mind and you know all the players."

"Aw shucks, Dan."

"I have another question for you. What are you doing Saturday?"

"That's easy. Let's plot out a strategy for the first week and the first month. What do you want to call this bank, anyway?"

Dan leaned forward in his chair and squared his shoulders as he spoke. "Corda."

"You kill me." I peered at him over my glasses. "You want to name it after rope?"

"Well, it's how we met." As an afterthought, he added, "and it's a metaphor with industry implications." It dawned on me that Catherine would always be a part of our interactions. The rope that had brought us together couldn't be escaped. And even with that understanding, I wasn't deterred. I had craved a leadership role like Jon's, and with this opportunity, I would take his place and clean up his messes, without having to lie for him or take his shit. It seemed like an acceptable trade.

Catherine would be just another tool in my arsenal, for use internally and externally, when Amy needed backup. I was exhilarated. Things were coming together. My mind was racing with possibilities when Dan gripped my hand. 'You're feeling it, too, aren't you?"

"Feeling what?"

"Us. What we're building. What we're doing here." His pupils were dilated, and his eyes glistened.

"I'm excited." I paused, to give myself a moment to formulate a safe answer to such a provocative question. "Yeah. I'm feeling excited."

Dan kept my hand in his and gazed into my eyes. "When I asked what you were doing on Saturday, I meant on Saturday night. I fucked up. Let's go to Paris, back to Montreal, or anywhere you want."

I took a deep breath while gathering my thoughts further. Male egos are dangerous when slighted. "I wish I could, Dan. But I really don't want to mix business with pleasure. It's too confusing. I don't have your wiring." He gave me a long pleading look. "And besides, I need to get ready for Corda. My partner's a beast. He wants the impossible."

Dan released my hand and sat back in his chair. A switch had flipped. "Alright, Amy. See you tomorrow at my office. How's 8 a.m.?"

"Perfect Dan, and thanks." I shook his hand and made for the stairs. The four men still remaining in the dining room all stared as my Louboutins clacked against the wooden floor. Once my back was to the table, it felt safe to breathe normally again.

When I got to the lobby, I left a message for Rafael. "You are not going to believe what just happened. I got a job!!! I have an idea about where to celebrate tonight. Somewhere insanely romantic. Somewhere with an awesome view and great desserts. It'll be my treat. And I'll even wear that slutty red Gucci dress for you, so you can tear it off later . . . As soon I hang up, I'll see if I can get us a table at the River Café."

———

ACKNOWLEDGMENTS

While I spent an awful lot of time alone with this novel, there were many people who were extraordinarily generous and thoughtful as it came to fruition. Judith Regan is someone whose work I have admired for years, and her willingness to back women authors drawn to edgy topics is gutsy and incredibly helpful. She knows the traps, and she's been fantastic in helping me navigate them.

Once I had a draft, there were several readers whose comments and suggestions improved *Edge Play* substantially. I'm particularly grateful to Laura Yorke, Caitlin Fisher, Nikhil Bharadwaj and Jill Bruce for sharing their time and insights with me.

But before there was a draft, there were numerous Wall Streeters who helped me understand the jargon and the Big-Swinging-Dickitude. During the Financial Crisis, I lived near Wall Street and I often wondered what it must be like to be one of the people in my spinning class, whose work almost destroyed the economy.

There was a pair of Jeffs who helped me get the submissive men right. And perhaps my most fundamental thanks goes to my girlfriend Ilsa Strix, who was the inspiration for Erika. Years ago, she brought me into her world and let me observe what went on in her dungeon. I was rapt. While exploring the BDSM demimonde, I met some extraordinarily brave men and women whose passion for intensity led them to some fascinating places. What it takes to pursue a life like Ilsa's, one filled with intimate adventure and risk, is a puzzle I have tried to answer in *Edge Play*.

As a first-time novelist, the prospect of sharing my work was particularly daunting. When I studied engineering, there was no class called "The Novel," so the prospect of having made some fundamental mistake in style or structure haunted me. Fortunately, my very first reader was also the best editor I know—my husband, Norm Pearlstine. I handed that first draft over to him knowing I was also offering him a marital bomb. If he didn't like it or if he found it problematic, he'd have to figure out how to tell his wife it sucked. I trusted his finesse and judgment, and as always, he offered his best advice. To my relief, his reaction was positive, and to his relief, I found his suggestions encouraging and extremely helpful. While I knew he was special soon after we met, this experience has shown me just how extraordinary a partner he is.

Jane Boon lives in New York City and Los Angeles with her husband, Norm Pearlstine. She studied technology and policy at MIT and later received a Ph.D. in industrial engineering. Jane has written for publications like *The Wall Street Journal, Bloomberg Businessweek, Time.com, McSweeneys.net,* and *TravelandLeisure.com.* Jane enjoys improv and playing dress up, including the time she wore a corset, garters and thigh-high stockings as a dominatrix in the Fox TV series, *Gotham. Edge Play* is her first novel.